# Miss WRONG

# Mr and RIGHT

**Also by Robert Bryndza**

## The Coco Pinchard series

*The Not So Secret Emails Of Coco Pinchard*
*Coco Pinchard's Big Fat Tipsy Wedding.*
*Coco Pinchard, The Consequences of Love and Sex*
*A Very Coco Christmas*
*Coco Pinchard's Must-Have Toy Story*

## Stand alone novels

*Miss Wrong and Mr Right*
*Lost In Crazytown*

## The DCI Erika Foster Crime Thriller Series

*The Girl in The Ice*
*The Night Stalker*

Miss WRONG and MR RIGHT

ROBERT BRYNDZA

bookouture

Published by Bookouture

An imprint of StoryFire Ltd.
23 Sussex Road, Ickenham, UB10 8PN
United Kingdom

www.bookouture.com

ISBN: 978-1-78681-108-0
eBook ISBN: 978-1-78681-107-3

This book is a work of fiction. Names, characters, businesses,
organizations, places and events other than those clearly in the
public domain, are either the product of the author's imagination
or are used fictitiously. Any resemblance to actual persons, living or
dead, events or locales is entirely coincidental.

*This book is dedicated to all the people who dare to dream, and have the courage to make their dreams a reality.*

# THE PLAYERS

My wedding dress burned easily.

I stood in the field behind the farmhouse on that summer afternoon, the afternoon of my wedding day, with my Mum, my Gran, and my best friend Sharon. It was almost two o'clock.

My wedding invitations stated that at two the reception would begin. I should have been sitting at the top table with my gorgeous new husband Jamie, listening to my Dad make the speech he'd stressed over for the past few weeks. Instead, I was peering into an old oil drum, and watching with morbid curiosity as the satin and lace of my dress puckered and curled, appearing for a moment like caramel, before crinkling, singeing, and then igniting with a whoomph.

The flames shot up high, and our view of the hills beyond rippled and distorted in the heat.

'Natalie…What are you doing? This is madness!' cried my Mum.

'I didn't even get a photo of you in it,' said Sharon sadly, her camera hanging off her wrist. She was still wearing her peach-coloured bridesmaid dress.

'It vas just a dress Natalie, and it made you look like a cream cake,' said Gran lighting a cigarette. She snapped her gold lighter shut and stuffed it back in her fur coat. My Gran, Anouska, is Hungarian. She came to England as a young girl but has stubbornly held on to her accent.

'I don't know how you can say that. She looked beautiful!' said Mum.

'She did look beautiful, like a beautiful cream cake, offered up to be gobbled down,' said Gran. 'Is that how she vanted to begin her life as a married vooman, as a sugary insignificant object?'

'Do you know how long it took old Mrs Garret to sew all that lace?' asked Mum. 'It cost a fortune! If I'd got here five minutes earlier, I'd never have let you do this.'

The breeze changed direction, blowing a toxic plume of smoke at us. We coughed and flapped for a moment.

'Natalie didn't vant to get married!' snapped Gran. 'And I paid for the dress…'

'It doesn't mean you can burn it. I would have liked to have kept it,' said Mum.

'Yes, only to remind the poor girl you think she should hev gone through vith it,' said Gran. There was a fizzing popping noise as the flames worked their way down to the fake pearls on the bodice. I didn't say anything; I was still numb with shock. Mum went on.

'What were you thinking, Natalie? You walked down the aisle on your father's arm, in front of half the village, and two minutes later you run back up it and out of the church.'

'I thought you had a tummy upset, Nat,' said Sharon.

'How will I show my face in the village? And poor Jamie! That handsome lovely boy,' cried Mum.

'Annie, put things in perspective,' said Gran, flicking the butt of her cigarette into the oil drum. 'Didn't I say Natalie vas too young to get married? She's nineteen. She needs to get out into the world…' She squinted at me against the sun. 'You've got your whole life ahead of you my darlink. You need to try out some different men for size.'

'She's not trying any men out for size,' hissed Mum. 'She needs to…'

'What about what I want to do?' I shouted suddenly. 'You're all talking about me as if I'm not here! Can't you ever be a normal family, and try to understand how I feel? All you've done is shout and persuade me to set fire to my dress!'

'If you didn't vant me to burn the dress, you should hev opened your mouth, Natalie,' said Gran.

'Like the poor girl had a choice. Once you've got a bee in your bonnet there's no stopping you!' countered Mum. There was an awkward silence. Sharon leant over and grabbed my hand.

My Dad approached us, picking his way across the muddy field. He still had on his morning suit and smart shoes. When he reached us, he peered into the oil drum in disbelief. My dress was now a blackened lump.

'Bloody hell, is that…?' he began, but Mum cut him off.

'Martin, I thought you were going to get changed?' She slapped at his lapels, brushing imaginary dirt off his suit.

'I've been trying to sort out what to do with my parents,' he said, fending her off. 'I dropped them at the Travelodge, they want to know if we're still having the sit down meal at the pub?'

'Of course we're not still having the sit down meal at the pub!'

'I'm trying to get my head around this, Natalie, did Jamie do something?' asked Dad. They all turned to look at me. I opened my mouth. Nothing came out for a few seconds.

'I just, don't feel ready…'

It sounded whiny and pathetic.

'When would you feel ready?' shrilled Mum. 'Tomorrow? Next week? It would have been nice to know when we were booking the bloody wedding!'

'I'll pay you back, all the money,' I said.

'With what?' asked Mum. 'Money from the DSS? You've got no job. You failed all your exams because you were so in love with Jamie. Do you have any idea what you've done?'

'Of course I know what I've done!' I shouted. 'You think I did it just to spite you?'

'I wouldn't put anything past you right now!' roared Mum. 'I can't look at you.'

'You need to calm down, Annie,' said Dad putting a hand on my mother's shoulder.

'Don't you dare tell me to calm down,' said Mum shaking him off.

'She vas always highly strung as a child,' said Gran watching my mother impassively. 'Some mornings I'd sprinkle a little of my Valium in her Ready Brek, just for some peace and quiet…'

Mum pulled away from Dad and marched off back towards the farmhouse.

'I'm sorry I never got to hear your speech, Dad,' I said.

He took one look at the charred dress, shook his head, and followed. Tears began to stream silently down my face. Gran pulled a lace hanky from her handbag and handed it to me.

'Do you vant a moment, Natalie?' she asked. I took the hanky, pressed it to my face and nodded.

'Sharon, let's go back,' she said.

Sharon smiled and squeezed my hand. They followed after Mum and Dad, who were halfway across the field to the farmhouse in the distance. I grabbed a stick and poked at the now blackened lump in the oil drum. The tip of the stick caught, and as I pulled it away a string of melted material came too.

After running out of St Bathsheba's church, I had found myself on a deserted country lane. The local bus had stopped, probably because they didn't often see a bride in her wedding dress and veil, waving madly from the pavement. I didn't have any money, so had to exchange my bouquet for a ticket (the driver was off to see a sick aunt when his shift ended, and needed some flowers to take to the hospital). As brides, we're told it's so important to have something old, something new, something borrowed, something blue… but what about a bit of cash – if we don't go through with it?

When I walked into the kitchen, Mum was making a very angry cup of tea, furiously spooning leaves into the pot. Dad had changed out of his suit and was at the table with Sharon and Gran. They were sitting in silence, looking up at the three elaborate tiers of my wedding cake, which had been placed in the middle.

'The lady from the pub just brought it over,' said Sharon apologetically. I stared for a moment at the flawless royal icing, topped with a crown of delicate yellow sugar roses. Mum came up to me and held out a long knife.

'You want me to cut it? Now?' I asked.

'Yes, it'll have to be frozen. We won't get through it all,' said Mum.

'Annie, she doesn't have to do it right now,' said Dad.

'Well, when, Martin? She was happy to let her Gran chuck her wedding dress on the bonfire! When is an appropriate time to…?' Mum was cut off by a knock at the back door. Through the frosted glass was a peach-coloured blur.

'Micky! We forgot about Micky!' cried Mum, running to the door and opening it. My fourteen-year-old sister Micky was standing outside in her bridesmaid dress. She had a pair of white shoes in her hand, having taken them off to wade through the mud up the driveway.

'Micky, where did you go?' asked Mum. She put down some newspaper by the door and Micky hopped onto it.

'And she tells me I vas a bad mother,' muttered Gran lighting another cigarette.

'I had a wander through the graveyards, and then got a lift with the man who digs the graves. He had spades in his boot!' said Micky excitedly.

'You see Annie, Micky is just fourteen, and already she's seeking out interesting men,' said Gran.

'Oh will you shut up!' said Mum. She went to the sink, filled a bowl with warm water and set it down by the door. We watched Micky as she washed her feet.

'What's going on Nat?' asked Micky looking up at me. 'I thought you and Jamie were in love?'

There was a silence. I jumped as the phone rang. Dad went and answered then came back.

'It's for you, Natalie. It's Jamie.'

I shook my head.

'He's at the end of the drive, on his mobile phone. He says he won't leave until you talk to him,' explained Dad.

'That poor lad, you at least owe him the decency of an explanation,' said Mum.

'Okay… Tell him I'll come outside,' I said.

I pulled on some plastic wellies. Mum made a fuss about my hair. I batted her hand away and stepped outside.

Jamie was standing behind the gate at the end of the drive, tall, lean and heart-stoppingly handsome in his wedding suit. He was still wearing his rose buttonhole with a spray of gypsophila, and the sun glinted off his chestnut hair. I walked towards him, my wellies sloshing through the mud.

'What the hell Nat?' he said when I approached the gate.

'I know. I'm so sorry.'

'That's it? You're sorry?' He opened the gate and went to come in. I put my hand up and went through it joining him on the other side. I closed the gate behind me.

'I'm not ready…' I said.

'How aren't you ready? You put the dress on, you got in the car… You walked up the aisle?'

I just stared at him.

'Do you know how humiliating it was? They kept playing the Wedding March over and over again, expecting you to come back… I've got cousins who've come over from Canada. They've spent a fortune on their plane tickets!'

'When I said I wasn't ready, I meant…' I tried to explain, but Jamie went on.

'My cousins go back in a week. My aunt is already asking if we can do it on another day…'

'Do what on another day?'

'Get married. Auntie Jean said she had wedding jitters before she married my Uncle Paul. She said she nearly did what you did, and bolted for it, but they're still happily married after thirty-five years.'

I looked up at his handsome face. He wanted me to tell him it was just wedding jitters.

'This is different,' I said softly.

'How?'

'It wasn't just jitters. I don't want to get married. Well, I don't want to get married right now.'

'When do you want to get married?' he asked.

'It could be tomorrow, it could be next week, next month… I could be thirty-five, Jamie. But right now, I don't want to get married.'

His face clouded over.

'I thought we were in love,' he said in a matter-of-fact way.

'We are, but don't you think it feels different now we're not going to university together? We planned to leave home, get away from here and start a new life.'

'We can retake our exams,' he said. 'Try again for university next year.'

'The college where they do retakes is miles away. We've got no car, no money. What if I fall pregnant by accident?'

'Would that be a bad thing?'

'So we'd be jobless, homeless, with a baby too?'

'We could live with my parents.'

'What? In your bedroom with the beanbag and the Star Wars posters?'

'Or your parents.'

'I wouldn't expose a newborn child to those nutters…' I said.

Despite himself, Jamie laughed. A lock of his hair fell over his forehead and I reached up and tucked it behind his ear.

'I just feel that if we got married now, we'd miss out on life. We were so stupid. We did no work for our exams. We just spent all our time…'

'Shagging?' grinned Jamie weakly.

'We did other things too, like, the cinema, and we went for walks,' I added.

'And we did shag on several of those walks, and in the cinema. You seemed pretty happy,' he grinned. He leant in and went to kiss me.

'Jamie, please can you be mature about this. I'm trying to be serious…'

'I'm immature am I?' he said pulling back. 'Why didn't you open your gob about this before our families booked a whole bloody wedding?'

'Everyone got so excited and carried away, and there never seemed a right time… until…'

'Until you got to the altar?' he finished. I reached out and grabbed his hand.

'Don't you worry about the future? How your life is going to end up?' I asked.

He looked nonplussed.

'Dunno, I don't really think about it…'

'Well, I have been thinking about it. I want a decent life, with a career and prospects!'

'Oh, nice. So life with me isn't good enough?'

'It's not just about you. I don't want to be stuck here in bloody Sowerton! I don't want to just be your wife, and get trapped here!' I shouted, making a grey-haired lady wobble on her bike as she passed us on the road.

'Natalie. You agreed to marry me,' said Jamie losing his temper and gripping my arm. 'You can't do this! You can't back out!'

I pulled away, lost my balance and landed on my backside. I sat there for a moment, sinking into the mud and feeling the wet begin to seep through my trackies.

'I'm sorry,' he said, helping me up. I stood there for a moment. Jamie ran his finger round the collar of his shirt. He looked so good in his morning suit.

'So, that's your final answer. You won't marry me?'

'No,' I said softly.

'Fine,' he said. 'You'll never have to see me again.'

'That's not what I want!'

'It's simple. Either you want me or you don't,' he said defiantly.

'So you're going to blackmail me? Wedding or nothing?' I asked.

'Yes, wedding or nothing,' he said.

We stared at each other for a few moments. He was waiting for an answer, but I couldn't give it. He turned suddenly and walked away, crossing the road to the green by the pub.

I should have gone after him. I should have gone after him and stopped him, but something held me back. I watched him cross the green, and vanish round the corner into the pub. I burst into tears and for a few minutes had to hold onto the gate until I had composed myself. Then I trudged my way back up the drive. When I reached the back door my mother pulled it open.

'Well?' she said grinning hopefully. She grabbed my arm so I could balance and pull off the wellies.

'It's over,' I said.

Mum hit the roof. She ranted whilst everyone looked on. She said I'd never find anyone as good as Jamie, that I'd made a fool of myself and the family, and that she might as well go up to bed and die of shame.

'Okay Annie,' said Dad firmly taking my mother's arm. 'That's enough.'

'I think this vill be the making of Natalie,' said Gran, stubbing out her cigarette in the fruit bowl. 'She needs to see the vorld! I vas lucky enough to, ven my family had to flee persecution from the Nazis…'

'You didn't have to flee,' shouted Mum. 'The Hungarians were Nazi allies! And you always said how handsome you thought Hitler was.'

'Don't be so ridiculous, Annie…' snapped Gran. 'I thought Himmler vas the handsome one. If Himmler had been in charge, the Nazis vould have done so much better.'

'Do you hear this Martin?' Mum said to Dad. 'This is the woman I had to grow up around. No wonder my nerves are shot!'

Gran stood up. She eyed my wedding cake for a moment.

'Natalie, I vas planning to go on to London after your vedding, to stay with my friend Paulo; he has a flat right in the middle of everything… You could come vith me?'

'London!' said Mum. 'Why would she want to go all the way there?'

'I think Natalie needs some time away, so the dust can settle,' said Gran.

'What? A holiday?' I asked. The thought of staying in Devon and watching the mushroom cloud rise above the wreck of a wedding was giving me anxiety.

'Think of it as a coming of age,' said Gran. 'Paulo runs an open house, everyone is velcome. He plays clarinet for the London Symphony Orchestra.'

'And who's going to pay for this?' asked Mum.

'I vill take care of Natalie,' said Gran.

'Maybe I could go? Just for a bit?' I said, the idea suddenly seeming like my saviour. Mum's lips thinned.

'She is an adult now,' said Dad.

'You could bring your friend too,' said Gran gesturing to Sharon.

'Really?' said Sharon. 'Wow, I've never been to London before.'

'What about me?' asked Micky. 'Can I go to London?'

'You've got school Micky,' said Mum.

'That's not fair! Why does Natalie get to go to London? I hate you!' cried Micky.

'Micky love, you can go to London with your Gran, when you're older,' said Dad.

'Even if I don't leave someone at the altar?' asked Micky.

'Um… yes,' said Dad.

There was a silence. Gran came over and put her arms around me and Sharon.

'So that's decided. You are coming to London, vith me, yes?'

I looked at Sharon's excited face and I nodded.

'Ok, let's go to London,' I said.


That evening, we went to London. And since then, I've rarely been back.

# ACT ONE

Fifteen years later…

# THE KEY

I woke early with the summer sunshine pouring through the window, marking out squares on the bedroom wall of my flat. I stretched and sat up in bed. My boyfriend Benjamin was still asleep beside me. I watched him for a moment, and traced my fingers lightly over his muscular back. His eyelids flickered under his long dark lashes, but he didn't stir. A rush of excitement for the day ahead propelled me out of bed. I took a quick shower, pulled on a loose summer dress, and then went to make breakfast.

My flat is tiny, and the kitchen is a little like the galley of a ship, thin and narrow with everything on the walls; cooker, fridge, washing machine, microwave. I closed the kitchen door quietly, so I wouldn't wake Benjamin. Under a long window at the end, overlooking the communal garden is a small breakfast bar where I'd laid out my makeup, hairdryer, and hair straighteners. I popped a capsule into the coffee machine and plugged in the straighteners to heat up. I loathe my frizzy hair and spend a fortune on product to tame it. I have it down to a fine art, and can do it in twenty minutes. I switched on the radio quietly and jiggled along to the music as I drank my coffee, and dried and styled my hair.

As I was gathering up my Blackberry, Kindle, and laptop from their unofficial charging station on the floor beside the fridge, the kitchen door opened and Benjamin came in. He had on just his boxer shorts and he was rubbing his eyes.

'Sorry, did I wake you up?' I asked shoving everything into my oversized handbag.

'No. Mmmm. You look nice. Namaste,' he growled putting his hands around my waist and pulling me against him. He is very tall; I reach up to his shoulder. He was warm and firm against me, and I put my hand up and ran it through his short salt and pepper hair. His hands moved down to my thigh and started to slide up the material of my skirt. He leant down and kissed me, then pulled away a tiny bit and flashed me a wicked smile.

'You've brushed your teeth before breakfast,' I said.

'Yes,' he said and pulled me against him.

'I can't, Benjamin,' I said. 'I have to get to work…'

'Busy girl,' he said, releasing me with a sulky pout.

'I'm hardly a girl Benjamin,' I said, checking my bag again and locating my sunglasses.

'Yes, you are knocking forty… hang on,' he said and left the kitchen.

'I'm only thirty-five!' I said peering at my reflection in the chrome kettle. I waited for a couple of minutes, then seeing the time, went through to the bedroom.

'What are you doing? I have to go,' I snapped. He was perched on the end of the bed with his backpack open, pulling out clothes, his laptop, shoes, a tightly packed wash bag.

'Why don't you at least leave your wash bag here?' I said. 'And I could leave mine at yours? And maybe my hair straighteners? We lug so much stuff across London to see each other…'

'Natalie,' sighed Benjamin still rummaging through his bag. 'It's important to have our own space. Keeps it exciting…'

'I'd find it exciting not to pack a mini suitcase on wheels every time I stay over,' I said. He carried on rummaging through his backpack, a pile of stuff growing on the carpet beside him.

At the bottom he found a plastic wallet. He opened it and extracted a biro and one of the leaflets he'd had printed for the yoga studio he runs. Under the 'BENJI YOGA' logo he scrawled his email address and wrote, 'ATTN: Ryan Harrison - discretion assured.' He held it out to me.

'Benjamin,' I said crossing my arms.

'Natalie you promised me you would give this to Ryan Harrison,' he said.

'Yes… But, jeez not today. Give it a few days.'

'Yes, and then he finds somewhere else to practise yoga.'

'We don't even know if he does yoga?'

'He's a hugely famous television actor from Los Angeles. Believe me. He does yoga.'

Benjamin stood up, and took my head in his hands.

'You are the theatre manager Natalie, the boss. I trust you to do the right thing… It will be good for me, and in turn good for us. Maybe I could reconsider you leaving some things at my flat.'

'Okay,' I said taking the leaflet. 'I'll do my best.'

'Thank you Natalie. Namaste.' He leant in and kissed me, then started to repack his bag.

'You know, you could still come along tonight to the launch party. Sharon's coming too…'

'I won't miss my meditation workshop. It's important to me,' said Benjamin.

'This is important to me,' I countered.

'It's nice that we both have important things in our lives Natalie,' he said, not getting what I meant. He zipped up his backpack and came with me to the front door. I grabbed the dress garment bag containing my outfit for later, and checked in my bag that I had my keys.

'Why don't I give you a key,' I said impulsively, seeing the spare on my bunch of keys. Benjamin paused.

'Um, okay,' he said. There was an awkward silence as I wrestled it off the key ring. I finally got it free and handed it to him.

'There, now you're…'

'Able to open the door myself,' he finished. I killed some time putting the keys back in my bag, hoping he might offer to give me a key to his place in return, but he lost patience, leant across and opened the door.

'Right, well I'll see you?'

'Soon Natalie, soon. And don't forget the leaflet. Namaste,' he smiled, and closed the door.

It was still early when I came out of the security gate onto Beak Street. The late July sun was dazzling, promising a hot day. I made my way past the pub next door. The cobbled terrace out front was being hosed down, and a rainbow hung in the air as a little of the spray landed on my bare arms with a delicious prickling cool. Further along, a lorry was idling by the kerb and there was a clinking of beer barrels being unloaded. I slipped on my shades and crossed the road.

Raven Street is in the heart of Soho and I walked past the glittery gay bars, restaurants, sex shops, all shuttered up and sleeping after another late night. Only the coffee shops were open this early. I nipped into Grande, my regular, and ordered a takeaway Americano from the pale dreadlocked guy behind the counter, then waited with the bike couriers and office workers as the machines hissed. Through the picture window I could see the crisp, white art deco I of the Raven Street Theatre opposite.

It was built in 1919 and was a functioning theatre until the Second World War. It then went into decline, closed, and over the years was used as a soup kitchen, a pornographic cinema, and a huge second-hand bookshop. It was then boarded up and almost became a theme pub. My proudest achievement so far is that I was involved in raising money to save and restore it to its former glory, and now I am the manager.

Eek!

I say eek, because every time I walk through the doors, into the hush of the box office with its art deco mouldings and brass lamps, I feel a thrill, a little fear, and a lot of pressure to make it succeed.

I reached the front of the queue and the pale dreadlocked guy handed me my coffee.

I left Grande, crossed the road, and entered the theatre through the main entrance. I always take the stairs up to my office. Photos of our most successful productions are displayed on the staircase walls, and it gives me confidence as I climb the five flights. Halfway up, I stopped on a step beside my favourite picture of all: me with Kim Cattrall. It was taken at a charity gala evening we hosted last year. The highlight for me was looking after Ms Cattrall (who was lovely and insisted I call her Kim) before she performed in the evening of monologues. In the photo she looks gorgeous, so sleek and polished... I look a little washed-out beside her, the dreaded frizz beginning in my hair, and what I was wearing was rather thrown together. Like a social worker who'd just spent her Christmas vouchers on a decent outfit.

When I went into the open plan part of the office, Xander, our new office assistant, was being versed in the alchemy of coffee ordering by Nicky, my business partner of five years. She's had a long career in London's West End. She knows everyone and everything there is to know about theatre. She was involved in putting together the complex financial package to bring the theatre back to life, and where I manage the day-to-day running of the theatre, she is head of PR and publicity.

'It's a tall, decaf, extra-hot, Colombian blend coffee with two pumps of hazelnut syrup, soy milk and a Sweet'N Low... And I'll know if it's sugar or Canderel,' she drawled in her Texan accent. She was wearing a hot pink trouser suit, nipped in at the waist, accentuating her considerable curves. Her sleek dark hair was tied back and she wore glasses with matching hot pink frames.

'Right, no problem,' said Xander scribbling furiously on a post-it. Nicky turned when she saw me.

'Nat. I love Xander. He's so cute. He's like a puppy dog!' She ruffled his shiny chestnut hair playfully. 'When did you get him?'

Xander's large brown eyes registered shock.

'Morning Xander,' I said apologetically, and then to Nicky, 'Xander started when you were away on holiday.'

She peered down at him sat neatly behind his desk as if he were a little dog.

'Xander, what a cute name!'

'It's Alexander, but my little brother couldn't say it properly so I became Xander,' he said, his deep Scottish accent belying his youth.

'Oh my God, and an accent,' said Nicky playing with the silver chain nestled between her impressive bosom. 'Welcome to the Raven Street Theatre honey. You are just adorable!'

She went to the printer and opened the paper drawer. For a moment I thought she was going to pull out a sheet of inkjet paper and put it down for him to pee on, but seeing it was full, she closed the drawer and turned.

'Xander honey. That coffee isn't gonna cross the street by itself...'

'Yes, of course,' he said grabbing his phone and getting up. 'Natalie?'

'I'm good thanks,' I said holding up my Americano. He left, and Nicky followed me through into the office we share and closed the glass door.

'So Xander, is he…?'

'Yes, he's got a partner called Paul,' I said.

'Perfect. Guilt-free ogling.'

'How was your holiday?' I asked as I put my bag down on my desk.

'Nat. The resort was amazing, the only downside was that Bart made my wrist ache…'

'Men can be so disgusting,' I said. I realised she was talking about something else when she held out her wrist to reveal a dazzling bracelet.

'Oh my gosh, are they real?' I asked.

'Yes. Diamonds. Yes,' she said wiggling her wrist with a grin. 'So many carats I'll never have to eat my five-a-day again!'

'Blimey Nicky. Your husband is still so romantic after twenty years…'

I pulled out my laptop, and the BenjiYoga leaflet fluttered to the floor. Nicky picked it up.

'Attention Ryan Harrison, discretion assured,' she read out loud. She raised a perfectly shaped eyebrow.

'Benjamin virtually forced it into my bag,' I said grabbing it back.

'Nat. Ryan Harrison is not going to BenjiYoga,' she said with an air of finality.

'Why not? Benjamin is a good yoga teacher.'

'And a good self-promoter, which is fine, but we need to protect Ryan…'

I went to protest. But Nicky went on.

'And Ryan Harrison's manager made us put in his contract that if he's sick, he is only seen by a Harley Street doctor...'

'What does that mean?'

'Nat. Didn't you get foot fungus from BenjiYoga?' asked Nicky.

'That was months ago, and it was athlete's foot...'

'That's just fancy talk for foot fungus. Do you know how much a Harley Street doctor charges to treat foot fungus? Probably a good chunk of our Arts Council funding for the next quarter.'

'Okay, okay,' I said folding the leaflet and stuffing it back in my bag. Nicky put her hand on my arm.

'Honey, I get the attraction to Benjamin. He's tall, well-built, arrogant. I'm sure he can reach the places other men can't reach... But there is a great guy out there for you, I'm sure of it.'

'I gave him a key this morning,' I said defiantly.

'A key to what?' she asked.

'To my flat...'

I didn't get to hear her response as there was a loud bang from outside, and then a squealing of metal. We went to the window and saw a lorry parked by the kerb. A massive pile of crash barriers was being unloaded onto the road below.

'Do you really think we'll need all these tonight?' I asked.

'Nat. This is Ryan Harrison,' said Nicky. 'He has crazy fame. When the costume department on his TV show take his clothes to the laundry it has to be in an armoured truck. A woman from Ohio bid ten thousand dollars for a pint of his bath water in a charity auction. Allegedly his stalker has a stalker...'

'Well, tonight's crowd should be a bit more demure. We've invited press and theatre people,' I said.

'You'd be surprised,' said Nicky.

There was a knock at the door. Val, the box office manager, poked her head of short grey hair around the door.

'Morning ladies, there's a group of muscly men in the foyer downstairs. Either it's an early birthday present for me, or the security guys you hired,' she said.

'We've already bought you slippers for your birthday,' I said with a wink. 'Xander should be back soon, he can deal with them.'

'Okay, I'll put them in the bar, and when Xander is back I'll get him to do a coffee run,' said Val leaving with a smile.

'Right. Let's go through our to-do list for tonight, and make sure nothing is forgotten,' I said.

'First I wanna know what you're wearing?' asked Nicky. I unzipped the garment bag, and pulled out a black pencil skirt and an orange blouse. The second it was out, Nicky wrinkled her brow.

'Did you choose this, or did a sales assistant railroad you into it?'

'I don't get railroaded!' I protested.

'Honey, you're British. Half your wardrobe is what you've bought to be polite.'

'I chose it. From that place off Carnaby Street where the girls all dress like they did during the Blitz... It's vintage!'

Nicky sucked in her teeth and shook her head. 'The skirt I can cope with. It's the colour of that blouse. Two words: Easy Jet.'

'EasyJet is one word,' I said.

'Either way, you're wearing the uniform of a budget airline... This is probably the most important night of our careers. If you wear this people won't be saying, oh look there's Natalie Love, she runs this joint, they'll be asking you for Pringles and charity scratch cards.'

'It's not EasyJet orange. Is it?' I said holding it up to me in front of the mirror by the door. Nicky nodded.

'What are you wearing?' I asked. She went out and came back with a beautiful pearl-white Alexander McQueen dress.

'Oh, wow, that's stunning,' I said.

'Bart got it for me, to go with my bracelet… I'd offer to lend you something but you know I've got a big fat ass and huge…'

'Okay, I know,' I said hanging the outfit back up. 'I'll sort it. Sharon will probably lend me something… Now, let's talk about tonight.'

'Just one more thing,' said Nicky.

'What?'

'How much is priority boarding?'

I couldn't help but laugh.

The rest of the morning, and first part of the afternoon, was spent in meetings, briefing our theatre staff, and ticking the seemingly endless list of tasks off our to-do list. By three pm there were a couple of hours free so I ducked out to get my replacement outfit from Sharon. I hurried through Covent Garden and down to Charing Cross where I jumped on a train to New Cross. Twenty-five minutes later I emerged onto New Cross Road.

I walked past the big Sainsbury's supermarket, and knocked on a bright green door in a row of terraced houses set back a little from the traffic roaring past. The door opened. Sharon was stood in the hallway, her hair slicked back with foam, and a towel round her shoulders.

'Have you seen Ryan Harrison yet?' she asked excitedly. 'Have you? What's he like?'

'Muzzle yourself. He's not arriving until five,' I said. There was a yell from down the hall.

'Stay by the sink Amy!' shouted Sharon over her shoulder. 'Come through Nat.'

I followed her into the big kitchen overlooking her cosy little garden. Her ten-year-old son Felix was sat at the kitchen table, also with his hair slicked back with foam. He was wearing a superman towel tied under his chin like a cape. Her daughter Amy's eight-year-old legs were only just long enough so she could lean up and over the sink as her hair dripped.

'Nits, Nat,' said Sharon. 'We've all got bloody nits.' She picked up a small silver comb and started combing through Amy's thick wet hair.

'Oh no!' I said putting my bag down on the table. 'How?'

'We got them from Laura Dalton, Aunt Nat,' said Amy. Even aged eight she had her disapproving face down to a tee.

'We don't know it was Laura Dalton,' said Sharon.

'She's always in the playground, flicking her hair around the boys,' said Amy. 'She was bound to get something from them.'

'Girls have nits too!' shouted Felix.

'The dress you want to borrow is on the back of the bedroom door,' said Sharon pulling the comb through a knot in Amy's hair. 'Do you mind grabbing it?'

'No probs,' I said. As I went through Amy yelled,

'Ow! This is all Felix's fault. He kissed Laura yesterday!'

'I didn't!' shouted Felix.


I always feel a little envious when I wander round Sharon's house. It's so cosy: pictures drawn by the kids, framed holiday photos, a little clay Homer Simpson ashtray made by Felix for his Dad, Fred, who is small, handsome and very Italian. It always reminds me I might just miss the boat as far as kids were concerned. Benjamin couldn't commit to leaving a toothbrush in my flat, let alone impregnating me…

'It's just water you twit. I haven't even put the nit shampoo on yet!' I heard Sharon saying from the kitchen. A beautiful green silk wrap-around dress was hung in plastic on the back of the door. I grabbed it and went back through.

'Is that okay Nat?' asked Sharon.

'It's perfect, thank you,' I said.

'I'm wearing my black galaxy dress,' said Sharon. 'I know it's a bit 2007, but it pushes me up and pulls me in in all the right places…' She tailed off when she realised the kids were staring. Amy rolled her brown eyes under her foamy hair line,

'Mother, you're like married, and Ryan Harrison is so out of your league,' she said.

'Where does she get this at such an early age?' asked Sharon. 'Out of my league… I love your father. I just like looking at Ryan Harrison… and I might get to touch him!'

'Steady on Sharon,' I said. 'I've had to book security guards for the theatre.'

Sharon wiped her hands and opened the pantry door. On the inside hung the Official Ryan Harrison Calendar. It was turned to July, which was a broody black and white shot of Ryan lying shirtless on a beach in Speedos, with sand artfully dusting his taut six pack.

'Look at him, smouldering in my pantry with all the dried lentils and Weetabix… And tonight I get to see him for real! Do you fancy a glass of wine Nat?'

'I'd love to, but I've got to get back,' I said.

'Ok, we'll make up for it later… Is it still a free bar?'

'Yes. We've hired a mixologist to make cocktails.'

'Ooh super!' said Sharon. 'Felix what does it say to do next?'

Felix unfolded the nit lotion leaflet and started to read out loud.

'After applying lotion allow eight hours, and then rinse thorror…thur..'

'Thoroughly!' shouted Amy. Sharon paused, closing the pantry door.

'Don't you mean eight minutes Felix?'

'No Mummy. It says eight hours…'

Sharon went over to Felix and grabbed the leaflet.

'Eight hours? Why didn't that bloody woman in the chemist say! I didn't want the eight hour one! Eight hours takes us to…'

'Midnight,' I said.

'Yay, yay, yay! Can we stay up?' shouted Amy. 'We've only ever stayed up till midnight on New Year's Eve!'

'Cool!' shouted Felix, joining in with Amy jumping up and down in excitement. Sharon stood with the leaflet, tears starting to prick her eyes.

'It's all right. Just rinse it off and do it again tomorrow,' I said. Sharon bit her lip.

'No, because I will still have nits, and I'll have to do them again, and it says you shouldn't use these chemical shampoos more than once a month… And I can't take them to school tomorrow if they haven't been done.'

'Really?' I asked.

'There's virtually been a witch hunt to find whose children are responsible for the nit outbreak. And I can't come to your fancy launch party with nits! What if I gave Ryan Harrison nits? I'd be mortified!'

Sharon grabbed a tissue, wiped her eyes and blew her nose.

'Can we have a Dr Who marathon Mummy?' asked Felix. Sharon sighed and nodded. The kids both screamed and ran through to the living room.

'BUT DON'T SIT RIGHT BACK ON THE SOFA CUSHIONS!' she shouted after them. 'This shampoo smells like industrial solvent.'

'Are you sure you won't come? You could stay at mine and…'

'Thanks, but no,' she sighed. 'Mummy duty comes first.'

'There will be plenty of time to meet Ryan. He's going to be at the theatre for five weeks. Plenty of time, I promise,' I said giving her a hug.

'I even had my tits measured at Marks and Spencer's, and bought an expensive new bra,' sniffed Sharon. 'Turns out my tits are bigger than I thought. God I could have seen Ryan tonight with my new big tits. He must like big ones, he's from Los Angeles…'

I peered at her breasts to see if they looked any different. Sharon blew her nose and dabbed her eyes.

'Will you be okay Nat, if I don't come? Is Benjamin coming?'

'He was invited but he's got his meditation group…' I said. Sharon turned to the fridge and pulled out a bottle of wine.

'I know you're pulling a face,' I added.

'I'm not doing anything,' she lied.

'I know you think Benjamin is selfish… And I suppose he is, sometimes, but he's just focused on his yoga and his meditation and… And we all need things to focus on. I focus on my job.'

Sharon nodded unconvincingly and poured herself a huge glass of wine.

'I gave him a key this morning,' I added.

'To what?'

'Nicky asked the same thing. To my flat, of course…'

Sharon went to say something when the Dr Who theme wound down and we heard the unmistakable sound of the Daleks.

'They are not watching that episode, Felix won't sleep. He's terrified of the Daleks,' said Sharon jumping up. I followed her into the living room and watched her go into Mum mode, commandeering the remote and choosing a different episode. I realised that I had to go. She gave me a hug by the door.

'Phone me later, and tell me everything,' she said.

'Of course,' I promised. 'And thanks for the dress.'

I felt a twang of envy as I made my way back to the train station. Not that I wanted nits or to watch Dr Who… I just envied Sharon's life, with her full house.

# RYAN HARRISON

The sky was heavy with cloud as I made my way up from Charing Cross Station and back to Soho. The rush hour was reaching its peak. I expertly weaved my way through the crowds, the plastic-wrapped dress sticking to my skin in the thick afternoon heat.

When I reached the theatre I was shocked to see a huge crowd had formed. The pavement and part of the road directly outside the main entrance had now been blocked off with a long line of crash barriers. The front row had been nabbed by members of the press and paparazzi, who were leaning languidly against the barriers, seemingly used to the routine of waiting for a famous person to materialise. In contrast, the Ryan Harrison fans behind them were whipping themselves into a frenzy, with an excited babble of chatter, shrieks and laughter.

There were teenage girls and guys, and some women a similar age to me and Sharon. Phone camera flashes went off as they took group selfies, and there were some elaborate homemade signs being held up with things like: 'WE LOVE YOU RYAN!', 'I LOVE YOU RYAN!', 'RYAN! I WANT YOUR BABIES!' And a group of older ladies were all wearing pink t-shirts reading, 'WE'RE MORMONS, RYAN. MARRY US ALL!'

Six uniformed police officers were stationed at intervals along the crash barriers, watching over the growing crowd. Inside the enclosed area on the pavement, Nicky was supervising Xander and a couple of the guys who worked in the box office as they straightened and vacuumed a huge roll of red carpet leading up to the main entrance.

I reached the barrier and tapped one of the police officers on the shoulder. He wouldn't believe who I was and I had to shout for Nicky to come over and vouch for me. The police officer wordlessly opened the barrier and I slid through.

'Sorry Nat, I meant to give you a pass before you left,' she said handing me a laminated square with my name and staff photo. 'Ryan Harrison's people have been in contact. He's running half an hour late.'

I checked my watch. It was five thirty-five. There was a rumble of thunder, and the crowd screamed. Xander came over with a clipboard for Nicky.

'This is the final guest list,' he said. 'Everyone who comes in will be verified three times. Once out front, once in the foyer when they get their goody bag, and then once more when they enter the bar.'

The thunder rumbled again, and the sky seemed to grow heavier.

'Have we got umbrellas?' I asked.

'Yes, we've got a load upstairs, I'll move them down to the foyer,' said Xander and went back inside.

'Can I see the dress?' asked Nicky. I unhooked it from my shoulder and she gave me an approving smile.

'It's perfect,' she said. 'This is crazy, huh?'

'I know. The crash barriers, the press, the fans... All at our theatre!'

Nicky grinned and squeezed my hand. 'It's what we've been working towards Nat, for so long... Look, we've even got press here from America.' She pointed to a blonde lady in an immaculate trouser suit as she did a piece to camera with her microphone.

We went back inside and I went up to one of the spare dressing rooms to get ready. The green dress from Sharon was beautiful, simple and elegant with a bit of cleavage on show for good measure. I gave my hair a touch up with the straighteners, and vamped up my make-up a little. It was one of those occasions when everything went right. My eyes were dramatic and smoky; my hair was sleek and straight with just enough volume. Why could I never pull this off on a date? The last couple of times I had been out with Benjamin, I'd been bloated and had an attack of the frizz.

I pulled out my mobile and called Benjamin, but after a couple of rings his phone went to voicemail. I stared at the screen. He'd cancelled my call… Maybe he was just about to meditate, I thought. A knock roused me out of my thoughts and Nicky entered.

'Nat. Ryan Harrison's car will be here in ten minutes.'

'Okay. I'll be down in a sec,' I said. I suddenly felt very nervous.

When Nicky and I went back out of the theatre, the atmosphere on the street was crazed. The air was hot and thick, and black clouds hung low above the rooftops. Streetlights were flickering on, even though it wouldn't get dark for a few more hours. The crowds had now swollen to fill Raven Street, and we were met by a policewoman who explained they'd made the decision to close it in both directions, and divert traffic. 'The Metropolitan Police have taken control of the crowd management and all public areas, please do not interfere,' she added sternly. We nodded obediently. The radio on her lapel hissed and crackled and a tinny voice said, 'incoming.'

The screaming suddenly intensified, and camera flashes started to fire off, lighting up the crazed faces of the crowd whose heads were snapping back and forward trying to see what was happening.

'This is it Natalie. That's Ryan's car!' shouted Nicky over the mayhem.

A black people carrier was waved through the barrier, which had been erected halfway along Raven Street. Four police officers flanked it, moving fans out of the way as it crept through the crowd. It stopped at the crash barrier and, holding the fans back, the police officers made a small opening near the rear door. A few seconds passed and then it slid open.

Ryan Harrison emerged to an epilepsy-inducing strobe of camera flashes. He posed for a moment on the pavement outside the theatre, pouting in his Ray Bans and looking fashionably dishevelled. He was gorgeous dressed in simple blue jeans and a tight white t-shirt, but as with most famous male heartthrobs, he was tiny.

Ryan's 'people' emerged behind him from the aptly named people carrier; a huge woman with jet-black hair pulled back from her pale face, and two serious-looking younger women in dark blue trouser suits. The huge woman moved quickly to the theatre entrance and vanished inside. One of the younger women approached me, whilst the other shadowed Ryan as he made his way along the barriers, posing for pictures and selfies with the press and fans.

'Who is Natalie Love?' shouted the woman above the noise from the crowd.

'Hello that's me,' I said.

'Wait here,' she snapped, pointing at the piece of pavement where we stood. She went back to Ryan and guided him to the end of the line, speeding things along.

'Who are all those women?' I said bristling a little from her attitude.

'The big dark-haired woman is Terri, Ryan's manager, the other two are her assistants,' explained Nicky. After about ten minutes, they decided Ryan had been paraded long enough. He posed for a final group photo with the 'MARRY US WE'RE MORMONS' ladies, then bade them farewell, gliding past us and into the foyer. We hurried in after them.

The theatre foyer was packed. Five of our beefy security men milled about, Terri stood in the corner, still wearing the grim scowl. Her two assistants were leaning in, whispering to her intently. The doorway leading to the rest of the theatre was blocked by a huge trolley piled high with goody bags, which were being unloaded by Xander and a couple of girls we'd hired. Ryan stood in the middle of the box office, still wearing his Ray Bans. As we approached him, I could see our faces reflected in them, like staring at the back of a teaspoon. Nicky and I introduced ourselves with manic smiles. He didn't remove his Ray Bans, and just nodded politely. One of Terri's assistants came over.

'Nadia… We need to move Ryan out of here,' she said indicating the cameras still flashing outside, illuminating the foyer.

'It's Natalie,' I said. 'And of course, we'll show you up to the dressing room we've had put aside.'

We got Xander to move the goody bag trolley. We went through and I pressed the button for the lifts.

There was a silence as we rode up. Terri and her assistants stared straight ahead with the same grim concentration you see from secret service agents. Ryan remained behind his shades.

'How was your flight?' I said to Ryan.

'Loooong,' he said. There was another silence.

'We were worried something had happened to you… I was wringing my hands a little like Lady Macbeth!' I said.

'Who?' asked Ryan. I went to say something but the lift pinged. We all piled out onto the third floor.

'As requested, we've set up our number one dressing room for your exclusive use,' said Nicky.

'Hey! Hello America,' said Ryan perking up at the sound of Nicky's voice. He pulled off his shades to reveal dark circles around his piercing green eyes. He gave us a cute smile revealing perfect white teeth.

'Yeah. I'm from Dallas, Texas,' said Nicky.

'Cuyahoga Falls, Ohio,' he said.

'Sowerton, Devon!' I quipped. There was a crashing silence. Thankfully we arrived at the dressing room.

'Okay, make yourselves comfortable,' said Nicky opening the door.

'Thanks,' said Ryan. He went in followed by the two assistants. I went to file in after Terri's enormous bottom, but she reached behind her and closed the door in our faces.

'Charming,' I said.

'Your terrible jokes didn't help Nat…'

'Didn't it worry you he didn't know who Lady Macbeth was?' I hissed as we made our way back down the corridor.

'They've all just come off a sixteen hour flight,' said Nicky diplomatically.

'But he's agreed to be Macbeth in Macbeth! How could he not get what I was saying?'

'Isn't it bad luck to mention the Scottish play?' asked Nicky.

'Oh crap. It is, isn't it? What happens if you say Mac… the name of the Scottish play?'

Nicky started to tap at her phone. 'Here in Google it says, using the M-word is like a curse on a theatre, which may cause disaster, plaguing theatre productions with accidents, bad luck, and misfortune…'

'That's all we need,' I said.

'There is, however, a cleansing ritual we can do,' said Nicky swiping at her phone.

'A cleansing ritual?'

'To reverse the bad luck. It won't take a sec, but we have to go back outside.'

Despite the stupidity of it all, I followed her back downstairs and out onto the pavement. The crowds behind the barriers were staying put, now looking up at the windows and chanting for Ryan.

'What do I have to do?' I asked.

'Turn around three times,' said Nicky. I turned around three times.

'Okay then what?'

'Then spit over your left shoulder…'

I went to spit.

'Not on the red carpet!' scolded Nicky. 'Do it in the gutter!'

I moved to the kerb and surreptitiously spat over my left shoulder.

'And you need to say the line from Hamlet, "Angels and ministers of grace defend us…"'

'Angels and ministers of grace defend us,' I repeated.

'There, it's all going to be fine,' said Nicky. I looked at the crazed faces of the crowds screaming hysterically for Ryan. Thunder rumbled and there was a flash of lightning.

'Ok. I'll go inside and check everything is running smoothly,' I said.

'And I'll get ready to be door bitch,' said Nicky giving me a hug. 'And let's have fun tonight, Nat, yeah? Enjoy our moment.'

'I couldn't have done it without you,' I said.

'And vice-versa honey,' she smiled.

When I got back inside I saw my phone battery was low, so I went up to the office. I was rummaging around in my bag for my charger when there was a knock at the door. It was Xander with a serious look on his face.

'Sorry to bother you. One of Ryan's assistants is asking if I can get him a Mountain Jew. I don't know what that is? Is she asking for a Rabbi?'

'I think he means Mountain Dew. It's a soft drink Xander. 'Dew' as in a light film of water on the grass, as opposed to someone of the Jewish faith…' I couldn't help smiling.

'Oh. Ok,' he said blushing. 'Do we have it at the bar?'

'No. You can get it at the international newsagent on the corner. Can you spare a moment to run out?'

'The girls need more goody bags in the foyer,' he said. I went to the petty cash tin, pulled out a twenty and handed it to Xander.

'Go and get Ryan a load of Mountain Dews, and I'll sort out the goody bags,' I said.

'I'll be quick as I can,' he promised.

I went downstairs to the foyer where guests had started to arrive. The two girls handing out the goody bags were already down to a last few on their table. I went and unlocked the store cupboard behind them, flicked on the light and saw the rest of the goody bags were piled up on a long flat loading trolley. The trolley had been tucked in behind the door and I had to close it and work it backwards and forwards on its wheels to manoeuvre it into the centre of the storeroom. I turned to open the door and stopped dead… through the strip of glass in the door, standing by the goody bag table was… Jamie Dawson.

He was dressed in a sharp black suit, opened-necked shirt, a loose fitting tie and trainers. I ducked to one side and flicked off the light in the storeroom. What the hell? I thought. I hadn't eaten much all day, but would it make me hallucinate Jamie Dawson? Did he even live in London? The last I'd heard was that he was working in Canada.

I peered back through the glass in the door. Yes, it was Jamie Dawson, chatting away to the goody bag girls. He laughed and his wide smile was bookended by dimples. A lock of chestnut hair fell across his face. I noticed next to him stood a beautiful dark-haired girl with ghostly pale skin. Her dress was pink lace, so tight, it looked as if it had been painted onto her hourglass figure. Her skin was like flawless porcelain. I recognised her from somewhere… She reached up tucking the stray hair behind Jamie's ear. My heart began to race; fear flooded through me and I ducked back out of sight, pressing my head against the cool wood of the door.

Why tonight did I have to see Jamie? Why had he come to the launch party? Who'd invited him? I took some deep breaths and waited a few moments. I peered back through the glass and saw that Jamie and his companion had moved off. I flicked on the light and pushed the trolley out to them.

'We just saw Tuppence Halfpenny,' said the first goody bag girl excitedly.

'The one in the pink lace dress?' I asked.

'Yes, she's like the British Dita Von Teese,' said the second. 'I've just started doing a burlesque course and…'

'Did you see? I think she had on real diamonds,' interrupted the first. A couple more people approached the table.

'We're not paying you to stand here and gossip,' I snapped. I went out onto the street where Nicky was standing behind a little lectern. Under her glare, people were queuing up on the red carpet, flashing their teeth and invitations. The crowd behind was still chanting 'RY-AN RY-AN RY-AN…'

'Hi Nat, everything okay?' asked Nicky.

'I just want to check we invited someone called Tuppence Halfpenny?' I asked.

'Yeah, the photographers went mad when she arrived. She's very hot right now, she's like the British…'

'Dita Von Teese, yes,' I said.

'Is there a problem? She's getting a ton of press – especially London press.'

'No, it's fine. And the guy she was with?'

'Jamie um, Dyson?'

'Dawson.'

'Yes, Jamie Dawson.'

'And he was her plus one?' I asked.

'Yes,' said Nicky. 'Do you know him?'

'Me? No, um just doing a head count…' I lied.

Nicky narrowed her eyes. 'Are you okay Nat? You've gone very pale.'

'I'm fine. Give me a buzz when everyone's in,' I said. I went back inside, past the goody bag girls, and took the stairs two at a time up to my office.

I closed the door and leant against it for a minute. My legs were shaking. I grabbed my handbag, pushed down the bar of the fire door in the corner of my office, and went out onto a now-defunct fire escape. The platform remained, but the metal stairs leading five storeys down to the street below had been neatly clipped off during the renovations. I climbed the set of stairs they hadn't removed, and stepped up onto the flat roof of the theatre. I leant against the huge chimney stack and took some deep breaths.

Jamie looked great. So many feelings were surging through me… like my past had caught up with me. Jamie and I never finished our conversation that day, the day he walked away from me outside my parents' house.

It was like his question still hung in the air after all these years…

Wedding or nothing?

What would I say if we carried on the conversation today? Wedding? Nothing? I had to admit things had changed. Jamie was still gorgeous, and he'd appreciated in value over the years. When I was nineteen it was easy to meet a guy like him. Now I'm almost thirty-five, and men of his calibre are never single. And if they are, they're snapped up, just as fast as a house in a desirable area.

Wedding or nothing?

Of course, it wouldn't be 'wedding', but would it be 'nothing'? I remembered how he'd made me laugh, just how good we were together. I shook those thoughts away. I was with Benjamin. I had the career and life I'd always dreamed of. I was just feeling the stupid jitters after seeing an ex for the first time in fifteen years.

There was a rumble of thunder and a large raindrop burst on my bare arm, then another on the back of my neck. There was a few seconds' pause and then the rain came splattering down on the flat asphalt roof. I yelped and ran back to the steps and down to the fire door – which was shut. I had forgotten to wedge it open, and there was no handle on the outside!

'NO!' I cried feeling uselessly at the edges of the door. Rain was pouring down, soaking my hair and large drops were clinging onto my bare shoulders. I grabbed my mobile and called Nicky, it rang once and then my phone gave three bleeps and the battery died.

'NOOOOO!' I shouted staring at the blank screen. I put my handbag above my head and hammered on the fire door. The rain cranked up a notch, roaring as it came down on the buildings packed close around me. I banged on the door again and shouted. The beautiful green dress was now sticking to my thighs. I dashed up the steps and back onto the roof.

Raindrops had rapidly pooled like patches of mercury on the smooth asphalt, reflecting the pink and blue neon signs from the bar next door. I dashed across the roof, trying not to slip, and leant over the edge to yell down to Nicky. The rain fell in sheets to the road below, which had rapidly emptied, save for a police van, the row of crash barriers, and a group of die-hard Ryan Harrison fans. The rain was hitting the road so hard, the tarmac was a pale blur. I couldn't see Nicky on the red carpet, she must have moved inside, and people were hurrying into the theatre under umbrellas.

'Nicky! NICKY!' I shouted, but my voice was lost in the noise of the rain. My handbag slithered off my head, and as my arm took the weight of it, I was nearly pulled over the side.

I pulled myself back and landed on my arse, in several inches of freezing rainwater.

# THE M WORD

After twenty minutes banging against the fire door, it was finally opened by Nicky.

'I've been looking for you everywhere,' she said. I rushed inside past her, drenched. My wet dress was now stuck to me.

'Thank God, my phone died, I could have been out there all night!' I said my teeth chattering. Nicky stared, horrified.

'Nat, I have to introduce you in ten minutes,' she said.

'Look!' I cried. 'What am I going to do?' Water was pouring off me, leaving dark wet patches on the carpet. On one side my hair was plastered to my cheek.

'There's your other outfit,' said Nicky going to the garment bag on the coat stand.

'The EasyJet air hostess?'

'I was just kidding,' said Nicky 'And I'm not sure what else we've got? Do you want me to run down to the costume department? What play is on at the moment?'

'*Dangerous Liaisons…*' I said.

'We'd never get the corset done up in time,' said Nicky. She went to her gym bag and pulled out a towel.

'Here, it's clean,' she said. I took it gratefully.

'Can you turn round, I'm gonna have to take off my underwear,' I said.

Nicky turned. I pulled off my knickers and unhooked my bra, and wrung them out in the plant in the corner.

'That's a plastic plant,' said Nicky still with her back to me. I laughed. It sounded like the crazed yip of a hyena. I dried off with the towel and put my underwear back on. Nicky passed me the pencil skirt and I stepped into it and zipped up.

'You can turn round,' I said. I pulled on the orange blouse. Nicky quickly did up the long row of tiny buttons as I towelled my hair. I had no choice but to twist it into a bun at the nape of my neck. I then grabbed a mirror and saw mascara had run down as far as my chin. I rummaged in my bag, found my make-up remover and cleaned off my face. The radio Nicky was carrying hissed and Xander's voice came through saying Ryan was waiting.

'Natalie we have to go,' she said.

'Can you stall him for at least a minute? Just let me put something on my face.'


Nicky went off and I hastily applied some make-up. I then dashed down to the third floor, where Nicky and Xander were waiting in the corridor with Ryan Harrison, Terri, and the two assistants, who I'd learned from Nicky were called Beth and Mindy. Ryan was leaning against the wall holding a can of Mountain Dew. He'd changed into black jeans, designer trainers, and a tight t-shirt showing off his impressive biceps. His muscled chest was on display through three horizontal rips in the t-shirt – as if he had been swiped at by something with sharp claws.

'Sorry I'm late. Did you find everything alright?' I asked. Ryan ran his hand through his dark hair and shrugged.

'Your Mountain Dew tastes different,' he said.

'Um. Well, we've got different mountains here in the UK,' I said.

'Yeah, there are some really nice ones in Scotland,' added Nicky.

'So I'm like getting a taste of your country?' said Ryan seriously.

'Yes, they use the water from Loch Lomond,' grinned Xander. This seemed to please Ryan and we made our way down the stairs. We went through the empty restaurant kitchen then stopped at a door. Nicky excused herself and went through.

'This leads to the bar. I'll say a few words, then introduce you Ryan,' I explained to Beth and Mindy. Terri leant against one of the steel work surfaces and scowled.

'Did you change your outfit?' asked Ryan. I didn't get to answer as I heard Nicky introduce me. I took a deep breath, opened the door and went out into the bar.

Every inch of the floor was crowded. The gold lamps reflected the red velvet walls and carpets, giving everything a warm cosy feel. Our two hundred guests were sipping cocktails whilst waiters circulated with trays. The band we had hired for the party were propping up the bar, their instruments waiting neatly on the back half of the stage. I climbed the small set of steps to the stage, and Nicky handed me the microphone.

'Good evening everyone and thank you for attending the launch of… *the Scottish play*,' I said. The crowd laughed knowingly. I went on to explain how I had uttered the M-word by mistake and they laughed again.

I suddenly spied Jamie, he was at the back of the crowd. Tuppence Halfpenny was stood beside him, swiping away at her phone. She was wearing fingerless lace gloves that matched her dress. Our eyes locked and he gave me a nod. I realised I'd paused too long; smiles were fading on faces in the audience.

'Ok, so, the Raven Street Theatre is staging *Macbe… the Scottish play…*'

Jamie leant down and whispered something in Tuppence's ear. She looked up and smirked. I struggled to keep on track.

'Um, and I'm thrilled to introduce the man who will be starring in… it…'

I just couldn't take my eyes off Jamie. He leant down and whispered something else to Tuppence, she gave a coquettish little smile and rubbed herself against him.

'Sluttish… I mean, the Scottish play…'

I could hear people begin to mutter at the back. Tuppence was still intent on her phone, swiping languidly at the screen. Jamie looked at me again. His beautiful brown eyes stared deep into mine. I gripped the microphone.

'Right, well I'm thrilled to introduce, Ryan Harrison!' I finally said. Ryan came bounding up onto the stage and the crowd clapped and wolf-whistled. Arms were raised with phone cameras and as they started to flash, Jamie was obscured. I moved down off the stage and stood back by the door. Ryan took the microphone and waited for the applause to subside.

'Thanks Nadia. It's great to be here at the Raymond Street Theatre,' I stood with a smile plastered to my face and my hair still plastered to my head.

'Um, I'm really excited to be here in London. I wanna drink tea, eat cake, and get lost in the fog! I wanna show my fans a different side to me… Dark, savage. I'm really looking forward to sinking my teeth into Hamish Macbeth!'

He then kissed his fingers and gave them the peace sign. There were hysterical screams from the audience. The cameras fired more flashes and Ryan came back off the stage. Terri, Beth and Mindy were on hand to get Ryan through the door and into the empty kitchen.

'I love the Great British people!' he cried. Mindy handed him a fresh Mountain Dew with a bendy straw. He drank greedily as if he'd just done a three-hour concert in Carnegie Hall and not a thirty-second speech. I caught sight of my reflection in one of the huge stainless steel fridges. I totally looked like an EasyJet air hostess. My make-up looked like it had been applied during an earth tremor, and a halo of frizzy was sticking up.

'Are we okay to go up to the conference room?' asked Nicky. 'We've arranged for Ryan to do some press interviews and meet some of our staff and financial donors.'

Over the next three hours we didn't stop. Ryan did loads of press interviews, met the staff of the theatre, our board of directors, our financial donors, three men from Westminster Council, and even the wife of the man who had supplied the crash barriers. Everyone wanted a photo and to tell him how much they loved him. I was amazed how many of them watched Ryan's TV show, *Manhattan Beach*.

Finally we took Ryan, Terri, Mindy and Beth down to the front entrance, where their people carrier was waiting. Terri heaved herself in wordlessly, followed by Beth and Mindy. Ryan stopped to shake hands with Xander and Nicky. Then he reached me.

'Thank you Ryan. Tickets go on sale tomorrow at nine am,' I said. 'We're expecting them to sell out fast.'

'Cool,' grinned Ryan. 'And it's Natalie right? Not Nadia.'

'Yes,' I said.

'Catch you later Natalie,' he grinned and climbed into the car. Xander went back inside, and we stopped under the awning of the theatre. Nicky beckoned to a waiter through the window and he came out with a couple of cocktails. We each took a long grateful sip. The rain continued to pour down.

'Thanks I needed that,' I said. 'What time is it?'

'Half ten,' said Nicky. 'I think most people have cleared out now,' she said craning her neck to peer through into the bar. 'It's just the reality TV crowd hoovering up the free booze.'

'I'm knackered,' I said finishing the last of my cocktail. 'I think I'm going to head ho…' but I didn't manage to finish as I heard a voice.

'Natalie, hello…'

We turned to see Jamie standing with Tuppence Halfpenny under a giant black umbrella. She had his coat draped around her shoulders and was shivering as she held his arm.

'Jamie,' I said. There was an awkward moment and then he leant in and pecked me on the cheek. His slightly stubbly cheek brushed mine and for a moment I could smell his hair, rich and clean…

'Umbrella!' shrilled Tuppence as it shifted and the rain caught her.

Jamie stood back and we stared at each other.

'Sorry Nicky, this is Jamie Dawson,' I said. Nicky smiled and shook his hand.

'And I know who you are,' said Nicky to Tuppence. 'We were so pleased you could attend, didn't I say that Natalie?'

'Um yeah, you did… '

Nicky gave me a puzzled look as to why I was suddenly not enthusiastic about Tuppence Halfpenny.

Tuppence pulled her face into what she must have thought was an appropriate smile. The wind whipped round, rattling rain on their umbrella. A couple of stray photographers emerged from an awning over the road and took a few shots, and she turned to face the flashes, her pale skin shimmering.

'Jamie, I can't get this dress wet. It's vintage,' she said moving closer to him.

'And it's a beautiful dress honey,' said Nicky. 'How do you two know each other?' I looked at Tuppence, then realised Nicky was talking about me and Jamie. There was a pause and we both laughed.

'Believe it or not Natalie and I were once engaged to be married,' said Jamie. Tuppence's nostrils flared and she looked me up and down, I self-consciously smoothed down my hair. Nicky burst out laughing.

'She went as far as leaving me at the altar...'

There was a silence.

'What? Seriously? You're not joking?' said Nicky looking between me and Jamie. I gulped trying to gain my composure.

'It was all a *very* long time ago, and I'm happy to see that you've found someone else Jamie... Are you two...?'

'We are lovers, yes,' said Tuppence icily. 'And Jamie is producing my new show.'

'I loved your *Burlesque Kicks* show at the Garrick Theatre,' said Nicky. 'Where's your new one going to be?'

'There,' said Tuppence, pointing with a thin lace glove. We both stupidly followed her finger.

'The Palladium?' asked Nicky.

'No. There,' repeated Tuppence rolling her eyes. She was pointing at the building over the road, which sat dark and swathed in tarpaulin.

'But that's the Old Library, it's been closed for years,' I said.

'Jamie's company has just leased it as a pop-up burlesque venue. I'm his first show,' said Tuppence putting her hand to his chest. A taxi came roaring up to the pavement. Jamie opened the door. Tuppence murmured goodbye over a slender shoulder and slid in. Jamie closed the door.

'Wow. You're opening a theatre opposite?' I said.

'Yeah. Well, a pop-up venue, you know it's more temporary,' clarified Jamie.

'I know what a pop-up venue is,' I snapped.

'What's it going to be called?' asked Nicky.

'The Big O,' grinned Jamie. My mouth was still open when he got in the other side and the taxi drove off. We watched the tail lights as they moved off into the rain.

'The Big O,' said Nicky. She turned to me. 'Nat, I have like a million questions…'

She was interrupted by a journalist from the *Guardian* who came out of the entrance to ask if he could do some fact checking.

'Nat, stay where you are, I'll be back, with drinks…'

She went inside. I stared across the road at the Old Library, dark and shrouded in faded plastic. Without thinking about the rain pouring down, I went off into the dark street.

# A LONELY SALMON

The rain continued to pour as I made my way home. Most of Soho had retreated to shelter under the shop and restaurant awnings dotted along the street, and the pavements were crowded with smokers and drinkers. I was close to crying and didn't want anyone to see me, so I put my head down and walked in the road. The volume of rain had swamped the drains, and they were overflowing, grey water frothing up to join the flow, zooming along almost as high as the kerb. I walked against the current, the force of the water spilling up and over my shoes, spraying against my legs and soaking the bottom of my skirt. In my orange blouse I was a very wet air hostess, or for a better metaphor, a lonely salmon, swimming against the tide.

When I reached my building I rummaged in my bag for my security card and scanned it on the gate. It opened with a buzz and a click, and I hurried through the communal garden to my front door. Wind whipped the rain against my face as I found my key, slipped it into the lock, and went inside.

The temperature had dropped, and my flat was cold. Shivering, I flicked on the light, went to the tiny airing cupboard and turned on the central heating. There were clicks and clanks and a whoomph as it went into action. The dust from the unused boiler burnt off, filling the hall with a dry stale smell. I dropped my handbag on the floor and leant down to pull off my shoe, shrieking when I saw I had picked up a used condom from the road river. It was milky white and had been nestling inside under the arch of my foot. I recoiled and dropped the shoe. The condom fell out, and sat lying bent over on itself on the bristles of the mat. I started to cry; tears poured down my face and I felt alone, and ugly. All I could bring home from my day was a disgusting used condom.

I wiped my tears away angrily, went to the bathroom and grabbed a wodge of toilet paper. I went back into the hall, scooped up the condom, and then did what you should never do – I flushed it down the loo. I then took a long hot shower, washing all the filth and sweat away. Afterwards I pulled on my huge squashy robe and went into the kitchen. I opened the freezer, took out a bottle of vodka crusted with ice and poured half a tumbler. I was about to take a sip when the door buzzer went. My heart lifted when I thought it might be Benjamin, but I could see on the little screen of the intercom phone by the fridge that Nicky was outside, huddled under an umbrella. I reached out to let her in, then pulled my hand back. I wasn't in the mood for Nicky's positive attitude. I didn't want to be told to look forward, and stay in the present because it's a gift, nor did I want to take my lemons and make lemonade. I wanted to be British and wallow in my misery.

I saw on the screen Nicky press the buzzer again. She hung about for another minute and then walked away. I stared at the space where she'd been, the rain even showing up on the tiny black and white screen, then it flicked off.

Seeing Jamie tonight had put my life in a different context, or, dare I admit it, had made my life seem hollow. For the first time I felt genuinely old, I felt my mortality.

Fifteen years ago we were engaged. If I'd gone through with it, we would have a house, and memories. We could have a fourteen-year-old child – or more! And I'd have pictures on the fridge made by the kids at school. I got up and looked at my fridge. It was bare save for a magnet. The only thing Benjamin had ever given me. On it was a silhouette of a lady sitting cross-legged. Superimposed on top was a quote from a famous Yogi called Ram Dass.

*'The quieter you become, the more you can hear...'*

'Isn't that just fancy talk, Benjamin, for shut the fuck up and listen?' I said out loud. I took the magnet off, but the fridge door was now completely bare, which seemed even worse. I rummaged in a drawer wondering if I had something to replace it with. A magnet from a trip to a cathedral gift shop maybe, but all I could find was an old prescription for thrush cream and a takeaway leaflet. I fixed the Planet Poppadom menu to the fridge, so it concealed the magnet in its folds. I gave up and poured myself more vodka.

I realised that in another fifteen years I'd be fifty. Which I know is by no means old, but where had my life gone? The past fifteen years had felt like two. And time seems to speed up as you grow older. And I was growing older. I looked such a state tonight. Jamie seemed hardly to have aged, he'd just got sexier. And now he was dating that Tuppence Halfpenny, a younger woman projecting an almost ethereal femininity.

Over the years I had filed Jamie at the back of my mind. Life in London was fab, my career was my focus and I had no regrets. After this weird night with Ryan Harrison, and Jamie popping up, the regrets washed over me one after another. It terrified me.

I went back out to the hall, retrieved my bag and went back to the kitchen. My phone was still dead and I put it on charge.

I pulled my laptop from my bag, and switched it on. I typed 'Jamie Dawson' into Facebook. Thirty-six names came up.

'You see, you're not that unique mister,' I said gulping more vodka. I scrolled down the names and found him. His profile picture was black and white and quite arty with him smiling, his eyes against the sun, but his profile was limited if you weren't his friend. I'm not a frequent Facebooker; I remembered he had friended me a couple of years back, and I had never accepted. Why didn't I?

'I'm *not* friending you now,' I said to his picture. I then logged on to Twitter, but again there were too many Jamie Dawsons. Several had no pictures and were just eggs.

'Which egg are you?' I said finishing my second vodka and pouring a third.

I then tried LinkedIn. Again his profile was limited. I became a bit crazed then and after some more manic googling, I found an article from the Canadian version of *The Stage* newspaper.

Jamie had spent three years working in theatre production in Toronto, and then another three organising tours around Canada and the States. Then he was artistic director of a theatre in Vancouver, before establishing a successful production company in Toronto. The article finished with a quote:

*'I will always love Canada, and I am thankful for the amazing opportunities I have had here, but England is my home, and I've been given an opportunity to establish a presence in London's West End.'*

He must have known I run the Raven Street Theatre. My mother still bumps into his parents every now and again.

I sat back in my chair with just the sound of the rain hammering against the windows. So many emotions came flooding back. What got me most was the smell of Jamie's hair when he'd leant in to kiss me…Rich and warm, it gave me a rush of happiness and desire I hadn't felt in years. I wiped my tears with the back of my hand. I thought about ringing Sharon, but it was late. Amy and Felix would be asleep.

I realised I just wanted to sleep. Going to sleep is a full stop for the day, and there is always the possibility of being able to start afresh with the next one.

I remembered I had some sleeping pills in the bathroom cabinet. I went through and took one with a mouthful of water from the tap. By the time I had put everything on charge, washed my glass and tidied away my things I was drowsy.

I barely made it to the bedroom and slid under the covers, when I was asleep.

# SOLD OUT

I woke up with my face stuck to the pillow. I rolled over, opened my eyes and saw it was ten-thirty in the morning. I staggered out of bed and went through to the kitchen. I saw the takeaway leaflet on the fridge and remembered everything that had happened last night. I switched on the coffee machine, and then went to the fridge to get milk. The red light was blinking on the landline and I pressed play.

'Morning Natalie,' purred Benjamin. 'It's nine twenty-three am. I'm calling to see how things went last night. Will I be seeing Ryan Harrison at BenjiYoga? I do hope so. *Namaste.*'

There was a bleep and the message ended. It was a passive aggressive message… and a passive aggressive *realize*. Benjamin seems to use that word a lot. He uses it when he wants something. He uses it sarcastically when someone does something he dislikes. He even yells it just before he ejaculates.

*Oh yes! Natalie, oh yes! I'm going to! Ugh! NAMASTE!*

I burst out laughing as I popped a coffee capsule in the machine. I went to my laptop and googled the word '*Namaste*' to see what it really meant. Wikipedia had it down as, '*a respectful form of greeting or welcoming, the translation being, I bow to the divine you.*'

'He lectures me on being more spiritual and he doesn't even use it properly!' I said out loud. My mind went back to Jamie. He really used to make me laugh. I can't think of a day when we were together that we didn't laugh…

That's the problem with Benjamin, he's never made me laugh. In fact he doesn't seem to have a sense of humour. I never realised how important a sense of humour is in a relationship. I once made the mistake of putting on an episode of *Absolutely Fabulous*. Benjamin regarded it in horror, as if it were a gritty documentary on two women in the fashion industry.

'These are awful people,' he said, staring at the screen. 'Why is everyone laughing?'

I was laughing along too with the studio audience, as Patsy staggered out of a taxi, realised and wearing her knickers outside her clothes.

'It's a sitcom,' I explained.

'But Natalie, these women have terrible substance abuse problems… The tall one…'

'Patsy…'

'Yes, she's the enabler for the dark-haired one…'

'Edina,' I added helpfully. On the screen Patsy opened the taxi door, and Edina fell out backwards onto the road.

'Don't they need help? Not our laughter!' said Benjamin seriously, which made me laugh even more. I realised you can't explain *why* something is funny. You either have a sense of humour or you don't.

I debated calling him back, but thought I needed a coffee first. Then the landline rang, and thinking I should get it over with, I picked up.

'Oh. Hello? Is that you, Natalie?' said my mother.

'Hi Mum,' I said.

'Natalie *hello!* I didn't expect to speak to you. I was going to leave a message.'

'I'm not working today,' I said. There was a silence.

'Right, well, the reason I'm ringing is that your sister Micky is organising to have Dexter christened for his first birthday.'

I realised it had been a long time since I'd last spoken to Mum. Was Dexter really already one year old? She went on,

'It's going to be on a Sunday, in two weeks' time.'

'Look, Mum, I'm really busy here…' I said.

'Surely you can't be working Sundays, Natalie? And we'd love to meet this Benjamin chappie who you've been going out with. And we'd love to see you,' she pleaded.

'I don't know…'

'Your sister wants to get an invitation in the post to you asap. The printers are holding the presses.'

'Doesn't Micky print her own invitations at home?'

'It's a figure of speech Natalie. We would love it if you could come to the christening. I've forgotten what you look like. And Dad misses you like mad. A visit from you would perk him up.'

'If, and I mean *if* I come, it would only be for a few hours. I'd have to do it there and back in a day,' I said.

'And you'll bring this Benjamin?' asked Mum brightly.

'I'd have to ask him…'

'Does he like trifle?'

'Mum, I said I'll ask him, I don't know if he's free…'

'But you'll also ask him if he likes trifle? I'm planning a big one; proper custard, real sponge. No bought boudoir biscuits!'

'Yes,' I said.

'How is it going with the theatre?' she asked. I suddenly remembered that tickets for *Macbeth* had been on sale since nine am. How could I have forgotten? I managed to get off the phone, promising Mum I'd let her know about the christening.


I switched my mobile on, and grabbing my laptop, went onto the theatre website. A few weeks back, we'd sent a photographer over to LA to do a photo shoot with Ryan for our poster. It appeared on the screen, a full-length image of Ryan, wearing just a kilt and black boots. His bare torso was sweaty and artfully smeared in mud – we'd figured, Macbeth does do battle after all – and he stared back at me with slicked-back hair and piercing green eyes. Above his head was written:

THE RAVEN STREET THEATRE PRESENTS

**RYAN HARRISON**
AS
**MACBETH**

*Limited Season! Book Now!*
AUG 1st - SEP 7th

I was just navigating my way through to the ticket portal when my mobile rang. It was Nicky.

'Nat! You're alive! I was gonna call the cops, but then I figured Benjamin might have given you a booty call…'

'No, that's not really his style,' I said. 'I was so tired, I came home…' I didn't add that the only time Benjamin had given me a booty call, he'd reversed the charges.

'Okay, let's put getting stuck in the rain and seeing the ex-fiancé to one side. Have you *seen* the ticket sales? Fuck-a-doodle-doo!' she cried. 'The first four weeks of shows have sold out in two hours!'

On my screen, I got into the ticketing portal and saw that there were only tickets left for the last few performances.

'Fuck-a-doodle-doo indeed!' I said.

'I've emailed you links to *Heat World,* the *Sun,* the *Guardian,* the *Mail Online…* The press all came good, honey. Sure there's a bit of trash talk about putting movie stars on West End stages, blah blah blah and how gimmicky it is… But the *Guardian* quoted my response to that. Have you got it on your screen?'

'Hang on,' I said. I logged into my email, and clicked on the *Guardian* article link. There were several pictures of Ryan arriving at the theatre last night, meeting fans, and then inside the party. He looked gorgeous, and I'm pleased to say, so did the theatre bar, so elegant and posh. I started to read out loud.

'"Ryan Harrison, star of teen drama *Manhattan Beach*, arrived in London last night for…"'

'No honey, further down,' interrupted Nicky.

'"Nicky Bathgate, publicity manager, countered, 'West End theatres have been hiring celebrities for years. *Chicago* has seen Kelly Osborne, David Hasselhoff, and Jerry Springer. And last year Lindsay Lohan was dried out like a lump of old coconut matting and shoved on stage… Ryan Harrison may be a heart-throb, but he trained at Juilliard.'" Nice one,' I said.

Nicky screamed. I held the phone away from my ear. 'What?'

'We've sold out. Nat! We've sold out!'

I refreshed the ticket portal and saw that all our shows were now sold out. I screamed along with her for a moment.

'That's two hours and four minutes,' said Nicky. 'It must be a record, I'm gonna go and put the word out there. Let's have a drink soon, yes?'

When I came off the phone, I clicked through the rest of the links. I was shocked to see how much Tuppence Halfpenny featured in the articles. In several she was pictured in her pink lace dress posing on the red carpet outside the theatre. In one, Jamie was pictured at her side. They looked so good together.

I switched off the computer, determined to be happy about *Macbeth* selling out.

# THAT SUNDAY FEELING

I had such cause to celebrate, but no one to celebrate with. I phoned Sharon but she was just on her way to take the kids swimming.

'Come over tomorrow for Sunday lunch, you can tell me all…' she said, then shouted, 'Felix! Stop kicking your sister! I don't care who started it!… Sorry Nat I have to go, see you tomorrow at one?'

I then tried Benjamin, but his phone went to voicemail. I left a breezy gabbling message asking what he was up to, and said I hadn't managed to give the BenjiYoga leaflet to Ryan, but I would, soon. I tried Nicky's phone, but she was engaged for the rest of the day.

I did my laundry, tidied the flat, threw away some dead plants – all with one ear out for my phone, but Benjamin didn't return my call. At six I was starving. I opened a bottle of wine and ordered a load of food from the Indian takeaway menu on the fridge. When I hung up, I realised I had ordered too much, and I had a thought. Would it be crazy to invite Ryan Harrison over? He must be lonely in London. It would be good to get to know him, talk about the show. I could also give him the BenjiYoga leaflet.

I scrolled through my emails and found the details of where he was staying for the six weeks he was in London. I noted the number for the Langham Hotel, and the name he had been booked in under, 'Samuel Heathcliff'.

I looked at my phone for a moment and called the front desk, asking if I could speak to Samuel Heathcliff. There was a pause.

'And who is calling?' intoned the man on reception.

'I'm Natalie Love, the manager of the Raven Street Theatre, where Ry, I mean Mr Heathcliff is working.'

'One moment please.'

Classical music played, and then Ryan came on the line.

'Hello?'

'Hello. I just wanted to say congratulations. All the tickets for *Macbeth* have sold out…' I trilled. There was a pause.

'Who is this?'

'It's Natalie… Love… Theatre manager… Raven Street?'

'Oh sure, hey! Sorry,' he said. 'What's up Natalie?'

'Well, I thought you're here in London…'

There was a scratching sound as the phone was covered, and I heard muffled voices. He came back on the line.

'Sorry Natalie, I've got a buddy visiting, we're just about to head out…'

'Of course, yes. I just phoned to say thank you for being so famous that all our tickets sold out in a morning.'

'Yeah it's far out. I'm so excited to start work on the play… Look, I'm really sorry, but we have reservations…'

'Oh yes, you go. It's Saturday night, I'm just off out too…' I lied. He said goodbye and hung up. I cringed, went and poured another glass of wine, and checked to see what was on TV.


I woke up early on Sunday morning. There was still no message from Benjamin, so I decided to go to his nine am yoga class.

I got off the tube at half eight, with my yoga mat slung over my shoulder. The roads were quiet and deserted. The BenjiYoga studio is in the basement of a tall office block, a short walk from Old Street station. I went through the tiny entrance and down the steps into the reception area. It was manned by Laura. She's worked for Benjamin for a few months now. She's early twenties, rather bony and her head is always shaved bald and shiny with a razor. Her face, ears, and God knows what else, are covered in piercings. I've always wanted to ask her what happens when she has to go through airport security, but she seems the type who wouldn't find that funny. I can't stand her, and I don't think she's too fond of me either.

There was a strong smell of incense, and some mystical sitar music was playing on the PA system. Laura sat behind the desk surfing the net on an elderly iMac. Taped to the back of the flat screen so it faced the customers was a quote:

'The fragrance always remains on the hand that gives the rose,' - Mahatma Gandhi.

However, Laura had her hand buried in some pickled onion crisps which weren't giving off a rose-like aroma.

'Natalie,' she said wryly. I slid a twenty pound note across the desk.

'Morning Laura. Is Benjamin here?' I asked with a forced smile. She slid a fiver back to me, her pickled onion hand covered in yellow butterfly tattoos.

'Of course he is,' she said. 'This is BenjiYoga. It wouldn't be BenjiYoga without Benjamin, would it?'

I was about to have a go at her when Laura's eyes flicked over my shoulder and she bowed her head saying, '*Namaste.*'

Benjamin had appeared behind us wearing a black towelling dressing gown.

'Hey you,' I said.

'*Namaste*, Natalie,' he said raising an eyebrow.

'Yes, hello, *Namaste*,' I said. I made a show of giving him a kiss. Benjamin cocked his head and seemed to sniff the air.

'It's Laura's pickled onion crisps,' I said.

'No… That music, it's wonderful. Good choice Laura,' he said. Laura smiled and bowed her bald head. She had a blue catering plaster stuck to the top where she must have nicked herself with the razor.

'Benjamin, can I talk to you for a minute?' I said. He nodded and we went along the corridor into the large yoga studio with the mirror along one wall. Several of the hardcore regulars were unrolling mats and limbering up for the class. They bowed to Benjamin as we walked through. We carried on to a tiny room in the corner, which Benjamin uses as an office. I closed the door and he sat behind his desk.

'Did you get my messages?' I asked, taking the seat opposite.

'I did…' he said. There was a pause.

'And this is the bit where you explain why you didn't call me back,' I said.

'Natalie, you're being very First World,' he said.

'I'm being First World? Well you're being an arse!'

'Natalie, I won't have raised voices in a yoga environment,' he said with an irritating calm. I took a deep breath.

'I'm not raising my voice…Is this about the leaflet? Because I *will* give Ryan Harrison your leaflet, but I couldn't during the launch party…'

Benjamin stared at me.

'*Namaste* Natalie! You gave me your word,' he said.

'Yes, and I will…'

'Do I ever ask you for anything?'

'Yes. You asked me for ketchup when we had chips the other night…'

'I'm not in the mood for your childish silliness,' he said. 'I need to prepare for class. Go through.' He waved me away with the back of his hand. I went to say something, but he'd sat back in his chair and closed his eyes.

I got up and went through to the studio. I was furious. I hadn't expected him to be such an idiot. I found my usual place at the front and unrolled my mat. The studio soon filled up, and by two minutes to nine we were packed in like sardines. Just before the class began, two very pretty girls, who can't have been more than twenty, came in and put their mats right at the front. One was blonde, and one dark. They were stripping down to little string bikinis just as Benjamin came in.

'Welcome ladies,' he said his eyes lighting up. 'I see you're newbies, I'll keep my eye on you both.'

They giggled and flicked their hair. He stood at the front and shrugged off his robe. Underneath he was wearing a tiny black thong.

Benjamin usually wears sports gear to teach his class… And so do all his pupils. But a *thong*!

I was in shock, but felt unable to say anything as the class began. I kept trying to catch his eye and give him a look, asking what the hell he was doing strutting about in a thong which clearly showed the outline of everything in front, and, when he turned to open a window with the long window pole, the little string vanishing between his bare backside!

However, Benjamin ignored me for the whole class. Several times he went to the two girls in the skimpy bikinis and adjusted their yoga positions, placing his hand on an upper thigh.

After the class I took a shower, fuming under the water as I listened to the two girls giggling in the changing room, saying how hot they thought the yoga teacher was… I waited until they'd left the changing room before I came out of the shower.

When I'd changed, I found Benjamin in his office. He had his robe back on and was tapping away at his computer.

'Natalie, you're still here?' he said. I sat down opposite.

'Benjamin. What was with the thong?' I asked.

'What?'

'The tiny posing pouch. The floss up your arse!'

'What?' he said seeming genuinely confused.

'What do you mean what? You might as well have been naked!'

'Natalie. In many cultures yoga is practised naked…'

'But this is London. And you were kitted out like one of the guys from *Magic Mike*. Which is fine for strippers, but…'

'The sports shorts were inhibiting my movement,' he said.

'And why didn't you correct any of my postures?' I asked.

'Your postures were fine.'

'No, they weren't. I deliberately hunched my back during downward facing dog.'

'Did you?'

'So you weren't even looking at me! Obviously those two girls in bikinis were more important…'

'Natalie, they were new. Do you remember what it was like when you first started? I had to adjust your postures.'

'Yes. And that's how it began with us, isn't it? And I fell for it hook line and sinker… Are you a proper yoga teacher, or is this just a pickup joint for you?'

Benjamin sat back and regarded me.

'I'm sorry. I didn't mean that. You are a very good yoga teacher,' I said.

'I think you should go home Natalie. I don't like your energy right now,' he said.

'I'm sorry. Look, let's go and get a coffee. I have loads to tell you. Our tickets have…'

'Natalie. I have another class.'

'Do you want to come with me for lunch at Sharon's?' I said. He shook his head. 'How about coming over tonight then?' He didn't say anything.

'You'll give me a call, yeah?'

He nodded his head. I picked up my bag and left his office.

On my way out Laura flashed me a horrible smile. She had big chunks of pickled onion crisps between her teeth.

'Nata-lee-a,' said Sharon's husband Fred when he opened their front door. He is quite short and dark with scruffy hair and warm caramel-coloured eyes. He's Italian, his grandparents came over to London after the war. He doesn't have an accent like his father, but he still cries '*Nata-lee-a*' whenever he sees me. I gave him a kiss on the cheek and followed him through to the kitchen. The French doors had been thrown open and a warm breeze wafted through the kitchen. Sharon was buzzing about laying the table for lunch.

'Hey Nat,' she said swooping in for a kiss on her way to the fridge. 'You want a glass of rosé?'

'More than anything else right now…' I said.

'Oh dear,' said Fred taking a chilled bottle of New Zealand rosé from her and grabbing the cork screw.

'AMY! FELIX! Lunch is in ten minutes,' yelled Sharon. From the depths of the living room I could hear the sound of a computer game being played and grunts of acknowledgement.

'Benjamin not coming?' asked Sharon.

'Um, no,' I said. I've given up making excuses, and Fred and Sharon don't expect them. I noticed that the table was set for five. They'd guessed correctly he wouldn't show.

There was a lovely clean sounding pop as Fred opened the wine. He poured three glasses and handed one each to me and Sharon.

'Cheers,' he said and we clinked. After I'd taken a good gulp I told them about the launch party, and about seeing Jamie.

'Jamie Dawson?' asked Sharon.

'Yes,' I said.

'And he's dating Tuppence Halfpenny… She's like the British…'

'Dita Von Teese, yes,' I finished.

'God I picked a right night to get nits…' said Sharon.

'She's pretty nice stuff that Tuppence Halfpenny. All that lace, and those suspenders,' grinned Fred.

'Steady on mister,' said Sharon tossing a salad briskly with two long plastic spoons.

'What? You can have pictures of Ryan Harrison in the pantry, and I can't appreciate the curves of Miss Halfpenny?' grinned Fred.

'No. Is the simple answer,' said Sharon. 'The crushes women experience are so much more elegant and romantic. If Ryan Harrison walked in here right now, I would offer him some salad and a glass of fine wine… If Tuppence walked in right now, your eyes would go all glassy, you'd drool, and no doubt have to adjust your trousers…'

'No, no. I'm class all the way,' protested Fred. 'The only trouser adjusting I do is for you.' He leant in and kissed her. I looked at them, they are still so in love after all these years. Sharon gave me a grin and took the salad over to the table.

'So how did Jamie look after all these years?' she asked.

'He still looks so good. He's like a fine wine, he's aged well,' I said.

'Like Fred. He's a vintage,' laughed Sharon rubbing the balding patch in Fred's dark hair.

'Hey! She was lucky to marry me, wasn't she?' he smiled. I grinned and nodded.

'Do you ever wish you'd married Jamie?' asked Sharon.

'God no! No… No, no, no, no, no…' I said. I took a gulp of wine. There was an awkward pause.

'Okay, I think we're ready to eat,' said Sharon.


I loved going for lunch at Sharon's, but today I felt out of sorts. All the talk of Jamie and what might have been made me see their happy family in a different light. They were such a tight, loving little unit. They never make me feel out of place, but today I did.

After we'd eaten the first course of cold meats, cheese and salad, I excused myself and went upstairs to the bathroom. I turned on the taps and tried Benjamin on my mobile, to my surprise he answered.

'Benjamin hi,' I said cupping my hand around the phone.

'Are you by the sea?' he asked. I turned off the taps.

'No. I'm at Sharon's. In the bathroom.'

'Are you on the toilet? Because Natalie, that's just disrespectful.'

'I'm not on the toilet. I'm sitting on the edge of the bath, running the taps,' I regretted saying this because it hinted that I had somehow hidden myself away to phone him. 'I called to see what you're doing later?' I added.

'Nothing,' he said.

'Great. So do you want to come round? We can order some sushi, and we can put on a film you like. I've got *Ghandi* on DVD…'

'No, I'm planning on doing nothing. I need to think. Meditate.'

'About what?' I said hopefully.

'Natalie, what is this Western obsession with *doing things* and filling up your time with tasks?'

'But you said…'

'Natalie, I'm a free spirit, you knew this when you entered into a relationship with me…'

'I was going to ask you tonight, but because you're busy doing nothing, I have to ask you now. How would you like to come to my sister Micky's christening?' I asked.

'I thought your sister was in her late twenties?'

'It's her son Dexter's christening,' I clarified.

There was a pause.

'Natalie, you know I despise organised religion.'

'There's nothing really religious about it, it'll just be a load of middle-class people showing off their children.'

'Fine,' he said.

'Fine what?'

'I'll come to the christening.'

'Really?' I said, shocked.

'Of course, Natalie. We're in an adult relationship. This is what adults do.'

'Well that's fab, thank you, I mean that's great. And if you want to do some adult stuff, I can come over after all… Before you do nothing, we could do somethi…'

'Natalie, please give me some space. *Namaste.*' And then he hung up.

I turned off the taps. I quickly wrote a triumphant text message to my mother:

I WILL BE COMING TO THE CHRISTENING WITH BENJAMIN
CAN'T WAIT TO SEE YOU ALL & FOR U TO MEET HIM :) NAT x
P.S FORGOT TO ASK ABOUT TRIFLE. WILL FIND OUT.

I heard Sharon from downstairs asking one of the kids to come and get me for dessert. I washed my hands and came out of the bathroom. Amy and Felix leapt back from where they had been listening outside the door.

'Hello, what are you two up to?' I asked. Amy threw her arms around my waist and gave me a huge hug.

'WE love you Aunt Nat... don't we Felix?' she said. He nodded sagely beside her.

'And I love you both too,' I said.

'Benjamin doesn't deserve you,' Amy added. 'We just heard you on the phone.'

'He does sound like a commitment probe,' said Felix nodding.

'Not a *probe* Felix, Mum said commitment *phobe*,' corrected Amy.

'What's a probe?' asked Felix.

'That's the thing they put up daddy's bottom, when he had the health check... A 'phobe' is someone who is scared of something...' said Amy. 'Benjamin is scared to commit to Aunt Nat, and that's not her fault, he's just making her feel that it is. That's what commitment phobes do.'

I looked at her, shocked at her insight and maturity.

'He's just agreed to come to a christening with me,' I said, realising I was seeking the approval of an eight and ten year old.

'Mum thinks Benjamin is a wanker,' said Felix. 'We overheard her saying that to Daddy. And she said that you think you're not good enough for him, but actually you are way better...'

'And Mummy said you shouldn't be afraid to be single and stay in the relationship just because you don't want to be alone...' added Amy.

Sharon appeared at the bottom of the stairs.

'There you all are. Who wants pavlova?'

'Yayyayayayayayyy!' The kids screamed and ran down the stairs.

'Nat?'

'I'd love some, and some more of that wine,' I said.

I left mid-afternoon, and after saying bye to the kids and Fred, Sharon came with me to the front door.

'Thanks again for lunch,' I said giving her a hug. 'Benjamin has agreed to come to Dexter's christening. He's going to meet my family.'

'That's nice,' she said. 'It's only taken him a year, is it?'

'Eleven and a half months... Do you like Benjamin?' Sharon opened her mouth then closed it. 'Be honest, please,' I added.

She came out onto the front step and pulled the door closed behind her.

'Nat. Whoever you love, I will love, or I will try my best to... I just think that Benjamin, I think he...'

'Is a commitment phobe and a wanker?'

'I may have said that off the record...' said Sharon uncomfortably. 'But seriously, I think you are a catch Nat. You're clever, and funny and so loyal. You are my best friend who I want the best for. And I don't know if Benjamin is the best.'

'He can be different when I get him on his own... And he sees the world differently...'

'Look, Nat. If you can make it work with Benjamin, then I support you all the way, and I will love him because you love him. Hell, he can even babysit!'

I smiled.

'So on another subject,' she said. 'When do I get to meet Ryan Harrison?'

'We start rehearsals tomorrow,' I said. 'Let me get the first day over with and then I'll sort something. I promise.'

'Love you,' she said giving me a big hug. As I made my way to the train station it kept going round in my head what, Sharon had said...

*If you can make it work with Benjamin, then I support you all the way...*

Maybe it was simple. I just had to make it work. Maybe I just needed to go with it, take risks. Benjamin agreeing to come to the christening was a real breakthrough. If that went well I could bring him to Sharon's for Sunday lunch, and we could babysit!

When I got home I made a decision. I had a shower, shaved my legs, straightened my hair and made myself look irresistible, best underwear and all. I packed my toothbrush and spare underwear in case things went very well and I stayed over. I then took the tube down to Benjamin's.

I spent the tube journey thinking what I would say. I'd tell him I was being spontaneous – that would be a word to appeal to Benjamin. I'd say that I'd come all the way for one kiss, and after that kiss I'd be on my way. He'd be unable to resist and pull me indoors.

With a buzz of confidence, I got off the train at Collier's Wood and walked round to his flat. He lives on the ground floor in a shabby chic area near the tube station, filled with organic shops and art galleries. When I got to the communal front door, the blinds were down in the front window. Light glossed from behind. I rang the doorbell and a few moments passed. I rang again. After another minute I heard, very softly, his twinkly sitar music coming from his flat.

I went round to the bay window at the front, which is his living room. The wooden blinds were drawn shut, but hadn't quite been lowered all the way. There was a two inch gap at the bottom. I crouched down to the window sill and peered through. I gave a little squeal of shock. On the living room floor Benjamin lay naked and sat astride him, also naked, was Laura! I could see in addition to her face, she had her nipples pierced and – where Benjamin's erection was buried between her legs – three more piercings.

I stared as they had sex, not quite able to turn my head away from it. The joint moans of ecstasy, the candles dotted around them, and the clinking sound of Laura's piercings. It was like hearing someone sorting through loose change in their trousers. Their movements became quicker, then I jumped as I heard Benjamin shout, '*NAMASTE*!'

I stood up, unsure of what to do. I was livid and terrified at the same time. I walked back down the path and through the gate, then went back. I walked up the path to the front door where I rang the bell holding my finger down on it. I was about to leave when the light flicked on in the hall and the door was pulled open.

Benjamin stood there in his dressing gown.

'Natalie. *Namaste*,' he said. He looked up and down and took in my short skirt and heels. The oversized bag. I was completely lost for words.

'What do you think you're doing?' I shrilled, sounding much like my mother. He looked furious.

'I told you. I'm meditating Natalie. Why did you go against my wishes? Why do you act so passive aggressive?'

'What? Me?'

'Yes! I tell you I am meditating. That I want peace and quiet and you turn up unannounced, dressed provocatively so I can't say no. And I have to let you in. Well I'm not going to bow to your passive aggressive behaviour!' he said raising his voice. I stood there with my mouth open.

'I just wanted to come and see you…' I squeaked.

'And I just want a bit of space. Maybe I want to be alone.' He stared at me and I'm ashamed to say I didn't speak. I opened my mouth again but nothing came out.

'Now it's still light. Go and get on the tube, and go home, and text me to let me know you're home safe, ok?' he said.

He smiled and closed the door. I stood there for a moment, but all my energy was gone. Defeated I walked back to the tube station, got on the train, and went home.

# THE WOMAN IN BLACK

I went back to the flat and lay on my bed in the darkness, staring up at the ceiling. My building was very quiet, save for the pipes gurgling as water whooshed through the walls. As the time passed, the pipes fell silent until all I could hear was the ticking clock in the kitchen. I tried to convince myself I had imagined it all. But the image of them having sex wouldn't leave me.

I spent a sleepless night trying to work out why. *What does Laura have that I don't? Tattoos and piercings... What do I have that she doesn't?* Hair. It went round and round in my head... Is that what Benjamin wanted?

I tried to picture myself with a shaved head, but I could never do it voluntarily, and as for all that body piercing... How often have I caught a hang-nail on a rug? All that metal attached to delicate skin didn't bear thinking about.

I was glad when morning came and I could focus back on work. It was the first day of rehearsals for *Macbeth*. I walked to the theatre, popping in to Grande, where I met Nicky. She was dressed in an electric blue trouser suit with matching blue heels and blue glasses.

'No honey, get a pen and write it down...' she said, berating a new barista, who wasn't versed in the alchemy of her coffee ordering. 'Decaf Colombian flat white soy, no foam, two pumps of hazelnut syrup, a little soy whip on top with a dusting of fair trade cocoa, and can you pour this Sweet'N'Low *slowly* into the soy milk as you steam.' She handed him a little sachet of sweetener. He nodded. Sweat had broken out on his forehead.

'Just a small Americano,' I said to the poor chap.

'Hey Nat. I'm all in blue, but you look blue,' she said giving me a hug.

'I didn't sleep all that well,' I explained.

'Don't be worried about today… it's gonna be great,' she said. The barista handed over a huge coffee and she peered over her glasses, giving it the once over. I realised I had been obsessing over Benjamin when there were far more exciting things happening. Why was I putting so much emphasis on him and our dysfunctional relationship?

Nicky pronounced herself satisfied with the coffee. I grabbed my Americano, and we made our way to the theatre. I stopped for a moment outside the Old Library. A skip was being lowered by the kerb, and a group of guys in hard hats were filing in through a gap in the faded tarpaulin covering the building. I tried to see inside.

'Honey, that will keep,' said Nicky. She pointed across the road. 'The Raven Street Theatre is the place to be right now.'

Outside the main entrance a small group of press stood huddled, and slightly apart were some die-hard Ryan Harrison fans. They consisted of teenage girls, a couple of greasy old men, and a thin camp guy leaning onto the handles of a wheelchair in which a small blonde girl sat. They moved to one side to let us in.

'What time does Ryan arrive?' asked the thin guy.

'Dunno. I'm just the cleaning lady,' lied Nicky pulling open the door.

Beside the thin guy with the wheelchair, a sweet little girl, who couldn't have been more than twelve, was waiting with her mother. Her mother, who was rather buxom and bursting out of a short red dress a few sizes too small, grabbed my arm saying,

'Beffany 'as got a cuddly toy fer Ryan 'arrison…' She nudged Bethany, who held out a small stuffed bear cradling a heart. Bethany smiled with a tooth gapped smile.

'Okay, I'll see he gets it,' I said, taking it.

'Thank you,' grinned Bethany sweetly. I went inside where Nicky was waiting.

'Nat, honey. Don't engage with the crazies,' she said.

'I know, but she was so sweet.'

'It's eight thirty on a weekday and she's stood in Soho. What about school?'

'She could be on the way to school?' I said.

'Trust me, they're crazy, like the rest of them.'

'But look, that guy has brought his friend in the wheelchair, she's clutching her autograph book,' I said.

Nicky peered through the glass door. She rolled her eyes.

'That's the oldest trick in the book, bring the friend in a wheelchair…'

'Nicky!'

'I've met Bruce Springsteen four times. You know how? Thanks to Connie Bouvier…'

'Who's Connie Bouvier?' I asked.

'A girl from high school who was in a wheelchair. We stalked Bruce on his *Born in the USA* tour… Even managed to get into his dressing room. No one ever questioned us when I was pushing Connie in her wheelchair. All fans are crazy, Nat. Remember that.'

I looked down at the cute little cuddly toy bear, and followed her up the stairs.

*

We were meeting at eight thirty in the rehearsal room on the fourth floor. It's large and bare with high ceilings. The parquet floor glistened under the fluorescent strip lights, and the row of windows along one wall was painted black.

Byron, the stage manager, was adjusting a big circle of folding chairs which had been set up in the middle of the room. She nodded hello to us. Her mousy waist-length hair was pulled back into a ponytail, and she had a ZZ Top t-shirt tucked neatly into her high-waisted stonewashed jeans. We were lucky to have Byron working on *Macbeth*. She's a no-nonsense New Zealander who has worked in every theatre in the West End.

Xander was in the corner setting up a tea urn on a table with plastic cups, tea bags, and instant coffee. He came over and showed off a tartan waistcoat he was wearing in honour of the occasion. Craig, the director, was next to arrive. He's a short, dark, rather intense-looking guy, but he has a wicked sense of humour, and when he laughs, which is often, his whole face comes alive. He's directed loads of our plays over the years and is, like Byron, one of the best.

Byron stationed herself by the door as the actors started to arrive. They drifted in, saying hello, and made a beeline for the tea urn, talking in small groups. When Ryan came in, the atmosphere in the room changed, and became a bit heightened. He was wearing a grey tracksuit and carrying a backpack. Byron shook his hand and started to talk to him.

'Awww. He looks really scared,' said Xander.

'You never said he was so short!' added Craig.

'Hollywood stars are like Christmas trees, you pay by the foot,' said Nicky wryly.

'Do you know how loud you all are?' I hissed. A tall dark girl swanned in and joined the conversation with Ryan and Byron.

'Look. Lady Macbeth is a foot taller than Ryan,' said Craig indicating the girl. 'We'll have to talk to costume about shoes, maybe we can put a big crown on his head…'

'It's cool Craig,' said Nicky. 'Lady Macbeth could make a joke about them all being the same height when they're lying down.'

'You can't add bits to the Bard,' grinned Craig in mock out-rage. Ryan turned to us, smiled and walked over.

'Hey guys, what's new?' he said.

'We were just saying how excited we are to have you on board,' I said. The room fell silent, they seemed to think that I was starting a speech. I went on.

'Good morning everybody, hello, please help yourselves to tea and coffee. For those of you who don't know us yet, I'm Natalie Love, I'm the theatre manager and artistic director, this is Nicky Bathgate our head of publicity, and Xander Campbell our office administrator…'

The actors all gave us a round of applause. Nicky stepped forward and gave a little curtsey which got a big laugh. I grinned and went on.

'Nicky and I started this theatre five years ago, and we're very excited about the buzz this production has generated. Tickets are sold out across the run, thanks to the hugely talented Ryan Harrison.'

I paused as the actors all whooped and clapped, Ryan smiled bashfully.

'And I'd like to add that Craig our director has found a truly talented group of actors, we're so pleased to welcome you all here, and we can't wait to watch the play on opening night!'

Everyone applauded.

'And!' I added. 'Last but not least, Ryan, when I got here this morning I met one of your fans waiting outside. A sweet young girl called Bethany. She wanted me to give you this… To wish you luck.'

I handed the teddy bear to Ryan and everyone went 'Ahhhh'.

'Gee thanks,' said Ryan looking at the toy. 'I'm real pleased to be here too, and I'm looking forward to working with you all!' He squeezed the little heart the bear was holding, and Bethany's mother's tinny recorded voice echoed throughout the rehearsal room.

*'Me name's Dawn Matthews 'an I love you Ryan. I can be really slutty in bed, 'an me 'usband works nights. Text me on 07984567341…'*

Everyone fell silent. I was mortified. Byron moved into the middle of the room,

'Cin I just say that this has highlighted the need to be vigilant about fans of Mr Hirrison,' she said in her broad New Zealand accent. She held out a small metal bin and Ryan dropped the teddy in. He had turned rather pale. Byron went on, 'If you see something or someone suspicious please talk to me, or theatre management. And I'll need all company mimbers to switch *awf* their mobile phones in the rehearsal room and hind them over to me.'

'What did I tell you Nat?' said Nicky when we were back in the office. 'Crazy fans…'

'I'm mortified,' I said peering out of the window at the road below. 'I've a good mind to go back down and tell that woman…'

'Tell her what? We've got so much to do Nat. And there are a million more crazier fans out there.'

I sat at my desk and logged into my laptop.

'I'm gonna call Val on box office,' I said. 'Make sure that no one gets past her and inside.'

The rest of the day was spent catching up on emails, opening post, and checking over contracts for everyone involved in *Macbeth*. I had meetings with the bar and box office managers to go over their figures, and I spent a few hours going through our budgets with the finance manager. Late afternoon, over another coffee, Xander went over the shows we were booked in to see during the week. Nicky and I try to see as much theatre as we can, to keep in the loop, and we often go along to see an actor we could cast in one of our future plays. Nicky had been due to come with me that evening to see an actor who was starring in *The Woman in Black* at the Fortune Theatre, but she managed to get a dinner date with the showbiz editor of *Heat* magazine, so I phoned Sharon to come and see it with me instead.

I met her at six thirty in the dark little pub opposite the Fortune Theatre. She had come straight from work, where she manages the Royal Mail sorting office in New Cross.

'Hello Nat,' she grinned giving me a hug. 'I'm having a very large glass of wine. We had an anthrax alert today. Turned out to be a parcel full of Yardley talcum powder for some old biddy.'

'Okay, I'm buying,' I said. Sharon went to grab a table and I pushed my way through the crowded pub to the bar. I came back with two glasses of wine, and told her everything that had happened that day, which made her laugh, and then everything that had happened with Benjamin the previous night, which she didn't laugh at. When I'd finished, she took a sip of her wine, and played with the stem of her glass for a moment.

'Nat. In a horrible way I'm relieved, because he's a wanker and a commitment phobe. He's also a bastard, a git, and so wrong for you. I mean what's the deal? Is it just lust and loneliness on your part? How can someone so pretentious do anything for you?'

'Okay Sharon…' I said, but she went on.

'He has no sense of humour. He's self-centred and vain. He pretends to be so deep, but in reality he's as shallow as a puddle.'

'Sharon!'

'I'm sorry Nat.'

'What was that speech yesterday? "*If you can make it work with Benjamin, then I support you all the way... I'll love him because you love him.*"' I asked.

'Now he's cheated on you I can be honest. *Namaste* indeed. You know what? Every time he said *Namaste*, you should have called him a twat. That would have cut down on his use of the word!'

Tears started to form in my eyes and I wiped them with the back of my hand.

'Now come on Nat,' said Sharon reaching inside her bag and pulling out a clump of tissues. 'I'm sorry. I should have slagged him off in instalments. I just can't stand to see you unhappy. Everything else in your life is going so well, and he's taking that away from you.'

'You're right,' I said wiping my face with a tissue. 'I just don't know what to do?'

'Well, I hope the first thing involves the tip of one of your pointiest shoes connecting swiftly with his bollocks.'

I laughed and then dissolved into more tears.

'You don't know what it's like Sharon. I feel alone so much of the time. You've got an amazing family...'

'Which I wouldn't have if I hadn't met Fred? He was the one. And you are going to meet the one...'

'I'm running out of time to meet the one,' I said, adding quietly, 'What if Jamie was the one?'

'Jamie wasn't the one,' said Sharon. 'And did you really think you could *marry* Benjamin?'

'No. But he was going to come to the christening with me.'

Sharon snorted.

'What should I do?' I asked.

'He can't get away with this. Have you got a key to his flat? We could go over when he's out and cut up all his clothes and throw them out of the window!'

'I haven't even got a key… I gave him a key, and he didn't give me one back!'

'Then it's remarkably simple. Tell him to go jump off a cliff and then get on with your life. How many people would kill to have such an uncomplicated separation?'

She gave me a hug. 'Now I'm getting us more drinks, and then you're going to tell me again about the obscene-talking teddy bear…I wish I'd thought of that as a gift for Ryan Harrison. Only last week I took Amy to the build-a-bear factory in Westfield.'


Sharon managed to cheer me up over another glass of wine and then we crossed the road to watch the show. Despite it being the story of a mad spinster who goes insane through loneliness, *The Woman in Black* was fab. I hadn't seen the show for years, and had forgotten just how terrifying it was. Staged with minimal props, the actors draw the audience in, recounting the story of the haunted house on the marshes by the sea. Sharon and I had seats down in the stalls, and during the show, the Woman in Black walked through the audience, brushing past the end of the row where we were sat! Sharon nearly died of fright, shrieking and spraying a group of Japanese tourists in front with half a box of Smarties.

After the show I felt a lot better. We had that wonderful feeling that comes after a good scare, and we went round to the stage door to meet the actor I had been there to watch. We had a nice chat and told him how much we'd loved the show.

Half an hour later we left him to finish taking off his make-up and went back downstairs. The Fortune is a very old theatre, and it was deserted as we made our way down the long creaky flight of stairs. Halfway down all the lights went out. I felt Sharon behind grab at my arm.

'What the hell! I can't see a thing!' she hissed. A couple of seconds later the emergency lights kicked in, casting a green pallid glow over the gloomy stairway.

'If we run into the Woman in Black I will shit myself,' said Sharon.

'Even if we do, she'll have taken off her make-up,' I said. Our feet echoed as we climbed down.

'Where is everyone?' asked Sharon, still holding on to me.

'Gone home probably,' I said. We reached the bottom of the stairs and went out of the stage door into the alley beside the theatre. It was eerily quiet and the moon was shrouded in cloud. When we emerged onto Russell Street it was empty and the streetlights were off. The outside of the theatre was now deserted, and the pub was closed.

'I don't like this, it's creepy,' said Sharon.

'It's just a power cut,' I said.

'But it's weird for all the street lights and the traffic lights to be off,' she said pulling her coat around her neck.

'Why don't you get a cab home?' I said. 'The theatre will give me it back on expenses, and you've got further to go.'

'You're going to walk on your own Nat?' said Sharon.

'It's five minutes, it's fine,' I said. A black cab rounded the corner with its light on. I stuck my arm out and it came to a stop beside us.

'We can go by your place,' suggested Sharon.

'That'll take an age with all the one-way streets. Take the taxi and get a receipt,' I said.

'I'll take it, if you take this,' said Sharon rummaging around in her bag. She pulled out a small back canister.

'It's pepper spray,' she added.

'Why have you got pepper spray?' I said, quickly taking it so the taxi driver couldn't see.

'Fred likes me to carry it when I'm walking home from work.'

The window slid down a few inches.

'How much longer are you two going to chat? The clock is on,' said the driver.

'She's coming now,' I said pushing her in.

'Make sure you have the nozzle facing the right way,' said Sharon tilting her head towards the pepper spray in my pocket. 'You don't want it in your face.'

'I'll be fine,' I said.

'And call me if you need me, anytime. You can't let Benjamin get away with what he's done.' She blew me a kiss and closed the door. I waved as the taxi pulled away and vanished round the bend.

The road was dark and quiet. Damp air seemed to descend onto me in the silence. A wisp of mist floated past. I thought of the misty marshland in *The Woman in Black,* and remembered the sound of the horses screaming as the carriage got lost in the fog and sank into the marsh.

I pulled my coat up around my neck and started to walk home. The five minutes seemed to extend far longer, and I barely saw a soul as I walked up to Soho. None of the street lights were working and all the shops and restaurants were dark.

Beak Street was quiet as I approached my building. I went to scan my card on the gate but as I touched the sensor it swung open with a creak. As I walked through the dark communal garden, a car out on the road backfired and I'm ashamed to say I ran to my front door, shoved in the key, and dashed inside slamming the door behind me. I flicked the switch in the hall but nothing happened. It remained dark.

I pulled out my phone, put on the light, and went through to the kitchen. I rummaged around in the drawers and found a stub of a candle. I lit it and placed it on a saucer.

As I pulled a glass from the cupboard, there was a scratching sound coming from the hall... I froze. It came again. I crept through, and in the gloom I could hear someone outside the front door murmuring, and the noise of a key being tried in the lock.

I panicked and scrabbled about for my coat. I barely had the pepper spray out when the front door opened a few inches. The door juddered as the security chain stopped it opening further. A hand came groping round to try and unfasten it. I screamed, rushed at the door, and fired pepper spray into the gap.

'Aaargh! *Namaste!*' shouted a voice.

Suddenly the power came back on. I went to the gap in the door, and saw it was Benjamin. He had dropped to his knees on the doorstep and was clutching his face in agony. His cheeks and eyes were rapidly swelling and tears were streaming down his face.

# THE STING

Benjamin was shouting and thrashing around in agony. I took the security chain off the door and guided him inside through to the bathroom.

'*Namaste*!' he cried, clutching at his face. I opened the shower door and guided him into the cubicle. 'Jeez!' he said as I leant round him and turned on the water. 'What did you do to me?'

'I pepper sprayed you, I thought you were an intruder,' I said.

'But I bought you flowers!' he cried reaching into his jacket like a blind magician, and pulling out a bunch of carnations. He thrust them in my direction, and clamped his large hands back over his face rubbing furiously at his swollen eyes.

'Well? Are you going to say thank you?' he snapped.

'Yes, thank you,' I said dropping them down the side of the toilet. It didn't feel like a good time to tell him I'm allergic to carnations, they make my eyes run.

'Put your head under the water,' I said pushing him gently under the shower head and switching on the tap. 'Let the water run over your face, I'll just go and see what to do next.'

'Oh my GOD! *Namaste*, this HURTS!' he shouted and slammed his hand against the tiles of the shower. I hurried through to the kitchen, grabbed my phone and googled what you should do to relieve the symptoms of being pepper sprayed. It said that pepper spray is oil based, and to mix up a very weak solution of dish detergent. I found a bowl and mixed a tiny spot of Fairy Liquid into warm water and took it to the bathroom.

'Nat! Natalie! Where are you? Don't you leave me!' Benjamin was shouting. He was standing under the running water still in all his clothes, and denim jacket.

'I'm here,' I said grabbing his flailing hand. 'I've got a bowl of very weak washing up liquid water. You need to dunk your face in and open your eyes so the pepper spray can wash away.'

'Washing up liquid?'

'Yes.'

'I hope it's the eco stuff I bought you for your birthday?'

'Yes, that was a lovely present,' I said. 'Now you need to do it fast, or you could go blind.'

'Blind?' he whimpered groping around for the bowl. I placed it in his hands. He held it in out in front of him, and taking deep breaths, dunked his face in for a few seconds before dramatically coming up for air. I almost laughed. He reminded me of a contestant on *I'm A Celebrity* where they have to dunk their faces in slime and pick out plastic stars… Then he started to sob, and I felt dreadful.

'It hurts so much Natalie!'

After I had changed the water a few times, I guided him out of the shower and through to the living room. As he sunk into the sofa, still dripping wet, I realised with concern that he didn't seem to be getting any better… His face seemed even more swollen.

I grabbed my phone again and scrolled through the advice page on what to do after being pepper sprayed. Another tip was to use dairy. Dairy products like plain yoghurt are good for relieving stinging and swelling, so I went to the fridge to try and rustle something up.

I didn't have plain yoghurt, but I did have vanilla yoghurt. I grabbed it, thinking it would have to do. I went back to where Benjamin was on the sofa. His nose and eyes were streaming, and as I put my hand up close to his face to dab it with a tissue, I could feel the heat beating back against my palm.

'Did you manage to find anything?' he said, opening his eyes just a tiny bit and wincing. The whites had turned pink, and were criss-crossed with a spider web of veins.

'Yes, I've got yoghurt,' I said. 'Yoghurt will relieve the pain.'

I peeled off the lid, scooped up a teaspoon of the vanilla yoghurt and dabbed it gently around his eyes. He was silent for a moment and then began to groan.

'What?' I said. He groaned louder. Then his face started to puff up even more. And then I remembered. Benjamin is allergic to soya. I looked at the label.

It was soya yoghurt!

# TO BE, OR NOT TO BE?

The ambulance arrived within minutes of me calling, but in that short time Benjamin had swollen up like the Incredible Hulk and was having trouble breathing. I hurriedly buzzed in two paramedics, a man and a woman who were carrying big green medical boxes and pulling a stretcher. There was a film of rain on their fluorescent jackets.

We went through to the living room where Benjamin was propped up on the sofa; he looked gruesome, like he was wearing a fat suit. They rushed over and began firing questions at me. What's his name? What triggered the allergy? Was it a sex act with latex? Peanuts?

'It was soya yoghurt,' I blurted. 'And we weren't using it in a sex act... I pepper sprayed him...'

'So this is an intruder?' asked the woman prising Benjamin's puffy lips apart and shining a torch in his mouth. 'You defended yourself with a soya yoghurt, then pepper spray?'

'No. He's my boyfriend, we've been together for a year... He has a soya allergy... I pepper sprayed him, then tried to soothe it with soya yoghurt,' I explained.

'And you didn't know about his allergy?' asked the male paramedic.

'Men never tell you anything! You have to wrestle the most basic things out of them...' I said. It hung in the air for a moment. The woman unwrapped a plastic syringe and gave Benjamin a shot of adrenalin; he took a sharp intake of breath.

'Benjamin, can you hear me?' asked the woman. 'You've had a nasty reaction and we're going to take you to hospital…'

Benjamin murmured something through a thick tongue. They positioned the stretcher beside the sofa, swung him round and heaved him over and onto it.

'Airway is now relaxed and open,' said the woman unwrapping another needle from a plastic pack and sliding it into Benjamin's arm. She worked quickly attaching a tube which led up to a bag of clear fluid.

'Is he going to die?' I asked, now very scared. I thought even Sharon would agree that Macing Benjamin, then death through anaphylactic shock was revenge too far. The man opened out a rod connected to the pop-up stretcher and hooked up the fluid bag.

'We got here in time. He's stable now,' he said.

'Right let's move,' said the woman throwing a red blanket over Benjamin. I grabbed my bag and followed them out into the communal garden.

'Does Benjamin have an EpiPen?' asked the man as they lifted the stretcher up the three small steps leading to the path.

'I don't know,' I said running along beside. 'He's only got a toothbrush here… I wanted him to bring more stuff, but he always refused…'

Benjamin's hand emerged from under the blanket.

'He wants your hand,' said the woman. I cottoned on and grabbed it, but had to let go again as they swung the stretcher round to the ambulance. With a thunk of the wheels collapsing, the stretcher was in. I went to follow but they said there was no room and I was to meet them at the hospital.

'Do you want me to come?' I asked.

'You're his girlfriend, yes?' asked the woman.

'Um, well it's kind of…'

'We have to go. We'll be at Guy's and Tommy's,' she said and slammed the doors. The ambulance streaked away with the sirens and lights on. I flagged down a cab and got to Guy's and St. Thomas' Hospital twenty minutes later.

The accident and emergency department was crowded. Babies were crying, an elderly lady was sitting with a huge swollen ankle. Another woman was leaning against the wall clutching at her head, blood seeping from a wound and staining her white t-shirt. Two receptionists were answering phones, and I joined a queue at the desk. I got to the front a few minutes later and asked the younger, friendlier receptionist where I could find Benjamin Jarvis. She tapped away at her computer then asked me to take a seat.

'Could you tell me what's going on? Is he okay?' I asked.

'The doctor is assessing him now,' she said.

'Is he going to be all right?'

'We'll know more when the doctor has assessed him, please take a seat,' she said firmly. I stood there for a moment and saw a woman with a tiny baby behind me. I sat and began to think, should I contact Benjamin's parents? Where would I get their number? I knew he had a sister called Emma, and she lived in Reading but I'd never met her either. I didn't even have a key to go and get him some stuff. I felt very odd. I watched the clock go round once, and then my name was called out.

'Please go through there, and ask for Dr Best,' said the receptionist, pointing to a set of swing doors opposite. I went through into a huge room divided up into cubicles. A tall thin man turned from staring at a bank of X-rays.

'Natalie Love?'

'Yes,' I said. 'I'm here for Benjamin Jarvis, is he okay?'

'Follow me,' he said. He took me to a cubicle on the end of the row, and pulled the curtain open. Benjamin was lying propped up in bed. He was wearing a green hospital gown, and now had two IV lines in his arm. His face was still swollen to twice its size, and he still looked as if he was wearing a fat suit.

'He had a very nasty reaction, but he should make a full recovery,' said Dr Best. 'It was a rather odd mixture of pepper and vanilla yoghurt on his face…'

'Yes,' I said. There was a pause and the doctor went on.

'Is that something I could perhaps find in Waitrose? My wife loves their Heston Blumenthal range, is it something new?'

'No, it was pepper spray.'

'Oh, right…'

'No. It was just a misunderstanding…'

The doctor was now looking at me differently. Like I had gone down in his estimation. I wasn't a fellow Waitrose shopper. I was a trouble-making chav.

'Right… Well I'll want to keep him in until morning for observation,' he added and then scuttled out. I went to the bed and took Benjamin's hand.

'Hello Benjamin, it's Natalie, I'm so sorry…' I said. A nurse came in and adjusted the IV fluid going into his arm.

'His belongings are in the plastic bag in the bedside cabinet,' she said. 'Do you want a cot?'

'We haven't got a baby,' I said.

'No. For you dear. If you want to grab a few hours' sleep? Once this IV has gone in, he'll probably be free to go home in the morning…' she peered at Benjamin. 'He's asleep now, we gave him a sedative too.'

I agreed to have a cot and thanked the nurse.

'Why don't you get a drink whilst he's asleep? I'll be around.' She pointed me in the direction of the cafeteria, and I went and grabbed a large Americano, and took it outside the main entrance.

\*

It was a warm summer night, and moths were swarming around the orange streetlights. There were small groups of nurses smoking. An old man in a wheelchair came to a stop beside me.

'I could get into trouble bringing you out so late, Gerald. You've got five minutes,' said a nurse. She secured his brakes and went back inside. The old man's face was plump with jaundice, and he fumbled around under his blankets, pulling out a creased pack of cigarettes. He teased one out with a swollen hand. He located a lighter amongst his blankets, and eased the cigarette into his mouth. Big black bruises dotted his arm, presumably from attempts to find a vein. Despite using both hands on the lighter, his swollen fingers couldn't get it to work.

'Do you want a hand?' I asked. He nodded gratefully. I took the lighter and lit his cigarette.

'I shouldn't really,' he said breaking into a hacking cough. 'Ooh that's lovely though.' I took a swig of my coffee.

'You all right lass?' he asked.

'Um, I don't know,' I said. 'How are you?'

The old man looked down at his walking frame, the bags of fluid hanging off it.

'Sorry that was…'

'Don't worry lass,' he wheezed. 'I've had a bloody good life. I'm nearly ninety…' He reached into his blankets again, pulling out one of those purses where you have to squeeze the top so the edges part. He held it out towards me with a shaky hand.

'Do you want something from the shop?' I asked. He shook his head and then went into a coughing fit, turning almost blue before he recovered.

'Look inside,' he said finally. I took the purse and gently squeezed it open. I could feel something rigid, and I pulled out a stack of bankcards held together with a couple of rubber bands.

'Turn it over,' he said. I did, and inside a cloudy square of plastic wrapper was an old black and white photo. I carefully took it out. It was of a young couple, sat on the ledge of a window, looking out over the backdrop of a fishing village.

'Tuscany… Nineteen fifty-four…' he wheezed taking another drag.

'She's very beautiful,' I said looking at the woman. Her long brown hair shone in the sun, and she was wearing a plain blouse buttoned up almost to the neck. You could still see she had an amazing figure. Beside her was a dark, lean, handsome man in a roll neck jumper. He had his arm slung over her shoulder and was smiling into the sun.

'Is this you?' I asked.

'Can you believe it?' he said. 'I can remember that photo like it was last week, seems like it was only last bloody week!'

'Was she your girlfriend?' I asked, still holding the photo.

'Girlfriend? I bloody married her!' he said. 'You think I'd let her get away! We were together sixty-three years.' He seemed like he was going to cough, but didn't. He was quiet for a moment, then his eyes filled up. I found a tissue and passed it to him.

'I'm a daft bastard, aren't I?'

'No!' I protested. 'She was the one, yes?'

'Oh she was indeed,' he said wistfully. 'Claire was the one…'

I gently packed the photo back in its plastic in the purse, and handed it back to him. He tucked it carefully in his blankets.

'Even ten years ago I could have given any bloke a run for his money,' he said coughing again. 'You got a husband?'

'No,' I said.

'Boyfriend?'

'Um. Not sure,' I said.

'Well, if you want your mind made up I'm in Ward 69, for want of a better number!'

I laughed. The nurse appeared behind us.

'Ah, here's my prison warder,' he said. She smiled and nodded at me.

'Has he been behaving himself?'

'He's been a gentleman,' I said.

What am I going to do with you Gerald?' said the nurse. She was pretty with black hair, and she looked good in her uniform.

'You can join us. My dying wish is a threesome!' he said, winking at me. The nurse gave me a wry look and then wheeled him away.


I went back inside to the cubicle where Benjamin slept. A mattress had been delivered, and was rolled up and propped against the wall. I could unroll that mattress, and stay the night or… A realisation fell on me from a great height. Benjamin wasn't the one. How had it taken me so long to realise the obvious?

I opened the locker beside the bed, and gently pulled his phone out of the plastic bag. I switched it on, muffling the start-up tone with my hand. After a moment, it asked me to enter a PIN. I stared at the little box with four underscored lines… I tried my birthday, but it was incorrect. I had two attempts remaining. I had no clue when Laura's birthday was, then I realised that the only person Benjamin was really in love with was Benjamin. I keyed in his birthday, and was shocked when the phone unlocked.

I looked up, he was still asleep.

I scrolled through texts, and emails, and saw that Laura featured heavily. It seemed things had been going on for some time, and there were even pictures, taken over the last couple of months, unappetising Readers Wives-style pictures. I won't go into too much detail, but I can tell you that Laura has fifteen piercings. Eight of which are below her neck.

I took out my phone and wrote Laura a text message, telling her she was welcome to Benjamin, and to claim her prize she would have to pick him up from the hospital tomorrow. I then went back to Benjamin's phone, opened his Facebook account and found the BenjiYoga page. After a moment's debate, I wrote the following message and posted it to his five thousand followers:

'Apologies, but all BenjiYoga classes are
cancelled until further notice.
My girlfriend caught me sleeping around with my students,
which has resulted in me catching something nasty.
*Namaste.* BenjiYoga.'

I tweeted the same message on the BenjiYoga Twitter page. I then changed the password for both, switched off the phone and stuffed it back in the locker. Benjamin's swelling seemed to be going down.

I took one last look at him, then left quietly and took a cab home.

# ACT TWO

One week later.

# IT'S JUST PR, DARLING

'Do I look all right? I don't look like a sad mum?' asked Sharon eyeing herself in a small make-up mirror and applying lipstick. We were outside the *Macbeth* rehearsal room on the third floor of the theatre, waiting for Ryan Harrison to break for lunch.

Sharon had rushed over in her lunch break, still wearing her Royal Mail uniform of grey trousers, red blouse, and a multi-coloured neckerchief. She jumped as the door opened, but it was just a member of the crew. He nodded hello and gave Sharon an odd look as he passed.

'I should have brought something to change into, I look like a right twerp!' she hissed, smoothing down her uniform and pulling at bits of fluff on her trouser leg.

'You look fine, but maybe take off the neckerchief,' I said. She untied it, and stuffed it in her handbag.

'How's that?' she asked.

'Perfect. And this is just a casual hello, yes?'

'Of course! I don't want to seem like a crazy fan, like the obscene teddy bear woman… Should I compliment him on *Manhattan Beach* first? Then ask about his dogs?'

'He's got dogs? I wonder who's looking after them?' I asked.

'He's got a dog walker and house sitter, they all do in LA. They're called Bella and Edward.'

'You know the names of his house sitter and dog walker?'

'No. That's what his dogs are called…' said Sharon. We were silent for a moment. Voices murmured behind the rehearsal room door and there was the scrape of a chair leg on the parquet floor.

'Have you heard anything more from Benjamin?' she asked. It had been a week since I'd left Benjamin in hospital.

'He left me another message, which escalated to shouting insults.'

'Looks like his yoga calm has gone the same way as his thong. Halfway up his arse!' she laughed. 'Don't acknowledge him, you've moved on…'

'I've returned ownership of his Facebook and his Twitter account,' I said.

'But you had them long enough for everyone to realise what a cheating bastard he is…' said Sharon gleefully.

The door suddenly opened and Byron emerged with Ryan. He was carrying a script of *Macbeth* that was covered in biro scrawls, stage directions, and doodles. He had on tracksuit bottoms and his beefy biceps were shown off by a sleeveless white t-shirt. Sharon gripped my hand, nearly breaking my fingers.

'Can I hilp you?' asked Byron, looking suspiciously at Sharon in her Royal Mail uniform. 'Do you want me to sign for a peckidge?'

'I haven't got a peckidge… Package. I'm here for Ryan,' said Sharon.

'You'll need to see Val downstairs, all postage for Mr Hirrison goes through Val…'

'She isn't delivering any post, this is my friend Sharon,' I explained. 'I hope you don't mind but she was passing and is a huge fan of yours Ryan.'

The door opened again and the rest of the actors and crew streamed past, as if the dinner bell had just rung.

'Sure, hey…' said Ryan his face breaking into a smile.

'Hello, I'm Sharon Lombardo,' said Sharon. She stared across at him with a bizarre love light in her eyes. Ryan leant in and gave her a kiss on each cheek.

'Oh goodness. Thank you,' she said touching her cheek where his lips had been.

'Lombardo is an Italian name?' asked Ryan. 'You don't look Italian.'

'No I'm not. My hus… husband is Italian,' she looked down at her wedding ring and stuffed her hand in her pocket. There was a silence.

'How are Bella and Edward?' she asked. Ryan looked surprised.

'Wow, you know your stuff. They're good. How are your…?'

'Amy and Felix,' grinned Sharon.

'Cool names, what breed are they?' asked Ryan.

'No. They're not dogs, I love dogs… but I got children instead. I mean they're my children. I didn't get them from a breeder, a surrogate, I gave birth to them…'

Ryan nodded. Sharon went on.

'I love *Manhattan Beach*, I've seen every episode. I just can't believe you're not a real dentist… I mean I know you play a dentist, but I'm having to stop myself from asking for a checkup!'

Ryan was nodding along gamely at Sharon's babbling.

'Not that I need a checkup. I've just been, only one filling, I splashed out on a white one,' she pulled open her mouth and leant in to show him.

'Sharon!' I said, but Ryan seemed used to this.

'Your dentist did a great job. If you ever came to Manhattan Beach I would try and do the same!' he said.

'Ryan only has thirty minutes for lunch,' said Byron. What she really wanted to say was *this woman could have a gun.* Sharon sensed he was about to go and started to gabble.

'Nat, Natalie told me that they're unveiling the huge billboard picture of you above the theatre today, for *Macbeth*!'

'Yeah. It's really cool. Natalie tells me it'll be on the front page of some London newspaper?' grinned Ryan.

'The *Evening Standard*?' asked Sharon. Ryan went to answer, but Byron indicated they had to get going.

'Okay, Sharon, well it's been real cool to meet you,' he said. 'But I have to go and do an interview…'

'I'm not just any old fan,' blurted Sharon. 'I *am* a fan, but I'm Natalie's best friend. She knows I would never stalk you, or go through your bins. Well, I'd take your bins out for you…'

'Ryan has to eat lunch and thin he has an interview,' said Byron who was now looking annoyed.

'Sharon, if you're Natalie's friend I'm sure I'll be seeing more of you, and you'll have to come and see the premiere,' said Ryan.

'I'm coming!' cried Sharon as he walked away. He turned, blew her a kiss and then disappeared round the corner with Byron.

'BYE!' she shouted down the empty corridor.

'Jeez Sharon,' I said.

'Oh my god, I met him. Natalie, I met Ryan Harrison… He's beautiful and he kissed me… He invited me to the premiere!'

'I know, I was here too. You also showed him your fillings and offered to take out his bins.'

'Oh shut up. It was just nerves…' she looked at her watch. 'Crap. I am *so* late back to work. I'm going to have to have a lie down in the sorting office, in the parcel bin.'

We took the stairs down, and emerged into the sunshine on Raven Street. All five storeys of the theatre had been covered with our most dramatic poster yet. Xander was standing on the pavement coordinating three guys in cherry pickers who were assembling large pieces of canvas which made up a giant Ryan Harrison.

'Look at those legs,' said Sharon. Our eyes travelled up Ryan's huge hairy footballer's legs, standing astride the main door.

'Can you see up his kilt?' she said moving to stand in the entrance and look up. I smiled and shook my head. Ryan's kilt took up the second and third floor of the building, and his torso the fourth and the fifth. His head and shoulders were still to be assembled.

Sharon stopped for a moment and looked at the Old Library opposite. It remained stubbornly swathed in plastic. A small gap had been made, and builders had been moving in and out for the past few days.

'So any more info on Jamie's pop-up venue The Big O?' asked Sharon.

'No. It's very hush-hush. I've managed to find out he's secured public liability insurance and a liquor licence, and they launched a Facebook page a few days ago.' I looked troubled for a moment.

'Cheer up Nat! You get to spend the day with Ryan Harrison... I have to go back and change the pads which moisten stamps,' she said. I gave her a hug. 'Thanks so much. When do I get to see him again?'

'I'll see what I can do,' I grinned, and with a wave goodbye, Sharon went off towards Charing Cross.


I stopped outside the theatre and stared across at The Big O. A couple of guys in hard hats approached the plastic, pulled it to one side and filed in. They had forgotten to fasten it shut. It flapped in the light summer breeze. I waited for a car to pass, then crossed Raven Street to the other side of the pavement. I approached the gap, trying to nonchalantly peer inside, but the sun was bright and I couldn't see anything in the gloom. Suddenly Jamie emerged almost crashing into me.

'Whoa, Nat. Hello there,' he grinned. He was wearing a tight black t-shirt and blue jeans, and was holding a long roll of paper in one hand. He looked effortlessly gorgeous.

'Hi!' I trilled. There was a silence.

'Trying to get a sneak peek?' he asked.

'Yes, busted… Can I see?' I asked, making to go through the gap.

'All will be revealed,' he smiled moving to block my path. I stared up at him for a moment then looked away.

'Impressive poster,' he said pointing behind me to Ryan's huge head, which was being slowly unfurled and stuck to the fifth floor of the building.

'Thanks,' I said. There was another awkward pause.

'Look, Nat. We're going to be bumping into each other quite a lot over the next few weeks. Do you fancy a coffee?' he asked.

'Um, sure,' I said, surprised. 'There's a coffee place a few doors down.'

'Hang on,' he said and ducked between the plastic, returning without the roll of paper. He leant down, and I thought he was going to kiss me on the cheek, but as I offered my left side, I realised he was ducking under a scaffolding pole. He hesitated, laughed, and then gave me a swift peck. As his warm stubbly cheek pressed against mine I caught the rich, warm smell of his hair… I was taken back to the night before our wedding, as we lay in bed and I pressed my face into the crook of his neck, the same smell of his skin, his hair… Jamie pulled away and we started to walk towards Grande in an awkward silence, passing several gay bars.

A couple of the barmen were opening up for the early shift, and the sight of Jamie made their heads snap round. A couple of women did double takes too, although much more subtly.

A voice in my head started to scold me.

*'You're a fool Natalie Love… He's even better looking than he used to be… You should have married him… If you'd gone through with it, you'd have kids, and a house!'*

*'Don't be ridiculous!'* I replied to the voice, still in my head. *'We'd be stuck living in Sowerton with no prospects, our kids might have ASBOs, how would that be any fun?'*

'Are you okay Nat?' asked Jamie. We had reached the entrance to Grande, and Jamie was holding open the huge glass door.

'What?' I said, coming back to the present.

'You were rolling your eyes and muttering to yourself…'

'I'm making a mental note, about work,' I lied.

'You should use the memo app on your phone… looks less weird,' he said. We reached the counter and Jamie said hi to the skinny pale barista with dreadlocks.

'Hi Jamie,' he grinned. 'How's it going?'

'You know, swings and roundabouts,' said Jamie reaching inside the pocket of his jeans and pulling out a wad of notes. 'This is Nat,' he added introducing me to the man I've wordlessly bought coffee off for the past five years.

'Hi,' he said cautiously.

'Hello,' I said.

'Me and Nat go way back,' said Jamie. 'I was meant to marry her, but I have no clue what kind of coffee she drinks?'

I looked at Jamie in disbelief.

'It was a long time ago. We were just teenagers!' I cried.

'Tall Americano, right?' said the barista.

'Yes,' I said, and scuttled off to find a table. I was so annoyed. Why did Jamie have to introduce me to the coffee guy, and tell him about our past? We say hello and he knows my order, I even tip, and that's enough for me. I grabbed a table at the back, facing a side street through the window. Jamie came over a few moments later with our coffees.

'Are you going to blurt that out to everyone?' I asked.

'You left me at the altar Nat, do you know what that does to a guy?' he said.

'For what it's worth… I'm sorry…' I said.

'Thank you. Although, you're only saying sorry because you've bumped into me.'

'Have I just bumped into you?' I asked.

'*Of all the theatres in all the cities in all the world… You choose to walk into mine,*' he said, doing a terrible Humphrey Bogart impression. Despite myself I laughed.

'I thought you were happy living in Canada?' I asked.

'I was, but I've been back a few times, and now I'm back for good, so you can stop avoiding me.'

'I have never avoided you. Sharon invited you to her wedding, but you never came.'

'You were invited to mum and dad's fiftieth birthday… My nan's eightieth… You were invited to them all!'

'I was busy…' This wasn't true. I had chickened out of seeing him on all three occasions. The latter made me feel very guilty. I had always loved Jamie's nan. 'Okay Jamie. Cards on the table, I'm really sorry. I should never have let things go so far and then have done what I did… But I was right back then, wasn't I? Would either of us be doing what we do now if… if we'd got married?' I paused and took a sip of coffee. Jamie smiled.

'I accept your apology Nat… It's just, I never quite got over it and the past fifteen years have been tough,' he said.

'They have?'

Jamie nodded and took a sip of coffee.

'That day, when I left you, I went straight to the pub on the green and started to drink… I didn't stop for days. I carried on and then got into drugs. Marijuana, crack, smack…'

I put my hand to my mouth in horror. 'Really? Crack and smack?' I asked. He nodded.

'After that I spiralled out of control. I missed my rent, and ended up homeless on the streets…' He looked around and lowered his voice. 'I even ended up giving blow jobs on the street, for cash.'

'What?' I whispered wide-eyed.

'Which is tough in Devon, 'cos it's all country lanes…' he said.

'Hang on. I heard you lived with your mum and dad… They wouldn't have let you…'

Jamie dissolved into fits of laughter.

'Your face Nat… was a picture!'

'What? It's not true?' I said, blushing.

'Course it's not true!' he guffawed. 'I moved to Canada, got into theatre production, and started up my own company. A few months ago I sold it for a fortune. *Cher-Ching*!'

I stared at him with my mouth still wide open. I went to protest, but heads were turning in Grande, as the big glass door was pushed open by Tuppence Halfpenny.

Despite the balmy weather, she was dressed in a floor-length fur coat of soft pink. Her caramel-coloured hair tumbled down her back and she was immaculately made up, with huge lashes and her glossy lips slightly parted.

'Hello,' she said icily looking between me and Jamie. She placed a small square Louis Vuitton case on the table.

'Hey sexy,' he said leaping up. She raised her palm in front of his face.

'No Jamie, I'm camera-ready. I can't be smudged.'

'Are you going to be on camera?' I asked.

'It's a figure of speech. Shouldn't you know that, working in the theatre?' she said.

'I *do* know that, but seeing as you don't have a theatre yet, I presumed otherwise,' I said, bristling.

'You see, she doesn't know today is our launch!' said Tuppence.

'I told you it's…' started Jamie, but Tuppence cut him off.

'The ex-fiancée, who probably stalks you on social media, *doesn't know about our launch*! What hope do the ticket-buying public have?'

'Tuppence, I told you. It's a soft launch,' said Jamie looking between us.

'Any softer Jamie, and it'll be through the eye of a bloody needle!' snapped Tuppence. 'I hope this flash mob thing doesn't leave us with egg on our faces. If there are less than a thousand I am NOT going up on that…'

Jamie stood up and went to put a hand to her mouth.

'It's all in hand sexy girl… You just worry about looking gorgeous and I'll…'

She pushed him away again.

'I mean it Jamie. It has to be perfect. I'm taking a chance on you…'

She eyeballed him for a moment, then threw her shoulders back. Her coat fell open to reveal a show-stopping showgirl outfit of black corset, stockings and suspenders. Again I marvelled at her figure, how did she manage to pull in her corset so tight? Did she eat? Jamie slid his hand inside the coat and round her tiny waist.

'You are going to be the biggest thing in the West End,' he said puckering up and leaning in. Tuppence eyed me, sitting awkwardly in my jeans and blouse and grinned. Despite her perfect shaped mouth and straight teeth, it was a hungry grin. I wondered if she ate bog roll.

'Bigger than *Macbeth*?' she said spitting the words out cattily. Jamie laughed.

'God, that puts me between a rock and a hard place,' he said looking at both of us.

'Tell her what she wants to hear, Jamie,' I said. 'Or you'll be left to deal with your own hard place…'

Tuppence narrowed her eyes at me.

'I'm going to go Jamie,' she said. She pulled a business card out of her coat and slid it across the table.

'I have a friend who is great with waxing,' she said tapping it with a manicured finger, and with a swish of her coat strode off to the door. Jamie followed, opening it for her and she allowed him a light kiss. He came back to the table.

'Wow, she's got being a bitch down to a tee,' I said, still reeling. We watched as Tuppence stalked past the picture window.

'Sorry about that, you know how it is, managing the talent,' he said.

'I think the talent is managing you,' I said. 'You two are an item?'

'Yeah, I went to one of her shows, and…'

'Spare me the details,' I said.

'What about you? How's *Benjamin*?'

'How do you know about Benjamin?' I asked sharply.

'It's on Facebook Nat, your relationship status… By the way I friended you a few days back.'

'Thanks, I haven't been online for a while.'

I realised I had to make myself single on my Facebook page.

'So what does Benjamin do?' asked Jamie.

'He's a yoga teacher. Runs his own yoga studio.'

'So how did you meet?'

'I went to one of his classes and…'

'*Spare me the details…*' shrieked Jamie mimicking my voice. Despite myself I laughed. We regarded each other for a minute.

'Well, I should go, I've got a huge poster to deal with,' I said, getting up.

'Yes, I should too,' he said. He held the door open for me and we walked slowly over to our theatres.

'She's different at home, Tuppence,' said Jamie. 'Under all that make-up she's…'

'A Rottweiler?' I finished.

'Very funny Nat. You wait till I meet this Benjamin…' it hung in the air for a moment. I had a million questions: did they live together? Was it serious? Had Tuppence met his mum?

We reached the tarpaulin still covering The Big O. A blond-haired guy with glasses perched on his thin ratty face emerged through the gap, and closed the plastic carefully after himself. He looked me up and down, then turned to Jamie.

'Tuppence is in her dressing room, and…' he saw me listening.

'Sorry Natalie, this is Brendan my PR manager,' said Jamie. I held out my hand, and he took it gingerly.

'Hi I'm Natalie Love, I manage the Raven Street Theatre,' I said. Brendan dropped my hand mid-shake.

'I don't fraternise with the competition,' he said cattily and walked away to talk to a group of builders parked by the kerb. It was breathtakingly rude.

'Nice team you've got Jamie,' I said.

'Everyone is just worried,' he said looking embarrassed. I'd had enough.

'Grow a pair Jamie, or they'll leave you…' I closed my mouth. 'Like you left me?'

He stared at me for a moment and then went inside the huge blue tarpaulin. I stood for a moment in the sunshine.

'Alright love,' said a scratchy smoker's voice. I turned and Eva Castle, a journalist from the *Evening Standard*, was standing beside me looking up at the giant image of Ryan. His head was just being uncurled and stuck in place.

'Hi Eva,' I said. She leant in for an air kiss. She was dressed in a crumpled beige trouser suit and had a pair of glasses, two mobile phones, and three e-cigarettes on lanyards around her neck. She pushed her hand through her short dark bob and squinted.

'Is he ready for the interview? Cos I've got other appointments.'

'Yes,' I said. 'I'll take you up to meet Ryan.'

# THE BIG O

Ryan's interview seemed to go well. Nicky and I sat in on it, as he chatted to Eva in our conference room. She was bullish, and in the mood to provoke, with questions like:

*Shakespeare is an ambitious leap for the star of a teen drama, do you think you're up to it?*

And

*Do you think you'd be as successful if you weren't so attractive?*

Ryan was a pro, batting her hostility to one side and managing to keep a professional level of cheer. When the interview was over he thanked her warmly and Byron escorted him back down to rehearsals. We walked Eva to the main entrance.

'I think Ryan really enjoyed it,' said Nicky pressing the button for the lift.

'He's very short,' said Eva sounding unimpressed and tucking her notepad back in her bag.

'He's eighty feet tall on the front of the building,' I said. She gave a half laugh and puffed at one of her e-cigarettes.

'I'll make something out of it,' she said. 'He came across as too polished, too cautious… That's why I love interviewing people like Lily Allen or Noel Gallagher. You only have to bait them a little and they go off on one, slagging someone off. The story writes itself.'

'So what do you think about us having tonight's front page on the *Standard*? Online and print?' asked Nicky.

'There's no *absolute* guarantee darling,' said Eva taking another puff. 'If the dear old Queen pops her clogs, or someone declares war we'll have to clear the front page.'

'Of course,' said Nicky.

'We've sold out all the tickets for the run, but we'd like to use this as an opportunity to increase our social media audience,' I said. 'You've got our Instagram and Facebook links?'

'Insta-arsing-gram, Face-bloody-book, ugh,' said Eva rummaging in her bag. She popped her glasses on her nose and read out the address for our Facebook page, and the handle for the new Instagram account.

'Like it or not we need social media,' I said. We all got in the lift and it began to descend.

'I meant to ask. Off the record, of course. Is Ryan Harrison a poofter?' said Eva.

'I don't think so,' I said.

'He's not,' said Nicky firmly.

'I've heard he is,' said Eva. 'Apparently he's had a thing going with one of the other actors on *Manhattan Beach*. They've even bought dogs.'

'Dogs?' I said.

'Yeah,' said Eva. 'Bella and Edward – named after the *Twilight* idiots. Now that would be a story.'

'My friend Sharon mentioned the dogs earlier,' I said.

'I can confirm he's not gay,' said Nicky shooting me a look.

'Easy love, I'm not gonna write about it. Can't. The press commission makes it tricky for us to out people. Bloody European Court of Human Rights,' said Eva.

The lift came to a stop and we got out.

'What do you know about The Big O?' I asked as we reached the main entrance.

'I haven't had one of them for years,' she quipped. We went outside where a grey-haired photographer was waiting. He had a camera slung around his neck, and he was fiddling with his balls.

'Leave them alone, for fuck's sake Larry,' said Eva.

'Is this it?' muttered Larry staring up. The giant, smouldering image of Ryan Harrison towered above the street. He stood against a backdrop of dark mountains, storm clouds hanging ominously above. His hair was sexily tousled, his bare torso was artfully oiled and covered in mud. He had on a kilt, sporran and black boots. He stared into the camera with a crackling intensity in his piercing green eyes. Above his head was written 'RYAN HARRISON IS MACBETH'.

Larry started snapping away. Several people in the street had stopped and were staring, pulling out their mobile phones and taking pictures. It looked incredible.

'Isn't he a bit boy band to play *Macbeth*?' asked Eva. Larry clicked away for another minute and then pronounced himself satisfied.

'Boy band sells, honey,' said Nicky.

'Okay, that's enough Larry. Keep your eyes peeled for the late edition,' muttered Eva and she walked off up the road. Larry gave us a nod and made off in the other direction.

'Are you okay Nat?' said Nicky.

'It does look great doesn't it?' I said.

'It looks awesome. It's going to be awesome,' said Nicky and she gave me a hug. 'She's a hardened journalist Nat… and who cares what that old ball scratcher thinks!'

Over Nicky's shoulder I saw Eva in the distance. She had stopped, and then I saw Brendan standing waiting for her. They hugged like they were old friends and went into one of the restaurants, deep in conversation.

'What do you know about Brendan O'Connor?' I asked. Nicky pulled away.

'Has Jamie hired *Brendan O'Connor*?'

'Yes, why do you say his name like that?'

Nicky furrowed her brow.

'He gets results, but he's a real snake, Nat... However, as I said, we've sold out our show. We're different beasts, an established theatre and a pop-up venue... Don't let it being run by your ex-fiancé distract you, or cloud your judgement.'

'Yes, you're right,' I said.

'Now come on. We've got a meeting with the costume department about how short the guys' kilts should be...'

Ok, I vote we show lots of leg,' I grinned.


A little while later, Nicky and I were just finishing up in the costume department when Xander popped his head round the door.

'You need to come and see this,' he said. We went back out onto the street. The plastic had been removed from the Old Library opposite. It had been covered for so many years that I struggled to remember what the building was like before.

The five-storey building in front of us was now completely covered by the most incredible frontage, a wall of video screens. The whole building had been turned into a giant video screen, with just a small gap left at the bottom for the huge double doors, upholstered in red velvet with THE BIG O inlaid in gold.

The screens were blank, and then in the top corner, a pinprick appeared which grew into a full moon at night... Twinkling stars began to appear all across the building, clouds rushed across the moon and then a massive image of Tuppence Halfpenny came gliding across the building. She was sat on a swing, legs thrown out in front, wearing black knickers and suspenders. Her impossibly pert breasts were each covered with a little red heart. She threw her head back and laughed, glitter trailing in her wake.

She froze for a second with her eyes half-closed, then the video ran backwards for a few seconds, and then the building became a multi-coloured test card. People in the street had stopped, a car honked to clear them out of the road.

'Fuck-a-doodle-doo,' said Nicky bathed in the coloured reflection from the video screen. Jamie emerged from the huge double doors. He came across the road to where we were standing.

'What do you think ladies, and gent?' he asked.

'It's remarkable,' said Nicky.

'Genius,' said Xander.

'I know, it's a bit extravagant for a pop-up venue, but I'm banking on us being around for a while,' said Jamie. 'My mate from Canada owns a company who makes these huge video screen frontages…'

'Well, I hope you've got your TV licence,' I said. But the joke fell flat and made me sound bitter.

# BAPS

We went back up to the office. The only drawback of the huge Ryan Harrison poster was that all the windows in the building were now covered. I was dying to peer out and see what was going on in the street below, but all I could see was a dingy square of canvas covered with Ryan's giant left eye. Over the next hour the street filled up with increasingly excited voices. Nicky went off to attend a telephone conference with *Heat* magazine about making Ryan 'Torso of the Week'. As she left she turned to me.

'Stop obsessing about The Big O…'

'Said the actress to the bishop,' I joked.

'I'm serious, Nat. You need to move past this,' she said leaving with a pointed look. However, it wasn't Nicky's ex- fiancé who had rocked up and opened a theatre over the road. I got up and paced round my office. Running the theatre is a constant source of stress and such hard work. Jamie's theatre was at the very least another option for punters to not buy tickets for our productions.

Xander knocked on the door.

'Hi Natalie, I'm doing a late lunch run, do you want anything?'

'I could murder pastrami and mustard on a rye bap,' I said. 'And get me one of their floury baps with cheese and Marmite for later on.'

Xander added my order to his list then went off. I sat back in my chair. It now sounded like there were hundreds of people on the road below. Cursing the canvas blocking my window, I opened the fire door and climbed up onto the roof, making sure this time that I blocked the fire door open.

It was very warm, the asphalt having soaked up the morning sun. A flock of pigeons was huddled at one side of the roof, basking in the heat. I moved slowly to the edge and looked down. Raven Street was full of women dressed in burlesque outfits. There seemed to be hundreds, all shapes and sizes, wearing different-coloured corsets, and full make-up. They were chatting excitedly and watching Tuppence Halfpenny on the video wall.

Suddenly the velvet doors of The Big O were flung open and Jamie emerged holding a microphone. He was dressed in tight black trousers and he was shirtless! He'd bulked up considerably in the fifteen years since I last saw his naked torso. A small square stage had been set up on the pavement, and Jamie climbed up, elevating himself above the crowd so he could be seen.

'Good afternoon ladies,' boomed his voice. The women in the street started to cheer and whistle. He shielded his eyes from the sun to peer up and down.

'Wow! You all look amazing. We're so grateful you are all giving up time to be with us today. Are you ready to flash mob burlesque?'

The women went wild, shouting and whistling. There was a large group of photographers and journalists, including Eva Castle, who was standing with Brendan O'Connor on the pavement. Jamie went on.

'To launch her new show here at The Big O – *Halfpenny Dreadful*... Please welcome, the one and only, the fabulous, *Tuppence Halfpenny!*'

Tuppence appeared through the doors behind and joined him on the little stage. The crowd went wild. She wore a silver boned corset, with matching 1950s style knickers; this was coupled with stockings, suspenders, silver glittery heels, and long silver gloves.

'Hello ladies!' she cried. They screamed hello in response. 'Are you ready to burlesque?' They screamed again. I had to stop myself from joining in, such was the atmosphere.

'Okay, now the routine we are all going to do goes left glove, right glove, then final showstopper, the corset… Have we all secured our nipple tassels?' she asked.

The crowd responded in the positive. I noticed a swing was being lowered down to Tuppence. I followed the two steel cables up, to where a guy had appeared on the roof opposite. He was operating a small winch, fastened to the edge of the roof, lowering the swing. I looked back down and the swing stopped beside Tuppence at waist height.

'Okay, now you all follow me,' she said. 'The choreography may be simple, but burlesque is slow… it's all about the tease!' She handed the microphone back to Jamie and gently perched on the swing.

'You're certainly teasing me Tuppence,' said Jamie. 'Are you ready to TEASE?'

The crowd screamed that indeed they were.

'Sexy Back' by Justin Timberlake began to boom out. Slowly, Tuppence was raised on the swing, to hysterical screams from the crowd below. She began to glide from side to side on the swing, against the video screen of the moon and stars, glitter trailing her movements back and forward. It was incredible.

Xander returned from the sandwich run, climbed up onto the roof, and came towards me carrying a huge basket of sandwiches, rolls, and baps. I turned back as the crowd below cheered.

Tuppence was removing one of her long gloves, teasing off each finger with her perfect teeth. I imagined those teeth biting into Jamie's smooth muscles… She had the glove off and she dropped it with a wide-eyed pout. The crowd below were all mirroring her, and they threw their gloves in the air, in unison, with a scream.

Tuppence was now travelling rapidly side to side; she arched her back, smiled, then stood up on the swing in a racticed move. The crowd below drew gasps and applauded. She pulled off the other glove and the hundreds of ladies below followed suit. Tuppence turned her head, and for a moment, our eyes met as she whooshed back and forth.

Xander was now standing beside me with the lunch basket packed with rolls, artfully displayed in neat rows. He said something, but I couldn't hear him, the music was too loud. I don't know if it was the smell of the fresh bread and all the fillings, but the flock of pigeons in the corner of the roof, which had up until now been snoozing in the sun, started to wake up, and peck around near us. Xander noticed them and went pale.

'No! I hate pigeons!' he shouted, skipping around to try and avoid them. I grabbed him, worried that he might fall over the edge. The pigeons started waddling round his feet and flapping up towards the basket. Xander panicked, lifting it up above his head, but then he lost his grip. The whole basket of filled rolls went flying over the side of the roof, separating in mid-air, and showering the burlesque ladies below in bread, salad, filling, and mayonnaise.

I don't know if you've ever been in a park and dropped a crisp or a piece of a sandwich, and suddenly from nowhere pigeons besiege you?

A giant flock of pigeons appeared from one of the rooftops and zoomed towards all the free food on the floor below. They didn't take into account that a half-naked lady would be suspended on a swing in mid-air, and they started to flap around Tuppence who lost all composure, screamed, and nearly fell off her swing. Bird poo dotted her black corset as she screamed even louder. The pigeons flocked and started to crash into the video wall. Screams erupted from the ladies below, as pigeons swooped down between them to get at the bread. The music stopped and people started to stare up to where the sandwiches had appeared from. Xander had scarpered, so it was just me leaning over the edge of the roof. Jamie looked up at me, still holding his microphone, and I made a dash for it, down into my office slamming the fire door.

I sat sweating in my dark office, unsure of what to do. I listened to the voices from the street below. One woman's shrieks were very loud, moaning that her corset was ruined, now it was covered in coronation chicken. Nicky opened the door.

'Hey Nat… Do you know if Ryan would be willing to shave his chest for 'Torso of the Week'?' I opened my mouth to speak, but I heard shouting, and Xander's voice.

'You can't just barge up here!'

Jamie appeared behind Nicky. He was still shirtless and had a small slice of cucumber balanced on his head, like a weird little fascinator.

'Sorry ladies,' said Xander appearing shortly afterwards. 'I tried to stop him but he wouldn't take no…'

'What the hell did you do, Natalie?' interrupted Jamie. Nicky and Xander stood there for a moment looking between us. Then Brendan O' Connor barged in. He was equally furious, and had mayonnaise smeared on the lenses of his glasses.

'Hey! What's this? I thought we had people on the door, stopping just anyone coming in!' cried Nicky.

'It was my fault,' said Xander.

'No Xander, let me deal with this,' I said. 'Guys, I'm so sorry, it was a freak accident…'

'Freak accident?' shouted Jamie. 'Lobbing a load of filled rolls off your roof! What you just did was dangerous. Tuppence said you were waiting up there to deliberately scare those pigeons… She could have fallen off that swing! She could have died! She got pigeon poo in her mouth!'

The little slice of cucumber was flapping around on his head, and when he mentioned pigeon poo. I couldn't help it. I laughed.

'You think this is *funny?*' shouted Brendan. 'Cos you don't want to go down that road girlfriend.'

'Hey! You don't want to go down that road either, Brendan,' said Nicky.

The mayonnaise eye patch made him look slightly less threatening, but I didn't like the look in his other eye. It was vindictive.

'Where is she?' came a voice from the corridor. 'Which one is her bloody office?'

Tuppence Halfpenny burst in, barefoot, wearing a long towelling dressing gown. Pigeon poo clung to her hairdo, which was askew. One of our big burly security guards came in just behind, and attempted to guide her back out.

'You get your hands off me! Do you want an assault charge against your name?' she cried. The security guard stepped back, visibly scared.

'No. You do your job! She's trespassing,' said Nicky. The security guard moved towards her again.

'Oh no mister, you keep your hands off me… I won't be here long!' cried Tuppence. 'I am *so* going to sue you Natalie Love!'

'What are you going to sue me for? It was an accident!' I said.

'Oh, I have lawyers *Natalie Love*. You assaulted me with… you threw that bread!'

'What, you were traumatised by all those carbohydrates coming towards you at once?' I said.

'Yes!' she shouted. 'And I am billing you for cleaning this corset, it's covered in seven thousand pounds worth of Swarovski crystal!' Tuppence pulled open the dressing gown. The corset was ruined.

'We're not paying for an act of God, which is what 'birds flocking' comes under,' said Nicky.

'What if I don't believe in God?' replied Tuppence.

'What if I don't believe burlesque is anything more than a fancy word for stripper?' said Nicky challengingly.

'You take that back now,' said Tuppence.

'I will not,' growled Nicky.

'You need to leave. Now,' I said moving between Nicky and Tuppence.

The security guard took a step closer and Tuppence closed her dressing gown knotting it tightly.

'I'm leaving. This isn't over,' she said and stormed out.

'You too, lads,' said the security guard, finally finding his voice.

'You've chosen to screw with the wrong person, Natalie… You screw with my clients, you screw with me,' said Brendan and he stalked out of the office.

'Natalie. Do you know how hard we worked on putting that together? On our launch, the flash mob?' asked Jamie.

'Jamie. It really was an accident, I'm sorry,' I said again. He shook his head and left.

*

When the door was closed, Nicky rounded on me and Xander. I explained what had happened, and then Nicky asked Xander to leave.

'And you think this isn't getting personal?' said Nicky, when he was gone.

'It was a freak accident!' I said.

'Yes, but why you were up on the roof spying on him?'

'I was watching their launch… They *are* the competition," I said.

'The only competition we have is with ourselves, Nat. We look to better ourselves and what we do, yes?'

I nodded, she was right.

'Ok, I'm gonna go down there and do some damage limitation. And so help Tuppence Halfpenny if she gets in my face,' added Nicky. I nodded and she left the office.

I *had* to find a way of dealing with Jamie being back in my life.

# REGIONAL NEWS

I sat in the dingy office for the rest of the afternoon, unable to work. For the first time I wished I hadn't removed the anti-pigeon spikes on the edge of the roof. The council had fitted them when the theatre was renovated. I had quietly removed them one day, after finding a pigeon with a bad leg impaled on one of the spikes.

By five-thirty the noise outside had died down, and Nicky phoned to say she was going home, and the coast was clear. She sounded rather cold on the phone.

I waited until six, then left the theatre. The normal evening crowds were milling around, as the bars and restaurants opened. The Big O was deserted, the video screens were off, and it had blended back into the street furniture. I didn't stick around to bump into anyone, I quickly walked past and made a detour down to Charing Cross where I picked up a copy of the *Evening Standard.*

Half of the front page was taken up with news of a tube strike, and the other half read: *FLASH MOB CHAOS IN SOHO!* With a series of pictures under the subheading '*Popular British Burlesque star attacked by pigeons …*' My phone rang in my pocket and I pulled it out. It was Nicky.

'Have you seen the *Standard*?' she asked. I told her I had a copy in my hand. 'You know the worst thing? I'd been sent proofs of our Ryan Harrison billboard as the front cover image…If this hadn't happened we'd be front page news.'

'Where are we now?' I said, putting the phone under my chin and rifling through the newspaper.

'Page eight,' we said in unison.

'What about online?' I asked.

'Buried low down on the sidebar,' she said. 'Maybe we should fire Xander?'

'No, it was a genuine accident. And he's a good worker... And what if he took us to a tribunal? They'd have a field day with the reason why we fired him. Dropping baps from a great height?'

'We've lost a real opportunity here,' said Nicky pointedly. 'We could've collected thousands of new social media followers, and you know...'

'Yes, I know how important that is,' I snapped.

'Good, because whilst you get to go home, I've got to keep this from turning sour in the press, and we've got that Brendan on the war path, he's a poisonous queen...'

'Well, do your best,' I said trying to lighten the mood.

'I always do,' said Nicky and hung up.


I got back to the flat just before six-thirty. I closed the front door and leant against it with my heart pounding. I thought about phoning Sharon, but I could imagine telling her what had happened and her finding it hilarious. Just the word 'bap' reduces her to hysterics. I wasn't ready to laugh just yet.

I had a shower, and poured myself a large drink, but still felt tense and wound up. I picked up the post from the doormat and came through to the kitchen. There were some bits of junk mail, a bank statement, and a cream envelope with my sister's unmistakable scrawl on the front. I opened it and an invitation fell out.

Dear **Natalie and Benjamin,**

Micky, Dave, House, and the twins Downton and Abbey cordially invite you to the Christening of baby Dexter. The Christening will be held at St. Bathsheba's Church, Sowerton, Devon on Sunday 26th July at 11am.

An informal luncheon buffet will be held afterwards at Hill Farm. Due to the current financial crisis, I'm sure guests appreciate that money is tite. So therefore we are asking if each guest can bring a something to con-trabute to the buffet table. Therefore I have put you down for... **A rotary chicken, a tube of barbecue Pringles and a bottle of Proscuttio**

With love, Micky and Dave Lamb.

(Enclosed is a map with parking and a list of local B & B's)

**Ps Looking forward to seeing you, Nat and meeting Benjamin! Is he fit? ;) Are you staying with Mum and Dad? Since I printed the map there's been a salmannella scare at the Pig & Whistle, and it's closed for a deep clean, so don't stay there.**

**Micky x**

Everything about the invitation gave me angst. I would have to show up alone and try to play down another failed relationship. And why did the guests have to bring food? Surely the ones having the bloody christening should stump up for lunch! And Micky's spelling was awful. What was a rotary chicken? And did she want a bottle of prosecco or a bottle of prosciutto ham? I made up my mind I was going to cancel. I just had to come up with an excuse.

I went through to the living room with my drink and flopped down on the sofa. I flicked on the TV and caught the end of the *BBC News*.

'And now let's see what's happening in your region,' purred the newsreader condescendingly. Growing up in Sowerton in Devon, I always resented the way BBC newsreaders said this, as if my little corner of Great Britain was inferior. Back then it was Anna Ford who read the *BBC News* from London and I idolising her; she was so cool, calm and clever. When I heard she'd thrown a drink over a TV executive at a party I loved her even more.

But Anna Ford was the master at delivering the line '*And now let's see what's happening in your region…*' It was as if we'd all been invited into her cosmopolitan London world for half an hour, and then just as things got interesting, we were being shooed away.

When *BBC Spotlight* came on, the difference was stark. I used to sit in the living room at the farmhouse scorning the inevitable announcements that Bideford had won a 'Loo of the Year' award, or that someone or somewhere was in urgent need of a bypass.

I wondered if Anna Ford waited until all the regions had vanished and then carried on talking to the London people?

'*Now let me tell you all about the time I threw a drink over someone important at a very important party…*' I imagined her saying.

Of course, when I came to London it turned out that Londoners were shooed away by Anna Ford just like the rest of the country, and had to endure *BBC London Tonight,* which always tries to make London, with its nine million inhabitants, feel like a village.

I suddenly realised what I was watching on *BBC London Tonight*. On the screen, grainy mobile phone footage was playing of a flock of pigeons swooping down, and attacking a group of ladies dressed in burlesque corsets. There were tinny screams, and the image lurched to show a wobbly view of feet on moving pavement. I turned up the volume.

'What began as a carefully orchestrated flash mob, rapidly turned into chaos...' intoned the news reporter. The camera cut to two enormous ladies bursting out of their corsets, stood outside a bar in Soho.

'We were having a great time, and then this flock of pigeons were attacking us...' said one, tucking in her flesh, which was escaping over the edge of her corset.

'I was pecked on the nose,' said her thinner friend, who unfortunately had the kind of nose a pigeon couldn't miss. More grainy mobile phone footage was shown, this time a view of Tuppence Halfpenny on her swing, filmed from below. The flock of pigeons surrounding her as she flailed about.

And then the camera cut to Brendan! He was standing outside The Big O. He had cleaned the mayonnaise off his glasses.

'And how is Tuppence Halfpenny doing?' asked the reporter.

'She's in shock,' said Brendan. 'Luckily her burlesque training kicked in and she managed to keep hold of the swing... We believe it was an act of corporate sabotage,' he added.

'Sabotage in Soho?' intoned the reporter, with an edge of excitement to her voice.

'Yes, the Raven Street Theatre opposite has blocked us at every turn, as we try to establish this new venue... At a crucial moment of her routine, several kilos of bread were thrown off the roof opposite, inciting the pigeons to violence. I'm just relieved no one died…'

As the report concluded, there was a shot of a thin girl in burlesque gear with a cut on the side of her head. A lady from St John Ambulance was pressing a large bandage to it. It ended with the news reporter standing in Raven Street. Our giant billboard of Ryan Harrison was lit up behind her, and LIVE FROM SOHO was written across the bottom of the screen.

'The St John's Ambulance service is advising everyone who was pecked, or came into contact with pigeon faeces, to have a tetanus booster,' she said. 'As far as corporate sabotage is concerned, one can only speculate. The artistic director of the Raven Street Theatre, Nancy Love, was contacted, but declined to comment. This is Rita Cochrane, in Soho, for *BBC London Tonight*.'

The report went back to the studio as I shouted at the screen.

'What do you mean declined to comment? No one asked me, and *Nancy* Love?'

I grabbed my phone and rang Nicky.

'Have you seen the news?' I asked.

'Yes. You're welcome honey,' she replied.

'What do you mean?'

'Did you really want to be interviewed on *London Tonight*?'

'Well, no…' I said.

'Good, because it could lead to more nonsense about corporate sabotage. I can see Brendan is using this as best he can, for publicity. We just don't give him anymore, okay?'

'Of course not.'

Nicky hung up. I paced round the flat for a bit, then as a distraction, ordered a huge Chinese and a bottle of wine. It had just arrived when my phone rang. It was the operator asking if I would accept a reverse charge call. Was this a desperate attempt from Benjamin, another booty call? Intrigued, I said I would accept the charge. There were some beeps and then a voice.

'Natalie my darlink!'

'Gran? Hi!' I said tucking the phone under my chin and paying the delivery guy. I closed the front door and went through to the kitchen. 'Gran, what a surprise, how are you?'

'Ayayay Natalie. I have had my heart broken again. Stefan ended our love affair...'

I started to unpack my Chinese onto the table, racking my brains to try and remember Stefan... Was he the artist, or the sculptor?

'I caught him vith another vooman...' she said.

'I'm sorry Gran. Are you okay?'

'Yes, my darlink,' she said wearily. 'The sex vas tip top, but he didn't make me laugh. I think that's so important...'

'I can agree with you on that,' I said. 'But what I meant was, are you okay? Why are you reversing the charges?'

'Natalie. I call to say I am coming to this christening for Micky's baby with the funny name. She vants me to bring Sousa-gez!'

'What's Sousa-gez?' I asked.

'You know the little rolled up tubes of meat, from a pig. Sousa-gez!'

'You mean sausages,' I laughed.

'Ayayayy, my accent huh?'

'I've been asked to bring ham in a bottle,' I said spooning out Chinese onto a plate. Gran laughed.

'Vat planet does Micky live on? I vasn't going to fly to London today with a suitcase full of Sousa-get. Vat am I? A refugee?'

I paused with my hand hovering over the egg fried rice.

'Fly to London. Today?' I repeated.

'Yes, Natalie. I am in London, at the Heathrow. Terrible place, no vonder it rhymes with death row...'

On cue there was a bing bong in the background and an announcement.

'So where are you staying tonight?' I asked looking at my watch. It was almost eight.

'Vith you!' she laughed, as if I had made a joke. 'Now Natalie, I am at the terminal five. Vat time will you be here?'

My heart sank. Why does she always do this? She just shows up, what if I was out? What would she do? My brain started whirring, where were the clean sheets? Where would she sleep?

'Terminal five is on the Piccadilly Line,' I said. 'If you go down to the tube, find the eastbound platform, it will take you all the way to Leicester Square where I can meet you…'

'Natalie. Vill you be a darlink and come to get me? I hev many bags, and I am vearing all of my mother's gold, the nice stuff she vore when she escaped the Nazis…'

'Okay,' I said. 'I'll be there in, I don't know, an hour?'

'Thank you my darlink,' she said and hung up. I crammed in a few mouthfuls of Chinese, then put the rest in the oven on a low heat. I grabbed my bag and went off to the tube.


I arrived at terminal five an hour later, and found Gran, sat in an empty Starbucks. She was surrounded by suitcases piled high. She was dripping with gold jewellery and wearing her huge fur coat. There was a walking stick against her chair.

'Natalie! My darlink!' she cried standing awkwardly to give me a hug. 'You look more beautiful as time goes by!'

Despite her rocking up unannounced, I was pleased to see her. She looked the same, a little older, her long blonde hair was piled high on her head and fixed with several gold combs.

'You've got so much luggage!' I said surveying the pile of suitcases and her vanity case propped on top.

'Yes. I never know what to vear, so I bring it all!' she laughed. I went and found a trolley, then heaved all her suitcases on. We moved slowly down to the Piccadilly Line, as Gran was limping badly, leaning heavily on her stick.

'What have you done to your foot?' I asked.

'I hev a terrible bunion,' she said indicating her misshapen foot, which was crammed into a gold heel.

'Should you be wearing heels?' I asked. She just laughed and paused, leaning on her stick.

'Even if I vas shot in the foot I would choose heels!'

We made it down to the tube, and the guard opened the ticket barrier for Gran with her stick, and me with the trolley. A train had just arrived. Gran took a seat, and left me to pile in all the suitcases; several times the doors beeped and I had to keep stopping them closing to get it all in. Finally everything was in, and the train pulled away.

She asked me all about work, and I started to tell her about Benjamin, and Jamie, and what was happening at the theatre. Then a ticket inspector boarded and I realised, Gran didn't have a ticket.


'I'm so sorry my darlink,' she said as we travelled up in the lift at Leicester Square station. 'I vill pay you back the thirty pounds fine… when I get some pounds,' she added vaguely. We took a taxi back to the flat, and by the time I had all her suitcases in-doors, it was gone ten o'clock. I put the leftover Chinese on two plates and came into the living room.

'Thank you. I am famished,' she said as I handed her a plate. 'I love your place Natalie, it vill do nicely…'

I was about to question what that meant when she handed me a duty-free bag. I took it, and inside was a bottle of Chanel No.5 and a litre of plum brandy.

'Thank you, I thought you didn't have any money?' I asked.

'I hev plastic money... Let's have a toast,' she said. I grabbed glasses and poured us each a measure. We clinked.

'To my favourite granddaughter,' she said.

'So, where have you been living?' I asked taking a big mouthful of chicken chow mein.

'Spain. In Torremolinos, by the sea, with Stefan who is a film maker,' she said cramming prawn crackers into her mouth; she crunched them and washed them down with brandy.

'What kind of films does he make?' I asked.

'The kind that nobody understands,' said Gran wryly. 'I vas in his latest, *The Song of the Floundering Mermaid*.'

'You did some acting?'

'Yes! He cast me as the High Empress Mermaid.'

'Sounds glamorous,' I said.

'It vasn't. I spent three veeks sat topless on a rock in Benálmadena, buffeted by the freezing tide. I ended up with a vater infection.'

'You were topless?' I said.

'Yes, all the ladies in Stefan's films are topless... I caught him one night vith another mermaid, unzipping her flipper. We're over now. Done. Kaput.'

'I'm so sorry Gran,' I said.

'It vas my own fault. I thought I vas his muse, but in reality he vanted my money to pay his production costs...There's nothing that parts a fool vith her money quicker than having a toy boy.'

'How old is Stefan?' I asked.

'Fifty-three,' said Gran, shoving more prawn crackers in her mouth. I took another forkful of Chinese and tried to process all that information.

'I've had a similar experience, well, I wasn't a topless mermaid or anything, but I started seeing my yoga instructor, Benjamin...' I told her all about it, leaving out none of the details.

'This is men,' said Gran. 'When they vant you, but you don't vant them, they stay. But let them know you vant them, they no longer need you, and they go! It's like that movie, *Nanny McPhee*.'

I burst out laughing.

'It's nothing like *Nanny McPhee*!'

'But you get the gist,' she grinned leaning over and topping up my brandy. 'I've missed you Natalie. I feel I can tell you about my life… All your mother vants to talk about on the phone is how to make hot vater crust pastry.'

'Well, I have something else to tell you,' I said. 'Jamie is back on the scene. He's decided to open a theatre opposite mine.'

'Interesting… You think he vants you back?'

'No. He's got a gorgeous girlfriend, far prettier than me… No I think he wants to show off.'

'First of all Natalie, you are the prettiest girl in the vorld, don't forget that, and second you were right not to marry him. He would never have coped with you being more successful than him… Think of the life you've made for yourself. Vould you have done that back in Sowerton?'

I shrugged.

'Natalie. I do regret making you burn your vedding dress. In my own crazy way I did it so you wouldn't change your mind, and marry him after all…'

I grabbed her hand and smiled.

'I've calmed down a lot since then,' she said pouring us more brandy.

'Have you? I can't think of anyone else's gran who would play a topless mermaid in a film!'


She regaled me with more tales, and then I offered to run her a bath. I waited until I heard her get in the water and then I went into the kitchen and rang my mother.

'She just showed up?' said Mum. 'I thought she wasn't coming to the christening?'

'Well, she is,' I said.

'I thought she was gallivanting around Spain with Stephen?'

'Stefan... and that's over,' I said. Mum sighed.

'How are you going to get her here?'

'I'll drive,' I said.

'Will there be room for you and her *and* Benjamin?'

I was too exhausted to go into detail, so I just said yes.

'It will be lovely to see you Natalie, and well, I'll just have to deal with Mum I suppose...Did you find out if Benjamin likes trifle?'

'No, he doesn't,' I lied, cringing.

'What kind of a person doesn't like trifle? Is he from a special religion?'

I racked my brains to think of a religion which abstained from eating homemade trifle, but she went on.

'It doesn't matter. I'm making a huge one. All from scratch. No boudoir biscuits, proper sponge. I bet you if Benjamin has a bowl he'll be a convert! Looking forward to meeting him. Bye!'


When Gran came out of the bath she was wearing a long nightgown. Her face was free of make-up and her hair was down. Without the make-up and jewellery she looked vulnerable. She refused to take my bed so I made up the sofa bed for her in the living room. When the sheets were on she got in, and I found myself tucking her in for the night.

'This is great Natalie,' she said snuggling down under the covers. 'It's lovely to see you, I am sorry I didn't let you know sooner... I lost my phone and...' her eyes welled up. 'I am so tired.'

'It's fine. You're always welcome here,' I said. I leant down and gave her a kiss. 'Sleep tight.'

'God bless Natalie,' she murmured and she was asleep. I watched her for a moment and then crept out and switched off the light.

# AFTERMATH

When I woke the next morning I tiptoed about, so as not to wake Gran who was fast asleep on the sofa. She was still snoring as I left the flat, so I scribbled a quick note, leaving my work number. I realised bloody Benjamin still had my spare key, so I added that if she wanted to go anywhere, I would come back and drop off my key. Ugh, ex-boyfriends!

Outside the sun was blazing, and it was promising to be another hot day. When I arrived at the theatre, Raven Street was bustling; bike couriers sped past, swearing at tourists who were too transfixed with the tacky glitz of Soho to look both ways before crossing; white vans were dotted along the road, unloading their deliveries for the shops, bars, and restaurants; and a huge refuse truck rumbled along, stopping every few metres to collect bins and hold up the traffic.

The screens of The Big O opposite were still blank. A ladder was propped against the building, and one of the square screens making up the video wall had been removed to reveal a tangle of multi-coloured wires. A man in dungarees and a cap stood on the ladder, tinkering with a screwdriver. Outside the theatre, Val from the box office was trying to move a group of Ryan fans, who were blocking the entrance.

'Are any of you lot listening to me? Move to one side, let this poor bloke do his job!' she was shouting. A greying man was waiting with a trolley piled high with bottles he needed to deliver to the bar. The fans ignored her, using the opportunity of the open door to peer past her into the gloom of the box office. Some took pictures on their phones.

'Ryan Harrison is *not* in there!' she cried. One of our security chaps materialised and shooed the fans to one side.

'Morning,' I said to Val and the delivery man.

'Gawd, haven't they got anything better to do with their lives?' muttered Val, and then followed the delivery man inside.

I was about to go in after her, when a small figure in a pink tracksuit and baseball cap emerged from the doorway of The Big O. It was Tuppence Halfpenny; she pulled a box of cigarettes from the front pocket of her hoodie and lit up. Contrary to what Brendan had said on the news, she seemed fine.

'Jamie, Jamie!' she snapped. 'How long are you gonna be up there? I want you to watch my rehearsal…'

It was Jamie on the ladder with the screwdriver.

'Give me ten more minutes,' he said.

'You shouldn't be fiddling with that, let's call in the engineer,' she snapped, taking a drag of her fag.

'I know what I'm doing, Tuppence,' he said. I realised that if you took away the video screen and replaced it with an old car, they were just like any other couple. I went inside the theatre before they saw me.

I was in the office first, and Nicky followed a few minutes later. She was clutching her iPad, and seemed to be in a better mood than last night on the phone.

'Morning honey. It seems this pigeon thing is already fizzling out… I was real worried the national media would grab hold of it,' she said.

'And they haven't?' I asked nervously.

'Not really, in fact there's very little about their launch yesterday… Look, just a small piece in the *Sun* and *Mail Online*.' She handed me her iPad. The *Sun* had an unflattering shot of Tuppence toppling off her swing, and a pigeon hovering above her head in the process of having a crap.

'*Going arse over Tuppence*,' I said, reading the headline.

'And look at this,' added Nicky swiping at the iPad. 'Our delicious little golden goose Ryan Harrison is *everywhere*. The national newspapers took up Eva Castle's interview with him. Doesn't he look great!'

'What about Brendan?' I asked.

'Who'd want to interview Brendan?'

'No. I'm worried Brendan is out there, plotting against us,' I explained.

'Honey, there will always be someone out there plotting against us. What's the worst that can happen? Ryan gets photographed picking his boogers? He's a cool kid. Clean cut and media savvy, and more importantly so are we.'

I looked back at the awful picture of Tuppence mid-fall, and remembered the vindictive look on Brendan's face yesterday. I didn't share Nicky's sudden confidence.

At lunchtime I had a call from Gran to say she wanted to go out shopping, so she could cook dinner tonight. I popped home and found her standing in the middle of the kitchen. She was still in her nightgown and looked confused.

'Are you okay?' I asked.

'How do I make a bloody coffee?' she grumbled. 'All these shiny machines! I tried the hole in the front of your fridge, but it showered me in little pieces of ice, and that other thing vants me to insert a capsule?'

'You sit, I'll make us a nice strong coffee,' I said. Gran perched on the chair. I made us coffee and cheese sandwiches, and gave her a twenty pound note, which she didn't want to take.

'I should be back about five,' I said, when we'd finished our lunch. 'You will be careful out there?'

'My God Natalie, I am not a baby. I vas the one who first brought you to Soho!' she said. I gave her a hug and left the flat. On the way back to the theatre I made a phone call to Benjamin. I was relieved when it went to answer phone, and I left a short message asking him to return my key.


When I got back to the theatre, Nicky, Xander and I went up to the rehearsal room to watch a run-through of the first act of *Macbeth*. We sat on some folding chairs arranged facing a square marked out to represent the stage, as Craig and Byron bustled about checking the actors were all ready. Then there was a nervous excitement in the air as the lights in the rehearsal room flickered off, and we were plunged into darkness.

There was a little shuffling around from the actors, and Byron's chair squeaked as she settled down in the tech booth, then it was silent. A distant bell tolled, and the three witches slowly materialised in the gloom. We watched rapt as they performed the opening scene, casting the spell that would doom Macbeth.

Even at this early stage, the play seemed to have energy and drew us in. And when Ryan entered as Macbeth, returning from the battle – and he was reciting his lines in a British accent! And it wasn't a bad Dick Van Dyke cockney, or like the plummy one Madonna affected during her Guy Ritchie years; Ryan's accent was strong, masculine. He was brilliant.

'Look at Xander,' said Nicky leaning across to whisper in my ear. 'He's in love…'

We looked at one another and realised this play was going to be amazing. The first act was over all too soon and we gave them a loud applause. Then Craig took the actors down to the bar for a notes session. When they were gone, Byron joined us outside in the corridor. She had a serious look on her face.

'Is everything okay?' I asked. 'That run-through was brilliant.'

'No, this is more of a housekeeping matter,' said Byron. 'I hev a request from Mr Hirrison. He needs to move hoe-till.'

'Hoe-till?' repeated Nicky, confused. I was versed in Byron-speak so I understood it as 'hotel'.

'Yis. His hoe-till room is at the front of the building, and he's been having real trouble gitting down for some kip…'

'Sleep,' I translated for Nicky. 'Are all the fans camping outside his window?' I asked.

'Cimping, screaming, throwing up their brassieres… and they constantly chant obscenities, "shag me", "do me now", "I want to hiv your bubbies". The poor chap is exhausted.'

'Okay, I'll sort this,' I said.

'Do you hev his pseudonym for the hoe-till?' asked Byron. I said I did.

Byron said thanks and went back into the rehearsal room. Xander went off home and then it was just me and Nicky in the corridor.

'I don't know about you honey, but today was certainly better than yesterday,' said Nicky. 'I'm gonna go home early. It's date night for me and Bart.'

'Yes, go and have some fun,' I said. 'I think I'll go home early too. My Gran showed up last night.'

'The crazy communist one?' asked Nicky

'Well, she's not a communist, but yes.'

'Okay. Let's go home, have some time out, and make tomorrow an even better day,' said Nicky. She gave me a hug and then I made my way home.

When I got home there was a delicious smell coming from the kitchen. Gran was standing at my cooker stirring something in a huge pan.

'Natalie! Darlink. I'm making my famous goulash!' she cried. She was dressed in a smart pair of trousers, a red blouse, and was fully made up.

'Lovely, I'm starved,' I said giving her a hug.

'I visited that very good butcher shop on Raven Street, and I vent to the greengrocer too,' she said.

I pulled my laptop and phone out of my bag and started to put them on charge.

'Glass of vine?' she said moving slowly to the fridge.

'I can get that,' I said.

'Sit please, my darlink. The guest vill serve the host.'

I went to the table and sat. She came over with two glasses of red.

'Your butcher sells *vine,* can you believe it?' she said. We clinked glasses and I took a sip. It was amazing.

'Hang on, butcher? Do you mean the Rossi's Organic Store on Raven Street?' I asked.

'Yes. He did seem Italian,' said Gran going back to the pan and stirring. A beautiful smell of spice, tomatoes, and wine floated across.

'Gran, that place costs a fortune. I only left you twenty quid?'

'And here it is,' she said handing me back my money. 'I opened an account.'

'I didn't know you could even do that?'

'Darlink, I vore the gold, the furs, I vas a bit of a bitch. I got an account.'

She went and opened the fridge. It was considerably fuller, with packets of cheese and sliced meats shining through greaseproof paper bearing the Rossi's branding. She took out some plastic tubs of olives and stuffed bell peppers.

'Nibbles? The goulash needs time…'

'How big was this account he gave you?' I asked.

'Natalie, Natalie. I make this meal for you. Let me vorry about how it comes to the table. Just enjoy.' She leant over and popped an olive in my mouth before I could complain.

'Oh, hang on, I have to make one phone call for work,' I mumbled through the olive. I went to the landline and dialled the number for the Langham Hotel. I explained that 'Samuel Heathcliff' aka Ryan Harrison needed to be moved to a suite at the back of the hotel, away from his screaming fans. The man on the desk promised he would have Ryan moved immediately.

Over wine and nibbles, and Gran's mouth-watering goulash, I brought her up to speed with everything that had happened.

'And finally, Mum thinks I'm bringing Benjamin with me to the christening,' I said, a gloom suddenly descending over me.

'Natalie, Natalie, Natalie,' she said grabbing me in a hug. 'It's okay. I'm here my darlink…'

'Today was such a good day, and here I am worrying about a bloody man! I'm being silly aren't I?' I said, wiping a tear away.

'No. You hev all these men making you feel like Miss Wrong, but you are Miss Right, don't you forget that!' said Gran.

'It was really nice to come home and have someone cooking for me,' I grinned.

'It is a pleasure. Now, I didn't get any dessert. I bought soap because it hev less calorie.'

'We're going to eat soap?'

'No Natalie. I think you need a nice bath.'

I had more wine as she ran me the water.

'I put special boobles in,' she said emerging wiping her hands on a towel. 'For a nice booble bath…Your butcher also sells very good soap.'

'You bought soap from Rossi's, Gran? It costs a fortune!'

'Shhh. As I said, instead of a dessert…'

When I was in the bathroom I saw a wooden box of hand-milled soap sitting open on a chair beside the full bath. I'm pretty sure I had seen them in the shop priced at sixty quid. I slipped into the water and felt myself unwind in the warm soapy water. When I emerged an hour later I was sleepy and relaxed. Gran was just finishing washing up.

'Natalie, why don't you take an early night? I hev done the dishes, everything is done,' she said.

'Are you sure?'

'You are a beautiful girl, but you must have your beauty sleep…'

'I suppose I am a little tired,' I said. 'Goodnight, and thank you.'

'Good night my darlink… Vould you mind if I make a few phone calls? They are not international.'

'Course, the phone is by the fridge,' I said. 'Goodnight.'

'Night darlink,' she said, and gave me a hug. I crawled into bed and was asleep in minutes.

# THE INVITATION

The next morning I left Gran snoring, and went to work. Benjamin hadn't got back to me, so I sent Xander out to get a key cut, and asked him to post it through my front door in an envelope. The rest of the day was a series of meetings, ranging from the sublime to the ridiculous.

In the morning we had a staff meeting about whether or not we should reattach the anti-pigeon spikes to the roof, after the fiasco during the flash mob. It turned into a fierce debate about pigeons. Val from the box office was dead against it, saying her husband kept racing pigeons and they are highly intelligent creatures – in fact she thinks they are more intelligent than her husband. Byron was also dead against it; she is a devoted animal lover and spends most of her wages sponsoring animals around the world.

The theatre caretaker Len, along with Xander and Nicky, were all for it. Nicky hasn't been able to think of pigeons in the same light after she went on a booze cruise to Dublin, and a tour guide told her that pigeons in the capital eat three hundred tonnes of vomit off the streets each year.

I suggested that we look into more humane ways of keeping pigeons at bay. Craig proposed renting a bald eagle, and taking it up on the roof twice a day to scare them away, but we doubted the Arts Council would fork out for that.

Then we had a meeting with Craig, and Mhairi, the set designer for *Macbeth*. She pitched the idea to us that blood could cascade down the back wall of the stage when Lady Macbeth killed the King. It sounded fabulous, but we had to try and work out how we could do it, and then how much fake blood we'd need to do it every night for five weeks. Mhairi estimated it to be six hundred gallons. Then Nicky started telling her about the pigeons in Dublin, and Mhairi tried to work out what three hundred tonnes of vomit would be in gallons, which made us both laugh and feel sick.

I realised again that without my wonderful, unpredictable job, I would be lost.

Later in the afternoon, I was surfing the net to find competitively priced fake blood suppliers, when I realised I still hadn't phoned Mum to explain I would be coming to the christening tomorrow without Benjamin. I reached for the phone, but there was a knock at my door.

'Come in,' I said. The door opened and it was Ryan Harrison. He was dressed in jeans and a checked shirt, his hair fashionably tousled. He had a record bag over his shoulder. He looked like a student, a rather cute one at that.

'Ryan, hello,' I said. 'Is everything okay? Is Byron with you?'

'Yes, and no, it's just me,' he said.

'Is your new hotel room okay?' I asked. 'They said it would be overlooking the park.'

'Yeah, and it's a suite, it's so much better. I slept!'

'That's great,' I said. He was quiet for a moment and started to straighten up some books on my desk.

'You know, London is kinda weird, especially the weekends…' he said. 'I have friends here, but they're in the industry too. They wanna go to parties and… I've been and seen loads of shows. Have you seen *Matilda*?'

'Yes, it's fab,' I said. 'And I remember when I first came to London, how overwhelming it was, and that's for people who aren't famous!'

'Yes, that's why I really appreciate the invitation,' said Ryan.

'Invitation?'

'Yeah to um, Micky's christening.'

It was the weirdest moment, to hear my sister's name come out of Ryan Harrison's mouth. He went on.

'Your grandma, Anouska, sure is a character… Did she really grow up in Hungary with Zsa Zsa Gabor?'

'Apparently yes,' I said, with a fixed smile on my face.

'And did she really escape the Nazis?'

'Yes. Although sometimes we wish…' I shook away the thought. 'So, she invited you to the christening?'

'She said I should experience an "oldie English village and an oldie English church", but that she was no oldie! She's funny… She said you'd come by my hotel tomorrow morning at seven.'

'Of course, we'll see you at seven,' I said the smile still fixed to my face.

'Do I need to bring anything?' he asked. I was tempted to ask him to pick up a rotary chicken and a bottle of ham, but I wondered if he did his own shopping anymore, or if he even handled cash?

'Just bring yourself,' I smiled.

'Great, thanks Natalie,' he grinned and slipped out of the door.

I stormed back to the flat and found Gran lying on the sofa. She had a cold flannel pressed to her forehead.

'Natalie, I had a funny turn!' she said dramatically. I rushed to her and took her hand.

'What is it?'

'Angina. I think I overdid it hoovering.'

I looked around, but I couldn't see the hoover.

'You don't have to clean the flat,' I said.

'I am your guest Natalie, and I thank you from the bottom of my heart.'

I went and made her a cup of tea, no milk just a slice of lemon, and came back to where she was lying on the sofa.

'Oh that's better,' she said sitting up and taking a sip. 'I forget I am old. It sucks to be old.'

'Gran. Did you invite Ryan Harrison to Micky's christening?' I asked.

'Yes,' she said taking another sip of tea and coughing.

'Why? And how? And didn't you think you should ask me first?'

Gran looked thoughtful and sat up a little.

'Natalie. You get dumped by this Benjamin, before you can introduce him at the christening – vich ve both know is about as desirable an invitation to view an execution on death row...'

'Okay,' I said.

'However Micky and your mother think it's the next royal vedding...'

'Where are you going with this?' I asked.

'Do you vont to turn up man-less again? To see their pity?'

'No.'

'Of course not... And yet here you have vorking in your theatre, Ryan Harrison! A huge heart-throb!'

'You said you didn't have a clue who he was?'

'Vell, I looked at the goggle. On the computer... I goggled him,' she said.

'You *googled* him,' I corrected.

'Yes, he is certainly vat the Americans call candy for the eye.'

'Eye candy.'

'Yes, he's no Sean Connery, but there vill never be another Sean. However, those pictures of Ryan in the swim suit are hot stuff, no?'

I nodded in agreement.

'But this is Dexter's christening, Gran! It will be full of people from Sowerton…'

'Natalie, ven I vas your age I fantasised about coming back to my hometown in Hungary, with Sean Connery on my arm. That vould have shown all those potato-faced bitches who called me a slut! Ha!'

'He won't be on my arm. I work with him. He might even be gay! Anyway, how did you get him to agree?' I asked.

'Natalie. You phoned his hotel in front of me last night. Ven you vent to bed I dial 1471, called the hotel and ask for Mr Heathcliff! He is very keen to experience a little of England…' she gave me a wink.

'Gran, he's virtually a teenager, and…'

'Oh Natalie. You are too shy! Now, I von't hear anymore. I vill microvonk some goulash and ve vill decide vat you must vear.'

She got up off the sofa.

'I thought you had angina?' I said, seeing she suddenly had much more energy than when I'd arrived.

'It comes and it goes…' she said vaguely.


Despite my protests she fed me goulash, and this time didn't let me drink, so I could look my best. She went through my wardrobe and found me an outfit and then she sent me to bed, for my beauty sleep. I lay there in the dark for an hour, with my brain whirring. Unable to sleep, I phoned Sharon.

'What?' she cried when I'd told her everything. 'Life is so unfair! You know what I'm doing tomorrow? Taking Fred's dad, Giuseppe, to Lewisham hospital to get his ears syringed…'

'Sharon, it's going to be so embarrassing… Ryan Harrison meeting my weird family, and Gran will be trying to match-make the whole time…'

'You get no sympathy from me,' she said.

'It's going to look desperate, isn't it?' I asked. 'Showing up at Dexter's christening with Ryan Harrison. Maybe he's gay?'

'Dexter? I don't know Nat, he's only two years old,' said Sharon.

'Not Dexter, you twit, Ryan! If Ryan is gay, people might assume he's my GBF.'

'Wash your mouth out with soap and water, Natalie Love! He is *not* gay,' insisted Sharon.

'Let's look at the evidence,' I said. 'He's far too handsome to be straight, his dogs are named after *Twilight* characters. And I did hear a rumour he's dating someone on *Manhattan Beach*.'

'Who?' demanded Sharon.

'It's just a vague rumour…'

'WHO?' she growled.

'The guy who plays his best friend…'

'Jodie Pitch? Who plays Mitch Fitch, who's married to the rich bitch? NO WAY! Oh my god!'

'I hasten to add Sharon, that this is just a rumour. Anyway, if Ryan is gay, he's not going to out himself at a random family christening,' I said.

'Also Ryan does look good in Speedos,' she agreed. 'Not many straight guys look good in Speedos. Well, apart from Olympic divers… I am jealous as hell Nat. You have to take photos, document everything. Oh my God, I've just had an idea!'

'What?' I asked.

'You could make me my very own personalised Ryan Harrison calendar!'

'No.'

'Come on, you're always asking for ideas for what to get me for Christmas! And it's a family occasion. It's perfectly normal to have a camera at a christening. January could be Ryan with one of the llamas on your farm… Hot guys look so cute with cuddly animals.'

'No Sharon…'

But she wasn't listening.

'February could be Ryan on the green outside the Ramblers Rest pub, shirtless… I'll check the weather forecast for tomorrow. I'm sure he'd take off his shirt if it was hot. March could be…'

I finally got off the phone after fending off Sharon's requests for Ryan photos; she assured me she knows someone at Snappy Snaps who can be discreet. And Byron thought bunny boilers would be the strangers in the street!

# SUPER GRAN

It was a beautiful day when we left the flat early next morning. Gran had shown remarkable taste, helping me to choose a pair of skinny jeans and a cream-coloured sleeveless top, which showed just the right amount of cleavage for a christening. She had opted for a cream pair of close-fitting slacks with black patent heels, a matching cream blouse, a string of pearls, and a cashmere cardigan thrown around her shoulders. As we stepped into the lift down to the garage she slipped on a huge pair of Jackie Onassis sunglasses.

'You look amazing,' I said.

'Thank you darlink,' she said pulling down my top a little. I pulled it back up.

'He vill be looking at you, not me,' she protested.

'He doesn't need to see that much of me,' I said tartly. 'And besides I'm his boss, kind of.'

The lift opened to the underground garage, and she took my arm as we made our way over to my little Ford Fiesta. She grimaced, limping badly.

'Those shoes look three sizes too small,' I said noticing her feet crammed painfully into the black patent heels.

'I'll be fine. I took nine painkillers,' she said stopping for a moment and leaning on her stick.

'Gran!'

'Oh be quiet. I'd rather have liver failure than be seen in flat shoes by a man who has von *GQ*'s Sexiest Man of the Year three years in a row.'

'You have been busy on the goggle,' I said.

'Now stop fussing and let's go and get him,' she said. I tidied up the car and helped Gran into the back seat (she wanted Ryan to go in the front so he could talk to me). We drove out of the underground garage and made our way to the Langham Hotel.

It was quite difficult to navigate the winding streets and one-way system to reach the rear entrance of the hotel, and I wondered if Ryan was going to bail on us at the last minute. Would he want to get up so early? And there was a strong chance he could get a far better offer, but as I pulled into the set-down and drop-off area, I spied Ryan waiting in a doorway at the rear entrance of the hotel. He was dressed in a well-cut black suit, and holding a bag. A skinny teenage bellboy from the hotel stood beside him, holding a huge gift basket.

'Vich von is he?' asked Gran peering through the window.

'Take your sunglasses off. He's the one not wearing the bell-boy outfit,' I said.

'Ah yes, he looks even better than he does on the goggle,' said Gran lifting up her sunglasses. Ryan came down the steps, accompanied by the bellboy. I got out of the car and Gran wound down her window.

'Morning ladies,' said Ryan with a grin.

'Hello!' I trilled. 'This is my Gr…'

'It's Anouska, hello,' interrupted Gran through the window. Ryan leant in and pecked her on the cheek.

'I think that might have to go in the boot,' I said to the bell-boy carrying the gift basket.

'The *trunk* Natalie, speak his language,' said Gran. I went round to the back of the car, where Ryan gave me a kiss on the cheek. He smelt delicious and looked so handsome in his well-cut suit. The gift basket was enormous, and it contained a bottle of expensive champagne, chocolates, whisky, and cheeses.

'My goodness, you didn't have to do that,' I said.

'The basket is for Micky and Dave, I know how the Brits love to party,' he grinned. 'And this is for Dexter.'

He pulled out of the bag a boxed set of *Peter Rabbit* books by Beatrix Potter.

'Oh Ryan,' I said. 'They're beautiful.'

The bellboy placed both gifts carefully in the boot, and Ryan tipped him twenty pounds. I went back round and got in.

'He's got them such beautiful expensive presents,' I whispered quickly. 'What have we got?'

'A bottle of plonk and a rattle,' said Gran.

'I'll get some cash out at a petrol station on the way, Micky loves cash,' I said. Gran nodded in agreement as Ryan got in the car. As we pulled away from the hotel, he kept twisting round in his seat to look out of the back window.

'Is everything okay?' I asked.

'I've had this photographer dude following me over the past few days,' he said.

'Why didn't you tell us?' I asked, glancing in my rear view mirror.

'If I came to you, or my manager, every time the press followed me, you'd get so sick of hearing it!' he said. He watched for a moment, and, satisfied we weren't being followed, turned back in his seat.

'I'm really jazzed about going to Sowerton!' he said.

As we left London, and the houses began to thin out to fields, Ryan got more excited. He asked if my parents had a thatched house, and if Shakespeare had ever been to our village.

'No, but it is in the Domesday Book! It's a very beautiful old English village,' piped up Gran from the back. This was the first time I'd ever heard her say anything nice about the place. Her usual description is that Satan dug a big pit, filled it with shit, and on top he built Sowerton.

I didn't know how to behave around Ryan. It was as if my work life and personal life had collided. Every time I changed gear, my hand kept brushing against his leg, which was firm. After the fourth time saying sorry, I realised that he was just a guy, admittedly a very hot guy, but a normal guy to whom something extraordinary had happened. I've often read that when people become famous they don't change. It's the people around them who do.

'Hey Natalie, could we stop soon?' asked Ryan a few hours into the journey. 'I need to take a leak.'

'Yes, there's a service station in about a mile,' I said.

'Do you mind if we just, you know, pull over. I try to avoid public restrooms.'

'I know my darlink. I always hover over the seat, even with my bad hip,' said Gran from the back.

Ryan laughed.

'No, I get girls following me into public bathrooms, and sometimes guys too. Last week I had to get my manager Terri involved when this girl took a picture of my you-know-what with her camera phone, and tried to sell it to the press.'

I pulled over in a lay-by on a deserted stretch of the Motorway and Ryan got out and went to a row of bushes. We watched the back of him as he peed.

'He's nice, isn't he?' I said.

'Very,' agreed Gran. 'Did you think he vasn't?'

'No, but when we're at the theatre, we have to manage his time so carefully. He's always got to have someone with him. I thought he was a little high maintenance.'

'He's peeing in a bush. How high maintenance is that?' said Gran.

'You're right,' I said. We watched him for a moment longer.

'He really needed to go,' said Gran. 'Now I need to go too, but I'm not doing it in the bushes.'

*

We set off again, and pulled into the next petrol station. I drove past the petrol pumps through to the car park at the rear, where there was a block of toilets.

'Would you like anything from the shop?' I asked as Gran and I got out.

'No, it's cool, I'll just hang here and have a smoke,' he said getting out of the car with us. We left him smoking his cigarette and walked over to the toilet block. When we were done and washing our hands I realised I should call Mum and tell her I wasn't bringing Benjamin.

'Yes. You might be right,' said Gran reapplying her scarlet lipstick in the mirror. I pulled out my phone and dialled home. My mother answered sounding harassed.

'Where are you Natalie? Is Mum with you?'

'Yes, she is with me, and we're on the M5,' I said.

'Is Mum behaving? I hope she hasn't embarrassed you in front of Benjamin?' she asked.

'Mum, Benjamin isn't coming,' I said.

'Why not?'

'We broke up…'

There was a silence.

'When did this happen?' she asked.

'A week or so ago…'

Her response was not what I was expecting.

'Natalie I'm very sorry about that. I just wish you'd said sooner, because we'd renamed the dog.'

'What?' I asked.

'We got this little rescue dog a few weeks ago called Benjamin. I thought it might be rude if he had the same name as your partner…'

'*Partner?*'

'Well, you're a bit old for a boyfriend, Natalie… Anyway we've been training him to be called Nigel.'

'Nigel?'

'Yes, you know how much I love Nigella, well the dog is a boy so the obvious name was Nigel.'

'Obvious…' I said.

'Natalie, don't give me that tone. So do you think you and Benjamin will be getting back together?'

'I doubt it.'

'Then can we go back to Benjamin for Nigel, or should I say Benjamin?'

'Listen Mum…' I said.

'Ooh I'd best go. Mrs Rust is just banging on the window with a baked Alaska. Poor woman has dementia.'

'Mum, I just wanted to tell you I'm bringing someone else, the actor Ryan Harrison. The one I told you about at my theatre.'

'Jolly good… Hello Mrs Rust, oh no it's dripping… Look Natalie I have to go.'

And she hung up. Gran had been listening beside me.

'All that horse manure has gone to her head,' she said.

When we came out of the toilets, there was a group of teenagers shouting and rocking my car! Ryan had locked himself inside and was looking panicked.

'Hey!' I shouted. 'Stop!'

They ignored us and carried on shaking. There were two boys and two girls in their late teens, pale-faced and dressed in sports gear. Their shaking was building up momentum, and as the car lurched from side to side, two of the wheels came away from the tarmac.

'Stop! Or I'll call the police,' I said brandishing my phone, but they didn't look scared. Gran hobbled closer and stopped by the car bonnet, I put my hand on her arm, but she shook me off. The girls were now shrieking and goading the boys on. The tallest boy turned to face us.

'Hey, we've got some bitches,' he said. He looked us up and down, and spat on the floor.

'Please, stop,' said Gran taking a limping step forward. The tall boy motioned for them to stop, and the car ceased rocking with a creak.

'There you go, Grandma,' said the tall boy. 'Now what are you gonna do for me?' He looked her up and down, and the girls on the other side of the car gave a hyena-like laugh. Gran stood her ground.

'Come on, no harm done, let's go,' I said, terrified. Ryan was watching from inside the car with horror. The tall boy moved towards Gran.

'Old bitches know their way around a dick,' said the boy. The other three smirked nastily. He stopped near Gran, towering over her. 'You want some of this *Grandma*?' he leered grabbing his crotch. There was a pause as Gran regarded him.

'If I vanted a little maggot, I vould go to the fishing tackle shop…'

With a deft and powerful twist she brought her walking stick round in an arc, and it connected with a crack on the boy's nose.

His eyes opened wide in surprise and he crumpled to his knees, blood gushing down his chin and onto his white hooded top. She placed the rubber end of her walking stick against his chest and shoved. He toppled over onto his back. Gran stood over him, holding her stick against his chest and pinning him down.

'Vat's your name?' she said. The three teenagers stood with their mouths open in shock.

'Mike,' whimpered the tall boy, staring up at Gran with his back pressed against the tarmac.

'Does your mother know how you speak to old ladies?'

He shook his head.

'Vat?'

'No, no, she doesn't,' said Mike.

'If I vas your mother I vould smack your little bottom… Vat would I do Mike? Repeat,'

'You would… Smack my little bottom,' gulped Mike, wiping his bloody nose with a white sleeve.

'You,' said Gran clicking her fingers at the other boy who was in shock. 'Open the door for my granddaughter.'

Ryan undid the central locking and the boy rather awkwardly opened the driver's door for me.

'Get in Natalie,' said Gran. I moved quickly to the door and climbed in. Ryan gave me a sideways look.

'Now open my door,' she said. The boy did as he was told. Gran released Mike from being pinned under her stick.

'Now if no one else has anything nice to say, ve have a christening to attend,' she added. The girls silently stepped away from the car, the other boy looked at Mike still bleeding and followed suit. When Gran was in the car, I started the engine and drove away with a squeal of rubber.

'Jeez, way to go Anouska!' said Ryan looking out of the back window at Mike, who was being helped up by his mate. 'You are like the best bodyguard ever!'

'That was very risky Gran,' I said, my hands now shaking. 'What if he'd had a knife?'

'I have a Taser,' she said pulling a small black device from her handbag. 'I vould have shot him in the balls.'

Ryan looked at me and laughed.

'She's not exactly the apple-pie-making grandma, is she?'

'No,' I said still shaking. I hit the motorway ramp faster than I should.

'Hey Natalie, it's all good, we're okay,' said Ryan and he put his hand on mine. When the car started to scream, I realised I had to move my hand and change up to fifth. I caught Gran smiling at me in the rear view mirror.

For the rest of the journey, Ryan kept reliving the moment.

'That was so cool, you hit him hard! Kapoww!'

'Let's not mention this to Mum and Dad,' I said. 'We'll never hear the end of it…'

'Anouska you should have your own TV show, Super Gran!' added Ryan.

'There was a TV show here called *Super Gran*,' I said.

'Then we should totally remake it with Anouska!'

'I'm flattered but an actor's life is not for me…' said Gran. Luckily we passed some thatched cottages. Ryan started taking pictures on his iPhone, and we were saved from hearing about Gran's topless acting role in *The Song of the Floundering Mermaid.*

# THE FARM

We drove into Sowerton village around midday. The thatched cottages looked idyllic with their neatly mown lawns and gardens full of wild flowers. As we rounded the corner to the green, the Ramblers Rest pub came into view. A group of walkers sat outside, enjoying a drink in the sun. I had a sinking feeling, returning home. It always feels like I regress and I stop being the person I have worked so hard to become over the past few years. I go back to being the girl with the frizzy hair who is always being told off by her mother, the stupid girl who failed her exams and left her fiancé at the altar. I looked in the rear view mirror at Gran, she didn't seem happy to be back either.

Ryan opened his window, and the smell hit us.

'Wow. What's that?' he asked screwing up his face.

'Ten kinds of shit,' said Gran. 'Get used to it, it's relentless.'

I reached the gate to the farmhouse, and saw Dad had propped it open. The car churned and lurched slowly up the driveway through the mud, and I came to a stop alongside the house where the drive rose up to a grassy slope. Ryan was peering out of the window as if he had landed on the moon.

'What's that?' he asked, pointing in awe at a furry creature with long legs and a long neck standing in the field at the end of the garden.

'That's Rihanna,' I said.

'What?'

'She's my Dad's llama. My nieces and nephews named her,' I explained.

'Wow! I've never seen a llama before!' he said excitedly. We all got out of the car and Ryan sped off down the garden. I looked back at Gran who had a lace handkerchief pressed to her mouth and nose.

'Jesus, I'm back in shit city... I hate it here,' she said. She motioned to me to follow Ryan, and I caught up with him by the wooden fence. Rihanna had come to peer at the handsome man in the suit. The sun glinted off his dark hair, and his mouth spread into a smile showing perfect teeth.

'Do you want a photo with her?' I asked, thinking of Sharon's calendar request for January.

'Cool,' said Ryan. Rihanna moved towards him on her spindly legs, jutting her bottom teeth out and gurning. *Please don't spit,* I suddenly thought. Llamas will often spit if they are scared or provoked, and it's a revolting lump of green gunk which stinks. Rihanna snorted and pushed her head against Ryan. He gently reached out, and his hand disappeared into her coarse fur coat.

'Hey Rihanna, aren't you *pretty*?' said Ryan. She stared down through giant eyes with huge curling eyelashes. I took a photo of them, then I reached up and stroked her too. She gave a snort and opened her mouth showing a leathery tongue.

'They're like those creatures in *Star Wars*, the ones they ride in the desert. Could I ride her?' asked Ryan.

'They're not crazy about being ridden,' I said. 'And she's pregnant right now.'

'Wow, baby llamas,' said Ryan stroking her fur in wonderment.

\*

Gran came limping up to us by the fence, muttering swear words and Rihanna reared up. With a snorting hocking sound she spat at Gran. A lump of green goo shot out and landed on her cardigan. It all happened so fast.

'Whoa, what was that?' said Ryan stepping back in surprise. 'Is someone paintballing around here?'

'Bloody animals!' Gran shouted waving her stick at Rihanna. 'The only reason I never became a vegetarian vas so I could eat you all!' Rihanna eyeballed Gran and a long string of drool oozed from her mouth.

We heard a 'yoo-hoo' and Mum was running down from the house wearing a smart suit with a pinny over the top.

'Natalie! Oh Natalie!' she cried swooping in for a hug. She held me tight. 'It's lovely to see you!'

'Annie, your bloody animal just threw up on me!' said Gran, easing her way out of her cardigan.

'It's just llama spit. She must have sensed you didn't like her,' said Mum going to Gran and helping her off with the cardigan. 'Didn't you used to have a llama fur coat?'

'The second I set foot in this bloody place, I'm standing in shit and spat on!' Gran shouted. Then a little blond Labrador came bowling across the grass and crashed into her legs.

'And what the hell is that!' she cried almost losing balance. Mum grabbed her.

'That's Nigel, I mean Benjamin!' said Mum.

'Hello Mrs Love, it's great to meet you,' said Ryan.

'Oh. Hello,' said Mum suddenly noticing Ryan and approving at once. She handed Gran back her cardigan covered in llama spit. 'You're American!'

'Mum, this is Ryan Harrison. He's playing Macbeth at the theatre…'

'How lovely to meet you,' said Mum, quickly reaching round to untie her pinny.

'I really appreciate you including me in your special day, ma'am,' said Ryan leaning in and kissing her on the cheek.

'Oh, thank you,' blushed Mum.

'Get off me you little devil!' growled Gran as she tried to break away from Benjamin who was enthusiastically humping her leg.

'Nigel! I mean Benjamin, stop that,' said Mum pulling the little pup off Gran.

'Look at my bloody slacks!' said Gran.

'Don't make a fuss. It'll dry quickly, and then I'll give it a good stiff brush,' said Mum. She turned her attention back to Ryan.

'Why don't we go in for a nice cup of tea before we head off to the church?' trilled Mum excitedly. We started to walk up to the house and Mum mouthed '*very handsome*' behind Ryan. Gran followed with difficulty, still being humped by Benjamin the dog.

# AA VS RAC

When we came into the kitchen, Mum shouted up the stairs for my dad to come quickly. He came thundering down wearing just a towel round his waist, his face covered in shaving foam.

'What is it? Is everything okay?' he said breathlessly, spraying shaving foam everywhere. Mum looked horrified.

'Martin! What on earth are you doing?' she shrilled.

'What do you mean, what am I doing? You started shrieking up the stairs? Has someone had an accident?' He suddenly noticed me, Gran and Ryan and visibly relaxed.

'No one's had an accident Martin! I called you, because Natalie is here, and she's brought a gentleman friend... I thought you would at least be ready!'

She made it sound like I had never brought a man home before.

'Ah, yes, hello Benjamin,' said Dad offering his hand to Ryan and grinning through his beard of foam. There was an awkward pause.

'No, this is Ryan, he's from America,' corrected Mum, as if Dad were a moron.

'Pleased to meet you sir,' said Ryan stepping forward and shaking Dad's hand.

'Nice to meet you,' said Dad still confused.

'Hi Dad,' I said.

'Hello Nat, so what happened to?'

'Benjamin and I, um… we've… '

'She caught him having the sex vith another vooman,' said Gran, sitting at the kitchen table and lighting a cigarette.

'Ah, right-o,' said Dad. 'Well Ryan, it's lovely to meet you…'

'Martin, go and put some clothes on!' hissed Mum, giving him 'the look'. He went back upstairs, his bum crack showing over the top of the towel round his waist.

'Sorry Ryan,' trilled Mum. 'We don't usually gallivant around the house half-naked.'

When Dad came back down a little while later, he was dressed smartly in his best suit. Mum had brought out the fancy china, and was fussing over Ryan, asking him several times if he was in a draught. Dad said a proper hello to me and Gran and apologised again to Ryan.

'It's no problem sir,' said Ryan. Then when Mum handed him a cup of tea he said, 'Thank you ma'am.'

'Ooh isn't he polite?' squealed Mum. 'I wish we encouraged children in Britain to say 'sir' and 'ma'am'. Whenever I phone the bank they want to call me 'Annie' which is far too over fa-miliar if you ask me…'

For once I had to agree with her, although the way Ryan said *ma'am* in his deep American accent was making me go a little weak at the knees.

'Who fancies a drink before we head off to the church, Ryan?' asked Dad. 'I've got some malt whisky. You're not driving?'

'I'm in AA,' said Ryan.

'Ooh! We're in the RAC,' cooed Mum. 'They rung up and offered us a cheaper deal…'

'No, ma'am, I'm in recovery. I'm in Alcoholics Anonymous, I've been sober four months,' said Ryan.

There was a stunned silence. I looked at him in shock.

'I had no idea,' I said. 'You should have said, especially as this is a social occasion…'

'Goodness. I never would have guessed. You're too handsome to be an alcoholic,' said Mum.

'Mum!'

'Well, we don't know many alcoholics,' said Mum. 'There's only Ned and Jed who live in the village, and they look a fright.'

'I vill hev a large visky Martin,' said Gran.

'Hang on Gran,' I said.

'No, it's cool, really,' said Ryan. 'Anouska, you go ahead. I'm committed to the programme. Life is good. I'm here in the beautiful English countryside…'

Dad went and poured a whisky for Gran. He came back and placed it in front of her on the kitchen table. There was a silence as she took a sip.

'This is why I don't tell people,' said Ryan. 'It really isn't a problem. We're gonna have a great celebration for Dexter's christening.'

'Ok, well, that's great,' I said. There was another silence.

'May I use your bathroom?' asked Ryan.

'Of course you can dear, Martin would you show Ryan up,' trilled Mum. When Dad had gone upstairs with Ryan, Mum launched herself on me with a barrage of questions. *Where does Ryan live? Where did he go to school? How long have I known him?*

'He's just my guest Mum. He's not my boyfriend. He's starring in *Macbeth* at the theatre,' I explained.

'He's a very famous actor Annie,' said Gran. 'The star of a big television show in America. You must hev seen him in the papers?' Mum reached for the local paper on top of the fridge.

'My God Annie, I mean the national papers!'

'We don't read the national news,' said Mum.

'Of course not, and now you are so ignorant your brain has shrivelled to the size of a satsuma…'

'Gran, don't start,' I said. Dad came back in.

'Did he find it okay Martin?' asked Mum.

'Yes, I showed him to the bathroom, it's up to him what he does in there,' grinned Dad.

'Do you think he'll mind we don't have a bidet? All rich Americans have them. I knew we should have got a bidet when we had the new loo put in,' said Mum.

'Mum, it's fine,' I said.

'I think when Ryan comes back we should get going for the church,' said Dad.

'Annie, do you hev something I can borrow?' asked Gran who was watching her cardigan now going round in the washing machine.

'Yes, Mum, hang on,' she said.

Ryan came back down as Mum, Dad and Gran fussed about getting ready. He leant down and scratched Nigel behind the ears.

'Are we cool Natalie?' he asked.

'Yes, I'm just surprised you didn't say anything.'

'I never lie about my alcoholism, if people ask I'm honest. But I'm not going to walk into a room and announce I'm a recovering alcoholic, am I?'

'No, of course not,' I said. He grinned. I realised there was far more to Ryan than meets the eye.

# THE EPIC TRIFLE

I had missed the previous three christenings of House, Downton, and Abbey, so this was the first time I had been back in St Bathsheba's Church since my wedding day. Reverend Ball was at the huge oak doors, looking greasy in his creased cassock, and greeting the congregation. He was the same vicar who had presided over my wedding that never was.

'Hello Mr and Mrs Love,' he said, showing a huge amount of gums when he grinned.

'Hello Reverend Ball,' smiled Mum. 'You remember our eldest, Natalie?'

'Of course,' he chuckled. 'I hope you stay beyond the first hymn this time!'

'Haha,' I said.

'She's brought a famous television actor with her,' trilled Mum. 'This is Ryan Morrison.'

I went to correct her, but Ryan shot me a sideways glance.

'Pleased to meet you, Reverend,' he said.

It was cool inside when we entered the church. The sun streamed through the stained glass windows casting soft blocks of colour on the stone floor.

'Wow, how old is this place?' whispered Ryan.

'It was built in the fifteen hundreds,' I whispered back. Ryan mouthed 'wow' again and craned his head back to look at the carved cherubs on the vaulted stone ceiling high above.

Micky was stationed at the beginning of the aisle, giving out the orders of service to the guests as they arrived. Her husband Dave was beside her, cradling little Dexter who was dressed in a long lace christening gown, his black hair jutting out above a sleeping face. Since their wedding in Greece eight years ago they have both gained a huge amount of weight. Micky is now close to twenty stone and Dave must be more. They looked very happy though. Mum and Dad said hello to Dave and Micky and then went to bag a pew.

'Nat. You came,' said Micky giving me a kiss. 'Dave now owes me twenty quid…'

'No, thirty, the extra ten was if she brought a bloke!' added Dave.

'You bet on me not showing up?' I asked.

'Yeah, what do you expect? You never come to anything,' said Micky pointedly.

'Well, I'm here now… And this is Ryan,' I said. He shook hands with Dave, and gave Micky a kiss on the cheek.

'I recognise you from somewhere,' said Micky.

'He looks like the guy in that TV show about the beach,' said Dave.

'I am that guy in that TV show about the beach,' grinned Ryan.

'*Seriously*?' asked Micky, looking impressed. I nodded.

'I'm in London for a few weeks, I'm doing a play at Natalie's theatre,' explained Ryan.

'Fucking hell!' said Dave loudly.

'Dave, shut up! We're in the fucking church!' hissed Micky. They were both silent for a moment, just staring at Ryan.

'So your theatre must be, decent?' asked Dave, surprised.

'What do you mean?' I said coldly.

'Well, I thought you ran a pub venue out in South London…'

'That was ten years ago,' I said. There was an awkward silence.

'There are some really fit birds in your TV show mate,' said Dave.

'I hope they're not fitter than me?' asked Micky sharply.

'No one holds a candle to you, Micky,' added Dave hastily.

'They'd need a bloody big candle,' murmured Gran in my ear, having caught up with us.

'HELLO GRAN!' said Micky, using that loud voice reserved for the elderly. 'ARE YOU ALRIGHT?' Gran was now wearing one of my mother's cardigans, which was red and covered in green pom-poms.

'I'm very good dear. Little Dexter is such an angel,' said Gran stroking his soft dark hair.

'He shits like a train though,' said Dave.

'DAVE WAS JUST SAYING, DEXTER DOESN'T STOP POOING, GRAN...'

'I can hear you all perfectly,' said Gran, but Micky ploughed on.

'WE'VE GOT ALL THE GRANS AND GRANDDADS IN THEIR OWN SPECIAL PEW...' She pulled Gran off towards a pew filled with a row of grey heads. Gran looked back at me pleadingly, but the organ started to play and we had to hurriedly find somewhere to sit.

Mum and Dad had saved us a couple of seats in a pew near the front. I went in next to Mum, and Ryan sat next to me on the end. Then the church service began and Reverend Ball started to drone on about *The Parable of the Mustard Seed*. I looked across at Mum who had her 'I'm pretending to listen' face on, which is the same one as when she puts on mascara. Ryan gave me a sideways glance and grinned.

'When's half time?' he whispered.

'Sorry, there's no half time,' I whispered back.

'No hot dogs and beer? Root Beer for me, of course.'

'Shhh!' hissed Mum, giving me 'the look'. Ryan grinned and waggled his finger. He was squashed against me in the pew, and I felt the warmth of his leg against mine, the side of his rump, his arm... all of it felt so firm and warm, and he smelt delicious. I spent the rest of the service thrilled at his close proximity. Even Dexter's bloodcurdling screams as the vicar gently poured holy water over his head didn't bother me. Our connection was only broken when we stood to sing the final hymn, 'Who Built the Ark?'

After the christening everyone went back to the farm for the buffet. There must have been a hundred people crammed into the large dining room. Mum wasn't happy with Micky's arrangement that all the guests bring food. Most people had ignored her invitation, so we ended up with seventy Marks and Spencer's quiche lorraines, and sixty-five raspberry pavlovas. It made me wish I'd brought a bottle of ham and a rotary chicken.

It was great to have Ryan with me, and not to have everyone enquiring about my single status. They all assumed we were a couple, and none of them expected Ryan Harrison to be a guest at the christening of Dexter Lamb, so they regarded him with a mild curiosity.

We caught up with Micky and Dave by the buffet table. Dave was still holding Dexter who had fallen asleep.

'Congratulations on your beautiful family,' said Ryan. I looked over at Downton and Abbey who had quiche smeared over their faces, and were taking it in turns slamming the lid of the piano in the corner. House had pulled her skirt up over her head and it was caught on her tiara, unfortunately she wasn't wearing any knickers. Micky and Dave hesitated a moment to see if Ryan was taking the piss, but realised he was being nice and American.

'Thanks. I think four is enough,' said Micky before rushing over to help House with her wardrobe malfunction. Ryan then asked Dave what he did for a living. For the next half an hour we listened politely as Dave droned on about his job in IT. Companies hire him to hack into their computer systems and expose security flaws.

'What's been the hardest thing to hack into?' asked Ryan.

'I'm great with computers but terrible with women, so I'd say the hardest thing to hack into was Micky's knickers!' said Dave. We laughed politely.

Gran had been caught up in the herd of old people at the church, and brought back to the farm on the dial-a-ride minibus. She staggered into the living room amongst a group of grey old ladies.

'Are you okay?' I said.

'Help me,' she hissed, gripping my arm. 'They vant me to sit vith them and look at old photos!'

'Come on Anouska, we've saved you a seat on the sofa,' said a twinkly eyed old lady in a blue dress.

'I'll come and save you in ten minutes,' I promised. Gran reluctantly limped off to sit with them.


There was a clinking of glass and the room fell silent as my Dad stood to make a toast.

'Annie and I just want to thank you all for being here today, and we'd like to congratulate Micky and Dave. Little Dexter is another wonderful addition to our family, and now he is filled with God's love…'

There were some muted oohs and ahhs, and a clatter of applause. Dad went on.

'It's lovely to see so many familiar faces, and it's also wonderful to have a face here that we don't see often enough. Our eldest daughter, Natalie, has made time to be with us today, and she's brought her new boyfriend, who you probably know from the television, Ryan Harrison.'

There was a pause. I looked at Dad in horror.

'No Martin, he's not her boyfriend,' corrected Mum in a stage whisper.

'Oh, isn't he?' asked Dad. The whole room was looking at me and Ryan.

'No, Martin you missed that bit, when Natalie said Ryan was just a friend…' whispered Mum loudly.

'Did I?' asked Dad. I wanted the ground to swallow me up.

'Yes! You came down in the towel, but then went back up to get dressed… that's when she said he was just a friend.'

I don't know why she felt she had to whisper, everyone was watching.

'Ah, right then. Sorry. Correction, Natalie is *still* single and this chap is just a friend. Cheers,' said Dad. Everyone raised their glasses and there was an awkward silence.

'Everyone do help yourselves to the buffet,' said Mum. Slowly everyone started to talk again, but I felt eyes on me.

'Hey Natalie, are you okay? Do you want a time out?' asked Ryan.

'And they wonder why I never come home,' I muttered trying not to cry. Mum came over as if nothing had happened and asked Ryan if he wanted to try her trifle. It sat in the middle of the buffet table with multiple layers, custard and cream threatening to ooze over the rim of the giant crystal bowl.

'Is that a *real* English trifle?' asked Ryan.

'Yes,' said Mum proudly.

'Gee I'd love some, please ma'am.'

Mum grabbed a bowl, spooned out an enormous portion of trifle and handed it to Ryan. She watched proudly as he took a mouthful.

'I never thought a Hollywood superstar would be eating my trifle!' said Mum.

'Wow this is good,' said Ryan digging in. 'Ma'am you make the best English trifle.'

'Thank you,' she beamed. 'And those are homemade sponge fingers, no boudoir biscuits…' she went on to list the ingredients. I switched off, preferring to watch Downton and Abbey slide along on the parquet floor on their knees, until I heard Mum say, 'And almost a whole bottle of Harvey's Bristol Cream…'

Ryan had almost finished his trifle.

'What's that? Harvey's Bristol Cream.'

'Sherry, Ryan,' trilled Mum proudly. She saw someone she hadn't said hello to, and excused herself. Ryan's eyes were wide open and he was staring down at the remaining spoonful of trifle, as if it were a crack pipe.

'Four months,' he whispered.

'I didn't think,' I said.

'I can feel it… The high is coming!'

I had never heard Mum's trifle whispered about so intensely for its narcotic high, but I grabbed the bowl from Ryan and took his hand. There was the pop of a wine cork, and that delicious sound as the first wine glug-glugged into the glass.

'Come on, quick, make yourself sick,' I said pulling Ryan out into the hall and up the stairs. The landing outside the bathroom was crowded with people hammering on the door.

'Mrs Rust locked the door and climbed out the window,' said Ned swaying unsteadily at the back of the line.

'Have you got another bathroom?' asked Ryan.

'No, this is England,' I said.

'Would you like a drink lad?' said Ned pulling a hip flask from his tatty waistcoat. He flipped off the lid and a warm smell of whisky wafted over.

'Natalie,' gulped Ryan grabbing my hand.

'Come on, outside,' I said. I led him out of the house and down to the bottom of the garden; we went through the gate to the field, Ryan jogging beside me as he held my hand. We reached the pond at the bottom.

'Go round a bush and make yourself sick,' I said.

'Natalie, this is your sister's christening...'

'She's already had three, and a vomiting Hollywood star is the best it's gonna get.'

He slumped onto the bench by the pond.

'This is bad, I can feel it kicking in. I feel so chilled and... *Jeez* I know why I drank,' he said.

'But you haven't drunk, Ryan. You've had a big bowl of my mother's trifle. It's about as rock and roll as a night on the tiles with Marie Osmond.'

Ryan grinned. It was a loose grin, a slightly drunk grin which made me want him all of a sudden.

'Go! Stick your finger down your throat,' I said, snapping out of it.

Ryan went off and ducked behind a clump of reeds on the opposite side of the pond. I sat down on the bench. A few minutes passed, I heard a splash of water and he emerged wiping his face.

'That water is gross,' he said.

'You didn't rinse your mouth out with the pond water did you?' I asked. He nodded.

'Sorry, I meant to say that's where the run-off for the pig pen goes…'

I rummaged around in my bag and gave him a tissue and an extra strong mint. He sat beside me on the bench.

'Jeez I'm such a mess,' said Ryan, leaning forward on his knees. 'The show will fire me if they think I've relapsed… I've been in rehab three times and I'm twenty-five…'

'No one knows, apart from me, and I won't say anything,' I promised.

'*Macbeth* is supposed to be my chance to show people I can really act. And not be in some stupid show on TV.'

'You really can act,' I said. 'And *Manhattan Beach* isn't stupid.'

'I'm a millionaire dentist in a town where everyone has perfect teeth,' he said.

'People must still have to go for check-ups,' I said. He laughed.

'I'm a mess too. Have you heard what my family have to say about me?' I said. There was a pause. 'You know Jamie, the guy who has just opened The Big O venue opposite our theatre?'

'The handsome dude?' asked Ryan.

'Yes. He's the one I left at the altar of the church we were just in. We grew up together here. We used to sit on this bench and…'

'And…?'

'And talk. Dream, imagine our future together…'

'It must have been weird to see him again?'

'Yes, and he looks great, and he's dating that Tuppence Halfpenny woman, who I could never compete with…'

I realised I'd said too much.

'You wanna hear something to cheer you up?' asked Ryan giving me a sideways glance.

'What?'

'Tuppence Halfpenny showed up at my hotel, the night of the launch party. She was wearing a fur coat with nothing on underneath…'

'How did you know she had nothing on underneath?' I asked.

'She took it off…'

'Oh. And did you?'

'No.'

'Come on,' I said. 'She's gorgeous.'

'She is, but I'm just a few months' sober, and I can't get involved. I have a sponsor who I Skype in LA. And you know, she seems kinda mean.'

'So what did she say when you wouldn't sleep with her?'

'She threw my tea-making facilities at the wall,' he said. I laughed. 'I'm serious. That's what the dude at the hotel called them, "*So you've damaged your tea-making facilities sir*",'

'You do a really good British accent,' I said.

'My God, I can act,' he grinned. Ryan looked at me for a moment. A light breeze whipped round and blew a strand of my hair across my face. He tucked it back behind my ear.

'Thanks for inviting me here,' he said. 'I miss being part of a normal family.'

'Thanks for coming,' I said. 'And for thinking my family is normal.'

We stared at each other for a moment. Then Gran appeared, leaning on her stick. She didn't look happy.

'Gran, sorry, I forgot to come and save you!' I said.

'Do you know how many bloody photos of babies I've had to look at?' she snapped.

'You must have something in common with those ladies? You did live here for twenty years,' I said.

'The only thing ve have in common is that I dated all their husbands before they ver married… And I can't talk about that, can I?'

There was an awkward pause.

'Let's go back in and have something to eat, not trifle,' I said.

We went back up to the house and the rest of the afternoon went so fast. The potency of the trifle had loosened up the guests so they felt confident to approach Ryan for photographs and to tell him how much they loved his show. Late afternoon, people began to leave and at six, Micky, Dave and the kids were the last to go.

'How long are you two here?' said Micky as we said goodbye at the door.

'We're going back to London tonight,' I said. 'Ryan is taking part in the Gay Pride parade tomorrow afternoon…'

'You haven't even seen our new extension, and we had it done five years ago,' said Micky pointedly.

'You can come to London too, you know,' I snapped back.

'You're welcome to stay Natalie, you can leave early tomorrow instead?' suggested Mum. 'Ryan can have the spare room… Mum, you can share the attic room with Natalie.'

'Sure, thank you Mrs Love, that would be great,' said Ryan.

It looked like we were staying.

'Maybe we'll see you then, sometime,' said Micky, and she went off to the car with Dave and the kids.

'She just misses you,' said Mum, trying to smooth things over.

Ryan insisted on helping out with the washing up, and afterwards we went down the field with Dad to feed Rihanna. He answered all of Ryan's questions about llamas. As the sun sank down he said he was going to go back to the house.

'Natalie, sorry about earlier, my speech,' said Dad awkwardly. 'Crossed wires.'

'It's okay,' I said. 'Well, it's not okay, but I love you.'

'And we love you too Nat, and we just miss you,' said Dad giving me an awkward hug.

'Thanks for a great day Mr Love,' said Ryan. Dad said goodnight and left me and Ryan with Rihanna.

'Why did you ever leave here? This view…' said Ryan, after a long silence.

'I know, it's gorgeous,' I said. 'But you can't live on a view.'

'I hear that,' he agreed. 'My parents have a ranch. Horses. My twin brother runs it with them.'

'You have a twin?'

'Yeah, David.'

'Is he identical?' I asked.

'No. And I think he's really pleased about that,' Ryan laughed.

'Do you go back often?'

'Sometimes, not enough. I kind of wish right now Dave was the famous one. I would love to switch places. He's got a great boyfriend, and dogs. He's real happy… well, I'd want a girlfriend!'

'Hang on, what are the dogs called?' I asked.

'Bella and Edward. Why?'

'Ok, that clears up the gay rumour,' I said.

'There is always a gay rumour,' said Ryan wryly.

'So you're not at all?'

'No,' he said. 'I kissed a dude in a dream sequence on *Manhattan Beach*, but it did nothing for me, too scratchy…'

The vibe seemed to change between us. With the sinking sun and red-gold sky, the evening was suddenly filled with romance.

*

When it got dark, we went back up to the house. Mum and Dad were asleep and Gran was making hot chocolate in the kitchen. She put down three cups on the wooden kitchen table.

'Natalie and Ryan,' she said. 'I have a favour to ask.' We sat and blew on our hot chocolate. 'The stairs up to your attic room Natalie are too steep, and my bunion, it throbs like nothing you can imagine, so would you two mind to share? There are two single beds, of course...'

I opened my mouth but I didn't know what to say.

'I'm cool if you're cool, Natalie?' said Ryan.

'Yes, I'm cool...' I said.

When we'd finished our hot chocolate, Gran said goodnight and we went upstairs. My attic room has remained unchanged since I left for London.

It's big and airy with sloping ceilings and a small single bed in each corner, tucked under a skylight. My dressing table was still there, and perched on top of it was the obligatory jewellery box with a spinning ballerina on top.

'Gee this is cute,' said Ryan having to stay in the centre of the room so as not to bump his head on the sloping eaves.

'Kurt Cobain and Keanu Reeves?' asked Ryan peering at the posters on the wall.

'Yes. I was rather obsessed with Nirvana, and me and my friend Sharon used to watch *Point Break* constantly. Have you ever met them?'

'Keanu Reeves no, and Kurt Cobain died when I was four,' he said.

'Oh my God, I forgot, you're twenty-five,' I said. There was an awkward pause.

'I once had dinner with Courtney Love,' he said.

'What was that like?'

'Interesting… She could barely find her mouth with the fork…'

There was another pause.

'Do you have any pyjamas I could wear?' he asked.

'Sure I'll just go down and find you something,' I said. I opened the door and there was Gran stood outside.

'I found you some things,' she said, holding out some stripy pyjamas and a towel.

'Thanks Anouska,' said Ryan taking them.

'You can go first in the bathroom,' I said. 'It's down the stairs and to the left.' Ryan grinned and went off downstairs.

'What are you doing?' I said to Gran, when he was out of earshot. 'I thought you couldn't manage the stairs?'

'You are so I Natalie,' she said. 'Now, did you find out if he is gay?'

'He's not gay,' I said.

'Good, I had these in my handbag,' she added handing me a long foil strip.

'Condoms!' I said running them through my fingers. '*Six* condoms! Where did you get…?'

'Just because I'm old, doesn't mean I stop being a vooman,' said Gran. She then went on to tell me how difficult it used to be to get men to wear condoms… 'Now ve have problems to get them to vear a tie! Vat does that say about society?" she laughed. There was a creak on the stairs. 'He's coming back Natalie! I vill go.'

The door opened and Ryan came back wearing just the pyjama bottoms. His hair was wet from the shower, and so was his smooth muscled chest. He looked just like the pictures on Sharon's calendar. I quickly put the condoms behind my back.

'Natalie vas just giving me painkillers for my bunion, ayay-ayy it throbs,' said Gran suddenly affecting a limp.

'Do you want help back down the stairs Anouska?' asked Ryan.

'No. Natalie my darlink, vill you help me back down?' she said. I grabbed my stuff and helped her out and down the stairs.

'I can't believe you!' I hissed when we were out of earshot.

'My God did you see that body? I upgrade him to Sean Connery status.'

I went to protest, but she cut me off.

'Natalie, ven you get to my age, and gravity plays its cruel game, you vill vish you took every slutty opportunity. Now go and have some fun my darlink...'

'I am not... having this conversation with you, and... I am not...'

'All I ask of you Natalie is that you are safe. Goodnight,' said Gran patting my hand. She limped off to her room.

I went to the bathroom and took a shower. I pulled on a long t-shirt and looked at myself in the mirror.

'It's a bad idea isn't it?' I said to my reflection. I debated phoning Sharon, but I thought she would want to kill me for even sleeping in the same room as Ryan Harrison. I looked at myself in the mirror with my wet hair in a t-shirt.

'Anyway, who are you kidding? He turned down Tuppence Halfpenny. Sex on a stick.'


When I went back upstairs, Ryan was in bed tapping away at his iPhone.

'Hey, do your parents have Wi-Fi?' he asked.

'Yes,' I said putting my clothes on the dresser with the condoms bundled in the middle.

'Shoot, I can't find it, can you show me?' he said holding out his phone. I went over to his bed, pulling down the t-shirt which suddenly felt skimpy. I perched next to him and took his phone.

'Here we go,' I said scrolling through. 'It's LOVE27, password LOVE27.'

I handed him back his phone.

'That's a lot of love. Twenty-seven times?'

'It's the house number,' I said. I went to get back up, but he put his hand on mine.

'Thanks Natalie.'

'It's okay, they've got like a gigabyte a month, so use as much as…'

'No. Thanks for all this, it's been cool to be part of your family, even for a day. It's made me feel normal again.'

We looked at each other. He leant forward and kissed me. It was soft and tender. He pulled away and grinned. I didn't say we shouldn't, or that it was a bad idea, I leant in and kissed him again, harder. He put his hand on my leg and it moved up to my thigh. I put my hand on his leg and then laughed.

'Hey,' he said pulling back, a little hurt. 'What is it?'

'It's just the pyjamas. They're my Dad's, and it's a bit weird,' I said. He pulled up the covers, wiggled about underneath, then triumphantly pulled out the pyjama bottoms and dropped them on the floor.

'There. I'm now naked, and you don't have to call me Daddy,' he said with a grin. I laughed. He took my face in his hands and kissed me again, pulling me against him.

'You wanna get under the covers?' he whispered. I climbed in with him and we kissed some more. He was such a great kisser. His body was warm and firm. I ran my fingers across his washboard belly and down.

'What's that?' I said.

'That would be my dick,' he growled.

'No. Not that… *that*!'

'Oh… *That* is a consequence of a drunken night out in LA…'

He had a pierced penis.

We stopped for a moment.

'Does it turn you off?' he asked.

'No. It's just a surprise,' I said.

'Do you want to see it?'

'Okay…'

He pulled back the covers and his penis lay impressively erect against his stomach. The tip, resting against his belly button, had a silver ring. It wasn't huge and it fitted snugly on the end. I was surprised how much it excited me.

'Did it hurt?' I asked.

'Yes. Even after a bottle of Jack Daniels. Have you never seen one before?'

'A penis? Yes. I'm more than ten years older than you, remember…' I immediately wished I hadn't said that.

'I thought guys in Europe were more adventurous with piercings?' said Ryan.

'I've only seen one on a girl. Well, she didn't have a… she had her… you-know-what pierced.'

His face lit up.

'No nothing like that… It's a long story, which I'm not going to tell you now…' I said.

'Yes, we need to get to know each other better, before we tell each other stories,' he laughed. He slowly peeled off my t-shirt. I lay back and he moved on top of me, kissing me again. He felt so good, so warm. He stopped and fixed me with a mischievous grin.

'You wanna see how it feels?'

We had the most thrilling sex. We didn't quite use all the condoms Gran gave me – something I never thought I would say. It was getting light when we finally drifted off to sleep, my head resting on his shoulder.

'So now we know each other better, you want to tell me about the chick with the piercing?' he asked.

I told him about my relationship with Benjamin, and how I caught him in the middle of it with Laura.

'He's an idiot, I would never do that to you,' said Ryan, and he fell asleep.

# GUILT

I woke up a few hours later just before six am, with the sun streaming through the small windows of my attic room. Ryan was asleep, his head on my chest. He felt warm against me, and looked so peaceful sleeping. I traced the outline of his strong nose and long eyelashes. How did he manage to look so good first thing in the morning? His face wasn't crumpled, his skin shone… His hair had dried naturally and looked fashionably tousled. I reached up, and found my hair had dried into a mass of wonky frizz. Quietly, I took my phone from the bedside table, held it out and took a picture of me and Ryan.

Then I heard what had woken me, it was my mother.

'Coo-ee! Natalie!' came her voice. I heard a creak as she started up the small wooden staircase. I quickly slipped out from under Ryan's arm, and leapt into the bed on the other side of the room, pulling the covers over me just as the door opened.

'Morning Natalie! Oh…' she said, when she saw Ryan's sleeping form in the other bed.

'Morning, Mum. Gran couldn't make the stairs, not with her bunion, so Ryan bunked down on the other bed,' I said.

Mum surveyed the scene for a moment, and I felt this terrible guilt and embarrassment. I'm not sure why, I'm thirty-five for God's sake! But Ryan is ten years younger than me, and I'd had sex with him in my mother's house. I'd had an orgasm in my mother's house. Well, two!

'Is Ryan Jewish?' she whispered with a grin.

'I wouldn't know, I haven't seen!' I blurted guiltily.

'What?' asked Mum. 'Natalie, I'm making a fry-up. I wanted to know if Ryan eats bacon? Lots of these Hollywood types are Jewish. I wouldn't want to offend him…'

'Oh, I don't know,' I said.

'I'll come back when he's awake… The exercise on these stairs does me good.'

Ryan opened his eyes.

'Morning Ryan,' trilled Mum. 'Do you want bacon?'

Ryan rubbed his eyes, confused as to where he was. He saw me in the other bed.

'Are you going to make me come twice?' shrilled Mum just as Ryan remembered what had happened.

'What?' he asked.

'You don't need to come back Mum… Do you want bacon for breakfast, Ryan?' I asked.

'Yes, I love bacon,' he said. Mum was staring down at us like two friends. Much as she did with me and Sharon when she used to sleep over. I relaxed a little.

'So bacon sarnies all round? You'll need something in your tummies before you hit the road back to London,' she said.

'Wow, thanks Mrs Love,' said Ryan.

'Call me Annie, all Natalie's friends do! Breakfast in twenty minutes,' she said and went back downstairs closing the door.

We stared at each other for a minute, and then burst out laughing.

'Morning,' he grinned. 'Do you have a chair?'

'Yeah, there's one by the dressing table,' I said. Ryan got out of bed, still naked, and padded over to the dressing table. He carried the chair to the door and wedged it under the handle.

'What are you doing?' I asked. He came back over.

'I figure we've got twenty minutes to kill,' he said sliding into bed with me.

'What if my mother comes?' I said.

'I guarantee you will before she does,' he said leaning in to kiss me.


We had a really lovely breakfast, all sat down at the kitchen table, chatting and munching on a delicious pile of bacon sandwiches. Ryan sat next to me and kept pushing his leg against mine. Gran watched us with a knowing smile.

We left reluctantly just after seven-thirty, weighed down with several quiche lorraines and a pavlova. Mum and Dad came out to the car to wave us off.

'Do you think we'll be seeing you again, Ryan?' asked Mum.

'I'd love to visit again Mrs Love,' said Ryan getting in the car. 'But why don't you come up to London when *Macbeth* opens. You could come to the premiere?'

Mum looked at Dad.

'We could have a couple of days in London, couldn't we Martin?'

'Yes, I'm sure we could get Micky and Dave to feed the animals,' agreed Dad.

'Really, you'd come to London, to see the play?' I asked. They both nodded and I was a little overwhelmed.

'I'll book you tickets,' I said. 'Love you.'

'We love you too,' said Mum, giving me a kiss as I got in the car. She went to Gran who was looking pensive in the back seat. 'And where are you off to next Mum? Wherever the wind takes you I presume?' Gran mumbled something neutral and gave her and my Dad a hug.

*

As we hit the motorway, Gran fell asleep in the back of the car.

'There is so much I could show you in London when we get back,' I said excitedly. 'I go and watch plays all the time, you could come with me one night?'

'Yeah, and then I could take you back to my hotel and you can…'

'Enough of that joke,' I said. He grinned and kissed me. 'So, what about your sponsor, I thought you weren't meant to have a relationship?' I added.

'Wow, are we in a relationship?' he asked.

'I didn't mean that…'

I went to backtrack but Gran coughed and woke up.

'Darlink, could ve stop at the petrol station, I need to use the bathroom,' she said.

'Sure Gran, there's one in a couple of miles.'

When we got out of the car, Ryan said he was going to go to the petrol station shop. He gave me a big kiss in front of Gran and left with a dazzling smile.

When we were in the toilets, Gran quizzed me on what had happened. I told her as much as I felt comfortable about, even though she was what you might term a 'cool' Gran.

'Oh Natalie,' she said clasping her hands together. 'This could be the start of something beautiful.'

'We're not in a relationship,' I said. 'It was just…'

'Natalie. I see the love light in that boy's eyes. I think he has fallen for you, and you for him!'

'But he's at my theatre, and… he's in recovery…'

'You are both grown adults and single. You must follow your heart,' she said.

I was just trying to get my head around this, when we came back to the car. Ryan was standing by the open passenger door having a heated conversation on his phone. He looked up when we came back. The love light had gone from his eyes. He was furious. I noticed he'd bought a newspaper and a coffee.

'I pay Terri twenty percent to keep this shit out of the papers...' he was saying, 'Well maybe YOU should do your job better. Yeah I'm gonna have words with her. She's just here. Gotta go.'

He hung up and turned on me.

'What was this weekend all about?' he demanded, his eyes blazing.

'What?' I said.

'I let people in and they just want a piece of me...'

'Ryan, what's going on?' I said. He threw the newspaper across the car roof. I took it and looked at Gran who was equally confused.

'Page four,' he said. I opened the *Mail on Sunday* to see a big double page headline screaming out:

RYAN'S ALCOHOL SHAME!!!

It detailed how Ryan Harrison, star of popular teen drama *Manhattan Beach*, was an alcoholic. It revealed his stints in rehab, and how, despite assurances to producers of the show, he had started drinking again.

Below was a sequence of grainy, but still legible pictures of us taken yesterday by the pond at the farm; Ryan staggering and being held up by me, and then a hideous photo of him throwing up in the pond. The article went on to say that he was on his final warning with *Manhattan Beach* producers and he was almost certain to be fired. It talked of him as another Hollywood car crash coming to London to appear in a play. The article even cast doubt on his ability to take on a stage role such as Macbeth, and even his ability to act.

'Oh Ryan, I'm sorry,' I said.

'I bet you are!'

'You think I did this?'

'How the hell else did they find me? You said it was in the middle of nowhere!' he added to Gran.

'It *is* in the middle of nowhere,' insisted Gran. 'My God, I lived in Sowerton for twenty years! One bus a day to the nearest town,' she said looking nervously between us.

'So it was you, old woman, how much did they offer you?'

'Hey!' I said.

'You said she just showed up in London, with all her suitcases. These people pay big time for shit like this!' said Ryan.

'Enough!' I shouted. 'Say what you like to me, but you will leave my grandmother ALONE. Do you hear me?'

'Ok, well how do you explain this?' he said indicating the paper with tears forming in his eyes.

'It must have been someone at the christening. Look, an "unknown guest" is quoted as seeing you "worse for wear",' I said.

'I never liked your mother's trifle,' said Gran.

'This isn't the time for jokes,' I snapped.

'I want everyone's name who was at that fucking christening…' he said. 'Look at these photos. That's not a camera phone, these were taken by a long lens…'

We all stood for a moment in shock. It was still early in the morning and few cars were at the petrol station. Parked a little way away though was a grubby white van. The guy inside was just sitting there. He was plump and middle-aged, wearing a baseball cap. He didn't seem to be waiting for anyone, or anything… Ryan eyed him for a moment, and then went to Gran. He grabbed her handbag.

'Vat are you doing?' she said. He pulled out her Taser, and strode quickly towards the van. The guy inside panicked but Ryan reached his window, leant in, and pulled out his car keys.

'Get out of the car,' said Ryan. I rushed over to them.

'Ryan! How do you know this man has anything to do with…'

'I can spot them a mile off… Sleazy bastards with long lenses,' he said.

'I'm not getting out,' said the guy glaring at Ryan. I noticed a long lens camera on the passenger seat beside him.

'Are you a journalist? Have you been following us?' I asked incredulously.

'I think *journalist* is a bit generous. Shitty paparazzo fits better,' said Ryan.

'Fuck you pretty boy,' said the guy. 'Give me back my keys.'

Ryan suddenly reached through the open window and grabbed the guy in a headlock, pressing the Taser against his cheek. The guy looked shocked. The two prongs of the Taser dug into his pudgy white skin. Ryan flicked the power button, and it made a weird high-pitched squeaking sound as it powered up.

'Ever been Tasered before?'

'Hey now, look,' said the guy, his face squashed in Ryan's grip.

'Who do you work for?' said Ryan.

'I'm freelance…' whined the guy. 'If you let that thing off it will electrocute you too…'

'Do I look like I give a shit right now?' asked Ryan a crazed look in his eye. He tightened his grip on the guy's head.

'Ryan, are you mad?' I said.

'This weekend was a private thing. In my private life,' said Ryan his voice cracking. 'I was invited to a private family day!'

I really felt for him. The memory of the day, which had been so perfect, was now ruined. The guy gulped but stayed silent.

'I swear to God I will fire this in your face, and I will keep firing it if you don't tell me who you work for!' demanded Ryan.

'Ryan. Stop,' I said.

'Brendan O'Connor,' said the guy swallowing and shaking.

'Yes, I know who he is,' I said.

'How did he know where I would be?' asked Ryan.

'We've been following you around. We just followed you here…' whined the guy.

'Who's 'we'?' I asked.

'Me and some other guys Brendan hired…'

'Okay let him go Ryan,' I said. 'Let him go, now!'

Ryan was still furious, but I managed to get him to back off and release the guy from the headlock. I took the keys and handed them through the window.

'You go. NOW,' I said. The guy hurriedly put his keys in and started the engine. When he'd turned the van around he paused for a second and threw a parting shot.

'We see your type all the time. Pretty boys with no talent. Nobody will care about you in three years!'

Then he slammed down his foot and the van roared away. Ryan yelled after him, but it was lost in the heat of the engine as it sped away. Ryan started to run after the van, he stormed off down the slip road towards the motorway.

'Oh Natalie,' said Gran putting her hand on my arm.

'Ryan!' I shouted 'RYAN, COME BACK!'

But he carried on running towards the motorway.

'You think he's going to hitch a lift?' asked Gran.

'Who knows. Come on,' I said. We got in the car, turned it round, and started to follow.

'He's not going to catch that van, it's gone,' said Gran peering through the seats from the back. I put my foot down and drove towards Ryan who was nearly at the entrance to the motorway.

'What am I going to do? I can't stop when I'm on the dual carriageway,' I said as we neared the mouth of the motorway. I pulled the car in by a hedge.

'Stay here Gran,' I said. I jumped out just as a lorry roared past blaring its horn. Ryan had now reached the hard shoulder and was jogging along the motorway. I ran and caught him up.

'Stop! Ryan, stop! You can't walk on the motorway!' Cars were whipping past. I grabbed his arm. 'Stop!'

He stopped. He had tears in his eyes.

'Leave me alone!' he shouted above the sound of the traffic roaring past.

'Please. I swear on my life and the life of my nieces and nephews that I had nothing to do with this…'

'What? The nieces and nephews you barely see?'

'You can be angry, but don't walk on the motorway, come back to the car,' I said.

'No, I can hitch a ride.'

'Ryan, you're well known and in the papers. Do you want to be the crazy star found wandering on the M5?'

This seemed to make up his mind. He stopped.

'I'm only coming back with you because there isn't any other option,' he said.

'Fine. Now come on,' I said. I got him back in the car, and we set off to London. We drove in a horrible silence for a few minutes. Gran kept eyeballing me in the rear view mirror. Then Ryan's phone rang. It carried on ringing.

'Aren't you going to answer that?' I asked. He stuck out his bottom lip and stared out of the window. His annoying ringtone carried on blaring out. 'At least see who it is,' I added. He shot me a dark look and pulled it out of his jeans.

'Nicky,' he said cancelling the call.

'Oh crap,' I said under my breath. Seconds later my phone started to ring. It was in my bag on the back seat next to Gran.

'It's Nicky,' said Gran pulling out my phone.

'Pass it here,' I said.

'Darlink, you are driving… I vill hold it to your ear.' Gran answered and pressed the phone to my head.

'Fuck-a-doodle-doo, have you seen the *Mail on Sunday*' asked Nicky.

'Yes.'

'Where are you Nat? I'm outside your flat,' she added.

'I'm on the M5, coming back from Devon.'

'*Okay…* I'm trying to get hold of Ryan, but I presume he is with you? Seeing as you're both in these pictures. Care to share?'

'He came to the christening,' I said.

'I worked that part out, Nat. What I can't work out is *why*?'

'Because… he was invited.'

'I thought British family gatherings were kind of reserved. Why is he all over you? Why are you beside a pond? Why did he drink?'

'What you should know is that Brendan has had the press tailing Ryan for days. They followed us,' I explained.

'And they got a fabulous photo-op,' she said pointedly.

'Look Nicky, can we talk when I get back?'

There was a pause.

'Hand me over to Ryan. I need to brief him on this Gay Pride appearance.'

'You think he should still do it?'

'Of course he should still do it! He's agreed to be on the main float. After this shit in the papers he needs to show up, on time, and smile.'

I handed the phone over. Ryan listened for a minute, grunted a few times and hung up.

'You need to drop me back at my hotel. They're picking me up from there,' he said handing my phone back to Gran. We spent the rest of the journey in a horrible silence, Ryan staring out of the window.

'Is there anything I can do?' I said as we finally pulled up at the rear entrance of the Langham Hotel. He got out of the car.

'I think you've done enough,' he said and slammed the door. We watched him walk back to the service entrance of the hotel, ducking between the huge bins and in through the door.

I put the car in reverse and drove back to the flat, dreading what I would have to deal with when we got there.

# ACT THREE

Minutes later…

# PRIDE

Gran looked troubled as we drove back, we arrived in Soho around lunchtime. When we pulled into the underground garage and I turned off the engine there was a silence.

'I am so sorry Natalie,' said Gran. 'I really thought you and Ryan might…'

'Get married?'

'Be happy,' she sighed. When we got out of the car, her limp was more pronounced, and she let me help her to the lift. Gran said she needed to talk to me, but Nicky was waiting outside my front door with Xander and Craig.

'Honey, we need to have an emergency meeting,' said Nicky dispensing with any hellos. I noticed she had a big A1 notepad, plus a fold-up stand under her arm, and Xander was cradling copies of the *Mail on Sunday*.

'Can I meet you at the theatre in a bit? We've only just got back…' I said. Gran leant awkwardly on her stick. 'Sorry, Nicky, Craig and Xander, this is my grandmother Anouska.'

They all said hello.

'I know this sounds crazy, but I'm worried our office could be bugged,' explained Nicky.

'Are we really that paranoid?' I asked.

'I was the one who suggested it,' said Craig. He ran his fingers through his short brown hair, and looked worried.

'Would Brendan really go to that much effort?' I asked.

'He had you under surveillance all weekend,' said Nicky.

'Natalie, I need to get inside and sit,' said Gran who was leaning heavily on her stick with a white face.

'Okay, come on,' I said. I opened the door and we all went in.

'I really like your flat, Natalie,' said Xander as we went through to the kitchen. Gran limped to a chair and sat down gratefully. Xander placed the pile of papers on the table, and sat opposite.

'So, Ryan Harrison is an alcoholic?' asked Xander, picking up a newspaper and flicking to the article.

'It seems so,' I said.

'And is this where your parents live?' he asked, pointing to the pictures of the farm. I nodded. Xander went on. 'Was Ryan drinking at this christening?'

I started to tell them about the trifle, but Nicky interrupted saying,

'Listen, everyone. It doesn't matter if Ryan had nothing to drink, or one liqueur chocolate, or a bottle of whisky. These. Pictures. Show. Intoxication,' she tapped the paper to emphasise each word. Craig started to unfold the stand for the A1 flip chart.

'You're so lucky to have grown up on a farm. I grew up in Rainham, in a little two-up two-down…' said Xander. 'Are your parents rich? I'd love to live in Soho! This flat must have cost millions?'

'Xander, honey, stay on topic,' said Nicky.

'Natalie's flat is owned by the Peabody Trust, vat you call social housing,' explained Gran. 'Have you heard of Mr Peabody?'

'Is he like Mr Bean?' asked Xander.

'Okay people. Enough about Mr Bean and Mr Peabody, we need to brainstorm,' said Nicky. With a squeak of her marker pen she wrote Brendan's name in the middle of a clean sheet of A1 paper. Craig sat beside Xander. Gran ignored her and went on.

'Mr Peabody vas a very rich American business man…'

'Okay, what do we know about him?' asked Nicky.

'He set up a charitable foundation to provide affordable social housing for all,' explained Gran.

'Not Mr Peabody, Brendan O'Connor,' snapped Nicky. Gran shot her a dangerous look,

'My friend Pedro vas a fine musician vith the London Symphony Orchestra, ven Natalie first came to London, ve stayed here with Pedro…This vas his Peabody Foundation flat.'

'Nat, can you…' said Nicky but Gran cut her off.

'Pedro became very ill, and Natalie helped me nurse him until the end. He passed the tenancy over to Natalie in his vill, so she could afford to live in London and vork in the arts…'

There was a silence.

'Nat, you never mentioned this,' said Craig.

'It's not something that you just drop into the conversation,' I replied quietly.

'I'm sorry about your friend,' said Nicky.

'That's such a sweet, sad story,' said Xander. 'So, you're not rich…'

'No, I am not rich. But who is who works in the arts?' I asked.

'Ryan Harrison,' said Xander., 'I worked out that he's getting paid more than all of our salaries combined. I'd give anything to have his life…'

We all looked at the pictures of Ryan throwing up in the pond, and me with my arm around his shoulder. I could see my personal life was colliding with work, and it wasn't a good feeling.

'Okay. Here's what I think. I'll make us all a cup of coffee, and when we've settled down, we can properly discuss how to move forward,' I said indicating the flip chart.

When we had our coffee, we sat round Nicky's board, giving it our full attention.

'Okay, what do we know about him?' asked Nicky, pointing at Brendan's name, written in felt tip, as if we were all on a corporate training weekend.

'He is a man, yes?' asked Gran.

'Yes… *And?*' said Nicky, as if Gran were stating the obvious.

'You're not listening my darlink,' said Gran. 'Men are easy to manipulate. You need to find a way to push his buttons, kick him in the balls.'

'That's not really the most mature option,' said Nicky.

'I speak metaphorically of course. You must humiliate him,' explained Gran.

'How, Gran?' I asked. She went on.

'Someone did a survey recently. They asked many voomen vat scared them most about a man. Guess vat they all answered?'

'That he'd leave the toilet seat up?' said Xander. Gran gave him a look.

'That he'd leave them for a younger woman?" suggested Craig.

'No. That a man might attack or kill them,' said Gran. She went on, 'Guess vat the men answered ven they ver asked what most scared them about a vooman?'

'That she might do a Lorena Bobbitt? Chop his dick off?' asked Nicky.

Gran shook her head.

'Vat men said they ver most afraid of about a vooman, is that she might *laugh* at him…'

We took that in for a moment.

'And this is true?' I asked. Gran nodded.

'Let's ask the guys what they think of this?' suggested Nicky.

'I'm as bent as a butcher's hook, so you can count me out,' said Xander, sipping his coffee.

'Craig?' I asked. He looked uncomfortable and squirmed in his seat.

'It's a crude generalisation, but sort of true in many ways. The thought of a woman's mocking laugh directed at me is one of the worst things I can imagine,' he said.

'So you think we should all go and stand in front of Brendan O'Connor and laugh mockingly?' asked Nicky.

Gran shot her another look.

'Darlink, you are not taking this in. Vat is most precious to Brendan?'

'His reputation,' said Xander.

'His work,' added Craig. Gran indicated that Nicky should write it down. She did, her pen squeaking.

'Brendan's main client right now is The Big O,' I said. 'He's launching this new venue, I heard Tuppence Halfpenny say they were all taking a big chance…'

'We could go negative, put out some stories to counter what's been written about Ryan,' suggested Craig.

'Would that hit him in the balls?' asked Nicky. 'He would enjoy parrying them, and come back stronger.'

'Do we know what he's got planned for today, for Gay Pride?' I asked.

'He's got Tuppence Halfpenny back performing on her swing in front of the video wall, and they're running a text promotion on the wall. Text this number to get 20% off tickets… blah blah blah,' said Nicky.

'I'm not doing anything with pigeons and bread rolls again,' said Xander.

'If we think about it, Brendan's balls are the video screens,' I said ignoring him. 'And Jamie's balls too…'

'And Tuppence Halfpenny's too,' added Xander. 'She's such a feisty, strong, independent woman…'

'Okay honey, she's not Judy Garland,' said Nicky. She wrote VIDEO SCREEN at the top of her paper. 'That's it! We pull the plug on their screens!'

'How? We'd have to break in, which would be illegal, and they're a pop-up venue. They have all their own power. And what do any of us know about electrics?' asked Craig.

We reflected on that for a moment. Suddenly an idea popped into my head.

'I've got it!' I said. I jumped up and grabbed the pen from Nicky, and started scribbling.

'So let me get this straight,' said Nicky a few moments later. 'You want your brother-in-law…'

'Dave,' I said.

'Your brother-in-law, Dave, from Devon, to hack into the video screen at The Big O?' asked Nicky.

'Yes,' I said. 'We'll take down their video of Tuppence Halfpenny, and replace it with the YouTube video we've got of Ryan as Macbeth.'

'The yummy one with his shirt off?' said Xander.

'Yes!'

'So it's like we turn their venue into our billboard!' added Nicky.

'No. We turn their venue, into our venue,' I said.

'And there you hev it, that's his balls,' said Gran.

'And this Dave guy, he can do this?' asked Nicky.

'Yes, he spent ages droning on about his job at the christening,' I said. 'He's hired by banks and big corporations to hack into their computer systems, so they can anticipate weaknesses.'

'Let's phone him,' said Gran, pulling her little gold address book from her purse. I dialled Dave's number and put the phone on loudspeaker.

'Hello, Dave?' I said.

'Who is this?' asked Dave.

'It's Natalie… Nat… Your sister-in-law?'

'Hi Nat,' said Dave's tinny voice. He covered the phone shouting, 'Micky it's your sister, I dunno what she wants?'

We heard Micky in the background shout, 'I'm up on the loo! What does she want? I'm not going all the way up to bloody London to watch bloody Shakespeare, so you'll have to make up an excuse!'

Gran looked at me and rolled her eyes. Dave came back on the phone.

'Sorry Nat, Micky's…'

'It's you I wanted to talk to,' I said. I then went on to outline the plan. Dave sounded intrigued and promised he would check it out and rang off. I made some more coffee and we sat in silence.

'Sorry, how long do you think this meeting will take?' asked Xander bashfully. 'It's just, I promised to meet my friends Tim, Tim and Tim before the Gay Pride parade begins. We're on the Wonder Woman float, and I've got their capes and gold crowns in my rucksack.'

I went to answer him, but my phone rang. It was Dave. I put him on speaker again.

'Hi Nat, it was pathetically easy to hack into,' said Dave. 'People spend all this money on software and hardware but don't think to protect it. I'm in their system now. Do you want their email and phone records?'

Nicky shook her head.

'We don't want to steal anything. We just want to disrupt things,' I said. 'But before we do this. We need to know if it's illegal?'

'*Technically* yes, but what you're planning isn't necessarily malicious. You're not proposing we steal any data?' replied Dave.

'Could you lose your job?' I asked.

'I'm freelance Nat. And I might be a fat bastard in real life, but in online terms, I never leave a footprint,' he laughed. I looked at Nicky and Craig, they nodded their heads.

'What do you want to play on the big screen?' asked Dave. 'Revenge porn? A sinister message?'

'No! Nothing like that, we've got a video trailer for *Macbeth* we'd like to have playing on the screen,' I said.

'Find out Dave's email. I can send it over now,' whispered Nicky pulling out her iPad. Dave gave me his address, and Nicky emailed him the video to upload.

'And Dave?' I said. 'Can you make it that they are completely locked out of their computer systems until this evening, that's when the Gay Pride parade will be over.'

'They're not going to be getting back into their computer systems any time soon,' said Dave. 'I can get this up and running in the next hour, maybe sooner,' he finished.

We grabbed a late lunch of Gran's leftover goulash, and then Xander went to get changed into his Wonder Woman outfit.

'How do I look?' he asked coming back into the kitchen. He wore a long black wig, gold tiara, and the all-in-one bodice of red, gold and blue. I'd never ealized how skinny he was.

'It's a Cher wig, do you think it scans?' he asked.

'You've got such skinny legs,' said Gran.

'Thanks,' grinned Xander.

'Like two cigarettes poking out of the packet…' she added.

His face dropped.

'You look great,' I said encouraging the others, who all nodded and cooed appropriately.

'I'll look out for Ryan, our float is raising money for injured servicemen,' explained Xander.

'Oh darlink, I thought you ver just dressing up with a load of poofs to look for sex?' said Gran.

'No! Gay Pride is about more than that. It's about equality and charity,' explained Xander, pulling at strands of the Cher wig, which had caught in his mouth.

Gran rummaged in her handbag.

'There, I donate,' she said tucking a twenty pound note into his Wonder Woman bodice. We all scrabbled around for our purses and wallets and thrust notes at him, ashamed we'd been thinking the same thing.

'Thanks everyone,' he grinned. We left Xander on the corner of Beak Street where he joined an excited group of lads big and small, fat and thin, all dressed as Wonder Woman. Gran had decided to stay at the flat, saying she was feeling very tired.

'Give them a good kick in the balls from me…' she said.


Raven Street had been blocked off to traffic with crash barriers, in preparation for the afternoon's Gay Pride parade to pass. We heard whistles and drums banging a few streets away, and realised this was the calm before the storm.

Our huge Ryan Harrison billboard towered above the street and I looked up at him as we approached the theatre. I couldn't quite equate it with the guy I had spent last night with.

I looked across at The Big O. The video was playing of Tuppence Halfpenny on her swing, trailing back and forward with glitter. A 'text this number for tickets' message flashed up on the screen at intervals. Jamie and Brendan emerged from the doorway and lit up cigarettes. They saw us standing on the other side of the road.

'Afternoon chaps!' I said defiantly. They looked at me warily.

'Afternoon Natalie,' said Brendan. 'What did you get up to this weekend? Oh sorry, we read about it in the paper!'

Tuppence Halfpenny emerged in a red corset and matching fishnets.

'Natalie, hello,' she smirked. 'Are you here to turn a straight man gay?'

'I like those vintage knickers, where did you manage to tuck your penis?' I replied.

Nicky and Craig started to laugh. The sound of the drumming intensified. The Gay Pride parade had entered the top of Raven Street, and was advancing towards us.

'You guys should watch out. There's plenty more to come, isn't there, Brendan?' snarled Tuppence.

'You're underestimating us,' shouted Nicky. On cue, Tuppence and her swing disappeared. The giant screen above us went blank and a multi-coloured test card image covered the building. All three of them looked up and frowned.

With a crackle of distortion Ryan Harrison appeared on the screen. Twirling his sword, flexing his biceps, clouds roaring across the mountains and then 'RYAN HARRISON IS MAC-BETH' swirled into view above his head. Their mouths actually fell open.

'Sorry, we haven't got time to count your fillings,' I said, having to raise my voice over the advancing crowds. And then the parade was suddenly on us, filling the street, surging past with a happy colourful roar. A float full of men dressed as Spartacus, flexing their muscles cheered and whistled at the giant Ryan Harrisons on either side of the road. Brendan and Jamie rushed back inside with Tuppence in tow. A look of utter dismay on their faces.


We went up to the roof to watch the parade pass.

'I love this country!' shouted Nicky above the roar and the drums banging. 'Look at this: banks, major supermarkets, politicians. They're all part of Gay Pride, celebrating equality and raising money for charity. It's so positive!'

I went to answer but Tuppence and Brendan came out of The Big O, angrily peering up at Ryan on their screen. Nicky went on.

'And look at those bastards. They're screwed. Ha!'

I stared down at Brendan and Tuppence gesturing angrily at Jamie who had joined them on the pavement. Why on such a positive day, were we embroiled in something so horrible? This wasn't the reason I wanted to work in the theatre.

Xander's float of Wonder Women went past blaring out the Wonder Woman theme. We cheered and Xander waved up at us.

Ryan appeared on a float towards the end. The boys from the *Macbeth* cast were all dressed in kilts, and they had made a throne for Ryan, which he sat on, and waved to the crowd. The roar was deafening as he passed, and the parade actually ground to a halt as everyone wanted selfies with the real Ryan and the two massive Ryans either side of the street.

We waved from the roof, and some of the guys from the cast looked up and waved back. For some reason I really wanted Ryan to look up and notice me, but he didn't.

'Look!' shouted Craig thrusting his phone in my face. '#RyanHarrison is trending on Twitter!'

'Yes! Our fight back continues!' shouted Nicky pumping the air with her fist. Brendan emerged again on the street below, and

Nicky took the opportunity to give him the finger. He gave her the finger in return, then drew his finger slowly across his throat.

The parade started to wind down and despite our victory, I wasn't feeling victorious. Nicky and Craig said they were going on to watch what was happening on the stage in Trafalgar Square. I was exhausted and realised Gran was at home, alone, so I said I was going to head back.

'Amazing work today hun,' said Nicky as I hugged them goodbye. 'We should put your grandmother on the payroll!'

I headed home, and still felt uncomfortable about how things were going. I looked forward to seeing Gran, she could always cheer me up…

# A RIVER RUNS THROUGH IT

Gran was waiting for me when I came home. She was looking uncharacteristically nervous, and handed me a large glass of brandy.

'Natalie, I need to talk to you...' she said. We went through to the living room, and I perched on the sofa bed. Gran remained standing in front of the TV, leaning on her stick.

'Why don't you sit down? You look in agony with that foot,' I said.

'Natalie, my darlink. Do you remember receiving letters addressed to me from the National Health Service?' she asked.

'Yes, I forwarded them on to you in Spain,' I said. She moved to the big arm of the sofa bed, and perched on it awkwardly.

'I assumed they were about check-ups... What were they for? Gran? You're scaring me...'

'I hev to go into hospital,' she said dramatically. I went to her and took her hand.

'Are you ill?' I asked. She nodded.

'Is it serious?' I asked quietly. She nodded again and pressed a tissue to her mouth. My blood ran cold.

'Just know I'm here for you, Gran. Whatever you need, I'll stand by you,' I said.

'Thank you my darlink...'

'When do you have to go into hospital?' I asked.

'Tomorrow.'

'Tomorrow?' I repeated.

'Yes, the doctors want to operate before it grows any bigger,' she said. I studied her face, trying to find the words…

'Is it…?' I asked. Gran nodded.

'Oh no!' I cried, putting my hand to my mouth.

'My darlink, the doctor is confident it can be treated…'

'Oh Gran!'

'I hev put it off for years, but I must hev a bunionectomy,' she said. I went and grabbed a tissue from the box by the telly and stopped.

'Hang on, a *bunionectomy*? An operation on your bunion? On your foot?' I asked.

'Yes,' she said.

'I thought you meant you had something serious!'

'It *is* serious, Natalie. Vat if it goes wrong? I might never vear high heels again! Imagine, the rest of my life in flat shoes! And there is a long recuperation, six weeks at least.'

'So, if you're going in tomorrow, where will you recuperate?' I asked.

'Vith you, my darlink…' she said.

'What about Spain?'

'There is no Spain for me anymore, Natalie. No home. I am bankrupt. I came here because I hev nowhere else to go…'

I looked at her suitcases piled up behind the telly.

'How?' I asked.

'Stefan. He financed his films in my name. Last May he said he vas going to Cannes, and he never came back. I couldn't keep up the repayments. '

I just stared at her.

'So, I go in tomorrow morning for bunionectomy. I am vat is called a health tourist.'

I spied a letter on the coffee table. It was addressed to me, but had been opened. I picked it up and scanned the contents. It was from Rossi's organic store on Raven Street.

'You've no money, yet you open an account in *my* name with Rossi's and I get a bill for three hundred pounds!' I said.

'I vill pay you when I hev more money! I told you I vanted to treat you.'

'Three hundred pounds! You just gave Xander fifty quid. Have you got money, or not?'

'Natalie, vat is this hostile tone?'

'Hostile tone? There's a bloody *Tesco Metro* up the road.'

'A vat?'

'A *supermarket*. Do you know these words, supermarket? Bills? Or do you live in a world where you think you're a fading princess from the Ottoman Empire?'

'Natalie, of all the people in my life, you are the one I thought I could turn to. You just said vat ever I need, you could stand by me!'

'That was when I thought you had a terminal disease, not bloody bunion troubles!'

'I know my timing is bad…'

'Oh, you think?'

'I vas going to tell you when I arrived, and then you had the problem with the pigeons… and the Benjamin… And then I had the idea for you to bring Ryan to the christening. I thought if I could find you a handsome man, everything could be okay…'

'So you think it will all be solved by a man? Well, I've got news for you Gran, some of us make our own way in life!'

I slammed down the glass of brandy, grabbed my bag, and left the flat.


I walked and tried to clear things up in my head. I went down to the Thames Embankment and leant on the rail beside the river. There was a light breeze, and I watched the clipper boats, low in the water, swishing past packed with tourists. A tugboat chugged along in the middle, belching out smoke and pulling a huge flat rusting barge. My phone rang, and I pulled it from my bag. It was my mother.

'Dad has looked through the CCTV pictures from the camera on the back field. There was a fat little man with a baseball cap and a camera, lurking about all yesterday afternoon,' she said.

'Yes, that sounds like the guy,' I said. I then told her about Gran.

'I knew something was going on,' said Mum. 'A few weeks ago her Spanish mobile was cut off. She told me she'd dropped it in a vat of paella at the Mardi Gras... How much does she owe?'

'I didn't get that far. I shouted at her, and left the flat.'

'Now, Natalie. This might surprise you to hear it, but your Gran, under all those inappropriate clothes, and dubious morals is an ally,' said Mum.

'What do you mean?'

'She would never turn her back on you. Don't turn your back on her.'

'If she is such an ally, couldn't she phone and say she was coming to live with me for three months? She just landed at Heathrow and reversed the charges!'

'Natalie. She's old and proud, and she's never got over your Granddad dying. I think this crazy life she leads is driven by grief, and the hope that round the corner she'll find happiness again.'

'I didn't know,' I said.

'Well, you do now. And if she loses you, well I don't know what she'd do. Don't forget Natalie, she was the one who took you to London. I know I made a fuss at the time, but it was the best thing she could have done for you after that wedding malarkey.'

'I didn't know you cared so much about her,' I said.

'Of course I care about my own mother! Just don't you *dare* tell her that,' said Mum.

'Okay.'

'Promise me you will go home now and tell her she is welcome to stay. We can sort out the rest. I can come up to London and help out, and if money is tight, well, we can help with that too.'

'Thanks Mum,' I said.

'And I'm sorry about this Ryan. You looked like you were fond of him.'

'I don't know. He's a famous actor with issues. I should have known better.'

'You know, we're very proud of you Natalie. You went to London with nothing and now you're your own boss.'

'I don't know how much longer I will be, after this,' I said.

'Well, *fight* Natalie. You fight for what's yours and don't let anyone get the better of you.' There was a ping in the background. 'That's my sponge cake in the oven…'

'You go, Mum, thank you.'

'Chin up love,' she said, and she was gone.

I hung by the Thames for a while. I wondered how many people over the hundreds of years must have stood on its banks, with problems, big or small, or seemingly insurmountable? At the time they must have felt huge. And now they were dust. Their problems came and went and still the river flows. It's all just memories.

A group of guys dressed in hot pants and angel wings walked past laughing, on their way back from the Gay Pride parade. I took a deep breath, and went home.

*

When I got back, Gran was lugging a suitcase to join a pile in the hall. She was red in the face and her foot was obviously giving her pain.

'I vill be out of your hairdo soon,' said Gran.

'Where are you going to go?'

She blew her cheeks out, trying to come up with an answer. I put my hand on hers.

'Stay. I'm sorry. It's been an emotional day, and I overreacted,' I said.

'You don't vant an old vooman on your sofa for three months,' she said.

'But you're not just any old vooman. You're my Gran. And I think three months with you on my sofa could be fun...'

'Vat about gentleman callers?' she asked.

'You can use my bed, no problem,' I said.

'Not me! YOU,' she laughed.

'I think I'm going to abstain from gentlemen callers. The ones who knock at my door always seem to be trouble. Please. Stay.'

Gran stopped fiddling with her cases.

'What made you change your mind?'

'I went for a walk down to the Thames,' I said.

'Did you drink the vater?' she said eyeing me suspiciously.

'No, I didn't drink the water. I realised I was wrong. You looked after me when I needed help. Now I'm doing the same for you.'

'Vat if I die?' she asked.

'Then I hope I get first dibs on your jewellery box,' I said. Gran stayed serious. 'I'm being crass, sorry. You are not going to die,' I added. I grabbed her in a hug and kissed the top of her head.

'I have to be at the hospital at six tomorrow,' she said.

'Okay.'

'And if I do die, you are responsible for dressing my corpse. If your mother is in charge she vill make me look like Dot Cotton, on her vey to buy a tomato juice at the Queen Vic!'

'Fine,' I said. 'Now let's move your cases back and have a drink.'

# POSTAL CODE

That night I had a vivid dream.

*I was sitting with Ryan in the back of a huge stretch limousine. He was wearing a tuxedo. My mother was there also, sitting down the front next to the driver's partition. She was boiling a kettle to make us tea.*

*'It won't be a moment!' said my Mum, surrounded by steam. 'This water needs a good boil. I don't trust water from abroad.'*

*'This is Los Angeles, Mrs Love,' said Ryan. I opened my powder compact and saw in the mirror that my hair was a huge frizzy wig.*

*'Do you take milk and sugar, Ryan?' asked Mum.*

*'Do I take milk and sugar, Natalie?' asked Ryan.*

*'And how do you like your gravy, Ryan? Natalie, how does Ryan like his gravy? When I got married, that was the first thing my mother-in-law taught me… gravy!' trilled Mum.*

*I looked down and saw I was wearing a wedding dress. The dress we'd burned.*

*'Are we getting married?' I asked.*

*'Yes,' grinned Ryan. 'We've just got to make a stop on the way,' he added tipping his head behind us. I looked over the back seat. The limousine had turned into a hearse. Gran lay in a coffin with her eyes closed. She was ghostly pale and holding flowers.*

*'Gran's dead?' I said.*

*'That bunion got the better of her, she died on the operating table,' tutted Mum. 'It was her own fault, she spent her life wearing silly shoes.'*

*I climbed over the seat and touched Gran's face. It was cold.*

*The back of the limousine opened and Jamie stood, surrounded by steam. He was dressed in his morning suit, and he held out his hand.*

*'Natalie, come. They're waiting for us in church,' he said.*

*'I'm getting married,' I said.*

*'Yes, you're getting married to me,' he said. 'I'm the one, I've always been the one.'*

*Gran opened her eyes and sat up slowly in the coffin.*

*'Natalie, take these flowers,' she said holding them out to me. 'Vat do I need them for? I'm dead Natalie. Dead...'*

I woke with a yell and sat up, sweating. My alarm was going off. It was five o'clock. I sat back gulping and trying to catch my breath. I was drenched in sweat. There was a tap at my door and Gran poked her head round,

'Morning, my darlink, are you okay?'

I nodded.

'I try to make us coffee, but your machine!'

'It's the capsules, I'll come and make us a cup,' I said.

The roads were quiet as we drove towards Guy's and St. Thomas's Hospital. It was a grey day and a light drizzle covered the windscreen. I turned on the wipers and they dragged across the glass with a squeal.

'If I die on the operating table, I vant to be buried in my green dress,' announced Gran.

'Don't be daft. You are not going to die,' I said remembering my dream, her dead face talking to me.

'And I don't vant a vash and set. Some morticians just know how to do one kind of hairstyle. I don't vant to be lying there looking like any old biddy...'

'Gran…'

'And you vill do my make-up. Chanel red lipstick, Givenchy powder, and eye make-up like yours.'

'Gran!'

'I'm putting it all here in the glove compartment,' she said pulling out a little clear make-up bag and popping it in. 'And if I die before they finish, make sure they sew my foot up. I vant to be buried in heels… you promise.'

'Gran, please,' I said my eyes beginning to well up.

'Promise me, Natalie!'

'Okay. Yes, I promise. But you are not going to die!' I insisted.

I found a parking space and then we made our way into the hospital. When Gran was settled in her cubicle on the ward, a doctor appeared and closed the curtains behind him. He was very handsome with dark eyes.

'My, the NHS has improved since I was here last,' said Gran sitting up and patting her hair. The doctor took out a felt-tip pen and explained the operation. How he would cut out the piece of protruding bone in her big toe, which was causing the bunion, and then reset the foot.

'It's a very simple, routine procedure, so nothing to concern you. One of the nurses will phone you after the operation,' said the doctor. Then he moved onto the next cubicle leaving Gran with a scribble of felt tip pen on her foot.

'Natalie, look at that,' she whispered.

'At what?' I asked.

'That big toe he has drawn on my big toe…Is that how my new toe vill look? It's crap, even *I* can draw better…'

'He's not an artist, he's a surgeon.'

'Thank God he's not doing my tits! Imagine the kind of tit he'd draw?'

'Gran, it's fine,' I said.

'No, I vant to vear all of my nice shoes after this operation. Vat if I end up vith a huge toe like a Cumberland sausage? Go and find him, bring him back…'

With a red face, I called the doctor back. He was very nice, and explained that the toe he'd drawn was just for guidance, and that as well as being a surgeon he was a keen amateur paint- er. He summoned a nurse, who removed the felt tip ink from Gran's foot with an alcohol wipe, and he then redrew a much neater toe.

'Perfect, a toe Sophia Loren vould be proud of,' smiled Gran admiring his handiwork. The doctor grinned and went back to the next cubicle.

'I still vouldn't buy one of his paintings,' muttered Gran in a low voice.

'Do you want me to stay with you? I can take the day off work,' I asked.

'Don't fuss Natalie,' said Gran, settling down and opening a copy of *Vogue*. 'They knock me out, do the operation and I vake up. Bobby's your uncle. Now go to vork, I'm fine.'

I gave her a kiss and then made my way back to the car. I switched on my phone, seeing I had two missed calls from Sha- ron. Then it began to ring, it was Nicky.

'Morning Nat, where are you?' she asked.

'I'm at the hospital,' I said.

'So you've already heard?'

'Heard what?' I asked.

'About Ryan.'

'No, I haven't heard about Ryan. I'm dropping Gran off.'

'Okay, so Ryan, in his infinite wisdom, went out last night to a Gay Pride after-party at the Shadow Lounge. He got so drunk that an ambulance had to be called.'

'Is he okay?'

'Yes, he's in a private hospital, which we're paying for. He has a small amount of alcohol poisoning, but they think he will be fine after a few days on a drip…'

'Great,' I sighed.

'There's more. The Gay Pride after-party was hosted by our friends at The Big O. The concierge from Ryan's hotel said that Brendan O'Connor sent a car round to collect him.'

'That bastard,' I said.

'And there's pictures of Ryan drunk and out of it at the party on the *Mail, Mirror, Sun* and *Express* online.'

'I'll be at the office asap,' I said.


I drove home as fast as I dared and dropped off the car. I then ran over to the theatre. The doors of The Big O were shut, and our video of Ryan was still playing on the screens. The regular group of Ryan fans were blocking the main entrance. And I had to shove them out of the way to get to the door. One middle-aged woman handed me a pound of grapes and a get well soon card.

'See Ryan gets these,' she ordered.

'I'm not a delivery service,' I snapped, thrusting the paper bag of grapes back at the woman. One of our security guys opened the door for me, and I squeezed my way inside.

The *Macbeth* cast were all waiting in the bar, but I went straight up to the office. Byron, Craig, Nicky and Xander sat pensively in the open-plan office.

'The cast are downstairs. What's going on?' I asked, putting down my bag and pulling out my laptop.

'I've had Terri, Ryan's manager on the phone,' said Nicky. 'She wants to get him into rehab, which would be a disaster for us. We can't spare him for thirty days.'

'Shit!' I said.

'Terri is coming at it from an American perspective,' said Craig.

'What do you mean?' asked Nicky.

'We have a different view of drinking in the UK. Several of my friends have had alcohol poisoning after a big night out. No one ever told them they should go to rehab,' explained Craig.

'Ryan is in AA, he's got a sponsor,' I said.

'Let's just hold off until he's out of hospital. I can rehearse without him for a few days,' added Craig hopefully.

'Yis, we can go over all the bits Ryan isn't in,' agreed Byron.

'What other choice do we have?' I said. I looked to Nicky and she nodded.

'Keep us posted,' said Craig.

'Oh, and remind the cast that they signed confidentiality agreements, you know how actors love to gossip,' I said.

'I will devote today's housekeeping session to making this viry clear,' said Byron gravely, and she went off with Craig to get the actors.

For the rest of the morning we were in damage limitation mode, trying to tempt the press with positive stories about Ryan. We didn't have many takers.

One picture in particular had been picked up by all the news agencies. It was taken of Ryan sat in a booth at the Shadow Lounge, slumped back in his seat with his eyes rolling back. He was surrounded by unconcerned people, partying, the table in front of him littered with drinks.

'We should visit him in hospital,' I said, thinking about the fan outside the theatre with the pound of grapes.

'I will visit him, Nat. If you show up the press will make something of it. It's a miracle they haven't made more of you and him together by the pond,' said Nicky.

I then phoned Guy's and St Thomas', who said that Gran was in surgery. I tried Mum but she was out. I then tried Sharon, but it kept going straight to voicemail. After my fourth try a text message came through:

NOW YOU DECIDE TO PHONE ME?
AM TOO BUSY. CAN'T TALK.

I texted Sharon back, asking if she wanted to meet for lunch. Another brusque text message came through:

SERIOUSLY. I'M TOO BUSY.
SIX STAFF CALLED IN SICK & THE AREA MANAGER IS HERE!
I'M HAVING TO WORK ON THE POST OFFICE COUNTER.
NOT HAPPY.

I tapped my phone against my teeth. Was Sharon annoyed that I didn't call her after the christening? She is the queen of kisses and smiley faces in her text messages. I looked over at Xander, who was sorting out the mail.

'Anything you want franked for the post guy?' he asked. I eyed the big pile of letters in his hand.

'Let me take those,' I said.

'Okay,' he said. 'What would you like for lunch?'

'I'll be out for lunch,' I said. I took the pile of letters, grabbed my bag, and walked down to Charing Cross station. I made it on to a New Cross train just as the doors closed.

It had started to rain again when I reached the huge post office on New Cross Road. It was now close to lunchtime and people were streaming into the main entrance. The queue inside snaked back to the door, and I could see Sharon behind one of the windows beside the Bureau de Change.

I joined the end of the long line. Half of the windows were closed, and numbers flashed up on a screen, advancing the line forward. I reached the last turn in the zigzagging queue when Sharon spotted me from behind her window. She gave me a quizzical look, just as an old lady came forward to her window with a big pile of parcels. Another ten minutes passed and then I reached the front of the queue.

A man stood in front of me holding his electricity bill. Sharon finished with the old lady, and she delayed it so the man in front of me was called to another window, then she pressed her button. The computerized voice told me to go to her window.

'What are you doing here? Isn't there a post office in Charing Cross?' she asked.

'I'm sorry, so much has happened. I need to talk to you,' I said.

'Well, hand over those letters, I can't just sit here and chat,' she said adjusting her Royal Mail neckerchief. I passed them over and she sifted through.

'I have a life too, Nat. I've got kids, I had to take my father-in-law to have his ears syringed, yet I still manage to phone you!'

'I'm sorry. How was the ear syringing?' I asked.

'Vile. The doctor said he'd never seen so much ear wax come out of an ear,' she said. She printed off the last label for the letters and turned, placing them in a large grubby green sack.

'That's three pounds twenty,' she said. I handed over the correct change.

'So when I took Ryan back to the christening…' I started to say, but Sharon pressed the button on her desk. The computerized voice intoned, '*Next customer please.*'

'Sharon!' I hissed. 'I really need to talk to you about Ryan. Something happened between us, I slept with him!'

Sharon's eyes almost popped out of her head.

'Nat, you tell me this at the busiest time! One of the area managers is watching us all on the CCTV,' she said, glancing up at a tiny camera mounted on the ceiling.

'I feel out of my depth. I need to talk. Can you meet for lunch?' I pleaded.

A woman was approaching the window with a pile of parcels.

'Look, fill in this customer feedback form until I've served this woman,' said Sharon shoving a piece of paper and a pen through the gap. The woman reached the window.

'If you could stand to one side for me, madam,' trilled Sharon in her customer service voice. I stared down at the form as the woman said all her parcels needed to go to Jersey. Sharon started to weigh, and print labels. She glanced across at me with the pen hovering above the form.

'The first question on the form is about your most recent Royal Mail delivery. How would you rate the experience from one to five?' she said, still using her customer service voice.

'What?' I asked.

'*The lovely package from America* you were talking about, madam…'

'Oh, the lovely American package. He, I mean it, was a five,' I said cottoning on.

'So it was a *special* delivery?' asked Sharon.

'Yes, it was a special delivery. Very special,' I said.

'And how many times did he come? The postman.'

'He came twice…' I said.

'And he didn't have any trouble getting it through the letterbox?' said Sharon.

'No,' I said trying not to laugh.

'And did the postman know where your special place was? Where to leave a parcel if you're out?'

'He did. He knew exactly where my special place was,' I said. The woman with her Jersey parcels raised an eyebrow.

'So what do you wish to complain about, madam?' she asked. 'Did he leave you a card or anything to say he might be calling again?'

'No, but the problem is, I see this postman at my business address, and it's getting complicated,' I explained.

'And you don't want your business letters mixed up with your personal mail, is that correct madam?' asked Sharon.

'Exactly.'

'There we go, that's seventeen pounds and thirty pence,' said Sharon to the Jersey lady who paid and left, giving us an odd stare. I shifted back across to the window and shoved the form through.

'Please can you meet me for lunch?' I said. 'I've got so much to tell you, and I don't think our postal-based code will work for much longer.'

'Okay, Nat. You get points for coming all the way here to post your letters. Meet me in twenty minutes at the caff over the road.'

I had a cup of tea and a cheese and pickle sandwich waiting for Sharon when she arrived at the caff.

'I really have got only twenty minutes," she said, sitting down. 'Did I understand our postal code correctly? You slept with *Ryan Harrison*?!'

She started munching on the sandwich as I quickly told her everything that had happened, I finished up saying I thought I had feelings for Ryan.

'You need to get some perspective here, Nat. It just sounds like it was a fabulous one night stand...' she said.

'It felt more than a one night stand. He opened up to me...' I said.

'And you don't think you've bought into the whole thing that he's famous?'

'I'm telling you, we had a connection.'

'So now what? You're dating?'

'No. I think he hates me right now. Isn't it my fault he went back on the drink?'

'Nat, it's not as if you seduced him into doing shots, and lines of coke off your bare backside. He had some of your mother's trifle.'

Despite myself, I burst out laughing. Sharon went on.

'And you can't be responsible for someone's choice to go and get plastered. Yes, he's vulnerable, but where does it stop? If someone really wants to drink, they'll get drunk.'

'But what about everything else? It feels like it's all getting out of control. What if Nicky finds out?'

'Ryan made the choice to become an actor, and to a certain extent he has made the choice to be Ryan Harrison the heart-throb, he must know the deal? The press follow his every move, and Nicky knows the deal too, how the press twist things.'

'Should I go and see Ryan in hospital?"

'Nat, be a friend to him by all means, but remember you have your life and your career to think about. You have your Gran who needs you when she comes out of hospital. And you have a friend here who has missed you like crazy.'

She reached out and grabbed my hand.

'Thanks Sharon,' I smiled.

'Right, that's all the life coaching I've got time for. Now tell me, how many Ryan calendar pictures did you get me?'

'Just January,' I said sheepishly holding out my phone.

'Nice, with a llama,' said Sharon.

'Oh, I did get one of him asleep on me.' I took the phone and scrolled forward.

'He looks so gorgeous in the morning!' she said.

'I know. Look at me next to him…'

'Oh dear Nat, you look like Marge Simpson with all the colour rubbed off her!' said Sharon.

'You're a cow!' I laughed.

'You should see me in the morning, ugh!' said Sharon. 'Now, I've got a few minutes left. Tell me what it was like shagging a man with a pierced penis?'

'It wasn't horrible, it was exciting, and it felt good.'

'Do you think I should get Fred one for his birthday?'

'What? As a surprise?'

'Well, he would probably notice it being done!'

'No, you could arrange it as a surprise,' I said.

'Gosh, no. Fred has a very low pain threshold… anyway, I think he'd much prefer a subscription to the *National Geographic*,' said Sharon. Outside the window of the caff it started to rain harder. 'I hope this rain continues. Flooding water mains are just what we need,' she added.

'Is everything okay?'

'It's been very quiet on the work front for Fred. I think we're going to have to take in a lodger for the spare room.'

'Oh, I'm sorry,' I said.

'It's fine. We're not on the bread line just yet. If you hear of anyone who's looking, who's not a freak…'

'Of course, I'll let you know,' I said. Sharon looked at her watch, and drank the last of her tea.

'Crap. I have to go, Nat. Promise me you'll keep in touch?'

'I promise,' I said.

'And let me know how Anouska is doing, I'll try and come over and see her.'

She gave me a hug and we parted ways outside the post office. I walked back up to the train station, still with the weight of everything on my shoulders, but with the warm knowledge that I had a friend.

# SOPHIA LOREN'S TOE

When I got back to the theatre I ran into Val in the box office. She'd just come off the phone, and the theatre seating plan was open on her computer screen.

'Is everything okay?' I asked.

'I just had the headmistress of Our Lady of the Sacred Heart independent boarding school for girls on the blower,' she said. 'She's cancelled the school coming to one of the matinees.'

'Why?'

'Said she's seen the stuff in the papers, and parents don't want to fork out thirty quid a ticket to watch the understudy do Shakespeare.'

'How many seats?' I asked.

'Hundred and four,' she said pointing to the little rows of squares on the screen, which had reverted back to green, indicating they were available.

'Did you try and persuade her not to cancel?' I asked.

'Yes, but what is going on? Is Ryan fit to go on stage? And what do I do with all these flowers and teddy bears people keep leaving on the steps outside for Ryan?' Val got up and opened the store cupboard which was filled with soft toys. 'It's like Princess Diana's kiffed it all over again!'

I told her to send the teddy bears to Great Ormond Street Hospital, and that we would sort out an official statement about Ryan.

I went upstairs and filled Nicky in on what was happening. I noticed Xander was fiddling about with YouTube. I asked him what he was doing.

'We've been in touch with Dave. We thought we could further cripple them over the road by streaming the most boring videos on their screen,' he said.

'We've got a two-hour women's semi-professional curling match, and a three-hour North Korean victory parade,' explained Nicky gleefully.

At four-thirty, the gloom of our office with the blocked-up windows was getting to me, there was nothing more to report about Ryan, and I kept checking my phone every few minutes to see if the hospital had called about Gran.

'Honey, why don't you finish for today, go for a walk or something. I can hold the fort here,' said Nicky. 'Your Gran is gonna be great, and she's gonna love her new Sophia Loren toe!'

I gave her and Xander a hug and then left for the day.


When I came out of the theatre, the rain had stopped and Soho was buzzing with people. The sun was now blazing, and the puddles on the pavement rapidly shrinking. On the big screen the women's curling was reaching its climax, and a line of sturdy short-haired women were scrubbing at the ice madly with brooms. A group of lesbians were watching rapt from the terraced seating outside the bar next door.

When I got back to the flat I changed out of my work clothes into shorts and a t-shirt. I grabbed my iPod, made sure my phone was fully charged, and slung my rollerblades over my shoulder.

I walked through the crowds pouring out of work, all the way down to Charing Cross. As I crossed the Hungerford Bridge, warm air rushed at my face, and the sun sparkled on the Thames in front of the London Eye. I looked out at Big Ben and saw it was five-thirty. Surely by now Gran should have come round from the operation?

When I reached the slope on the other side of the bridge, I stopped by a guy busking on an old tinny-sounding guitar, and changed into my rollerblades. I stashed my trainers in my rucksack and set off, skating past the concrete block of Festival Hall, picking up speed along the Embankment.

I love this side of the river, as there is much more space to really get some speed up. I had my head down and was zooming towards the National Theatre, when a figure in black came gliding out ahead of me from one of the side roads. It was male and had on a black tracksuit and baseball cap. I clocked how good he looked from the back, but he was moving much faster and sped away in front.

I carried on at my own pace, enjoying the light breeze in my hair. The tide was low on the Thames, and a dog walker was picking her way along the exposed shingle with an elderly plodding Labrador. Up ahead, I saw the glint of the Italian coffee bike which always has great coffee. I slowed down to see the guy in black had also stopped. It was too late when I came to a stop by the gleaming handle bars of the bike, and realised it was Jamie.

I tried to turn and move off, but the bleary-eyed young lad asked me what I wanted. Jamie turned, and without missing a beat turned back.

'She drinks Americano.'

He reached inside his shiny tracksuit bottoms and pulled out a twenty pound note.

'No. I'll have a hot chocolate with whipped cream,' I said. 'And I'll pay.' The lad running the coffee bike was confused.

'Are you ordering together?' he said.

'I'm ordering two drinks. We are not together,' I said.

'We used to be, but she left me at the altar,' said Jamie.

'I left him at the altar, because of his obsession with having things shoved up his bottom,' I said. Jamie went bright red.

The coffee lad smiled nervously and started to make our coffees.

'Stooping really low now, aren't we, Natalie?' hissed Jamie.

'I can't believe you would stoop as low as to ply an alcoholic with drink! He's in hospital!' I hissed back.

'You've virtually destroyed my ticket sales!' said Jamie. 'Whatever you did, I want that video screen put back like it was. Then maybe Ryan will stay sober.'

'Is that a threat?'

'I don't make threats,' said Jamie.

'You had me followed!'

'No, Ryan was followed, you were just tagging along, like some sad middle-aged groupie.'

'I'm not a groupie, nor am I middle-aged. Even if I were, why am I sad and middle-aged? There's the same age difference between you and Tuppence, and it's okay for you to date her?'

'We're engaged, actually,' he said.

'Yeah, well next time she leaves the house in a fur coat, check what she's wearing underneath,' I muttered.

'What's that supposed to mean?'

'Nothing. This conversation is over. I don't want to be around you,' I said.

The coffee guy was finishing up with our drinks, and trying not to make it obvious he was enthralled by our conversation.

'I'll pay for these,' I said. Jamie raised an eyebrow as I pulled out the wallet I keep in my backpack for rollerblading, noting it had Dora the Explorer on the front.

'Planning on travelling?' he smirked.

'It was a present, from Sharon's daughter,' I said.

Jamie's face softened a little. 'How old is her daughter now?'

'Amy's ten,' I said. I handed him the coffee. He stood for a moment. 'Well, go on then, don't let me keep you…' I added.

We stared at each other for a moment, then Jamie did a spin on his wheels and skated away. I waited until he was a dot far ahead, then skated off sipping my hot chocolate, hating that it wasn't an Americano.

I began to skate faster, leaning forward into the breeze with my head down. I zipped between the boxes of books at the discount bookshop, past the National Theatre, and was really picking up speed, when I hit a piece of rough concrete on the Embankment. It happened so quickly, one minute I was speeding along, the next there was a squealing sound from my blades and I went over quite spectacularly, landing on my knee with a thunk, and then rolling, the lid coming off my hot chocolate and spilling all down my legs. I came to a stop by the wall of the Thames and sat there dazed. My leg was burning and throbbing, and blood was beginning to pour from a big gash in my knee, mingling horribly with the hot chocolate and cream. I started to sit up, and a pair of legs came to a squealing halt beside me.

'Nat? Are you okay?'

I squinted up into the sun at Jamie. He was looking down at me, concerned.

'What do you think?' I said. He knelt down and reached round into the back of his trackies, pulling out a little plastic pack of tissues. He shook one open and pressed it to my knee. I sat there fuming silently, as he held it against my leg.

'Ow!' I said. 'Easy.'

'I'm trying to stop the bleeding,' he explained. He had beads of sweat across his cheeks and forehead.

'It's just a scrape,' I said. I noticed people were hurrying past, but still staring. He pulled out another tissue and handed it to me, I began to wipe off the cream and hot chocolate.

'Bet you wish you'd had that lasagneo,' he joked.

'Jamie, leave me alone. Go.'

He finished wiping my leg.

'Let me help you up,' he said. He grasped my arms and pulled me up to a standing position. I perched on the lip of the concrete wall by the river, groaning at the new pain where I had landed on my backside. My phone began to ring. I tried to get my bag off my back, but it hurt too much.

'Where is it? Let me,' said Jamie, reaching round behind me.

'It's in the inside pocket, the tiny one at the front,' I said. Jamie began to fumble around. The phone kept ringing.

'The *inside* pocket!' I said.

'There's like twelve pockets on this thing!' snapped Jamie. I batted him away and gingerly took off the backpack. I scrabbled around for the phone but it had stopped ringing by the time I got it out of the pocket.

'Bollocks,' I said seeing it was a withheld number.

'What are you planning for me now?' he asked. 'You gonna burn down my venue?'

'I'm waiting to hear from the hospital. Gran's having an operation today,' I said, scrolling through my phone to find the number for the hospital. I pressed call and waited nervously whilst it rang. Jamie's forehead creased with concern. Finally a nurse answered, and after a moment gave me the good news that Gran had come round successfully from the operation, and she would be able to go home in a few hours.

'Thank God,' I said to the nurse, 'Thank you.'

'You can come and pick her up around eight,' she said. I came off the phone grinning madly, I felt such relief.

'What was the operation for?' asked Jamie.

'Bunionectomy, caused by years of high heels,' I said. Jamie smiled.

'Do you remember that year we all went surfing in Bude? She even wore her high heels in the sea!' he laughed. I laughed too.

'Didn't she manage to stand on a surf board in them too?'

'Yes. And she rode a wave for all of six seconds.'

'Yeah! She made you time her on your stopwatch…' I laughed.

'I've got a photo of it somewhere. I'll have to find it…' he said.

There was a pause.

'Nan isn't good right now,' he added, his face clouding over. I had fond memories of Jamie's nan. She was much more conservative than Gran, but a lovely, funny woman.

'I'm so sorry. What's wrong?' I asked.

'Pneumonia.'

'Please, give her my best won't you? I hope she gets better…'

'Yes, I will,' he said. His phone began to ring, he pulled it out.

'Hey babe,' he said. 'I'm just on the Embankment rollerblading… no I'm alone… What? It's now showing a North Korean victory parade? Okay I'll be there in ten…' Jamie hung up. He stared coldly, our previous conversation forgotten.

'You're going to destroy us,' he said. Then he turned on his wheels and skated off back towards Charing Cross.

I wondered for a moment who he meant by "us". I supposed the only real "us" was him, Brendan and Tuppence.

I arrived at the hospital at eight-thirty. When I went into the ward, Gran was sat up waiting in a wheelchair. She was back in her clothes with a huge bandage on her foot. On the other foot she had a high heel.

'Hello,' I said giving her a gentle hug. 'How are you?'

'I feel like I'm flying,' she grinned loosely. A kind-faced nurse came over with a big paper bag.

'She's on quite a lot of powerful pain medication,' said the nurse. 'It can affect the elderly in different ways.'

'Who you bloody calling "the elderly?"' snapped Gran.

'Gran!' I cried.

'Did that doctor make me a nice toe?' asked Gran in a loud voice. The nurse ignored her and handed me a paper bag.

'Here are some painkillers and antibiotics for Anouska. She'll need to have someone with her for the next twenty-four hours.'

'Don't you ignore me vooman! Have they made me a beautiful toe? A toe Sophia Loren vould be proud of?' cried Gran.

'Gran was a bit worried about the toe the doctor drew on her with the felt tip pen,' I explained.

'Don't worry, you've got a lovely new toe,' smiled the nurse using that sing-song voice reserved for the elderly.

'How do I know she's not lying? I vant to see my new toe before I leave!' insisted Gran. 'Once ve leave I von't be able to bring it back and get a refund!'

'You can't take the bandage off for a few days, Anouska!' said the nurse.

'Pfft, let's go Natalie. This nurse is an imbecile…' said Gran.

'I'm so sorry,' I said. The nurse didn't seem fazed and wished us well. God bless the NHS.

It was a bit of a nightmare to get Gran into the car from the wheelchair. She was a dead weight, and with my bad knee it wasn't great. I knocked her bandaged foot easing it back into the foot well of the passenger seat, but she was so full of painkillers she didn't notice.

'Let's go out Natalie. Let's go to a club!'

'We're going home,' I said firmly.

'Spoilsport,' muttered Gran, then fell asleep as I fastened her seatbelt.

Gran was still asleep when we arrived home. I drove down into the underground garage and then switched off the engine. I realised I had left the wheelchair in the hospital car park. How the hell was I going to get her up the four stairs to the lift, then in the lift, and then into the flat? I came round and opened the passenger door. Gran's eyes fluttered open.

'Oh hello Natalie,' she said. 'You look lovely, a little tired, but lovely.'

'Thank you Gran, can you walk or hop?'

I undid her seat belt and she tried to shift forward.

'I hev had an operation, yes?' asked Gran.

'Yes, on your foot,' I said.

'Oh, they had better hev done a good job. I vill be most unhappy if I get a man's toe. Vas there a brochure I flicked through? Which toe did I choose?'

'You chose the Sophia Loren toe,' I said humouring her.

'No, I didn't, the doctor drew it on. He couldn't fucking draw!' she cried.

'Excuse me? Is everything alright?' said a voice. I turned to see a huge muscly man, dressed in boots, leather trousers and a leather harness with studs. Beside him was a small skinny pale guy in a similar outfit, only he had the addition of a studded leather cap.

'Yes, fine,' I trilled, being all British.

'I hev had a foot operation. I spent my life in high heels, making my legs beautiful for the vorld and this is how God repays me!' cried Gran.

'Bunionectomy, was it love?' asked the huge muscly guy. I nodded.

'Lots of my friends do drag,' he said. 'It's a breeding ground for bunions… Can I help you?'

'Ok,' I said, unsure.

'Here Steve hold this,' he said handing a big brown paper bag to the smaller guy. He leant inside the car. 'Hello, I'm Kieron. If it's okay with you, may I carry you up?'

'Handsome men!' cried Gran, her eyes lighting up.

'Gawd, you must be on some strong pills love,' he laughed looking down at the leather harness and his nipples on display. I didn't know what to say.

Kieron leant into the car and gently lifted Gran out, with one strong forearm under her legs, and one supporting her back. I scuttled round and grabbed her stuff and my bag and locked up the car.

'Where to?' asked Kieron.

'We're on the first floor,' I said.

'I'm Steve,' said the skinny guy introducing himself. We followed as Kieron carried Gran up the steps. I pressed the button and we waited for the lift.

'Vere are you two boys off to?' asked Gran.

'We're having a party,' said Steve bashfully.

'Ooh a party!' said Gran. 'Natalie we have time, let's go and join in!'

'I don't think it's *quite* the party you'd enjoy,' grinned Kieron. 'But we'd love to have you over some other time, we're on the top floor.'

The lift arrived and opened with a ping. Kieron carefully manoeuvred Gran inside and the doors closed.

'Did you bring a bottle?' asked Gran, leaning over and reaching into the paper bag Steve was holding. She pulled out a giant pink dildo. We all froze as it flopped to one side in her hand.

'My God, whoever gets this vill have to bite down on a stick!' said Gran. Luckily the two guys were very kind, and found Gran hilarious. When we reached the flat, they took her into the living room, and gently put her on the sofa bed where she began to doze.

'Sleeping like a baby,' said Kieron.

'Thank you so much. Is there anything I can give you?' I asked.

'It's fine love,' said Kieron, 'Glad to help.'

'Do you guys like Ryan Harrison?' I asked.

'Ooh yes,' said Steve. 'We saw him at Pride, on the float.'

'It's such a shame about his booze problems. The good-looking ones always self-destruct,' said Kieron.

'I run the theatre where he's playing Macbeth. Let me comp you a couple of tickets, any night you like,' I said.

'That's still going ahead?' asked Kieron.

'Yes, of course,' I said.

'That's not what I read,' added Steve. 'They've fired him from that TV show, and his manager wants him checked into rehab…'

'Where did you read that?' I asked.

'It just came up on PerezHilton.com,' said Steve pulling a smartphone from the back of his leather trousers.

'Shit,' I said, reading.

'Sorry to be the bearer of bad news love,' said Kieron. I thanked them and they went off to their party on the top floor. I came back to Gran dozing on the bed.

'Are you okay Zsa Zsa?' I said, easing her out of her fur coat and slipping off the one shoe she had on.

'I didn't die, Natalie,' she muttered drowsily.

'No, you didn't Gran,' I smiled. 'You are very much alive.'

'I told that bitch nurse I vas forty-nine. She didn't believe me!'

'She probably had your notes, with your birth date,' I said helping her into a lying position.

'Vat vould I do vithout my favourite granddaughter?' she said, and then she was asleep.

I went through to pour myself a drink when my phone went. It was Mum, asking how things were. I told her that everything was okay and that Gran was asleep in the living room. Leaving out the part with the helpful dildo-toting leather boys.

'Just before you go, Mum,' I said. 'Did you know that Jamie's nan is ill? I bumped into him this afternoon.'

'Yes, I heard it from the lady at the butcher's. Mrs Dawson is in hospital; they took her in this afternoon. Pneumonia…' she said.

'Is it serious?' I asked.

'Pneumonia normally is Nat, but they're very good up at Devon North General…'

'Will you let me know if you hear any more?' I asked.

'Course love, and you keep me posted about your Gran. Make sure she eats lots of fruit and veg, and don't let her near the brandy.'

'Yes, Mum.'

'And don't let her wear any high heels.'

'I won't…'

'I'm serious Natalie. Find a high place on top of a cupboard and put them all up there, out of her reach. When she had her veins done she nearly got a clot from prancing around in stilettos the day after she'd been discharged from the hospital.'

'Yes, Mum.'

'And Natalie…'

'What?'

'It's never too late you know…. You and Jamie.'

'Oh Mum, that's… no, that's never going to happen,' I said. 'I'd better go, night, night.'

I hung up the phone, wondering where on earth that had come from.

# SNAKES ON A PLANE

I'd underestimated just how serious Gran's bunionectomy operation was. She was in constant pain and for the first few days she could barely walk. I moved her through to my bedroom, so she could recuperate in a proper bed and be nearer the bathroom. I also had to help her shower every morning with a plastic bag over her foot to keep the bandage dry. Gran insisted on choosing the plastic bag.

'Darlink! You scrubbing my backside with a sponge is bad enough, at least give me a Harrods bag to put over my foot and take my mind off it,' she said. Luckily I had one in the cupboard under the sink.

I'm so glad the theatre was only a few minutes away, so I could pop back home throughout the day. I bought her scores of magazines, and Gran likes fairytales so I downloaded *Tangled* and *Frozen*. She was adamant she didn't want to watch *Cinderella*.

'Is it because the older fairy tales have weak female role models?' I asked stupidly.

'No! I just don't vant to be reminded of my bad bloody foot,' she said.

'So *The Wizard of Oz* is out of the question too?' I asked.

'Yes, just the thought of ruby slippers makes me want to cry,' she grimaced, popping one of the super-strength painkillers from the hospital.

\*

On Wednesday, Ryan was discharged from hospital and came back to work. We were now in the middle of the second week of rehearsals, so time was very limited. I was hoping to get to talk to him, but when I approached the theatre there was an enormous queue running several hundred yards back from the main entrance. I thought at first it was Ryan fans, but then I saw it was mainly greasy older men and young girls with tattoos – and each one of them had one or more clear glass tank containing a snake!

When I reached the front door, Val was jotting down their names on a clipboard and showing them through to the auditorium.

'Gawd, these open auditions are always so popular,' she said rolling her eyes. She took the name of an old man with waist-length grey hair and an eye patch. He had an enormous snake in a tank. Its scaly body was pressed flat against the glass.

'Wanna see my python?' he growled to Val.

'Ooh, you sauce pot,' she giggled and motioned him to go through.

'What's going on?' I said as I watched him stride towards the doors of the theatre auditorium.

'The open auditions for *Snakes on a Plane: The Musical*,' said Val.

There was a whoosh of a hand dryer then a short woman with a pierced lip emerged from the ladies' loo with a giant white snake draped around her shoulders.

'You see that one, it got down to the last two for when Britney Spears performed at the MTV awards,' said Val. I stepped back with a shiver as the woman passed, the snake shooting out a black forked tongue.

'Who the hell is doing *Snakes on a Plane: The Musical?* And who said they could hire out the theatre for auditions?' I asked.

'*You* did,' said Val. She was about to let in a man and woman each cradling a clear tank with a colossal green and yellow snake.

'Sorry, could you wait a moment please,' I said. I pulled Val to one side.

'What do you mean *I* did?' I asked. Val rolled her eyes impatiently.

'You sent me the message, from yer new email address. I thought it was an odd musical to attempt, but I know you have to stay fresh and modern for the bloody Arts Council…'

'Can we please come in?' asked the woman whom I'd stopped. 'We've driven all the way from Thetford, and Molly and Mark need feeding.'

I nodded. They came into the foyer, and set down the tanks on the carpet. The woman pulled out a McDonald's Happy Meal carton, and lifted out some live mice by the tails. Molly and Mark shifted in their tanks, their heads rising to the vents in the top of the glass.

'What the hell is going on?' cried Nicky squeezing past the snake-toting queue and through the door. We all screamed as the woman lowered a live mouse into one of the tanks.

'I think this is Brendan's latest prank,' I said. There was a scream and Byron came running into the foyer.

'I'm sorry. I'm naught a squeamish person, but snakes are my Achilles' heel,' she said. She noticed the snakes in the tank and put her hands to her face.

'Three of our auditionees in the auditorium can't find their snakes. They're slithering loose in the theatre!' she said through her fingers.

The theatre had to be evacuated for the rest of the day, and a snake specialist was called in from London Zoo at a cost of £500 an hour! After five hours he finally rounded up the snakes. A grass snake and a python were found snoozing on a heater in the bar, and the rattle snake was located in the costume department, asleep in Macbeth's sporran.

I was given a long lecture by the snake specialist, saying how irresponsible and impractical staging *Snakes on a Plane: The Musical* would be. I think their careless owners should have been ticked off too. All one man had over the tank for his python was a sheet of cling film! When the theatre was finally safe to reopen for the evening, I set off home.

I phoned Dave and asked if he could locate a black-and-white snooker match from the sixties to put on the screen of The Big O.

That evening my mood lightened when Sharon came over with a homemade lasagne, and when Gran insisted I do her hair and make-up, I knew she was getting better. They thought the snake story was hilarious.

'I bet it was Jamie, cheeky bugger,' said Sharon. 'He always had such a great sense of humour…'

There was an awkward silence and Gran asked if Sharon could help her through to the bedroom. I made some coffee and then followed them through.

Sharon was perched on the end of the bed as Gran scrolled through her phone.

'Sharon, my darlink, your family is beautiful,' Gran was saying. 'Such beautiful dark hair, your little girl…'

'Amy is ten and Felix is eight. Fred is Italian,' said Sharon. 'They've inherited his dark looks.'

'I love Italian men. A little vain, yes?' asked Gran.

'Yes, Fred can be vain,' grinned Sharon.

'Does he vear his suit, just so, as Italian men do, a little louche?' asked Gran.

'He wishes! He's a plumber, so most of the time he's in overalls.'

'You have it all vorked out Sharon. You are in the post office, Fred unblocks toilets.'

'It doesn't sound glamorous when you say it like that,' moaned Sharon.

'But it's perfect, whatever happens in the vorld people always need to poop and post letters.'

'Well, things are a bit tight money-wise,' she said. 'We're looking for a lodger.'

'You need to find a nice ugly woman or a gay man,' said Gran. 'You don't want to upset your family dynamic.'


Later on, when Gran had fallen asleep, Sharon helped me in the kitchen with the washing up.

'Anouska hasn't changed,' said Sharon. 'Do you remember that first night when we came to London with her. She took us to that gay bar, Mr Bojangles.'

'I know. It was like a different world to Sowerton, so glamorous and exciting. We could be whoever we wanted,' I said.

'And *everyone* knew your Gran,' added Sharon.

'We were treated like royalty, free drinks all night…'

'Wasn't there even a drag queen who'd named himself after her?' asked Sharon.

'Anouska Temple,' I grinned.

'Yes! They got up and sang 'I've Got You Babe' together.'

'Gran insisted on singing the Cher part,' I added.

'She was good… *Dey say our lav vont pay de rent,*' sang Sharon, grabbing a banana as a microphone.

'Shhh!' I grinned. 'You'll wake her up.'

'She was so popular back then,' said Sharon putting the banana back in the fruit bowl. 'Where are all those people now?'

'What do you mean?' I asked.

'I dunno. She's turned up on your doorstep, homeless, with no money. There's no one here but you to help her out…'

'I don't know,' I said. There was a silence, I carried on washing up.

'It's got so crazy at work, Sharon. This stupid feud with Jamie's venue is getting in the way of what matters. And I ran into him the other day, and then fell over,' I said.

'Are you okay?'

'Yes, apart from a big bruise on my backside…'

Sharon's phone rang.

'Sorry hun, hang on it's the kids. Hold that thought…' She picked up her phone and said goodnight to Amy and Felix, checking they had had their baths and done their homework.

'What is it?' asked Sharon when she came off the phone and saw the sad look on my face.

'Do you think I'm going to end up like Gran?' I asked.

'What, with a bunion?'

'I'm being serious. What if I end up old and alone?' I said, wiping a tear away.

'Don't be silly. You've got me and Fred, and…'

'And?'

'And you will always be Amy and Felix's Godmother… If Fred, God forbid, were to die… I don't know, fall down a drain and if I licked a toxic stamp, you would be there for them,' she said.

I laughed.

'Joking apart, I'm serious, Nat…'

'Thank you,' I said.

'What were you talking about, before the kids rang?'

'Jamie… I fell over on my arse in front of him when I was rollerblading. It's hardly Jane Austen stuff.'

'Okay. And what about Ryan?' asked Sharon.

'I'm leaving that one alone for now.'

'You should talk to Ryan, Nat because…'

'My God! Jamie, Ryan, Benjamin! They're the kinds of relationships fifteen-year-old schoolgirls have. I don't think I'm cut out for a proper adult relationship. I'm too set in my ways now, I've missed the boat.'

'Natalie, that's rubbish. You haven't missed the boat!'

'Can you honestly say you believe that?' I asked. 'Look at my track record.'

'Oh Nat, you need to concentrate on what is good in your life. You've got your job.'

'That's a joke too! *Macbeth* opens next week, and our big star who I've gambled so much on isn't fit for purpose!' I snapped. 'And to complicate things further, I shagged him!'

Sharon was silent and started to place dry plates back in the cupboard.

'I think I'm done talking about this,' I said wiping my eyes. 'Here's your lasagne dish. Thank you.'

Sharon took it from me.

'Do you want me to stay over? I can,' she said.

'You go home, I've got work to do and that sofa bed isn't very comfy…'


When Sharon had gone, I checked on Gran who was sleeping peacefully and then went and lay on the sofa bed. I turned on the TV and they were showing Disney's *Cinderella*, just at the moment Prince Charming eased the glass slipper onto her foot.

'You're a stupid cow if you think that's your life sorted,' I said to the screen.

I switched it off, turned over, and tried to go to sleep.

# WHAT'S MY LINE?

On my way to work on Thursday morning I ran into Nicky in Grande. They'd hired a new barista, who she was laying into for using sugar instead of sweetener in her coffee.

'What if I were a diabetic? What if I have a sugar intolerance?' she was shouting.

'But you also asked for three pumps of syrup. That's like liquid sugar,' said the barista.

'Are you *back talking* me?' she growled.

'I ain't talking behind your back, *madam*. I'm saying to your face that your coffee is already loaded with sugar, so why ask for sweetener?'

Nicky opened her mouth to go nuclear, but I pulled her away and out into the street.

'Nat! What are you doing? I tell you, that kid wouldn't last three seconds back home in Texas…'

'Let's get coffee from the rehearsal room,' I said.

'What? That cremated stuff in the tin, with just hot water and milk?'

'Yes, it's how everyone else in Britain drinks their coffee,' I said. 'Maybe today we could keep some things simple…'

Nicky took a deep breath.

'Yeah, I'm really on the edge Nat. This run-through of *Macbeth*…'

'I know hun,' I said putting my arm round her.

'We've got five days until previews begin on Tuesday…'

'A lot can happen in four days,' I said.

'Did you get Val's email? We've had to refund eighteen percent of tickets now across the run…'

'Yes, and did you also read that her brother bought her a new calculator for her birthday with a percentage button,' I added.

'The board are sending someone to watch the run-through,' added Nicky.

'What? Why?'

'They're real concerned about the state of Ryan, all these refunds. You know how slim our margins of profit are on this show…' explained Nicky.

The run-through of *Macbeth* was a disaster. We sat in the rehearsal room behind Morag McKye, the fearsome little Scottish lady who heads our board of directors, and we watched as Ryan stumbled about the stage, forgetting his words and frequently having to shout out 'line' to Byron who sat with Craig in the sound booth, prompting.

Afterwards I went over to Craig sat in the sound booth.

'I'm going to talk to Ryan,' I said.

'Do you want me there?' he asked.

'No,' I said. I heard the door slam behind me and I looked round to see Morag McKye had left without saying a word. Nicky and Xander looked over at me with worried faces.

I went up to Ryan's dressing room and knocked on the door. A quiet voice inside said to come in. Ryan sat looking in the mirror. He just had his kilt on.

'Natalie!' he said. I closed the door and went in. He came towards me and grabbed me in a hug. At first I stood with my arms hanging at my side, unsure of what was happening, then I hugged him back. His bare skin was warm and firm. He pulled away and leant in to kiss me.

'Hey, what are you doing?' I said pulling back. His face darkened. He broke away and went to the little fridge by the window, pulling out an already-opened can of Mountain Dew.

'So when you feel bad I'm supposed to screw you, but when I feel bad…'

'Watch your mouth,' I snapped. 'The only people you should feel bad for are the poor actors, crew and all the people here who are working hard to…'

'Spare me the lecture Natalie.'

'*Spare you the lecture?*' I repeated. 'You've been rehearsing for almost two weeks, and you don't know your lines. You were shouting out 'line' more times than Kate Moss on a night out!'

He tipped the can back for a final swig and chucked it in the wastepaper bin under his dressing table. I moved swiftly, plucked it out of the bin and gave it a sniff, it stank of vodka.

'What are you calling this, *Mountain Brew?*' I asked.

'I told you, I'm an alcoholic,' he said.

'And I'm a bloody chocoholic but I control myself! You don't see me coming to work with Dairy Milk smeared over my bloody face!'

'You should watch your mouth too. Just because we screwed, doesn't mean you stop being professional,' he said. I laughed coldly. 'Oh, sorry, we made love, didn't we?' he said sarcastically. He went and pulled on a t-shirt. I was getting nowhere with him.

'Ryan. Listen. I care about you, I really do… and what we had was special. I don't know if we necessarily *had* anything, but I will always be a friend to you.'

He suddenly erupted.

'Then where have you been? I was fired from my show… Do you know how much I wanted to come over to your apartment, and just chill, get pizza, not be alone?'

He slumped back into his chair.

'I thought you hated me after what happened, with the papers, and that journalist?' I asked.

'I was angry.'

'Ryan, I know guys like to hide their feelings, but you take it to a whole other level.'

There was a pause. Ryan came over to me and knelt down. I thought he was going to tie his shoelace, but he took my hand.

'Natalie, I know this is crazy…' he said looking up at me.

'What are you doing?' I asked, looking down at him.

'Will you marry me?' he asked. I waited for him to laugh; he didn't.

'What?'

'Just hear me out Natalie. When I first met you I didn't notice you at all…'

'Right…'

'Then you kind of started to scratch at my brain. I'd see you in the corridor, scratch, scratch, and then at the first rehearsal, scratch, scratch, scratch, and then you invited me to the christening and you turned into such an itch. An itch only relieved by spending time with you. We had the most fun, and you treated me like a normal person. You're funny, you're real pretty, and you're really good at stuff in bed. And you remember when you told me the story of Benjamin, when we were in bed?'

'Yes.'

'I said I would never do that to you. That I would treat you right. I meant it. Let me treat you right.'

I looked down at him. Did he mean it? Or could he really act?

He pulled a plain silver band off his finger and held it out to me.

I stared at it…

I remembered Sharon telling me how Fred had proposed at the most unexpected time. It was an ordinary Saturday on the beach at Whitstable. Fred had gone to get chips and she was going to have a go at him when he got back, she had a cold bum from sitting on the sand, and he was taking ages… When he returned with her cone of chips there was a diamond ring on one of the chips. She'd not considered the possibility of marrying him, but instantly knew it was right.

Was this the same?

He was the second man to propose to me. How many more chances would I get?

And I've met a few of these feisty older single women, who tell stories of the numerous proposals they turned down. I never quite buy their belief that they made the right decision.

I looked down at Ryan, still kneeling. He had a shine in his eyes. Even slightly half-cut he was beautiful. Who could have begrudged me almost saying yes?

But I opened my mouth and the first thing came tumbling out was,

'I'm afraid it's a no from me.'

The light shining in Ryan's eyes faded. He slowly stood up and slid the ring back on his finger.

'Sorry, that came out wrong!' I said. 'You have to realise it would be crazy? It is crazy. Ryan? We've spent less than twenty-four hours together! You're a decade younger than me, and you're an alc…'

He went over to his dressing table, flicked off the bank of lights surrounding the mirror and grabbed his bag.

'What are you doing? Let's talk about this…' I said.

'I've been invited to Savile Row. They want to give me a suit for the *Femme Fatale* awards ceremony tonight.'

'Do you think it's the best thing for you to go to? There's going to be plenty of drink flowing…'

'I'm being paid to present an award Natalie. It's work,' he said and he left slamming the door. A few moments later there was a knock, it was Nicky.

'How did it go?' she asked.

'I gave him a good talking to. Told him to learn his lines,' was all I could answer.

# SHINE BRIGHT
# LIKE A DIAMOND

I went home and Gran helped me pick out an outfit for the *Femme Fatale* awards. I told her about Ryan's proposal.

'I hev had many proposals since your grandfather died,' said Gran, as I pulled on a blue dress.

'You have? How many?' I asked.

'Seven gay men, and three straight,' she said. She looked at me then shook her head. I unzipped the dress and chucked it on the growing pile next to her on the bed. 'I said no to all the straight ones, but I could hev married the gays…'

'Why didn't you then?' I asked pulling a black beaded dress off its hanger.

'Vell, I believe that marriage is about love and it should be for life. I loved your grandfather. He was the only man for me, forever…'

I paused; she wiped a tear from her eye. I stepped into the black dress and zipped it up

'Ah yes,' she cried clapping her hands. 'Natalie, that is the dress! You look beautiful.'

I smoothed it down and turned looking in the mirror. Gran had very good taste.

'But how many women get one man proposing to her, let alone two?' I asked.

'Just because a man proposes, doesn't mean anything. It's vat *you* vant… Now, bring me your jewellery box.'

I went to the bathroom and grabbed the little wooden box I keep bits and bobs in.

'But what if Ryan is the one? And I don't know it?' I asked bringing it back and handing it to Gran. 'But I did know it, because I didn't say yes, yes?'

'Natalie you are answering your own questions,' said Gran giving me a look. There was a pause as she raked her fingers through my jewellery box. She started tutting.

'Natalie, diamonds are a girl's best friend, all you have in this sad little box are enemies! Go and get my jewellery box, it's behind your television.'

I went and retrieved it from the top of her suitcases, still sitting unpacked, and brought it back. It was a huge heavy box of varnished wood with a built-in combination lock. I turned away politely as she entered the code. There was a click and a creaking sound. It was inlaid with purple, and three tiers popped up when the lid opened.

'Now, let me see,' she said sorting through an impressive array of jewels. 'Ah, yes. You *must* vear this.'

She held out a necklace inlaid with diamonds.

'Wow,' I said. 'I can't, they must be worth a fortune. Are they real diamonds?'

Gran snorted. 'This is white gold inlaid with *flawless* diamonds, exceptional purity,' she said. They blazed in the light from her reading lamp above.

'Where did you get these?'

'I vas courted by a rich Arab once. Gay proposal number two,' she said.

'And he let you keep the necklace?'

Gran snorted again. 'I got these on our second date. The engagement ring, I didn't keep. I could never hev gone through

vith it. I could never hev vorn a burka. I used to get panic at-
tacks ven I vore my snood!'

'You should write a book about your life,' I said.

'No. Writing about my life would mean it's over. I still have
many chapters I want to live through. Now try it on,' said Gran.
I leant down and she fastened it round my neck. I went to the
mirror. It looked stunning with my dress.

'I vant you to be the last person to vear this, and this awards
show is the perfect place,' she said.

'Last person, what do you mean?'

'I am going to sell it. I can pay the remainder of my debts
and find some place to live.'

'Gran, you can stay with me as long as you like,' I said.

'I know my darlink, but you hev a life, and hopefully I vill
hev one again soon.'

I turned back to the mirror.

'Just don't go valking about in the street. They vould be a
mugger's dream,' added Gran.


Nicky and Xander arrived in a taxi just before seven, and we
made the short journey over to the Royal Albert Hall.

'You look a lot better than you did at today's run-through!'
said Nicky admiring my outfit. She had on a fabulous red
gown which showed off her curves. Her dark hair was loose
down her back, and she had accessorised with dramatic red-
framed glasses.

'Thank you,' I said. 'I'm just trying to blot it out of my mind.'
She leant closer.

'Are those diamonds real, honey?' she asked.

'Yes, I borrowed them from Gran.'

'My God, what are they worth? They're proper Jackie O shit!'
cried Nicky.

'Who's Jackie O?' asked Xander who was sat beside her in a smart little tuxedo. We both screamed.

'This is what happens when we hire someone who thinks 1992 is in the past,' said Nicky.

'I wasn't born until 1995,' said Xander.

By the time we'd explained who Jackie O was, we were sweeping up to the Albert Hall. It sat like a colossal stack of terracotta sponge cakes, all lit up with blues and pinks. The road and the steps leading up to the pillared entrance were crawling with photographers and screaming fans.

'Is this really the best place for Ryan to be right now?' I said. 'He's got rehearsals again tomorrow at nine. And after what happened today…'

'Honey, this is his job,' said Nicky. 'And if he doesn't want to be Ryan Harrison anymore, there are plenty of other young guys lining up to take his place.'

We didn't walk the red carpet; the taxi dropped us off at a side entrance. The cavernous interior of the Albert Hall is ringed by a seemingly endless circular corridor, connecting floors via stairs and providing an entrance and exit to the hundreds of boxes on the second and third levels.

We got lost when we went in the side entrance, ending up on the second tier and emerging into a box. We stood for a moment and looked down at the tables. There were hundreds, and from above they looked like discs on a chequer board, all laid out with glasses and huge sprays of flowers. The lights were low, and cast a blue and pink glow across the white tablecloths.

My favourite part of the Albert Hall is the colossal ceiling with huge acoustic fibreglass discs suspended from the ceiling. They too reflected the red and blue lights.

At the front was a stage, with steps up to a glass podium where there was written FEMME FATALE AWARDS. People were already swarming into the hall, and finding where to sit.

'I've never been here before,' said Xander in awe.

'You should come back and see something better than the *Femme Fatale* magazine awards,' I said. 'I saw Adele here, she was incredible.'

'Ooh. There's Tuppence Halfpenny,' said Xander.

Tuppence was marching across the red carpeted floor wearing a black lace full-length gown, which somehow managed to completely cover her skin but also display everything she had on offer. A small television crew followed in her wake, the arc of a blinding white light enveloping her.

Jamie followed behind, deep in conversation with Brendan. They both had opted for a classic black tux.

'What's with the TV crew?' Nicky asked.


We left the box and went downstairs. We were met by a lady in a big rustling ball gown who pointed us to our table. We had been placed at a table right by the stage, but sitting with our backs to it. I was sandwiched between Nicky and Xander.

Tuppence, Jamie and Brendan were standing by the table next to us. They were in conference with the crew, made up of a handsome Indian cameraman and a blonde young girl with a clipboard and headphones.

Tuppence kept looking around, feverishly scanning the hall. A small black fascinator clung to the side of her head, defying gravity, and an almost transparent veil of thin black lace was meshed tightly against her face.

'She looks like she's stuck tights on her head to rob a bank,' murmured Nicky in my ear.

'Let's just go and break the ice,' I said. 'I don't want to be glaring at them the whole ceremony.'

'If there's no ice to break, we'll have to try something else,' murmured Nicky. We got up and went over. Tuppence noticed us, and I'm pleased to say my necklace threw her off her stride for a moment.

'Why are you all here?' she asked. 'I didn't think tinpot theatre staff were desirable guests for the *Femme Fatale* awards…'

'We're here with Ryan Harrison,' I said.

'Where is he then? Has he shrunk?' she laughed at her own joke.

'He's presenting an award for…' I looked to Nicky for help.

'Best Hair…' said Nicky.

'I've been nominated for Best Hair,' said Tuppence proudly.

'Is that for the hair on your head, or elsewhere?' I said.

'That's speed, and rolling,' said the cameraman pointing the lens at Tuppence. The light came on, and bathed in its glare she became paler. Brendan stepped in and adjusted her fascinator. Jamie stood back with a gaunt look on his face. I caught his eye briefly, and felt an overwhelming sadness coming from him.

'What's the camera for?' asked Xander.

'Tuppence has just signed a six-figure deal for her own reality show. *Totally Tuppence: Life of Burlesque Legend*,' said Brendan.

'Legend!' scoffed Nicky. 'My client is seen in a show sold to thirty-five countries. Yours takes off her knickers in the West End.'

'Your client has been fired from that show,' glowered Brendan. 'My client is about to break through!'

'Here he is! Quick. Are you filming?' squealed Tuppence. Ryan was weaving towards us between the tables with the woman in the big rustling dress. A band of photographers was following after him.

'Camera speed,' said the cameraman.

'Are you filming?' snapped Tuppence.

'We told you, camera speed means the camera is recording footage,' said the blonde girl.

'Ryan darling!' said Tuppence grabbing him as he reached our tables.

She pulled him against her and the photographers duly started clicking away. He was wearing a beautifully cut midnight-blue suit, and his hair had been artfully tousled. His faced was a little flushed.

'How are you Ryan?' cried Tuppence striking leg-kicking poses in full Moulin Rouge mode.

'Yeah, cool thanks Tuppence,' he said squinting into the terrible glare of the camera light.

'Who do you think is going to win?' she cried.

'Win what?' he asked.

'Best Hair of course, I'm nominated!' she cried.

'Oh you're all winners,' he said.

'Thank you,' she simpered. To her dismay Ryan moved away to where I was standing with Nicky and Xander. The camera lens started to follow but Tuppence reached out and pulled it back on her.

'Ryan is a very good friend, I've met his dogs too, Bella and Eduardo…' she said.

Ryan stopped beside our table and said hi to Nicky and Xander and muttered a hello to me. I went to say something, but the sound system blared out some jazzy music and a voice boomed, *Ladies and gentlemen please take your seats for the annual Femme Fatale Magazine Awards!'*

Everyone in the room moved and took their seats. Ryan was placed opposite us on the table, but he was obscured by a huge centrepiece of flowers. The ceremony was long, and watching it with our backs to the stage was uncomfortable.

Tara Reid presented Woman of the Year to Cher – who, surprisingly, '*couldn't be here tonight*' so Tara Reid accepted it on her behalf.

Then Jackie Stallone presented Best Dressed Woman to Gwyneth Paltrow who, surprisingly, '*couldn't be here tonight*' so Jackie Stallone accepted it on her behalf. No wonder they had been so keen to get Ryan to attend.

Then a voice boomed '*Please welcome to the stage Dean Gaffney!*'

'Who is Dean Gaffney?' asked Nicky.

'He's a soap star… Used to be in *EastEnders*… Had a pet dog called Wellard… Likes to date Page Three girls with enormous bosoms?' I said. Nicky still shrugged.

'We took my Nan to see him in panto in Gravesend,' said Xander. 'He played the prince.'

'He played the prince?' asked Nicky incredulously as Dean walked out onto the stage to present Best Cleavage to Kim Kardashian.

'My Nan loved him… Although she has got cataracts,' added Xander.

Kim Kardashian surprisingly '*couldn't be here tonight*', so Dean Gaffney accepted the award, and then went down the stairs to blag a photo with Ryan and Tuppence, which was filmed by her reality show crew.

About halfway through the ceremony, I stood up and looked over the giant flowers to see that Ryan's seat was empty.

'Where's Ryan?' I said to Nicky. On cue the announcer's voice boomed '*Please welcome to the stage Ryan Harrison and Yitta Bonn!*'

We craned our necks back round to the stage and Ryan entered holding hands with an absolute blonde bombshell of a girl. They walked to the podium and stopped, still holding hands.

'Who the hell is Yitta Bonn?' I asked. Nicky shrugged. Xander leant over.

'She once spoke to Prince Harry at a polo match…' he said excitedly.

'And?' I said.

'*And* they were photographed,' he added.

'A woman's crowning glory is the hair on her head,' said Yitta leaning into the microphone. She had a slight Swedish accent and huge baby-blue eyes.

'Do you know how many hairs a woman has on her head, Yitta?' asked Ryan, leaning into the other side of the microphone.

'I don't Ryan. I've never counted,' said Yitta seriously.

'It's millions Yitta, millions… All working together in unity to make a hairstyle,' answered Ryan.

'Jeez, someone should shoot the scriptwriter,' murmured Nicky from the corner of her mouth.

'Of all the millions of beautiful hairs on all the heads of all our nominees, I'm afraid only one can win though,' said Yitta gravely. She paused then she went on. 'The nominees are… *Jennifer Lawrence; Jennifer Aniston; Jennifer Love Hewitt; Jennifer Coolidge; Jennifer Lopez* and *Tuppence Halfpenny.*'

She leant against Ryan's shoulder as he opened the envelope.

'I wonder who will win?' I asked Nicky, sarcastically.

'My dog gets the same look in his eye when I'm about to give him a treat,' said Nicky, indicating Tuppence, who was leaning forward in her chair with an excited look on her face.

'And the award for Best Hair goes to *Tuppence Halfpenny!*' said Ryan.

Jazzy music began to play and Tuppence rose to her feet, manufacturing as much shock as if she'd just won the Oscar for

Best Actress. She walked up to the podium, stopping to wave back to her film crew. She thanked pretty much everyone she's ever spoken to, "her rock" Brendan O'Connor and "her baby" Jamie Dawson. The reality TV crew spun their camera round to Jamie and he looked on with love light in his eyes.

'When do you think we can leave?' I hissed.

'We have to stay and see if Ryan wins Best Hunk,' said Nicky.

'He is going to win, he's the only nominee who's turned up… I'll get more wine,' I said attracting the attention of a passing waiter.

After Tuppence's long-winded speech she went back to her table hefting her huge glass award for Best Hair. I think she had been hoping for Ryan to follow her back to their table, but he appeared a few moments later hand in hand with Yitta Bonn. She slinked along beside him and joined our table, everyone having to shuffle up as a chair was found for her to sit on. She ignored the chair and instead draped herself over him, stroking his hair. I was furious. I knew Ryan's marriage proposal was crazy, but it was barely five hours ago! Talk about moving on fast…

'Shall we have a bathroom break?' I said. Nicky nodded and we made our way out of the hall to the ladies' loo. I didn't look at Ryan and Yitta Bonn on our way past. Xander came with us too. I was feeling a bit tipsy, but instead of lifting my mood the alcohol had darkened it.

'What do you think will happen with Ryan and that Yitta Bonn?' I said putting my handbag on the sink and adjusting my hair.

'What do you care?' asked Nicky.

'Whatever happens, she'll make sure that it's photographed,' said Xander. 'They've apparently paid her thirty thousand pounds to be here tonight…'

'What?' I said. 'And the only thing she is famous for is talking to Prince Harry?'

Xander nodded.

'Lord! That makes me want to give up. You know how hard we had to work to get that Arts Council grant of twenty grand? And that was so we could take plays into local schools. It's depressing.'

'Unfortunately that's how the world works Nat,' said Nicky leaning into the mirror and reapplying her lipstick. 'Maybe we should bypass the Arts Council and go and find Prince Harry at a polo match!'

'Why are we even here?' I said. 'We could be doing something more worthwhile than watching bloody Tuppence Halfpenny win Best Hair. She only got it because she was the only one who showed up. And how is that best hair? It's all lacquered against her head like an old Brillo Pad!'

On cue, a toilet flushed and the cubicle behind us opened. Tuppence Halfpenny emerged with her film crew of two, swaying on her feet with her award under her arm.

'Did you just film her having a pee?' asked Nicky as the light from the camera glared in our eyes.

'It's called coverage,' slurred Tuppence. 'And my hair… is *great*…'

She slammed her award down next to the sink. It was a huge brick of glass with FEMME FATALE cut into the top. She attempted to open her lipstick but it slipped out of her hand and landed in the sink with a clink.

'You need to be on an angle,' said the blonde girl to the cameraman. 'We don't want to be seen in the reflection.'

We were all silent as the camera filmed. I straightened my hair and we went to leave.

'Your hair,' Tuppence laughed. 'It's like pubes isn't it? Pubic frizz.'

She began to fish her lipstick out of the plug hole. Nicky's eyebrows shot up.

'What did you just say?' I asked dangerously. I heard a little whirring sound as the camera lens watched us.

'Look at you. So stuck up. You think you're better than everyone.'

'No, I don't,' I said.

'Jamie confided something in me…' she said with a nasty drunken snarl. 'He said sleeping with you was like being with a dead cod. Apparently you're shit in bed!'

Before I knew what had happened I had slapped her hard round the face.

She reeled back in shock and felt her lip. Then she charged at me. Xander shrieked and jumped out of the way, Nicky tried to stop her but she managed to push past and launch herself on me. We both went crashing down onto the tiled floor. Tuppence grabbed at my necklace and pulled. The clasp snapped and there was a skittering sound as the diamonds scattered under the row of sinks.

Enraged, I reached up and grabbed her fascinator and pulled. Hard. It wouldn't budge. She screamed and started to rain down slaps on my head and face, but I held on fast and kept pulling.

Suddenly Tuppence and her hair separated, she fell back clutching at her head which was completely bald, less some strings of wig glue! We all looked in shock between her, and the full head of hair attached to the fascinator I was still holding in my hand.

The camera crew could hardly contain their glee.

'Oh my God. I'm sorry! Have you got…?' I said.

'You bitch! I have alopecia!' she shrilled. She grabbed her award for Best Hair, swung it round and hit me on the head. Then everything went black.

\*

I woke up in the back of an ambulance parked behind the Albert Hall. A short-haired St John's Ambulance lady in her sixties was leaning over me with a handsome male paramedic who was shining a light in my eyes. Xander and Nicky were standing behind him. Nicky was holding a brown McDonald's paper bag.

'Can you tell me your name please?' he asked.

'Yes, Natalie Love,' I said.

'And your surname?' he asked.

'No. Love is my surname.'

'Oh, I thought you were calling me love,' he grinned. He had a cute gap in his teeth. I went to sit up but he gently put his hand on my shoulder. Pain shot down the side of my face.

'Please lie still for now. Miss Love, you hit your head?'

'Yes,' I said.

'She was attacked by Tuppence Halfpenny, who was brandishing a *Femme Fatale* award!' said Xander excitedly. 'It was the award for Best Hair, but it turns out she's bald!'

Under the harsh lights in the ambulance it all sounded ridiculous.

'You were attacked?' asked the St John Ambulance lady nervously.

'No... no, it's fine,' I said waving it away dismissively.

'Oh Nat, here,' said Nicky handing over the brown McDonald's bag.

'Nothing to eat until you've been to A&E for a scan,' said the paramedic.

'No, these are her diamonds,' explained Nicky.

'We really scoured the toilet floor, we're pretty certain that's all of them,' said Xander. The paramedic took the bag and looked inside. He looked up in disbelief.

'Why does she keep diamonds in a McDonald's bag?' he asked.

'That was the only bag we could find, I got it from one of the stewards inside,' said Xander.

'My necklace broke... when I hit my head,' I said.

'Right...' said the paramedic. He was now looking at me as if I was a mad binge drinker.

'You missed the best bit!' cried Xander. 'Dean Gaffney burst in to the toilets desperate to be featured on *Totally Tuppence: Life of Burlesque Legend*, but Brendan followed saying he was too Z-list for the show... Then, Dean Gaffney gave Brendan a bog wash!'

We all stared at Xander.

'You know what a bog wash is? When someone sticks your head down the loo and flushes!'

'Yes, we know what a bog wash is,' I said.

'Well, it was so funny, and Brendan deserved it,' said Xander.

'It was pretty spectacular,' agreed Nicky.


Nicky came with me in the ambulance to the hospital. I was given an X-ray and had to lie still as it whirred and clicked and hummed. I was then wheeled back to a cubicle whilst the doctors pored over the results.

'I'm really embarrassed, getting into a scrap like that,' I said finally to Nicky who was sitting patiently in the corner with a magazine.

'She said some pretty horrible things to deserve it,' said Nicky.

'I didn't know she has to wear a wig... I still feel cruel.'

'You didn't know... Jeez the things people hide. It feels a bit like it's all getting out of control,' said Nicky.

'There's something I have to tell you…' I said. 'You know when you asked me if anything was going on with Ryan?'

Nicky put down her magazine and stared at me.

'Go on.'

'Well, I had a stupid one night stand. I slept with Ryan when he came to my sister's christening… Of course it was a mistake,' I added.

'You think?' said Nicky.

'Do you know how horrible it is to go to family gatherings single? I didn't mean for it to happen. We had such a good time, and then he had some of my mother's trifle, which was packed with sherry.'

'So you're the reason he's drinking?' said Nicky.

'The reason he is drinking is because he's an alcoholic! Which I didn't know about… Then today, he proposed to me.'

'Ryan Harrison *proposed* to you?' said Nicky disbelieving. 'Well, I suppose he is an alcoholic.'

'Thanks a lot,' I said.

'Why would you lie Nat, and not tell me?'

'Because, at the time I thought it should just remain private. I don't know who you sleep with.'

'Excuse me. I sleep with my husband and no one else,' said Nicky.

'What does that mean? I'm sorry if I haven't got a husband.'

'You've gone down in my estimation Natalie. I've given up so much to start this theatre with you. Ryan Harrison was a big deal for us, we've worked so hard to get here, and you jeopardise it by jumping into bed with him when you're feeling blue at a family gathering.'

'It was my Gran who invited him…' I shrilled, sounding like a kid.

'Did she lift him on top of you too?' said Nicky. She stood, rolled up the magazine and tried to stuff it into her tiny clutch bag.

'I don't think it's going to fit,' I said quietly. Nicky threw it on the bed.

'I'm going home to get some sleep. There are plenty of people here who can look after you,' she snapped.

'Nicky!'

'No, Natalie. It feels like you're losing it lately, all this crazy stuff isn't your style, and it certainly isn't mine.'

She slipped through the curtains and was gone.


A moment later a doctor came in with my X-ray. He slipped it into one of those light boxes and pointed out the inner workings of my head.

'You had a nasty blow, but there is no lasting damage, fracture, or swelling on the brain,' he said pointing here and there with the end of a biro.

'You seem to know more about what's going on in my head than I do,' I said.

'We'd like to keep you in overnight, merely as a precaution,' said the doctor flicking off the light box and taking the X-ray. When he'd gone I saw that it was almost two in the morning. I lay back but my head was now throbbing. A nurse came in and gave me some painkillers, and luckily I fell asleep.

# BOARDROOM DRAMA

I woke up at seven the next morning when a nurse came through the curtains and gave me more painkillers. My face was in agony as I swallowed them down.

'Where's the loo please?' I asked groggily. She pointed me to a door opposite. I picked up my bags and padded over in my bare feet. I had a shock when I looked in the mirror. One side of my forehead and cheek were puffed up and swollen. What's worse was that I had a black bruise which clearly read FAT.

'Oh my god, you are kidding,' I said gingerly touching the bruise and wincing as pain shot through my face. It wasn't ironic enough being hit in the face by an award for Best Hair by someone who had no hair, but fate had decided that the only letters of FEMME FATALE which would imprint on my face were FAT.

I came back out of the toilets and, keeping my head down, escaped into my little cubicle. I couldn't get comfy on the bed in my dress with the fine beads. I saw the nurse going past and asked for a gown. She returned ten minutes later with a neatly folded white hospital gown.

'You've been placed under observation until tonight, then the doctor will see if he wants to discharge you,' she explained.

'Tonight? It's not even nine in the morning. I've got work,' I said.

'You had a nasty bump, you're under observation for twenty-four hours,' she said and left closing the curtains. I was pulling on the hospital gown, and trying to get it to fasten at the back, when my phone rang. It was Xander.

'Hello Natalie, are you okay?' he said.

'Yes, and no,' I said. 'I'm still in hospital.'

'Oh…' he said. There was a pause. 'So you don't think you'll be in today?'

'No. What is it Xander?'

'Natalie, I'm not sure what's going on, but the board of directors are having a meeting here this morning. I've just had to prepare the agenda.'

He paused again.

'What is it Xander?' I asked.

'Okay, well I'll have to be quick. Ryan was found in the doorway of the theatre this morning.'

'Dead!?'

'No! No! Not dead, just drunk and looking a bit like a tramp. He's back at his hotel now, sleeping it off. Val found him when she came to open up… The Board of Directors are having a meeting to discuss firing him.'

'They can't fire him.' I said. 'I make that decision.'

'There's the other thing… I'm not supposed to tell you this, but they've had me put on the agenda that they want to discuss your position as theatre manager and artistic director.'

My blood went cold. 'Who asked you to do this?'

'The email I got came from the head of the board, Morag McKye…'

I thought about Nicky's reaction last night, but I didn't say anything.

'Right. So this meeting in my theatre that I've not been told about, what time is it?' I asked.

'In about forty minutes.'

'Thank you Xander. Don't tell them I know.'

I hung up and hurriedly put my dress back on. I passed the nurse as I was coming out of the curtain.

'Where are you going?' she said.

'Sorry, I have to go,' I said, and hurried past her.


I was in UCL Hospital on Warren Street, only a short cab ride into Soho, but the roads were jammed. A huge square of Warren Street had been dug up and traffic was at a standstill. I crossed the road and darted into the tube station. It took ages to get down onto the platform, and then the train seemed to crawl through the three stops to Leicester Square, pausing at each stop for what seemed like ages. By the time I was in the lift at Leicester Square, clanking up to street level, I was feeling terrible and getting looks.

I came out of the station, savouring the cool morning sunshine, and ran for it, across Leicester Square and through to Soho, making it to the theatre with about a minute to spare. I went inside, through the box office and up the stairs, stopping for a moment to look at the picture of me and Kim Cattrall… I gulped and carried on up to the top floor, barging into the conference room.

At the long table were sat the full twelve members of the board. The four I was best acquainted with were William, Larry, Craig, and Morag.

Morag's presence worried me the most. She's a tiny woman with cruel beady eyes. When I first started working in London's Theatreland, I found a job as assistant to her husband, Leonard McKye, who was a successful theatrical agent. He was a kind, brilliant man, and became a mentor to me, even coming on board as an investor in the Raven Street theatre. When he died suddenly two years ago, Morag had taken his place on our board, and she hated me.

They all exchanged surprised glances at me barging in. Right behind followed Nicky, who looked equally surprised.

'Did you know about this?' I said.

'I've just arrived and been told about this meeting. Nat? I thought you were in hospital?' said Nicky.

'Hospital?' said William.

'Natalie, it seems, was involved in a wee ruckus last night at the Albert Hall,' said Morag in her clipped Scottish tones. 'One of several incidents it seems.'

'So everyone decided to meet behind my back?' I said.

Xander sat in the corner, frantically minuting everything.

'I called this meeting… and you weren't invited,' said Morag.

'I wasn't invited?' I said in disbelief. 'I've devoted the past five years to this place. I found it, put forward the proposal to renovate, and I've delivered healthy returns on all your investments thus far… So if you want to throw me out, or fire me, then good luck, because no one can run this venue like I can.'

The board stared between me and Morag. She pulled out a pair of dark spectacles from a tartan case, gave them a polish and slipped them on.

'Natalie, we're all a wee bit worried you've rather *overexposed* the theatre,' she said peering over her glasses. 'Hiring this American television personality to perform Shakespeare.'

'He's an actor,' I said.

'But he's *American*.'

'He's bankable, Morag,' said Nicky.

'I for one can't *bear* to hear Americans recite Shakespeare,' said Morag. 'They tend to chew over the dialogue like a tough piece of brisket.'

'That's your main problem? You don't like to hear Americans recite Shakespeare? Do you know for certain how people used to recite Shakespeare when he was alive, Morag?' I asked.

'It's there in the script dearie,' said Morag looking around at the board with wry amusement. I went on.

'Some people believe Shakespearian plays were spoken in an accent much the same as our American friends', others think that old English was virtually impenetrable to our ears. Did you see the purist Shakespeare season Mark Rylance did over at the Globe in 2005?'

'I did,' said William. Craig nodded. Kyle, who had been silent in his shiny suit, also nodded, and crossed his legs nervously.

'What were you doing Morag?' I said. 'No doubt stood at Hadrian's Wall pelting some English ramblers with clootie dumplings.'

'How dare you!' said Morag.

'No!' I shouted slamming my hand on the conference table. 'How dare, YOU. As well as giving this theatre huge press exposure, I've got schools coming in to watch this play. Some of the kids will be seeing theatre for the first time. Most will be seeing Shakespeare for the first time.'

'What are you now Natalie? A UN ambassador?' said Morag. I suddenly remembered why I did this job, and it filled me with a fire I'd lost over the last couple of weeks.

'No, I'm someone who gives a shit Morag. *Macbeth* is on the school syllabus. Seeing someone like Ryan Harrison, who they can identify with, might help them understand the play, and pass their exams. I failed my exams and it has haunted me ever since... As we build up this theatre we're going to have to make tough choices, to cast celebrities or do media stunts. But always, my aim is to stage vibrant ground breaking theatre, and to bring people in who might not have seen a play before. To make this the best fucking theatre in London!'

There was a silence. I realised I was leaning over the table at them. I stood back.

'Natalie,' said Craig softly. 'I totally agree with you, but the fact is that Ryan has missed rehearsals and I don't think he's going to pull himself together and be ready… We open in a few days, and if he doesn't pull it off, people aren't going to want to see our understudy. We would have a colossal amount of returns at the box office.'

'And this brings me back to my point Natalie,' said Morag. 'We've spent hundreds of thousands of pounds. And it's highly likely that we will be forced to pay it back to ticket holders. I suggest we let this Ryan Harrison go. We have grounds to claim on our insurance policy. Isn't that right Nicky?'

'Well, yes…' said Nicky cautiously.

'And we would find it harder to get future insurance, our reputation would be badly damaged, we'd let everyone win!' I cried.

'I say we take a vote,' said Morag.

'Hang on,' I said. 'We have had some very trying weeks here at the theatre, but ticket sales are strong, isn't that right Nicky?'

'Yes… but we have had a lot of returns,' said Nicky.

'What if I said I can guarantee Ryan Harrison is back at rehearsals sober tomorrow?'

'He was found slumped in the doorway this morning by a road sweeper!' said Morag.

'Just give me a few more days. If you're going to claim on insurance and close it down, what does a few more days matter anyway? You can fire me too. Good luck finding someone who is happy to do two jobs for the price of one, who has the relationships at the Arts Council, who has a vision and passion for this theatre… I've just discharged myself from hospital with FAT stamped across my head!'

There was a silence.

'You're saying you can guarantee Ryan will be here tomorrow and sober?' asked Craig.

'I'll guarantee he's here this afternoon,' I said. Nicky glanced across at me.

'And he will come to rehearsals over the weekend, and he'll open next week word-perfect?' said Craig.

I nodded.

'This is getting tiresome, let's take a vote,' said Morag. 'All those in favour of cancelling the Scottish play starring the drunk American television personality...'

Morag raised her hand. So did two other members of the board. She looked shocked.

'All those against,' she said. Nine hands went into the air. William Boulderstone gave me a wink.

'Right then. Well, that seems to have delayed the hangman's noose... I look forward to personally handing over your P45 Miss Love,' snapped Morag. She pushed herself away from the table and stalked out of the conference room. Everyone followed after her staring at my forehead as they passed. Craig stopped to give me a hug on his way out.

'Nine am tomorrow, yes?'

'Yes,' I smiled. When everyone had gone, leaving Nicky and Xander, I sat down.

'I didn't know about this meeting,' she said. 'Nat. You really impressed me with what you said, when we're watching stupid award shows and haggling over the price of beer for the bar, you forget why you work at a theatre.'

'I meant it all,' I said.

'Just one question,' said Xander. 'How are you going to get Ryan on stage and sober?'

'I have to make a phone call,' I said.

# SHARON'S LODGER

I was dreading giving Gran back her diamond necklace, which was now in pieces in the grease-spotted McDonald's bag. When I got back to the flat, she seemed excited that I had stayed out all night.

'Did you *get lucky,* as the saying goes?' she asked.

I thought it best to tell the whole story, building up to the broken necklace. I made her laugh when I described the awards ceremony, and then gasp when I pulled off Tuppence Halfpenny's hair.

'My God! She's bald?' asked Gran.

'Yes, as a coot…'

'How did she react to you unmasking her?' Gran asked.

I placed the McDonald's bag on the breakfast bar. She looked puzzled and opened it. Her face clouded over as she pulled out the parts of the necklace. A few diamonds came skittering loose over the surface of the breakfast bar.

'I'm so sorry, I'll get it fixed… It will be as good as new. There's a guy in Hatton Garden I've looked up,' I said. Gran's mouth was set in a grim line.

'That bald bitch,' she growled finally.

'She can't help that,' I said. Gran noticed the bruise on the side of my face.

'Vat happened here?'

'She hit me with her award, for Best Hair…' I said.

Gran stared at the bruise for a moment, and started to laugh. Tears rolled down her cheeks, and she had to grab at a box of tissues and blow her nose.

'You couldn't make this stuff up Natalie!' she said, still laughing. 'Aren't you glad I brought you to London, all those years ago?'

'There's never a dull moment,' I said. 'Are we okay, about your diamonds? I'll get them fixed.'

'Of course. Diamonds are the toughest material known to vooman, your head is far more important. You should lie down.'

'I will do, but first I have to go and see Ryan…' I said.

I took a shower, got changed, and after a bowl of Gran's goulash felt better. Despite our best efforts with make-up I couldn't quite cover up the FAT bruise emblazoned on my forehead.

'I used to know a mortician from Whitechapel, but he killed himself drinking embalming fluid,' said Gran.

'How does that help me?' I asked, gently building up a layer of liquid foundation over the bruise.

'He could take a middle-aged car crash victim and make him look seventeen again… not that you're middle-aged my darlink,' she added.

I turned to show her my handy work.

'You look like a very beautiful girl with a touch of the mumps,' she said.


I drove over to the Langham Hotel, and went up to Ryan's room. When he answered the door, it was a tip of takeaway cartons and pizza boxes, cans of beer and empty bottles. He was bleary-eyed and still wearing the shirt and trousers from last night.

'Can I come in, please?' I said. He gave me a look and then let the door swing open. I followed him in. He went and sat down on the end of the bed. I opened the curtains, and saw the beautiful view across Green Park.

'We need to make a decision,' I said.

'About us?' he said shielding his eyes from the sunlight streaming in.

'No, Ryan. There is no us. I'm here to talk about you, and the theatre.'

He shrugged.

'What?'

'First I need to ask you if you want this job?'

'I've kind of got it already,' he said.

'Not for much longer…'

Ryan looked surprised.

'I've been showing up every day. I'm doing everything in my contract,' he said.

'There was a meeting this morning to discuss firing you,' I said.

'You can't afford to fire me,' said Ryan.

'The thing is, we *can* fire you. We've got good insurance. And then we'd stop paying for this hotel and your flights home…'

'What is this?'

'It would be a pity for you because you'll make most of your money when *Macbeth* opens. And then of course there will be all the casting directors and writers who will get to see you in a different light… Right now you're the drunk guy who's been fired. You have no manager anymore. This play is your last chance.'

Ryan suddenly burst into tears, his shoulders heaved as he sobbed. I went over and put my arm around him.

'What do I do?' he said.

'Have you spoken to your sponsor?' I asked. He shook his head. 'Well, you should.'

'Ok, then what? I just can't stop, I have no one to stop me,' he said.

'I thought you had friends in London?'

'They're party friends… And I had a mortifying experience with one of my fans.'

'I don't want to hear about any one night stands,' I said.

'No, it's nothing like that,' he explained. 'There's been this young girl who's shown up everywhere I go since I've been in London. She was at the airport when I arrived, she's been outside the theatre every day, and my hotel every night. A couple of days ago I saw her waiting on her own outside the hotel… And I was about to have dinner alone, again, so I thought heck why not? And I invited her to have dinner with me…'

'And what was that like?' I asked.

'Awkward. Her excitement slowly drained away during the entree, she was so disappointed in the real me. By the time they came round with the dessert menu, she made an excuse, saying she had to feed her cat. I've never seen her again. She's stopped waiting outside.'

There was a pause.

'Do you remember when we were at the farm, and you said you longed to be part of a family?' I asked.

He looked up and nodded.

'Well, I've arranged just that. For the rest of the play's run you'll be staying in my friend Sharon's back bedroom. She'll give you food, and you'll have to do chores. There will be a curfew, and you'll be driven to and from her house every day. There will be no alcohol or drugs. And if you are found with any, you'll be fired instantly.'

Ryan wiped his eyes and sniffed.

'So, do you want to carry on down this road to ruin? Or do you want a chance to change your life and your career?' I asked.

'I want a chance to change,' he said meekly.

An hour later Ryan had showered and changed and we heaved his suitcases down to my car. He was quiet as we drove from Green Park to New Cross, watching the majesty of Central London change to the unvarnished reality of Greater London.

'And this is still London?' He kept asking every few miles... 'Even this?' he added when we drove up the Old Kent Road, past houses with metal panels nailed over the doors and windows, and boarded up shops.

'Yep, still London,' I said. There was no space outside Sharon's house, so we went to the big Sainsbury's car park and I gave Ryan a pound, and told him to get a shopping trolley. We piled it up with his suitcases and he wheeled it round to her front door.

'This seems a nice house,' he said uneasily when I rang the doorbell.

A little gnome by the pond in the tiny front garden grinned at us over his fishing rod.


When I had phoned to ask Sharon this huge favour, she had been adamantly against it.

'I can't have *Ryan Harrison* living in my house!' she cried.

'Are you worried he might go on a drinking binge?' I asked.

'No. I'm thinking about everything embarrassing I have lying around. He'll see my frumpy old dressing gown with the cocoa stains on the back of the bathroom door, and I've got thrush cream in the bathroom cabinet. And my tea towels are a state. And then there's his calendar in the pantry.'

I explained that the theatre would no longer be paying his hotel bill, so we could pay for Ryan renting out her back bedroom.

'Please. We'd be helping each other out,' I said.

'I can't compete with the Langham Hotel, Nat! Amy and Felix get Coco Pops for breakfast, and there is always a queue for the bathroom… And often it's a no-go area after Fred has been, he never opens the window… No. I can't have my fantasy idol coming into the house and seeing all our reality.'

'Reality is what he needs right now,' I said. 'A routine. Everything is on the line for me Sharon. I'd have him at mine, but I've got Gran. We'll pay you the same rate as we've been paying for him to stay at the Langham Hotel…'

I told her how much it was.

'I'll have a quick tidy round, and make up the spare room for him,' she said.


When Sharon opened her front door, she stood in full make-up with her best skinny jeans and jumper combo. Amy and Felix stood shyly a little way behind her.

'Hello!' she said. 'Do come in Ryan. I'm Sharon, and this is Amy and Felix.'

'Hey, didn't we meet at the theatre?' asked Ryan.

We all bundled in, lugging in cases. I left the trolley in their front garden.

'Yes, we did. I had a bad reaction to antibiotics that day,' said Sharon blushing. 'All that gabbling rubbish…'

We all went through to the kitchen. Amy and Felix watched Ryan as he had a look round, noting the garden through the long windows at the back.

'Who'd like a drink? Cup of tea, or coffee?' asked Sharon.

'We've got loads of booze, too. Mum's been stashing it in the cupboard under the stairs,' said Felix.

'Is it true you enjoy drinking lots of booze?' said Amy shyly.

'Amy! Felix! What did I say?' trilled Sharon filling up the kettle.

'You look much more real than you do on the calendar Mum has,' said Felix.

'Dad reckons you stuffed a sock down your Speedos in March, did you?' said Amy opening the pantry. The Ryan Harrison calendar swung from side to side on its hook. She flicked to March.

Ryan laughed.

'They do a lot of airbrushing.'

'Airbrushing? Is that cockney for hair brushing?' asked Amy. Ryan laughed.

'No, it's when they make a picture look better using a computer. You see right now I have this zit on my nose,' he said leaning down to Amy and pointing at his nose. She peered at it.

'Euuuwww,' she said.

'Yeah it is euuuw. They can take a photo of me and with a computer and airbrushing make it disappear.'

'Wow,' said Amy.

The kids looked at Ryan weighing him up. Amy looked to Felix and gave him a nod.

'Do you want to see my remote controlled Dalek?' asked Felix.

'It's OURS!' said Amy. 'Do you want to see OUR remote control Dalek?'

'Kids, why don't you let Ryan settle in a bit first?' said Sharon.

'It's cool. I'd love to see a real Dalek,' said Ryan. 'I've heard so much about them.'

'Come on.' Amy grabbed Ryan's hand and led him out of the kitchen. Sharon poured me a cup of tea and added milk.

'What do you think Ryan Harrison will want for tea?' asked Sharon. 'God I never thought I'd say that! I'd planned egg, potato waffles and beans, but I can't give him that? He eats at Nobu in Los Angeles.'

'Cook him that, and make him wash up, it will do him good,' I said. I took a big gulp of tea and picked up my keys.

'You're going? Already?' asked Sharon. 'You're leaving me alone with him?!'

We could hear the sound of the robot Dalek in the living room and shrieks of laughter from Amy and Felix.

'This is the coolest robot!' we heard Ryan exclaim.

'He sounds like he's settling in. He's your lodger now. And I have a million and one things to do and a throbbing headache,' I said.

'Are you okay Nat?'

'I'm getting there. Just don't let Ryan leave the house on his own. I don't think he will, but to be on the safe side, tell him about the man next door, who killed his wife and buried her in the garden.'

'I don't know how I'll drop that into conversation,' said Sharon.

'Please,' I said. 'I want to discourage him from going out at night when he's here.'

'Ok… I know it was a dreadful thing to happen, but I really miss those neighbours. They kept themselves to themselves. The new ones are so bloody chirpy, always poking their heads over the fence for a chat!'


On my way out, we heard excited screams coming from the living room. An enormous old atlas had been propped up against the sofa cushion, and Ryan was using it as a ramp for the remote controlled Dalek.

'Amy! Felix! That's your father's! It's an antique!' cried Sharon. 'You'll get smacked bottoms the pair of you.'

'It was Ryan's idea,' said Felix.

'Yeah,' agreed Amy. 'Are you going to smack Ryan's bottom, Mummy?'

Ryan looked round.

'Gee sorry ma'am,' he said.

Sharon went bright red.

'Ryan is a guest and he didn't know! Now put it back on the shelf.'

'Ryan,' I said. 'You've got rehearsals at two this afternoon, and you'll be working this weekend too.'

'Will you be back for pizza night tonight?' asked Amy.

'And then it's DVD night tomorrow, you have to be here for that too, we're watching *Toy Story 3*?' added Felix.

'I can make sure a car has him back at seven,' I said.

'Yay yay yayyy!' shouted the kids.

'You're an instant hit in London, and you haven't done a show yet!' I said.

Ryan grinned and mouthed 'thank you'. I smiled, and Sharon showed me to the front door.

'Thanks so much for doing this,' I said. 'Just don't smack his bottom too hard…' I grinned, and before she could protest, ran off pushing the trolley back to the Sainsbury's car park, praying this gamble would work out for everyone.

# GENTLEMEN CALLERS

I phoned Nicky and Craig to say that we were back in business. I was going to come to the theatre, but Nicky told me to take the rest of the day off and go home.

'You must still have concussion honey,' she said. 'Let us handle it and we'll see you tomorrow.'

When I got back to the flat, Gran was hobbling round the kitchen dishing up some freshly made goulash.

'Come and eat, my darlink,' she said putting a big steaming bowl and some sliced bread on the table. I was suddenly starving, and wolfed down the bowl of goulash in minutes.

'My foot is feeling better,' she said watching me with amusement. 'On Monday ve have the big unveiling!'

'What?' I asked with a full mouth.

'Ve go to have my stitches out. Ve get to see my lovely new Sophia Loren toe,' she said. I was finishing my second bowl of goulash, when the buzzer for the door went. Gran got up and hobbled over to the entry phone.

'Natalie, there is a man outside!' said Gran. 'Do you know him? What should I do?'

I got up and joined her, peering at the tiny black and white screen.

'Bloody hell. That's Benjamin,' I said. He was looking up at the camera and was dressed in jeans, and a t-shirt with a picture of Ghandi sitting cross-legged.

'Shall I let him in?' she asked, her finger poised on the button.

'No, I'll go to the door,' I said.

'*Namaste*, Natalie, I'm here to get my toothbrush,' said Benjamin importantly when I opened the door. I ducked into the bathroom and came back with his toothbrush and the charger wound round it.

'Here,' I said thrusting it at him. Benjamin looked at it then at me.

'And I need my key back,' I said. He reached into his pocket and handed it over. We stood in silence for a moment.

'Is that it Natalie?' he said, surprised.

'Were there replacement heads for the toothbrush too?' I asked.

'No. Is that all you can say after our relationship?'

'Pretty much,' I said, and went to close the door. He put his hand out and stopped it.

'Laura's pregnant,' he said. 'Twins.'

'Congratulations,' I said. 'Just don't put her in charge of mealtimes. All I've ever seen her eat is pickled onion crisps.'

I went to close the door, but he stopped it again.

'We could try again, Nat? I think we fitted well together, we have similar interests, we want the same things…'

I stared at him in disbelief for a minute.

'I am nothing like you Benjamin. You are going to be a father, which frightens me. God help your twins. You are a deeply selfish, boring, humourless individual who finds himself so bloody interesting. You seem to think that yoga is some kind of calling or religion. But you know what it is?' I asked.

'What?' he said shocked.

'It's keep fit. It's a fucking workout class. You think you're the Dalai Lama, but in reality you're a second-rate Rosemary Conley. And for all the tantric sex you practise, you never gave me an orgasm in all the time we were together! Oh, and FYI, that's Ben Kingsley on your t-shirt. He *played* Ghandi.'

I slammed the door and went inside. Gran was in the kitchen still holding the video entry phone to her ear.

'Wow Natalie. I didn't think you had it in you,' said Gran.

'Gran, I just need a moment,' I said. I went to the bathroom and I splashed cold water on my face. I looked at myself in the mirror. I had no make-up on, bags under my eyes and my hair was a fright. I really needed a cocktail. I went back into the kitchen and the door buzzer went again.

'What does he want now?' I said.

'Natalie, it's not Benjamin,' said Gran. 'Look!' she said peering at the little screen. Jamie stood outside.

'I don't believe this,' I said. He buzzed again. He didn't look happy. 'Okay, now we're doing this, I've got some things I want to say to him too!' I said.

'Open the door! He's leaving,' said Gran pushing me in the direction of the front door. Jamie had turned to go, vanishing from the little black and white screen.

Jamie was near the gate when I opened my front door. He turned and came back towards me. I could see his eyes were red from crying.

'I'm sorry Nat, the gate was open,' he said. 'Can I come in for a sec?'

'Is this about Tuppence? She said some horrible things, and I didn't know all her hair would come off when I pulled…'

'It's not about that,' he said. The sky was grey and it had started to rain. I nodded and he followed me back inside. He slipped off his shoes and we went through to the kitchen where Gran was loading up a cocktail shaker with ice and vodka.

'My goodness, here is a sight for sore eyes!' she said limping over to give him a hug. He grasped her warmly and then she pulled away to look at his face.

'It has been a long time,' she said looking up into his eyes. 'And you're even more handsome than I remember… What's this? You've got fat like Natalie?'

I was about to protest that she was calling us both over-weight, when I saw Gran examining the side of his face. Faintly, Jamie had the same FAT bruise as me.

'Tuppence hit you with her award too?' I said.

'Yeah. We're on a break,' he said.

'I've never understood what *on a break* means,' said Gran.

'It means Tuppence wants to weigh up her options… Now she has a reality show, she doesn't want to waste her time doing theatre,' said Jamie.

'So why are you here?' I asked. Gran shot me a look. 'Sorry, I'm just being cautious,' I added. 'Things have got pretty nasty.'

Jamie nodded.

'This isn't about work or the theatres… It's my Nan, she's got worse. In fact, Mum rang to say she might not last the night,' he said. He stopped for a moment and had to wipe his face with the back of his hand. 'I have to get home to Devon, but there's engineering works on the trains… I haven't got a driving licence. I'm here to ask you, please, if you would consider getting me home…' he broke down crying. Gran reached out and grabbed his hand. She looked at me.

'Of course, I can take you,' I said. 'I've got a car… I'll have to come back though…'

'Just a lift,' he said. 'I'd owe you big time. Thank you. And I'll pay for the petrol and…'

'It's fine,' I said.

The skies opened as I pulled out of the underground car park onto Beak Street. Even with the windscreen wipers on full blast the window was an endless swirl of water. Jamie was quiet at first, then his phone rang. It was his mother.

I had seen Mrs Dawson once since our wedding that never was. It had been during a visit home, only a few months later, and she had been on the high street in Sowerton. I had seen her across the road coming towards me, and had ducked down the alleyway that led between two shops to a pay and display car park. At the last minute she had seen me, but I was in the process of darting away.

'Mum, Natalie is giving me a lift… Yes, Natalie Love.' Jamie covered the phone. 'She says to say thank you, and it will be lovely to see you again.'

'It's no worry… but I have to be back in London… I'll just drop you off,' I said.

I squirmed a little. Jamie chatted some more, and asked what was going on. The pauses got longer, and he said very little.

'Uh huh… Right… Ok.' Then he put the phone down. 'She says we need to hurry,' he said in a small voice.

We were now on the South Circular and the rain had eased a little. I took a left, signposting the entrance to the motorway. The windows steamed up and I put the fans on full blast to clear it. When we pulled onto the motorway I stayed in the fast lane and put my foot down.

We had hardly made any progress when the cars in front slowed, the red of their brake lights blurring in the water on the windscreen.

'I'll try and move us through this as quick as I can, but it's Friday,' I said peering at the three lanes of traffic to see which might be moving faster. I indicated and crossed to the middle lane. Then the traffic came to a standstill in all three lanes. We sat there for a few minutes, the sky darkening and the rain hammering down on the car roof. I turned the heater off and opened the window a crack. The air was chilly and smelt of ozone. My heart was pounding at the thought he might not get home in time.

'I've thought about you a lot over the years,' said Jamie suddenly.

'I've thought about you too,' I said, after a pause.

'Have you? Getting over you was tough… I went to Spain.'

'Mum told me, you'd gone to be a holiday rep?' I asked.

'Yeah, that lasted for about three days… Then I came home.'

'I had these visions of you sowing your wild oats in the Costa Brava.'

'No. I came home and spent the summer in Sowerton on anti-depressants,' he said.

I was shocked by his candour, and I felt guilty. I'd had the most incredible summer in London with Sharon and Gran.

'How did you end up in Canada?' I asked.

'My cousin, he ran a small chain of bookshops. It got to the point where I needed a change of scenery. There was nothing happening in Devon. So, I managed to get a work permit and I went and worked for him for a couple of years.'

'How did you start your theatre company?'

'That was just luck. I got into theatre through one of the guys who worked at the bookshop…'

'You made it all sound a lot better when we had coffee a couple of weeks ago.'

'I'm tired Natalie. Right now I don't care… I fired Brendan, and Tuppence went with him, she called off our engagement. They've got the reality show now.'

The rain continued to hammer on the roof. I scrabbled around for something to say.

'I recently spilt up with a guy called Benjamin, who runs his own yoga studio. I caught him having sex with his receptionist,' I said.

Jamie looked at me.

'It was going on for a while cos now she's pregnant with twins,' I said.

'Sorry, Nat.'

The cars started to move again, and I put my foot down.

'The thing is, I've had so many crap relationships. Before Benjamin, there was Michael. He had a weird fetish… He wanted me to balance salt and vinegar crisps on his bare bottom, and then smack him hard, breaking the crisps.'

'And did you?' asked Jamie.

'No! I told him it was a waste of good crisps! Then there was Stewart, Stew to his friends, who used to cry *uncontrollably* after sex, really grizzly like a toddler. It was disturbing. His face would go bright purple. Sharon nicknamed him Stewed Plum.'

Jamie wiped his face and laughed.

'And then there was John who had tons of pictures of his mother everywhere, and kept saying, "*Isn't me mammy beautiful…?*"'

'He was Irish?' asked Jamie.

'Yes.'

'That was a *terrible* Irish accent,' laughed Jamie.

'He wanted me to have my hair cut like her… "*Why don't you get a wee bob like me Mammy?*"'

Jamie laughed some more.

'The second John, he was nice, but gay… Kyle was lovely too, but dense. He attempted to rob a chip shop, and went to prison…'

My voice trailed off.

'Don't stop Nat, this is cheering me up…' he said, laughing.

'Well, I've reached you,' I said. Jamie laughed a little more and then stopped.

'Oh, I thought you were kidding. Go on, I might as well hear it, I've had a good laugh at all these other poor blokes.'

'There's not that many blokes! And, well you were perfect. I mean no one's perfect. You were great…'

There was a silence.

'Do you mean that?' he asked.

'Yeah. You ticked all the boxes. Funny, handsome, good in bed, treated me right.'

'Then why didn't you want to marry me?' he asked.

We were now zooming down the motorway towards Devon. The trees either side were whipping past.

'Jamie, let's not talk about this now. There are other things to think about... And it was such a long time ago.'

'It's something I've always carried with me,' he said. 'I know that sounds over-dramatic and self-indulgent.'

'It doesn't,' I said. I reached over and took his hand. 'If I had the choice today, I'd probably marry you like a shot.'

I grinned, but he remained serious. I pulled my hand away.

'Jamie! I'm talking with the benefit of hindsight! Could you imagine if we *had* got married? I was nineteen. I was clueless about life.'


Jamie's phone rang cutting through the silence. He scrabbled around in his pocket and pulled it out. My chest tightened thinking that we were too late, but it was his Mum, asking where we were.

'We're about an hour away,' I said seeing the sign for Oke-hampton swoop above the car. I put my foot down. The engine complained a little.

When Jamie came off the phone he was silent. He stared out of the window. The rain had stopped and there was a break in the clouds on the horizon, a blaze of white and gold with the sun and cloud attempting to cut through the storm.

It didn't seem appropriate to continue what I was saying. We passed the last of the journey in silence, the weather improved and we were basking in heat and early evening sunshine as I pulled up at the hospital.

I found a parking space, and told Jamie to go for it whilst I sorted out the parking meter. He slammed his door and ran off for the entrance. I grabbed my bag, and fished out my purse. I stuffed as many coins into the machine as it would let me, and stuck the ticket in the car window. The sun was so beautiful as it sank down, toward the hills leaving long shadows. It didn't seem right to be dying. My phone rang and it was Gran.

'Natalie darlink,' she whispered. 'Is everything okay?'

'We've just arrived at the hospital,' I said. 'Jamie's gone inside…'

'Where are you?'

'I'm in the car park.'

'You must go in. Support him…'

There was a muffled sound of a piano playing.

'Where are you?' I asked.

'Do you remember Kieron and Steve from upstairs, who helped me after my operation? They invited me over for a party.'

'What kind of party?'

'Nothing involving leather, it's a piano party. They've got a baby grand in the living room and another friend of theirs, Cecil, is playing beautifully. I'm just in the bathroom. There is a lot of Viagra in their medicine cabinet…'

My phone beeped. It was a text message from Jamie saying to go to Ward 4B on the first floor.

'Go, Natalie,' said Gran. 'Just let me know vat happens.'

'And you be careful,' I said.

'I'm a big girl. One drink and I'm going home,' she said.


I locked the car and made my way into the main entrance. There is something about the smell of hospitals on a hot day – the heat, mixed with the sterile bandages and illness. I found Ward 4B, the door was closed and you had to buzz to be let in. I pressed the button and peered through the little glass window, but there was no one there.

I waited a few minutes and then saw Jamie's mum and dad emerge from a room into the corridor with plastic cups. They sat on the bench and I could see the sadness on their faces. Jamie's mum, Cassandra, had aged a little in the last fifteen years, she had let her hair go from dark brown to an ash blonde and it suited her. His dad, Bob, had aged the most, his hair had thinned away, and he was fuller in the face. They noticed me peering through the glass and stood up smiling; they came over to the door and opened it.

'Oh Natalie,' said Cassandra. 'It's so lovely to see you, and thank you for bringing Jamie at the drop of a hat.'

'Nat, you look wonderful,' said Bob.

'I should go, I'm in the way,' I said.

'Nonsense!' said Bob. 'It's all a bit...' He looked at Cassandra. 'Well, it's all a bit touch and go...'

'Please stay,' said Cassandra taking my hand in hers. 'It's a case of waiting. Jamie is in there now with his brother, you remember Peter? Only two people allowed at one time so we came out to let them...' her voice trailed off.

I sat with them for a few minutes. A woman was lying in bed in a private room opposite. The door was open and we could hear the rhythmic hiss of her respirator.

'I heard you're very successful in London?' said Cassandra.

'Yes. I run the theatre opposite the place Jamie is renting.'

'And how has that been going?' said Bob.

'Oh it's been fun to catch up; we've only been across the road...' I lied.

I went to say more and Peter came out of the room. He looked sad, and he came and gave me a hug.

'Would you like to go in?' said Cassandra softly to me. 'Mum was always fond of you…'

I couldn't say no. They were sacrificing a little bit of the precious time they had left.

'I'll just pop in,' I said. 'Sorry that sounds wrong, I'll…'

'Natalie. You came. You brought Jamie. Nothing you could do is wrong,' said Cassandra. I smiled and went to the door. I knocked softly then went in.

The inside of the room was bare and white. The sinking sun came through the blinds, casting a ladder of light over the soft blue blanket covering Nan. I struggled to recall Jamie's grandmother's real name, but I couldn't remember. She would have to be Nan for now. The shape of her was small and thin under the blanket. Her face was peaceful and lined, but kindly so. Age hadn't ravaged her. I could imagine each line was caused by a life well lived, with lots of laughter, and a fair share of stress, as is all of life. Her white hair was soft and long against the pillow. When I saw her eyes closed I thought for a moment I was too late, but Jamie looked up from where he was sitting at her bedside, holding gently onto her hand. Very quietly I took the seat opposite, the bed between us.

'Hold her hand,' said Jamie softly. 'So she knows she's not on her own.'

I took her hand which was warm and soft. The underside of her fingers was so smooth. She opened her eyes and smiled.

'Hello,' I said.

'Natalie drove me here today, from London,' said Jamie. Nan's lips moved softly. Jamie leant in and she mouthed it again. Jamie laughed.

'What is it?' I asked.

'She wants us to hold hands…'

I looked back at Nan and she smiled and inclined her head. He reached over and I took his hand, making a circle. She tried to say something, but there was a rattling sound and she coughed. She closed her eyes and we watched her for a moment.

'Is she in pain?' I whispered.

'I don't know,' said Jamie.

We watched her for a few minutes more, listening to her rattling breathing. Then she breathed out and there was a horrible pause… and then she breathed in, her mouth opening wide. She breathed out and then there was another longer gap.

'What should we do?' asked Jamie.

'I'll go and get someone,' I said leaping up and opening the door. When Cassandra, Bob and Peter saw my face, they hurried into the room. I felt Jamie at my side as he grabbed my hand. Nan was breathing but with increasing gaps in between.

'The doctor said the morphine would let her slowly wind down,' said Cassandra softly. She leant over and stroked Nan's soft hair. 'It's okay Mum, you go, go and find Dad, he's waiting for you…'

I went to leave, but Jamie gripped my hand. Nan gave another soft inhale, she exhaled, and then we watched.

Cassandra and Bob started to say the Lord's Prayer, very softly; we all took hands and made a circle. As we spoke the words I watched as Nan began to go very white. I had thought she was pale when I saw her first, but all the colour seemed to drain away, so fast.

And then she was gone.

We stood in silence watching.

'She's not here anymore,' said Cassandra breaking the circle and wiping a tear with the back of her hand.

'Let me go and find a doctor,' I said. I was shaking as I went out into the corridor, and I flagged down a passing nurse.

I left in the aftermath of the doctors and nurses quietly organising what would happen next. Jamie came down with me to the hospital reception, which was eerily empty. We stopped by the doors.

'I'm sorry Jamie,' I said hugging him. 'I'm so sorry…'

'Thanks,' he said.

For a moment I rested my chin on his shoulder and smelt his hair, so warm and rich, just as I remembered it. We broke apart and he smiled weakly. I went to leave and then turned back.

'Jamie, what I want to say is that I'm sorry about everything. I'm sorry about so much. Of course, this isn't the time for that, but just know I'm here if you need me,' I said.

We stared at each other for a long moment and then I felt his strong arms around me again. He pulled me in close and kissed me. I hesitated and then kissed him back. His face was wet with tears, and he kissed me harder, taking my face in his hands. I slid my hand up and under his t-shirt feeling his warm skin… and then he pulled away.

'I'm sorry… I can't. This is wrong. Sorry, I have to go now Nat, thank you for everything,' he said.

I stood there, breathless from the kiss, and watched him walk away.


It was dark when I came out of the hospital to my car. The crickets were singing, and moths fluttered round the yellow street lamps above. My phone rang, it was Mum. She asked if I was okay and I burst into tears.

'You sound like you're in no state to drive back to London,' she said. 'You must come home. Don't drive. Wait there. I'll come with Dad, one of us can drive your car back here.'

When I came off the phone, I put my head against my car and sobbed.

I had never seen anyone die before.

# FAMILY

Mum and Dad picked me up from the hospital, and we drove back to the farm in convoy, with Dad driving my car behind. It was a very warm night and the sky was clear. The full moon was so bright, we barely needed headlights.

'Mum, do you believe in God?' I asked.

'What a silly question,' said Mum. We approached a red traffic light, and came to a halt at a deserted crossroad. Dad pipped the horn behind us. Mum wound down her window and stuck her head out.

'*NO! I'M NOT BREAKING THE LAW, MARTIN!*' Mum mouthed at him behind us. He pipped the horn again and revved the engine. Mum shook her head.

'So do you?' I asked.

'Do I what?' asked Mum. The lights went green and we moved off.

'Believe in God?'

'Why do you ask?'

'We said the Lord's Prayer as Jamie's Nan passed away. It got me thinking about where she went…'

'Of course we believe in God.'

'And do you think there's just one God?'

'Yes,' said Mum.

'What do you think he's like?'

'I think he's a nice man, he likes people, um, he made the earth in a week, and enjoys a nice rest on a Sunday,' said Mum.

'You make it sound like you're summing him up as a contestant on *Blind Date*,' I said. We reached the farm and Mum pulled into the drive followed by Dad. She switched off the engine.

'Natalie, you've obviously had a shock, being there when Jamie's Nan… departed. Why don't we open a nice bottle of wine, have something to eat and then you should rest.'

I nodded.

'And if you must know, I always say a little prayer, every evening when I wait for the milk to boil for the cocoa. It's silly, I know but I pray for Micky, Dave to lose weight, I pray your Dad will be safe when he's driving the tractor, and I pray for you up there in London, I pray for you to find a nice husband.'

'Do you pray for anything else?' I asked.

'Of course I'll pray for Jamie's Nan too.' She patted my hand and then shrieked as Dad appeared at her window. Mum wound it down.

'It's Friday isn't it?' he said. 'Who fancies fish and chips?'

'Ooh yes Martin! I could murder a nice piece of hake,' said Mum.

'*That's* your real religion,' I smiled. 'Fish and chips on a Friday night.'


It turned into quite a lively evening. Dad bumped into Micky and Dave at the chip shop, so they came back to the farm with Downton, Abbey, Dexter and House. There was a colossal mound of chips, beautiful fillets of lightly battered fish, mushy peas, pickled eggs.

It seemed for Micky's family, eating was extremely important and they were quiet whilst they consumed their heaps of food. I wasn't all that hungry, but I did seem thirsty for wine. When we'd finished, Downton piped up.

'Mummy, can we play Bears on the Stairs?'

'Yes, Mummy please?' asked Abbey her little blue eyes sparkling. Dexter and House jiggled up and down with excitement.

'Pleasepleasepleaseplease…'

Micky looked at Mum who nodded.

'Just take it slow, and be careful, you've got full tummies,' said Micky. The kids screamed and ran off.

'Is that a computer game? Bears on the Stairs?' I asked.

'No. They just slide down the stairs on their arses,' said Dave. Dad went off to check on the animals, and Mum started to clear away the plates.

I told them briefly what had happened with Jamie's Nan. I omitted the part about us kissing, which now seemed a bit weird. They were silent when I got to the end of the story.

'Life shouldn't be taken for granted,' said Micky reaching out to grab some leftover chips. Mum smacked her hand.

'Speaking of which, did you phone the woman on that Slimming World leaflet I gave you?'

'Leave it out Mum,' said Micky.

'Someone has to say it. I don't want you to end up like those people on the television, weighing two hundred stone. I don't want to be on some reality show where an American comes over and tells me what a bad mother I am and makes you drag a tractor tyre along with a huge rope.'

'Micky's beautiful,' said Dave shoving chips in his mouth. 'And her cholesterol and blood pressure are normal.'

'There's some tins of Slim Fast left over from the raffle at the fête,' said Mum.

'You gave away Slim Fast at the local fête?' I said.

Micky nodded.

'They charged a quid a ticket Nat. You can pick up three tins of Slim Fast at the 97p World shop.'

'What do you do Natalie, to stay slim?' said Mum.

I gulped back the mouthful of wine; Micky fixed me with a stare.

'Living on my own, I often can't be bothered to eat,' I said.

'That's not going to work for you Micky,' said Mum. 'You can always be bothered. How much do you weigh?'

'For God's sake Mum!' she said.

'Surely you can't be happy?' needled Mum.

'The thing is that I *am* happy. I have lovely kids, a lovely husband who likes me just as I am.'

Dave waggled his eyebrows to show us just how much.

'Think how much better life would be if you lost six stone?' said Mum.

'Life would be the same, I would just weigh six stone less, and I'd be miserable,' said Micky.

Mum huffed and puffed.

'I give up. And what about you Natalie?'

'What about me?' I asked.

'You need a man. Are we going to see a man in your future? What's happening with this Benjamin?'

'Nothing,' I said. Mum turned to the dishwasher. I leant into Micky and Dave.

'I caught him shagging his receptionist; she's now pregnant with twins!' I whispered.

Micky and Dave pulled a face.

'What about that Ryan Harrison, he was nice, what about him?' said Mum.

'He's ten years younger than me, and I'm his boss,' I said.

'Did you and him, you know?' whispered Micky. I nodded.

'He is so fit,' whispered Micky.

'Oi. What about me?' said Dave.

'What are you all laughing about?' said Mum coming back to wipe the table.

'I was just saying I'd love to go to Hollywood,' said Micky.

'It would set you back a fair penny my girl, you'd have to book two seats on the plane,' said Mum. Micky deliberately shoved a pile of chips in her mouth.

'Maybe you could go to Jamie's Nan's funeral!' exclaimed Mum, as if it were the best pickup joint. 'Did they give you an idea of when she'd be buried?' said Mum.

'Mum, you are unbelievable. What if I decide to be single? You can be single and happy. In fact that's what I'm going to do, I'm going to abstain from men,' I said.

'Oh, wayhayy…' said Dave.

'She's not saying she's going to be a lesbian!' said Micky slapping him on the arm.

'Will you stop talking about lesbians, the window is open!' said Mum diving over to close it. Just as she did Dad appeared knocking on the glass. Mum shrieked.

'Dad's head of the lesbian patrol,' joked Micky. I laughed. Dad banged on the window.

'Come on! Rihanna's given birth,' he said.


The kids were retrieved from playing Bears on the Stairs and we all went down to Rihanna's pen. Mum hastily donned her llama midwife outfit, which consisted of a hairband to pull back her fringe, an old Alton Towers t-shirt, and a pair of yellow marigolds. But it wasn't needed; a tiny furry llama was staggering around under Rihanna's long legs, attempting to suckle.

'I thought she wouldn't be due for a few more weeks,' said Dad. 'She must have had it late this afternoon.'

'They're very quick at giving birth,' said Mum. 'Unlike poor Micky, how long were you with Downton and Abbey?'

'Long enough,' said Micky.

'I know! You went in on the Monday and didn't come back out til the Thursday night!' said Mum. 'It's much easier for llamas – and they don't tend to put on much baby weight.'

'Now I have to be a llama,' said Micky.

'Is it a boy or a girl?' I asked.

'It's a girl,' said Dad with as much pride on his face as when we announced Micky's children.

Rihanna put her nose down and made a low humming noise to her tiny baby. It was so peaceful and sweet.

'What should we call her?' asked Dad. The kids, who were all standing in awe, shot their hands in the air as if they were at school.

'We have a great name,' said Downton, his eyes shining under his little mop of dark hair. 'What was it, Abbey?' he added.

'Llama Del Ray,' said Abbey proudly. We all laughed.

'That is the best name ever,' I said. 'You *have* to call her Llama Del Ray.'

'To think, Nat, you never made it for any of my kids' births, but you're here for the llama,' said Micky.

'Micky,' I said. 'Can I talk to you?'

We moved away from the others, cooing over Llama Del Ray in the pen. Micky flicked her hair back from her face and looked ready for a fight.

'I'm sorry,' I said.

'What for?' asked Micky, surprised.

'For being a crap sister, for buggering off to London all those years ago and not looking back…' I took her hand. 'We don't know each other really anymore, do we?'

'I missed you, I miss you,' said Micky, her eyes beginning to water.

'I miss you too, and I've been so stupid, I only just realised it. And I'm sorry I haven't been there for your kids, to see them grow up.'

'They've still got plenty of growing up to do… noisy little fuckers,' grinned Micky. 'You should come and stay with us, please. After we've been to see your play.'

'You're going to come and see the play?' I said.

'If you promise to come and stay…' said Micky with a wry smile.

'Deal,' I said. She gave me a huge hug. I hugged her back, but my arms didn't quite reach round her.

'Jeez, I think I am going to lose weight, just a little,' said Micky. 'But don't tell Mum, I'll never hear the end of it!'


I stayed the night at the farm, in my old attic bedroom. As I lay in bed I could see the night sky through the skylight above. It was clear and the stars were bright. It had been such a strange long day. I'd made peace with my sister, and perhaps some sort of peace with Jamie, but I had been there when his Nan had died.

And then the day had turned on its head, and I'd had the funniest, wonderful evening with my family, topped off with the birth of Llama Del Ray.

The parts of the day now seemed miles apart. I had started this morning beaten and battered, with a sense of impending doom, and now I felt profoundly changed. I realised my life was full and rich. I had a career I loved, I had friends and family. I had nieces and nephews, and Godchildren in Micky's and Sharon's kids, and back home I had a very cool lodger in the shape of Gran. And just maybe, with a little more fairy dust blown in my direction, *Macbeth* could end up turning into something truly special.

I was just drifting off to sleep when my Blackberry beeped. I was going to leave it, but I knew I wouldn't sleep with the little red message alert light flickering, lighting up the corner of the room. I clambered out of bed and grabbed it from the top of the pile of clothes I'd dumped on the chair. It was a text message from Jamie:

NAT. I'VE NEVER STOPPED LOVING YOU.
YOU WERE ALWAYS THE ONE. Jx

I felt a jolt go through me. A jolt of deep desire, of longing for him. That conversation we'd had all those years ago felt like it still hung in the air: *marriage or nothing, marriage or nothing…*

And we were older now; it didn't have to be marriage or nothing. It didn't have to be so black and white. It could be booty call, it could be date nights, boyfriend and girlfriend, living together… The floorboards creaked as I sat down. I looked back at my phone to reply, and realised he was in the grip of grief. I imagined how I would feel if Gran had just died. He was probably drunk, his mind all over the place. I couldn't let a late-night text message get to me. I wrote back:

AND I WILL ALWAYS LOVE YOU.

I pressed send. Then realised I should have phoned him. I'd wanted my reply to come across as kind and loving, acknowledging what we had, showing him that I cared. Leaving room for it to be a friendship gesture. However, I realised I'd just sent him the title of a Whitney Houston song. I waited five minutes, then realising that I had cramp from crouching on the floorboards, I quickly switched off my phone and climbed back into bed. Trying vainly to banish all erotic thoughts of Jamie Dawson…

# CURTAIN CALL

Five weeks later.

# THE WRAP PARTY

*Macbeth* was a hit. It never ceases to amaze me how a play can come together in the last few days of rehearsal. Chaos becomes calm, and everything clicks and starts to work. Of course, it helped that Ryan got sober, and worked so hard in the days leading up to it.

On opening night, Mum and Dad came with Micky and Dave, so did Sharon and Fred, with the kids, and of course Gran was there. Her stitches had only been removed that afternoon, and she was still on a high from seeing her new toe, which thankfully looked just like Sophia Loren's. She was still consigned to wearing flats for a couple of weeks, so I bought her a beautiful pair of jewelled sandals which she was thrilled with.

When I slipped into my seat beside Mum, I was almost having kittens with nerves. I looked back at the packed theatre auditorium, Nicky sat behind with her husband Bart, Xander and Val were a few rows back. Morag was in attendance with the rest of the board, and the press were taking photos before the play had even started. I'd never been to a Shakespeare performance where the audience had made banners, the most prominent being 'I LOVE MC BETH'. As the lights went down, the audience screamed and whistled, and my heart climbed into my throat. Then Mum smiled and leant into my ear.

'I've brought a bag of Revels, just tap me on the shoulder when you want one,' she whispered.

It brought me back down to earth and I relaxed. This was a fun night out for people. It was just a play.

During the curtain call there was a five-minute standing ovation, the audience went crazy. And I have to admit I shed a tear. Ryan and the cast were wonderful, the sets and production were stunning and atmospheric, I was so proud of the Raven Street Theatre.

My mother, whose attention span is non-existent, had been very drawn in during the play, forgetting about her bag of Revels and even shrieking loudly as blood started to slowly trickle, then cascade down the back wall of the stage when Lady Macbeth killed the King.

We all crowded into the bar afterwards, and there were smiling faces everywhere. Gran gave me a huge hug.

'My darlink! It was vonderful! Vonderful!' she cried. 'It was clever, and gripping – and those boys in the kilts, oh!'

'I really got into it, like I do with *Hollyoaks*,' said Micky, standing with a grinning Dave.

'Natalie, we're so proud of you,' added Dad, giving me a huge hug.

'How on earth will they get all that blood out of Lady Macbeth's dress?' asked Mum. 'They didn't have detergent back then.'

'It wasn't real Mum,' I said.

'Well, it felt real, well done love,' she said.

'Nat! I want to see it again already,' shouted Sharon, fighting her way through the crowds with Amy, Felix, Fred and an older greyer version of Fred in tow.

'Didn't we love it, kids?' asked Fred. Amy and Felix nodded shyly.

'Nat, meet Giuseppe,' said Sharon, introducing Fred's father,

'It was epic,' said Giuseppe in a thick Italian accent. 'Epic!' he repeated, throwing his arms open theatrically and knocking Gran's drink out of her hand, spilling wine all over her new sandals.

'Look vat you did you big oaf!' snapped Gran. Then she noticed just how handsome Giuseppe was for his age. 'All vill be forgiven if you buy me another drink,' she added raising an eyebrow. Giuseppe smiled and led her away to the bar.

'I've seen that look in her eye before,' said Mum to Fred and Sharon. 'Your father better watch out.'

'She doesn't look like she could hurt a fly,' said Fred, with a grin.

'It's not the flies I'm worried about,' said Mum.


Ryan emerged with the cast a few minutes later and made a bee line for my family. They all hugged him and slapped him on the back, and lined up for him to sign their programmes. Then Nicky came over.

'Fuck-a-doodle-doo, we did it honey,' she said. 'I've been talking to some of the press, and we're guaranteed five stars from all of them. The coverage is going to be awesome!'

'I'm sorry Nicky, for all the craziness that's gone down,' I said.

'It seems the craziness has done us good, Nat. Especially you, you seem younger, happier,' she said.

'Yes,' I grinned. My eyes flickered over her shoulder for a moment, scanning the people in the bar.

'Do you wish he'd come tonight?' said Nicky softly.

'What? Who?' I protested unconvincingly. Nicky smiled and raised an eyebrow.

'You know who I'm talking about... The gorgeous Jamie Dawson. I did get the girls in the box office to send him an invite.'

'I know... I didn't expect him to be here. His Nan's funeral was only yesterday, and I didn't really get much of a chance to talk to him... He was understandably distracted, and I had to come back to London straight away...'

'Give him time hun,' said Nicky. 'It's been fifteen years already, you can wait a little longer.'

'I don't even know what I'm waiting for, if there is anything to wait for...'

She gave me a hug and went off to talk to a group of journalists. I hung back for a moment and took a deep breath. This night was not going to be about pining for a man. It was about our success. I grabbed a drink and went to join in with the fun.


The reviews were wonderful, and for the next five weeks, through August and into the first week of September, *Macbeth* ran to packed houses. The day after the show ended was the eighth of September, and London seemed to switch over to autumn. It was blustery and cold, and there was the smell of wood smoke in the air. I hadn't heard anything from Jamie, and the idea of me and him had been pushed to the back of my mind as I buried myself in work at the theatre.

Ryan was due to fly back to LA the next day, so Sharon threw him a farewell party at her house in New Cross, to celebrate the successful conclusion of *Macbeth*, and that he'd reached thirty-nine days of sobriety.

Gran had been spending a lot of time with Giuseppe, since meeting him on the night of the premiere, so she was very keen to come to the party too. She assured me they were just friends, but I thought it could become something more. She was now fully recovered, back in heels, and her walking stick a distant memory. She'd sold all her jewellery and was trying to work out where she could afford to live – last week it was Rio, this week it was Scotland. I hoped it would take her a long time to make up her mind. I loved her being around. It made coming home to the flat less lonely.

At the party Ryan gave a toast to Fred and Sharon, and presented them with a personalised Ryan Harrison calendar. This one, however, was very funny and contained pictures of Ryan with Amy and Felix. My favourite was March, where Ryan was posing outside a phone box as Dr Who with his assistants Amy and Felix.

I was just in the hall retrieving my phone from my bag to take some pictures, when there was a knock on the front door. I opened it and there stood Jamie. He was dressed in jeans, a shirt and tie and was carrying a bottle of wine. He looked gorgeous.

'Hello,' I said.

'Hi Nat,' he grinned.

'I didn't know you were back in London? I mean obviously you are back in London, you're standing here on the doorstep which is in London…'

'Sharon invited me…' he said. 'I was supposed to be here earlier but, you know, engineering works on the train.'

'How are you doing? I left you a couple of messages…'

'Yeah, sorry I didn't reply. It's been a weird few weeks. I've needed to get my head round things.'

'Of course,' I said. There was an awkward pause.

'Thank you for the flowers, by the way, from you and your family, for Nan,' he added.

'You're welcome...' I said. There was an awkward silence. 'So, are you back in London permanently?' I asked.

'I don't know. I'm weighing up my options...' he said. 'You must have seen that Tuppence quit the show.'

'Yes, sorry about that. What's with all those adverts for iced tea and deodorant now running on the big screen?'

'I signed a year's lease on The Big O, and it was the only way I could pay the rent,' said Jamie. 'Although, ironically, I make more money showing adverts for iced tea and deodorant than I would if I put on a show.'

'And what's Tuppence up to?' I asked.

'She's finishing filming her reality show, and she's incorporated her alopecia into a new burlesque act. Now the final thing she takes off is her wig. She gets a guy up from the audience to polish her head with a lace handkerchief. She's a survivor.'

'That's not quite the word I'd use for her,' I said. There was a pause. He stared at me for a moment and then smiled.

'What?' I asked. 'Have I got something on my face?'

'No, I just realised something,' he said. 'You're thirty-five.'

'Gee thanks...'

'No, you look beautiful,' he added. 'It suits you.'

'You don't look bad yourself,' I said.

We stared at each other.

'Do you remember that day, our wedding that never was?'

'How could I forget?'

'I asked you when you might be ready to marry me, and you told me it wouldn't be until you were at least thirty-five...'

'That seemed like a hell of a long time in the future,' I said. Jamie nodded.

'And yet, here we are.'

'I should have said forty-five,' I added, only half joking. 'Anyway, Jamie, I was a different person back then. And you said wedding or nothing. It was kind of an extreme ultimatum.'

'You're right, it was,' he said. We paused again.

'This still feels all messed up,' I said. He hesitated and then put his hand out.

'Then let's start again,' he said. 'From the beginning. Hi, I'm Jamie Dawson.'

I looked at his hand for a moment and then took it in mine.

'Hello, I'm Natalie Love.'

'Pleased to meet you Natalie,' he said. Just then Sharon came bustling past.

'Jamie! I'm so glad you made it. What are you doing Nat, keeping him out on the doorstep? Come in, we're in the living room, about to cut the pavlova,' she said, and bustled off back down the corridor.

'So where do we start, getting to know each other?' I asked. He leant in and gave me a kiss. His lips were warm and firm and I felt a jolt of desire in my stomach. He slowly pulled away and smiled.

'That's a bit forward, for someone you've only just met,' I smiled.

'I'm almost thirty-six, time is ticking,' he replied.

'Well, you'd better come in then,' I said.

Jamie grinned and stepped inside to join the party, and I closed the door behind us.

# A NOTE FROM ROB

First of all, I want to say a huge thank you for choosing to read *Miss Wrong and Mr Right*. If you did enjoy it, I would be very grateful if you could write a review. I'd love to hear what you think, and reviews really help new readers to discover one of my books for the first time.

If you want to drop me a line, you can get in touch on my Facebook Page, through Twitter, Goodreads or my website www.robertbryndza.com. I love to hear from readers, and it blows me away every time I hear how much you've taken my books into your hearts. There are lots more to come (including, yes, more Erika Foster crime thrillers and more adventures from Coco Pinchard) so I hope you stay with me for the ride!

Rob Bryndza x

 bryndzarobert

robertbryndza

# ACKNOWLEDGEMENTS

Thanks to the fantastic team at Bookouture, for re-publishing *Miss Wrong and Mr Right* and giving it a new lease of life. I love working with you all, and you guy's rock!

Thanks to Araminta Whitley, Peta Nightingale, Jennifer Hunt and all at LAW, and thanks also to Stephanie Dagg and to Emma Gillett. Thank you to Emma Rogers for a brilliant cover.

To Ján – thank you as ever - your love, advice, encouragement, and support every step of the way is what keep me writing – and thank you to my amazing mother-in-law Vierka. And big hugs to Ricky and Lola.

I have drawn heavily on my own experiences in this book (well, saying that, I've never left a man called Jamie at the altar!) and before I became an author, I was an actor. I was lucky enough to work in so many fantastic theatres in London and around the UK. I'd like to thank all those actors, writers, directors, producers, stage managers, techies, and everyone who work to produce wonderful theatre productions.

Thank you also to my wonderful Mum and Dad, who gave me the opportunity and support to go to drama school, and who along with my amazing grandparents Les and Heather, travelled up and down the country to see me in all kinds of weird and wonderful plays.

The biggest thanks go to all my amazing readers and book bloggers who give me so much love and encouragement. Word of mouth is an incredible thing. Thank you for telling people about my books.

Printed in Great Britain
by Amazon